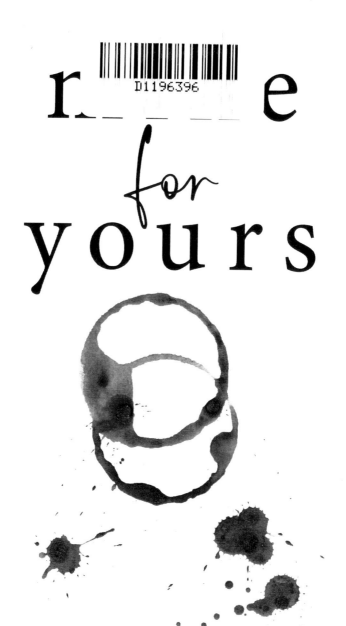

r___e

for

yours

HARLOE RAE

Editor: Infinite Well
Cover designer: Harloe Rae
Interior design: Champagne Book Design

To finding the one who makes the bad days better, the pain hurt less.
Also, for fireflies. Thanks for chasing off the shadows.

novels by
HARLOE RAE

Reclusive Standalones
Redefining Us
Forget You Not

#BitterSweetHeat Standalones
Gent
Miss
Lass

Silo Springs Standalones
Breaker
Keeper
Loner

Quad Pod Babe Squad Standalones
Leave Him Loved
Something Like Hate
There's Always Someday
Doing It Right

Complete Standalones
Watch Me Follow
Ask Me Why
Left for Wild
Lost in Him
Mine For Yours

Screwed Up (part of the Bayside Heroes standalones)

playlist

"It's OK" | Nightbirdie
"Run Away to Mars" | TALK
"Numb" | Marshmello and Khalid
"Tequila" | Dan + Shay
"Wait" | M83
"Glycerine" | Bush
"Trying My Best" | Anson Seabra
"Walk Out on Me" | Jonathan Roy
"Running Out" | Astrid S
"Almost Lover" | Jasmine Thompson
"Ain't Met Us Yet" | Matt Cooper
"I Guess I'm in Love" | Clinton Kane
"Walk Me Home" | P!nk
"Give You Love" | Forest Blakk

Mine For Yours

I didn't expect to see Rylee Creed after her brother's funeral.
That's the initial reason my jaw hangs slack when she walks
into Bent Pedal a month later.
The loss of my friend hit me hard, but that's nothing
compared to the crash she's endured.

Grief and misery still shadow her every move.
But she's not alone.
A little boy about the age of my daughter clings to her side.
Their shared pain is too ripe, salt in my raw wounds.

I assume we're about to make a deal and go our separate
ways.
But this bar was Trevor's pride and joy.
She wants to honor his final wishes.
How can I possibly stand in her way?

Simple. I don't.

Our paths collide after that point.
The journey forward is messy and complicated, much like us.
Maybe there's an exchange to be made after all.
Rylee just has to willingly accept the wager.
Then I'll trade her broken heart for mine.

"It's a beautiful sound when two broken pieces slide together to become whole."—Rylee Creed

mine
for
yours

prologue

RHODES

"**M**AY HE REST IN PEACE."

After that closing tribute from the officiant, a thunderous boom echoes across the sky. The clouds above finally make good on their brooding appearance. Furious, heavy sheets of rain soon follow. Whispered curses fight against the wind. Umbrellas open in a simultaneous wave—mine included. I could almost chuckle at the ironic cliché. A strangled cough escapes my tight throat instead.

Trevor Creed knew how to make a statement. My best friend rarely missed an opportunity, and it seems he's not taking this one for granted either. If only his presence wasn't just in spirit.

I stare without truly seeing as his casket begins to lower. White roses and damp soil litter the polished surface. More gets tossed on top from those gathered to pay their respects. My fellow mourners rush through the process to sooner escape the elements. I barely recognize the familiar faces shrouded in such anguish.

My fingers tremble when I scoop a fistful of earth from the pile. I can't seem to throw the so-called offering. It doesn't sit well with me that we're burying him. Twenty-nine is too young for the end.

The dirt remains clenched in my limp grip. Fuck tradition.

There's nothing right about this scene. Trevor had so much life left to live. So much to see, to do… to experience. I rub at the fresh sting assaulting my eyes. My vision has been a constant blur since I shuffled into the church earlier. That doesn't stop me from noticing her standing apart from the rest.

Rylee Creed doesn't bother to seek shelter. Trevor's sister stands in the rain with her face tipped to the angry clouds. She's getting soaked with each passing second. The chilled onslaught pebbles her pale skin, but she isn't shivering. Her red hair drips with sorrow. A black dress sticks to her body like glue, exposing a figure carved from fantasy. But those lush curves aren't what captivates me in this moment.

It's just her. The entire package. Period.

The riot thrashing in my chest matches the chaos looming above. Then our surroundings dissolve into a muted hue. I give myself just a brief beat of permission to lift the oppressive grief and admire how stunning Rylee is in her agony. Her presence grants me peace.

There's a quality in her I fumble to describe. Raw and vulnerable and free. She possesses the type of temptation that makes a man's will bend to hers. Even from this safe distance, I already feel the pull.

Her gaze doesn't stray from the clouds unleashing a downpour. Maybe she'll have more luck seeking answers than me. Even as I watch her, though, an alternative scenario manifests in my mind. Call it coping or a hallucination, but I envision her dancing in the rain. In this imagined version of events, a smile graces her lips rather than a painful grimace. Her movements reflect joy instead of misery. She crooks a finger at me to join her. I find it impossible to deny her in this blissful state.

Bright lightning breaks apart the gray, effectively smacking me from the somewhat serene reprieve. I wait for her to flinch or cower from the stormy conditions. Rylee's position doesn't falter, almost as if she's frozen.

No one approaches her. It's as if she's protected behind an

invisible wall that we can't climb. I'm transfixed on her slender throat as she struggles to swallow. A shudder racks her limbs. The rain has soaked her to the bone, sodden clothes suctioned to her skin. But it doesn't hide her inner light. She still brightens the darkness with short bursts. Flickers that can't be snuffed out. I find myself comparing her to a firefly in this moment— mighty beyond the oppressive shadows. Her display is as captivating as it is devastating. At any second, she might crumble into the wet ground.

The irrational urge to comfort her ripples through my limbs. But she doesn't need me to intrude. We're practically strangers. That truth churns my gut with a barbed spoon.

Under different circumstances, Rylee Creed might've become more significant than my best friend's younger sister. Between the gnarled threads of my grief, I find regret that I'll probably never see her again. Our paths rarely crossed even when Trevor was alive. With him gone, these moments in the same space are fleeting. It's a shame, but one I have no right to consider. Especially now.

That prompts a faded conversation with him to rise to the surface. The memory is startling enough to knock some much-needed sense into me.

There's no excuse to linger. I take one last glance for a selfish keepsake. The dirt forgotten in my fist falls to the ground. Then I'm turning on my heel and leaving the lure of Rylee Creed behind.

My loafers squelch across the grass as resignation clashes with doubt and guilt. I can only hope my friend forgives me.

chapter one

RHODES

ICE CLINKS IN MY GLASS, RIPPING ME FROM A BLIND DAZE. I BLINK at the spots dancing in my vision while the empty bar comes back into focus. But what I see is no surprise to me. Bent Pedal is in the same condition as it was before I drifted off.

Silent. Lonely. Abandoned.

The reminder only serves to sour my shitty mood. I'm wallowing, and I damn sure know it. This is becoming a habit as of late. But I only allow myself to let go while within these walls. My little girl will never witness this side of me.

The therapist I met with said it's a safe space. He told me that I need to grieve and find comfort in the pain. Loss is part of life. I should embrace the emotions ripping me apart. Cherish my memories. Once I hit a certain phase in the cycle, the healing can begin.

Sounds like a bunch of bullshit to me. I lasted all of one session before showing myself out.

The truth surrounds me, as it has for the past month. This place will never be the same without him. The same goes for me, but that impact is more complicated to grasp. Why Trevor's death is hitting me this hard remains a mystery. He was a good friend, one of the best I've had, but I'm not a stranger to loss. I've moved forward after a crisis before. It often feels like my job is one massive rescue scheme. And I'm damn good at it, until the one in need of saving is me.

A familiar ache spreads through my torso. I rub at the burn while drawing in a deep breath. I can't even force my own brain to figure out where to go from here. Thankfully, this weakness only plagues me when Bent Pedal is the topic.

That doesn't make it any easier to accept I'm failing our business, and him along with it.

My pity party comes to an abrupt end when the front door creaks open. Tension radiates across my shoulders in a tight squeeze. I didn't lock the damn deadbolt. Regardless, there are enough signs plastered on the windows to alert the public.

Footsteps pass the threshold and tread across the floor. Someone dares to enter this desolate cave I've allowed the bar to become.

My head drops low with a defeated sigh. "We're closed."

There's a brief hesitation clogged with doubt. Whoever lingers behind me doesn't immediately retreat. My eyes narrow on the abandoned glass of whiskey sitting exactly where I left it. I don't turn, leaving the intruder to decide.

"Rhodes?"

The soft voice has me swiveling on the stool fast enough to make me dizzy. I catch myself on the edge of the bar. My lips part with a wheeze as everything spins except her.

Rylee Creed hovers near the entrance with shadows dancing across her features. I never bothered to turn on the lights. Now I wish I had. Even in the darkened space, I see the uncertainty furrowing her brow. I take a moment to study her, if only to gather the scattered scraps of my dignity.

My gut sinks at her appearance. Not because she's any less striking, but because her vibrance has dimmed significantly. She's staring at me with a hollow gaze. Deep purple stains the skin beneath her red-rimmed eyes and the frown on her lips appears permanent. A noticeable slouch curves her shoulders inward, as if the load is too heavy to carry. It's all too familiar. Painfully so.

And she's not alone.

There's a boy about the age of my daughter clinging to her leg. Pain wafts from his small form, too strong for someone so young. This must be her son. Trevor used to brag about his nephew on a near-endless loop. He was so damn proud of this kid.

The crater in my chest expands. Their unexpected visit wages a stealthy attack on my lowered guard. I wasn't prepared to see them. Not sure I would be with advance warning either. That's the only viable excuse for why my vision is becoming a hot blur.

I avert my gaze with a silent curse, but there's no escaping the iron balloon my stomach has morphed into. That doesn't mean I can't deflect for a bit longer.

My attention shifts to the boy. Trevor's nickname for him filters into my muddled brain. "Are you Rage Gage?"

He buries his face into Rylee's thigh. When she loops an arm around him, he lifts his stricken expression to hers. Something passes between them without either one saying a word.

At his silence, she confirms what I already guessed. "The one and only."

A telltale sting burns at the bridge of my nose. "You hanging in there, little guy?"

"I'm not little," the kid grumbles.

A fissure—albeit thin—cracks through the pressure lodged in my chest. "Nah, of course not. You look about seven?"

He brightens, straightening from the safety of his mother's side. "Yep! My birthday is July twenty-third."

I rock back on my seat. "Ah, I missed it by a few months. Happy belated."

"Do I get a present?" His hands clasp in a pleading gesture.

"Gage," his mother scolds.

His bottom lip sticks out. "But he forgot my birthday."

"Ah, the guilt trip. Payton is almost famous for the exact same thing."

Rylee squints at me. "Payton?"

"My daughter. Payton isn't little either. Nothing short of a spitfire. She turned seven in August."

"You have a daughter?" She sounds shocked. Her reaction is a reflection of mine from all those years ago.

"I sure do. She keeps me humble and on my toes."

Rylee bites at her inner cheek while glancing at Gage. "Kids will do that. Such a blessing."

He sticks his tongue out. "Payton is a boy's name."

I wag a finger at him. "Don't let her hear you say that. She might challenge you to a rock, paper, scissors battle."

"I'll win. Where is she?" He slaps a fist against his open palm.

"Maybe next time, buddy. I dropped her off earlier for a sleepover. She'll be there until tomorrow."

His restored enthusiasm dims slightly. "What am I supposed to do now?"

"There are games over there in the corner. Trevor insisted we have an area for little—I mean, children." I blindly gesture at the place in mention.

"Smart man," Rylee chirps.

Gage stares at his mom. "Can I play with the stuff?"

She gives him a nudge. "Go on. Have fun."

That's all the prompting he needs. Gage darts across the room in search of proper entertainment. We watch in silence when he grabs a puzzle and settles on a chair.

"He wasn't at the funeral," I mumble absently.

"I let him stay with a friend. Maybe I'll regret shielding him from attending the ceremony, but it felt like the right decision in the moment. I was worried about how the open casket and burial would impact him. He's still so young. That sort of thing can be traumatic, especially when the person is your beloved uncle."

My head bobs along with her reasoning. "I understand. That's why I left Payton at home with her nanny."

Rylee crosses her arms tight across her middle. *"It's been really tough explaining death to him. That Trevor isn't coming back. I want to protect him from feeling such a major loss, but that's not fair. He's confused more than anything."*

The notion sinks like a boulder and I sag into the solid wood behind me. *"Fucking sucks."*

She moves forward, but her stride is cautious. *"Are you okay?"*

I bite back another foul phrase. *"You're asking me?"*

Damn, I'm a real schmuck.

"Can you blame me?" She offers a limp shrug. *"It's barely noon and you're sitting in an empty bar without the lights on. All by yourself, I might add."*

Thankfully, my failed attempt at drowning my sorrows doesn't make the list.

That's when I remember where we are, and who's in my company. *"What're you doing here?"*

"That's one way to kick off this conversation." When her head tilts, sunshine streaks through the window to dance over her reddish blonde hair. The shade is lighter than I remember.

For the first time in a month, I have the urge to laugh. Almost. I scrub at my bleary eyes instead. Maybe this is a warped dream, or I spaced out again.

But no. Rylee is still in front of me, waiting for a response. Her son stays in the toy corner, almost done with his puzzle.

The sigh I release is heavy. *"Would you prefer I continue staring in disbelief?"*

"Doesn't matter to me, so long as you ditch the wounded edge from your expression." Like she's one to talk. It's obvious she's struggling with this situation as well.

And I'm an asshole for ignoring the signs. *"Don't worry about me. Is there something I can help you with?"*

She fidgets for a beat. *"Not sure if you recall, but Trevor left this place to me."*

I nod. *"His half, yeah. Are you ready to sell?"*

"What?" Her tone is a bold smack, at complete odds with her sullen appearance.

"I just assumed…" My sentence trails off while I wait for her to fill in the blanks.

"You shouldn't." Rylee straightens her stance, confidence radiating from the subtle shift. "But maybe we should do this another time."

"Do what?"

Her nostrils flare with a noisy exhale. "Discuss the business."

"What about it?"

"You wanna hash out the details now? I figure you'll have customers soon."

I squeeze the back of my neck. "Not likely."

She seems to slot the pieces together while her eyes scan the barren space. "Why is the bar closed?"

"It has been," I mumble around the lump in my throat. My dress shirt becomes stifling, even with the sleeves rolled to my elbows. "Ever since his accident."

She sniffs and drops her gaze. "Can't run the place without him?"

"Something like that," I manage to rasp. In all honesty, there are days when Bent Pedal feels haunted. But that's my twisted psyche playing tricks. I hope, at least.

"How can you afford to just let it sit?"

I stand from the stool, no longer requiring the extra support. It's not like the whiskey was great company. "The rent is cheap. We're in a tiny town beyond the 'burbs."

Her forehead wrinkles. "I'm aware, but don't you rely on this place for income?"

The urge to scoff tickles my throat. That cocky reaction won't grant me any favors. Instead, I shake my head. "You don't know much about me, huh?"

Rylee mirrors my action. "Trevor didn't mention you very often."

A hollow pang thumps off my sternum. I almost clutch at

the inflicted area. "Damn, Firefly. Way to kick a man when he's already down."

She quirks a brow at the nickname but doesn't comment further. "Don't take it personally. He didn't share much about anything when it came to his life."

A cool balm settles over my bruised ego. The man felt like a brother to me more often than not. We met in college and bonded over being total opposites, but I can admit our conversations rarely scratched the surface. It didn't seem like an issue until his sister walked through the door.

"I'm an investor. My hand is in all sorts of pots. When Trevor came to me with this idea"—I point at the floor—"it seemed like a worthy project. Gave me an excuse to leave the city every now and then."

"So, this is nothing more than a side hustle for you. Super." The disgust in her voice is a rotten stench.

And I don't appreciate it aimed at my business. "Did you come all this way to ridicule me?"

She ignores my question. "Don't you have paid employees?"

A muscle pops in my jaw. "Yes."

Flames ignite in her green eyes, replacing the somber undercurrent. "You're fine just leaving them without a paycheck?"

I let my scoff loose. "Now who's making assumptions?"

"Is there an alternative?"

"They're on paid vacation," I drawl.

"For how long?"

I pinch the bridge of my nose. "Until I scoop my balls out of the meat grinder."

"Thanks for the delightful visual. Gross," she gags. Then her features smooth into a neutral mask. "Sounds like I arrived just in time."

That remains to be seen, but the day is young. "What took you so long?"

The spark in her gaze fizzles somewhat. "I didn't have the courage to come sooner."

Our situation crashes down on me. Bickering won't solve what's missing. We're little more than strangers, but that's about to change. Rapid and drastic if this woman has any control over the matter.

"Fuck," I spit. "I'm being a dick."

"Just the tip." She holds up a pinch between her thumb and index finger.

"You cracking a joke?"

Her wet lashes flutter in my direction. "The only other option is to cry."

My focus doesn't stray from the brittle cracks manifesting in her expression. Rylee's emotions are a boomerang whipping wildly at unpredictable speeds. This woman's suffering makes mine look tame.

Air whistles from between my clenched teeth. "I'm interested in hearing your plans."

She sputters out a sigh. "I honestly planned to just stop by and say hello. That's why I let him tag along."

I follow her meaningful glance to the corner, where Gage has moved on from the puzzle and is now building a tower of blocks. "And yet, you're ready to show me the door."

Her lips twitch. "Only after recent developments."

"This phase is temporary." Not sure who I'm trying to convince.

Rylee's bottomless stare renders me immobile. "His dreams don't have to die with him."

The sucker punch lands a direct hit to my gut. I narrow my eyes while wrestling with the accusations ready to be flung at her. "That's a shitty thing to say. I'm allowed to grieve in my own way."

She glares at the ceiling, her mouth forming silent words. Maybe to ask forgiveness—or for patience. "You are. I would never claim otherwise."

"Sure about that?"

"Yes," she snaps. "I didn't come here to strike low blows. Besides, this shouldn't be a battle."

"Something we can agree on."

"I'm not trying to cause problems for you," she continues.

"Try harder," I grunt.

It looks like she's biting her tongue. "Shutting the bar down isn't fair to his memory."

"Good thing that's not what I'm doing."

"Fine, whatever." She blows out a loud exhale. "Just let me share this burden with you."

I'd be more willing to cooperate if she quit jabbing at me. "Why did I think this would be a pleasant negotiation?"

Rylee presses her mouth into a firm line. "There's nothing to negotiate. Just let me take the lead. You can return to other investments that I'm sure take greater priority. We both win."

Stubborn pride flexes my muscles. "That's not happening. I'll maintain my role in this business."

"And that is…?"

"Owner, and a very involved one at that. I don't just sit back and let others decide how my money should be spent."

The slight curl in her upper lip suggests she wants to argue. "These principles extend to every pot your hand is dipped in?"

"Yes," I clip.

"Great. Glad to have you on the team." She wipes fake sweat from her brow. "But if it's all right with you, I'd like to fulfill Trevor's wishes."

"Which are?"

Her smile wobbles at the edges. "To keep this place running in his absence."

I yank at the loosened tie that's suddenly too tight around my neck. "Dammit, I can't fault you for that."

"Exactly." She sounds far too smug under the circumstances. But any positive boost in our situation is a win.

I recall a minor detail Trevor once told me. "Don't you live on the east coast? Minnesota is a long way from home."

"We actually moved to this 'tiny town beyond the 'burbs' a few weeks ago." Her brows lift as she recites my description from earlier. "I'm from this area originally, and always planned to return at some point. This is just sooner and far more tragic than anticipated."

Not to mention barely the beginning.

"Well, I guess this makes us partners." I extend my hand in a peace offering.

She nods while sliding her palm into mine for a quick shake. "Afraid you're stuck with me, honey."

Unlike her implication, I allow the endearment to bounce right off. "Should we seal the deal with a toast?"

"Looks like you started celebrating without me." Her gaze flicks to behind me where two glasses rest on the wood bar. "Were you expecting company?"

Both are neglected, untouched, and sweating into the coasters. Why I bothered making them on the rocks is beyond me. I didn't have the nerve to take a sip.

An odd tightness cinches around my lungs. The tradition has become second nature and I'd completely forgotten about it. Just one more pitfall this bar has carved into me. "Nah, I pour an extra for Trevor."

"Oh." Her eyes shimmer, reflecting the emotion I cough to hide. She lifts a trembling palm to her lips as a single tear trickles down her cheek. "That's very sweet."

"Or pathetic." I scoff at my own coping mechanisms that have formed lately. "His death has taken a toll on me. Not sure why."

But deep down, underneath the denial, I could find the truth. I'm just not at that stage yet.

Rylee shuffles forward until we're close enough to touch. "You guys were friends."

I cross my arms. "So what? I have plenty of those."

"Don't do the detached macho act. Not after that." She lifts her chin to the sentimental whiskey beside mine.

Discomfort churns in my stomach. This isn't an easy topic. Trevor might be gone, but I haven't forgotten. I'm suddenly trapped under the weight of it all. This is too strange.

"Maybe I should go. These walls are too damn loud." Which is the main reason I've kept others out.

"Do you mind if we stay?" She motions from Gage to herself.

"Knock yourself out." I lean over the counter for a spare set of keys stashed by the register. *"It's your place now, right? Just lock up when you're done."*

She snatches them from midair and twirls the ring around her finger. *"Um, okay."*

There's nothing left to say. Not now, at least. My shoes scuff against the floor in my hurry to get gone. Freedom beckons to me from just beyond these confines. Then I can breathe easier.

"Rhodes?" Her soft voice begs me to reconsider.

I pause in my retreat, but don't turn. *"Yeah?"*

"We have a lot to talk about."

That's a major understatement. *"Monday good for you?"*

"Sure." But only reluctant uncertainty strains from her tone.

I pretend not to hear it. I've already lingered long enough. *"See you then, partner."*

"Wait. Do you have my—?"

But I'm out the door before she can finish her sentence. There's only so much baggage I can juggle in an hour.

Rylee Creed was meant to be a faded memory. But now she's in the trenches with me.

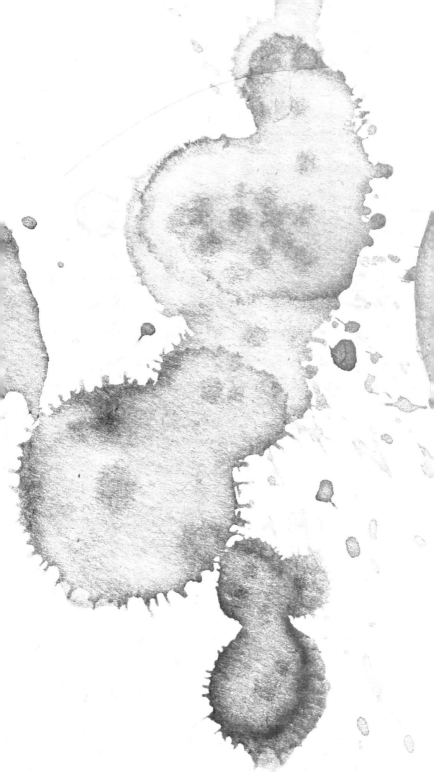

chapter two

Rylee

I'VE BARELY SHIFTED THE CAR INTO PARK WHEN A TELLTALE CLICK sounds from the backseat. My gaze locks on Gage, just waiting for an acknowledgment. It only takes a second or two for his eyes to find mine in the rearview mirror.

"What?" But his sheepish expression betrays him.

"You need to stay buckled until I've fully stopped."

"We are stopped," he protests. "You take too long. I wanna get out."

"Patience," I singsong.

"But Gramma is waiting for me." And he can hardly sit still under the anticipation.

As if on cue, my parents' front door opens and the woman in mention appears in the entryway. "What're you doing loitering in the driveway? Get your butts in here."

"See, Mom? She wants us to hurry." It's his turn to inject a heavy dose of scolding.

"Yeah, yeah." I step out and set him free.

A flurry of movement rushes past me. Gage might as well have springs on his soles with how fast he goes. I'm not sure his feet hit the pavement before he's running toward her.

She crouches as low as her creaky knees will allow. With more than a foot still separating them, my son launches himself into her arms. I wince at their collision, but my mom only laughs. Her arms automatically lift to wrap around him. A blissful smile shines on her weary features as they exchange a heartfelt embrace. Whenever Gage is near, some of her grief melts away.

My dad appears behind them to hop on the welcome wagon. He tousles Gage's hair and offers him a peppermint. My son eagerly pops the treat into his mouth. The scene is a natural comfort, and warmth spreads through my chest. The moisture that just cleared from my vision reappears with renewed vigor. Witnessing their bond is worth each ache and pain I suffered during our rush to move.

I'd already been planning on returning to our small town in Minnesota. Knox Creek owns my roots. Being separated by half the country never felt right. There was a hollow sensation that couldn't be filled. Besides, there wasn't anything or anyone tying me to South Carolina. I stuck around after graduating college to give Gage's father a chance to be more than a vengeful sperm donor, but my efforts were wasted. More than that, the itch to leave grew more irritating with each passing year. Although, to be fair, I didn't have much of a choice in the matter.

This, right here, is what I've missed. Family. True belonging.

If I could provide my parents with even a pinch of joy after losing their firstborn, I'd do it in a heartbeat. Trevor's death and gaining ownership of Bent Pedal just made the process a sprint.

Wood creaks in protest as I climb the porch stairs. My mom manages to wrangle Gage into another hug. He wiggles in her tight hold but doesn't put up much of a fuss. Once she's adequately smothered him in love and affection, her focus shifts to me. I'm encircled in her arms before I can register being drawn close. She smells like peaceful mornings and much-needed relief. My lungs drag in more of the calming scent while she squeezes me impossibly tighter.

"I'm so happy you're home." She recites a similar version of this sentiment each time I arrive.

That doesn't stop my body from sagging into her pillar of strength. *"Me too."*

"And you're here to stay." Her statement leaves zero room for argument.

"Yes, Momma." I've already provided reassurance on multiple occasions.

"Even if he—"

I'm quick to interject in case a certain pair of listening ears are tuned in. "He won't."

My mom pulls away to stare at me. *"Good. He doesn't deserve either of you."*

I scoff. "He never had us."

"That's enough of that," my dad cuts in. *"Let's get inside."*

I greedily accept his invitation, pressing a kiss to his scruffy cheek as I pass him. "Thanks, Dad."

He winks. *"I've got your back."*

And he does. That's precisely why Gage has a thoroughly padded college fund all set to spend when the time comes.

As a seamless unit, we stroll through the foyer and into the main hallway. Portraits line the walls, most of which are difficult to look at. I keep my gaze trained forward as we enter the kitchen. Dad sweeps an arm to the side. As if on autopilot, I follow the not-so-subtle request.

"Would you like some tea or coffee?" My mother is already moving toward the fridge. She knows me too well.

"Iced tea, please." I settle into one of the dining chairs.

My son pops up beside me as if springing out of a jack-in-the-box. The green in his eyes twinkles with mischief. *"Can I go play?"*

I boop his nose, a habit from when he was a baby. "Of course, Schmutz. Have fun."

"Yippppeeee!" Gage breaks off in a mad dash to the toy bin.

Momma laughs while watching him go. *"If only I had a quarter of his energy."*

Dad pours himself a cup of coffee and sits in the seat next to mine. "That's why we drink the good stuff."

My mom finishes fixing our drinks and heads for the table. "Ah, yes. Speaking of that…"

Oh, brother. Here we go.

I immediately cringe at the reference. The smile I paste on is wobbly at best. "What do you mean?"

Momma takes the chair on my other side. "You stopped by Bent Pedal yesterday, right?"

I take a sip from my glass, buying myself a few precious seconds. "Yep, we sure did."

She doesn't respond. Silence shrouds us, long enough for me to peek over. An expectant gleam rests on her features. I shift my focus to a safer trait. Her strawberry blonde hair is the same shade as mine, although hers is increasingly streaked with gray as of late. That almost makes me crack, but the stubborn streak I'm semi-famous for presses my lips into a sealed vault.

My mother huffs. She always folds faster than me, try as she might to change the pattern. "Did you go inside?"

I gulp past an unforgiving knot as my heart thumps a bit harder. "Well, yeah. Why wouldn't I?"

She exchanges a glance with my dad. Thick grief clings to their downturned mouths. Dark circles rim their eyes, much like mine. We smile less. Hug more. Cry often. It's a sad cycle, but we're healing. Slowly.

Dad clears his throat. "We've tried to visit several times, but the bar seems to be closed. Permanently."

The reminder steels my spine. "That's my first order of business."

Momma places a palm on mine. "Are you sure this is a good idea?"

"It's what Trevor wanted," I state with conviction.

"How about what you want?"

My gaze bounces between them. Any lingering doubt fades while their support frames me. "I'm looking at it."

"Oh." My mom clutches her chest.

"This is what I need to do. I was concerned about uprooting Gage so suddenly, but those fears weren't necessary. The condo we're renting—"

"You could've stayed with us," Momma interrupts.

I lift my brows in her direction. "Where exactly?"

She nibbles on her bottom lip, knowing full well they couldn't actually accommodate us. Best of intentions aside, they downsized in a major way once I left for college. Their two-bedroom isn't meant to house guests long-term. That's especially true when one of us is a rowdy boy with extra sugar content.

"Besides, our place is only a block from the park. He's very happy at his new school. Only two weeks in and he already has a bunch of friends. It's all good." I flash them a grin, lopsided as it might be.

Dad's stare is a bit too assessing for my taste. "We're glad he's adjusting well."

I nod, but the inkling that there's plenty left unsaid nudges me. "He's young and resilient. It helps that he knew we were going to move eventually. This was just sooner rather than later."

Now it's my mom studying me. "You didn't once mention how *you're* handling these abrupt changes."

And there it is. My confidence teeters, much like the unstable tilt in my stomach. "Don't worry. I'm doing just fine."

"That's not very convincing," she presses.

Which summons a deflection. "You're okay watching Gage for a few hours tomorrow? Maybe more. I'm not sure how long our meeting will take."

My conversation with Rhodes earlier this morning was a stellar example of cutting straight to the point. Turns out he does have my number. Trevor must have given it to him, or he found it buried somewhere. What's important is that he followed through. It's a quality I was beginning to believe men my age don't possess.

Momma scoffs, effectively severing my reverie. "Heavens, yes. You act like I'm the one doing you a favor."

"Because you are."

"Oh, please. I'm always willing and available to care for my grandson. He's my only one." Her bottom lip trembles. "Thanks for moving back."

I flip my hand to grip hers that's still covering mine. "You've been saying that since we pulled into town."

"And I'll continue saying it. Repetition isn't going to hurt in this case. I need you to understand how much you being home means to us. Especially now." There she goes again, but her actions are warranted.

I feel the love, and my watery eyes reflect in hers. She can repeat herself until most would claim insanity. My shoulders roll inward at the thought.

Will we ever get back to normal? No, that's not possible. Not without a vital piece missing. This is our new version. Eventually, we'll adapt. Maybe.

Ice melts in my glass, reminding me that time is trickling on. I catch a bead of condensation with my finger. "I only wish we'd moved sooner. Then I could've spent more time with Trevor. Maybe stop him before he—"

"Hey," my mother coos while cupping my cheek. "How about we try not to cry today?"

It's then I realize tears are streaking down my face. I swipe at the drops with a sigh. "Easier said than done."

Momma smiles, but the expression doesn't reach her eyes. "He loved you so much, Rylee. When you were little, he would carry you around everywhere we went. He told anyone in earshot that you were his. And when you got older, he chased off all the boys. No one came close to being good enough for his little sister."

I snort, but the sound is soggy and distorted. "That's precisely why I went to college halfway across the country."

Dad hums. "He was very protective. Learned from the best."

The ache in my chest is almost unbearable. "I wish he protected himself more."

My mom's stare wanders and grows unfocused, lost in a moment we can't see. "Reckless soul, that child. He couldn't be contained if he tried."

"There were plenty who tried," I muse.

My parents lock eyes, something heavy and secretive passing between them. It's my dad who replies. "He didn't meet the right one."

Momma blinks, swinging her eyes to mine. I brace myself for whatever comment she's about to make. It's no secret that I share my brother's terrible track record in the dating department. The urge to slink under the table twitches my muscles. In the end, she must notice the rigid shield my posture becomes—and thankfully relents.

"Does Gage ask about Trevor?" The question is soft, steeped in uncertainty.

I falter for a beat. That isn't a shift I could've predicted. "He has, but not recently. I think he understands that his uncle is gone."

Which hurts my heart more than I care to admit. But the alternative is my son suffering from this persistent gloom. It's a storm cloud I can't escape. Similar to the one at Trevor's funeral, ironically enough. I wouldn't wish that on anyone, especially Gage.

My mom sniffles and averts her gaze. "Maybe it's a blessing you didn't move before the accident. If they had a tighter bond, it would've been more devastating."

And I thought we weren't supposed to cry. Another wave of heat prickles my eyes. "I'm not sure what the correct answer is."

"There isn't one, kiddo." Dad's eyes are glassy when I glance over.

"But we'll always carry him with us. That's how Gage will remember him." I simultaneously tap my temple and chest.

"And his legacy," Momma murmurs.

We sit in silence for a brief moment, as husks of our former selves. I imagine we're recalling my brother's announcement about opening Bent Pedal. His laugh was infectious. Maybe that's why his absence has left us with this empty void.

A glimpse upward provides me with a glimmer of peace. Almost. I'll try to be ambitious and enthusiastic and wild for both of us. If nothing else, he would love to see me attempt the feat. It reminds me of the silly bets we'd make as kids. Trevor would accept before the stakes or wager were set. Ballsy odds aside, that's one thing I admired about him.

"I'm going to do right by him." The vow resonates deep within my cracked spirit.

My parents smile, strained though the expression might be. Dad pats my shoulder. "We'd love to see his dream prosper again. It's been too long."

Renewed purpose thrums through my veins. "I'll get the place up and running as soon as possible."

Momma clucks her tongue. "Don't force too much at once. Nobody expects you to take on the burden."

"Still worrying." But my chiding is in jest.

"It's my job."

"And this will be mine." Not like I have another one at the moment. Other than mommying, of course.

Her grin deflates. "Just be careful."

I brush off her concern with a shrug. "How hard can it be? It's just a bar. Well, maybe more of a restaurant."

The distinction gets mentally added to my list. I barely got a peek at the space, but food is definitely served in addition to alcohol. We only stayed about ten minutes after Rhodes left. The way he tore out of there freaked me out. Like maybe the bar is actually haunted. I shiver involuntarily.

Don't be ridiculous.

There's much to pick apart when it comes to Bent Pedal. My so-called partner will be responsible for explaining the essentials. A thrill—albeit tiny—zings at the thought of his broody smolder. The image of him in a white dress shirt with the tie loosened is stored someplace safe and private. He caught me off guard yesterday, but I'll be better prepared tomorrow.

Rhodes Walsh has no idea who he's dealing with. But he will. Soon.

"Gramma?" Gage's voice breaks into our dwindling discussion, immediately brightening the mood.

Momma turns her head, so as to not blast me with her reply. "Yes, baby boy?

The three of us share a much-needed laugh when he grumbles about not being a baby.

My father smirks, his sigh lighter than a feather. "Great for the soul, that kid."

Gage's affronted tone evaporates seconds later. "What's this weird rainbow thingy by the window?"

My mom stands from her chair with a few creaking joints. "That's my cue."

I get to my feet as well. "We'll go together."

Dad follows suit. "Yeah, enough talk. I'm ready to play."

Gage zooms into the room, screeching to a stop before colliding with me. "It's my turn to go first."

I savor a slow breath to trace the freckles on his nose. The smattered pattern is a family staple, but Trevor gets full credit for my son's tenacity. "I wouldn't have it any other way."

chapter three

RHODES

PAYTON'S GIGGLE PIERCES THE WARM AUTUMN AIR. "HIGHER, Daddy!"

"Okay, here comes a big one. Hold on." I'm quick to do her bidding. My palm meets the center of her back for a gentle shove.

"This is the best thing ever!" Her long hair blows in the breeze as she reaches for the sky.

She's capable of swinging by herself, but I plan to take advantage while she still demands that I do. Soon enough, she won't ask me to push her. I'll get a pity extension by begging and pleading. Then independence will reign beside her stubborn streak. And then before I know it, she'll abandon the playground altogether.

I'm not ready for that to happen. Such a small task gives me more purpose than a dozen lucrative investments combined. More than that, these genuine moments fill the cracks that attempt to shatter me. I soak in her unconditional happiness like it's my own.

Payton's laughter rises above the idle chatter of our fellow park goers. "Again!"

"Your wish is mine to grant." I get into position and send her soaring to the clouds.

She squeals while kicking her legs. "I can see the ocean from up here."

I snort at her antics. "Maybe the lake."

"Nope, it's the ocean." The willful spirit on this girl renders me speechless. Her word is the law these days.

Might as well join the fray. "Which ocean is it?"

"Ummm," she squints into the distance. "The super big one."

"Ah, that explains everything."

Payton quits pumping and drops her feet. A dust cloud billows in the dirt. "I'm bored."

I frown. "Already? You just got started."

"And now I'm done." She hops off the swing and crosses her arms.

My head spins trying to keep up. "How about the monkey bars?"

She glances in that direction. "Meh."

"Slides?"

"No."

I tug at my hat, flipping it backward. "Duck, Duck, Gray Duck?"

Her lips twist as she considers that option. "Not right now. Maybe later."

"Okay," I drawl. "What would you like to do?"

Pebbles skitter when she kicks the ground. "I dunno."

"You could make me one of your famous wood chip and mud smoothies at the café." I hitch a thumb over my shoulder to the empty counter tucked under a platform.

That's when I notice a trio of onlookers gawking at me. Hunger shines from their gazes. One bites her bottom lip. Another gives me a blatant once-over. I almost scowl, but offer a polite wave instead. There's no reason to create enemies at my daughter's beloved park. Even if their leers are shameless and objectifying.

"How about ice cream?" That gives me an excuse to get the hell away from these Rosy Palmers trying to score a daddy.

"Yes, yes!" Payton bounces in place, garnering more unwanted attention. "I want three scoops."

"Sure, Bumblebee. Sounds perfect." I begin guiding her to the exit.

She loops her arm through mine, leaning against me. "And extra sprinkles?"

"Uh-huh," I mumble while skirting around the drinking fountains.

My little girl skips with outward glee. "Whipped cream, caramel, and cherries?"

"Delicious."

"Wow, you're easy today."

I nearly choke on my tongue. She has no idea just how accurate that statement is. The vultures were about to swarm their prey. That's exactly what I'm trying to avoid while hauling ass along the sidewalk. I'm not in the market to get devoured. But solid effort.

As if on cue, a chorus of disgruntled grumbles chases us as we round the corner and disappear from their sight. Relief tugs at my lips, propelling me onward at a quick clip. Payton whines while tugging at my shirt.

"Daddy, why are we going so fast? Are they gonna sell outta ice cream?" If her tone is any indication, that thought is terrifying.

"Oh, sorry." I slow instantly. "Just in a hurry to satisfy my sweet tooth."

Her face scrunches into an adorable pinch. "Why is your tooth sweet?"

"It's just an expression."

"You're weird," she murmurs under her breath.

I bump her with my elbow. "That makes you weird too."

She gasps. "Am not!"

"Well, you're my kid. That means you inherit my weirdness."

Her prancing comes to a brief pause. "What's inherit?"

"Something you get from me, like a gift."

Her groan is thick with disappointment. "But I don't wanna have your weird stuff."

I chuckle and pull on her ponytail. "Don't worry, Bumblebee. You're immune. I only gave you the super awesome genes."

She just gapes at me. "Huh?"

"You're made from quality stock. The best parts."

"I don't get it."

"Never mind," I laugh. This random conversation has effectively scared off the funk.

Payton chews on the inside of her cheek. "Is that why I don't have a mom?"

Spoke too soon.

My head jerks to the side, as if I've been slapped. I falter with how to reply. There isn't a swift response to give. Not one that's been mentioned in the countless parenting books I've read. This isn't the first time she's broached the subject of her mother. I'm not foolish enough to assume this will be the last. Far from it. When she begins to deal with more… feminine issues, I'll be a lost cause.

If only I could be everything she needs. But that's wishful thinking, and selfish. My daughter deserves the truth, but I haven't found the courage to provide it.

I settle for a non-answer that might restore a fraction of my pride. "Who you have is even better."

Payton shrugs as we near Moos Truly. "You're pretty cool, I guess."

Sugar and spiked energy levels tickle my nostrils. "Even if I'm weird?"

"That's kinda my favorite part." Her smile could melt icebergs.

"Ah, the truth comes out." I yank the door open, cold air blasting me in the face.

She dashes to the row of display freezers. Her nose presses

to the glass while she peruses the choices. "Don't forget, I get three scoops."

"With caramel and cherries," I tack on.

"Whipped cream and extra sprinkles too," she replies.

A teenage girl appears behind the case. Her wide grin leads me to believe she's been sampling the products. "Hi! Thanks for stopping at Moos Truly. What can I get you?"

"I want ice cream," my daughter demands.

"Payton," I admonish.

She glues on a beaming smile. "Please."

The young scooper falls victim to my daughter's charm, which is entirely too familiar. She makes this awkward noise between a coo and babble. "You're the cutest little thing."

I cringe in preparation for the backlash. At the last second, I manage to squish a finger against Payton's lips. She glares up at me, but her upset fades in a blink. Meanwhile, the teenager is completely unaware of the hissy fit I just saved her from.

"Cup or cone?" The girl holds one in each hand.

"Both," my daughter states with authority.

"Oh?" The scooper lifts her gaze to me for approval.

"She puts the cone on top," I explain. "Something she learned from me."

Payton giggles when I wink at her. "Like the super awesome pants you gave me."

It's my turn to laugh at her version of my earlier statement. "Exactly, Bumblebee."

The teenager is silent during our exchange, scoop held at the ready. "Um, okay. Two of these then?"

"Yes, please." I point to the tubs and prattle off the specifics.

Payton is fascinated as the scooper gets to work. Her eyes are the size of dinner plates once the girl is done piling on toppings. "That's all for me?"

The scooper passes her the overflowing cup with a waffle cone perched on top. "Enjoy, cutie pie."

My brows almost reach my hairline. "I hope you're hungry."

Payton nods with added enthusiasm. *"My tummy is rumbling."*

After I pay and grab my ice cream, we find a table outside. My little girl is digging in before my ass even hits the chair. Pure delight spills from her while she stuffs her face. I'm far more civilized, savoring each small spoonful. The creamy vanilla, chocolate chips, and caramel create a groan-worthy combination. A large chunk of cookie dough melts in my mouth. This is almost better than sex. Almost.

Which is creepy as fuck, considering my present company. Maybe I'm weirder than I thought. Definitely more mangled after recent events.

Which leads me to a certain redhead and her insistent agenda.

"By the way, Melinda is picking you up from school tomorrow." I take a bite after delivering the nanny news.

"Why?" She pouts, but only momentarily. Payton's expression brightens before my suspicion kicks in. *"Do you have a date?"*

I choke on my recent mouthful. *"Absolutely not."*

"Oh." Her shoulders slump in defeat.

"You're the only girl for me. More sass than I can handle." I wink at her.

"Gross, Daddy. I'm your daughter. Just… yuck." She sticks a finger in her mouth, pretending to vomit. So literal, this one.

I shudder just thinking about the teenage years to come. *"You know what I mean, Bumblebee. My heart is already full, thanks to you. There's no room for anyone else."*

"Whatever. You need to fall in love and get married and have more babies." The twinkle in her eye is all too familiar.

"Pass." I tug at my collar, just picturing the park pack ready to pounce.

"Laaaaame. Even I have a boyfriend." She makes that flippant comment as if it's not devastating to my ears.

I wheeze through the thin straw my throat becomes. "Who?"

"A boy from class." She dips her chin, but there's no hiding her blush.

My gaze narrows. "What's his name?"

"Henry."

The plastic spoon bends in my grip. "He better keep his hands to himself."

"What's that mean? His hands are attached to his arms."

"And they'll stay that way so long as he doesn't touch you." Is it too intense to threaten a second grader? Maybe. But so is dating at their age. Fucking ridiculous.

"Gosh, it's not a big deal. He just smiles at me sometimes. But we barely talk." She doesn't seem too pleased about that.

"Sounds like the perfect relationship." I don't bother masking my smug tone.

"Maybe you should try it," Payton grumbles at her ice cream.

"Not interested." I swat all that nonsense away. "I'm working late tomorrow. No dates."

"Fine," she relents with a sigh. "Will you tell me the bumblebee story?"

"Didn't I already this week?" Not that I'd ever deny her.

"Doesn't matter. I wanna hear it again."

"Okay, okay." I sigh, as if this is some huge undertaking.

She giggles at my theatrics. "You love me."

"I do, which is why you have a cute nickname." There's a pause for dramatic effect. "When you were a baby, before you talked, you would make this buzzing sound."

Payton demonstrates, mashing her lips into a firm line. A distinct hum shortly follows. "Like that, Daddy?"

"Yep, exactly. You were my little bumblebee. Still are."

"That's a good story," she breathes.

"Want to hear another one?"

"About what?"

"The smelliest poop you ever pooped." I plug my nose and cough. "It stunk up the entire house for a week."

"Nuh-uh," she protests.

"Yep."

"Ewwww, no way." She's laughing so hard that tears drip from her eyes.

"Yes, way."

She whips her head left to right in sharp denial. "My poops aren't stinky."

"I strongly disagree. But I won't tell you if—"

Payton slaps a palm flat on the table, amusement dancing in her features. "Tell me!"

And so I do. Twice for good measure.

chapter four

Rylee

BENT PEDAL ISN'T THE SAME SPACE I LEFT ON SATURDAY. THAT'S why I find myself at a complete standstill after just crossing the threshold. I force my feet to shuffle forward, but there's no controlling my slack jaw.

A significant transformation has occurred since I locked the doors a scant forty-eight hours ago. The glossy wood surfaces sparkle under the overhead lighting. There isn't a speck of dust or smudge to be found. Chrome tables and cushioned chairs are arranged in a purposeful pattern across the open floor-plan. Several whiskey barrels are upcycled as additional surface space. Bold, artful décor hangs from the walls, giving the place a modern, rustic vibe. Framed black and white photographs join the collection. Upon closer inspection, the pictures appear to be taken from Knox Creek's very own Main Street—past and present. The entire package is very appealing. It's obvious my brother put extra care and effort into his business.

For once, the ache in my chest isn't excruciating. His dream is being revitalized right before my eyes. I would choose to come here often, which is ironic under the circumstances. The challenge of loving where I work won't be an issue in this case. And speaking of an upcoming battle…

The spotless, illuminated interior isn't the only thing that's different.

Rhodes is behind the bar polishing a beer mug. He fits the

scene seamlessly. In this instant, I can't envision a more accurate role for him to play. Then he holds the tall glass up to the light, checking for streaks. That gives me pause, thinking maybe psychic should be added to his job description. But either way, the brief lapse gives me a much-needed moment to admire his appearance.

Our paths have only crossed on a handful of occasions. He's previously proven that three-piece suits were invented for his broad build. Nobody had the courtesy to warn me about the threat of him in casual clothes. I nearly liquify at the sight of him.

Today, a plain white t-shirt clings to his upper body. The faded jeans gracing his lower half must've been stitched on directly by the designer. Denim hugs his ass and thighs as if glued on. As if that's not already spoiling my appetite for all other man meat, he's wearing his hat backward.

Most striking, however, is the calm confidence oozing from his movements. Even completing routine tasks, he seems lighter. Freer. Such a contrast to the shadows clinging to him the other day.

This package might be even more appealing than the one I walked into. I expel a humorless laugh. There's no question about it.

Rhodes pauses mid-scrub to lift his chin in my direction. "You doing okay over there?"

The question snaps me from my stupor. I've been asked that too many times to count lately. Even a passing glance from a self-absorbed socialite confirms I'm far from okay. It just so happens that this slip isn't related to grief.

I square my shoulders and approach him with a measured stride. "Why wouldn't I be?"

"The fact you've been frozen in the doorway for almost five minutes," he explains in a lazy drawl.

So much for my stealthy perusal. "I'm just peachy. How about you?"

"Hanging in there." He reaches for another glass to scrub.

My heels click against the stamped concrete. Another detail I missed before. "I'd be willing to give you more credit than that."

His brown gaze is fixed on me, just waiting for my remaining shock to dissipate. I suddenly have an intense craving for melted chocolate. But I have a sneaking suspicion this man isn't overly sweet.

"Glad you made it," Rhodes offers as an official greeting.

I'm not entirely sure how authentic that sentiment is, or the one I give in return. "Likewise."

He pins me with a scowl, the carefree cloak slipping for a beat. "Didn't expect me to show?"

My feet slide to a stop at the stools framing the bar. "I wasn't sure what to expect."

"And now?"

"Still processing," I admit honestly.

After a jerky nod, his eyes shift to a spot behind me. "No Gage?"

"He's very happily occupied elsewhere. My parents are taking him to the beach." Which might've been a wiser alternative. Pressure is already beginning to pulse at my temples. "How about Payton?"

His mouth twitches just at the mention of his daughter. "She's with her nanny. Melinda picks Payton up from school on the rare occasions I have to work late. I'm hoping to join them for dinner."

A frown tugs at my own lips. The insinuation that I would stop him is insulting. "This shouldn't take long."

He turns to grab yet another mug. "That's what I'm banking on."

"I can see that. You did all this today?" I motion to the noticeable changes.

"Sure did." His gravelly timbre should require a permit for public use. He's succeeded in jamming my circuits with a few standard phrases.

It's only then I realize my mouth is still gaping wide. My teeth clack with the urgency to regain some semblance of composure. "I have to say that I'm impressed."

"Only because you lacked faith in me."

Still do, but he doesn't need to hear that. "For what my opinion is worth, the place looks great. I feel like it's ready to open."

Rhodes snorts. "Not sure why it wouldn't. We were fully functioning, and quite well, a month ago. There isn't much that needs to be done."

"Right, okay. That makes sense." But I'm still chewing on the shock.

Creases form across his forehead as a lull settles between us. He seems perplexed by my stunned reaction. "Haven't you been here before?"

I'm ashamed to admit the truth. But that's my burden to carry. "Trevor invited me, of course. I didn't make the time. My visits home weren't long enough to stop at a bar. Now I see just how wrong that choice was."

"At least you're here now." The warmth in his tone is another unexpected shift.

The flutters in my belly are traitorous. "I didn't think you were pleased about my sudden involvement."

Rhodes almost smirks. "Another assumption? I thought we were past that."

"Oh, come on. Your initial reception was less than welcoming." I'm beginning to believe we could make this partnership work, though.

"That had little to do with you. This space kinda became a refuge for me after… well, you know." Rhodes averts his focus.

"I do." My response is barely a murmur in fear of shattering the fragile territory we're breaching.

There's a vulnerable shine in his eyes when he glances back at me. "I wasn't prepared to lose that."

A dense awareness thickens the air. Rhodes' confession is personal, along with the unguarded expression he pins on me.

I have a hunch that he doesn't allow many to witness the grief he's harboring.

Heat stings my vision, revealing the festering wound still eating at me. It's not a secret that I'm a mess—inside and out. The desire to clutch at my brother's memory had me moving halfway across the country in a matter of weeks. If anyone can appreciate his protective instincts when it comes to Bent Pedal, it's me. This place was special to Trevor, and I'm quickly realizing just how much it means to Rhodes as well. If I'm being honest, there's already an attachment taking root inside of me.

But that doesn't mean I want to hoard the treasure all to myself.

This is a topic that will always connect us. Even if we handle the process in completely opposite manners.

I shift closer until my thighs bump a stool. The obstacles between us are few, yet the barriers are paved in caution. "You aren't losing anything."

In an instant, the softness vanishes from his features. "Bullshit."

Just like that, our understanding is severed. But I won't let that dissuade me. "On the contrary, really. You're sharing the haven with others."

"Awesome," he clips.

Well, someone isn't a team player.

"I think getting Bent Pedal back to its former glory is far better than letting the space go to waste." And my brother's wishes along with it.

Rhodes returns to his polishing task, but the glasses are already squeaky. "You don't have to tell me, boss. It's a business above all else."

And for a second, I thought we could share our pain. Disbelief snorts from me instead. "Oh, I'm the boss?"

"Thought that was obvious."

"All right." This seems like an appropriate prompt to swerve us back on track. I slide my butt onto a seat, elbows resting on the wood counter. "Where do we begin?"

Rhodes exhales a noisy breath. In the same beat, his gaze fastens on me. A conflict begins to flicker behind the scenes. I watch the debate play across his stony expression. It only takes a breath for him to reach a decision.

Flames ignite from his molten eyes. The sizzle hisses between us when he mirrors my pose to lean on the bar top. Then he's cutting a feverish trail down my body. I feel exposed while his blatant interest skewers me.

Approval gleams from Rhodes' dark smolder. The man has no problem being forward with a thorough appraisal. "I have a few suggestions."

I've been starved too long, almost lightheaded from his thrice-over. My mouth goes dry. "Such as?"

"Do you like being in control?" He has the uncanny ability to make everything sound sexual. Or I'm just that deprived of male company. Probably the latter.

That doesn't stop me from feeding this sideways interaction. "It depends on the situation."

The heat in his gaze burns hotter, paying special attention to my breasts. "Does being the boss excite you?"

I almost rub at my skin to make sure I'm not on fire. "Are you flirting with me?"

"Wouldn't dream of it, Red." His gaze roves over me again, ending at my hair.

The messy bun is nothing to drool over. I pat at the sloppy updo, suddenly wishing I'd taken more care in my appearance. "Real creative."

"You have no idea," he rasps.

"Um, okay. Wow." I fan my face. "Are we planning to keep this professional?"

My question seems to knock Rhodes off the suave roll he'd been spinning on. He blinks, the action dipped in frayed composure. Something like guilt flashes across his expression.

Then he straightens while his face morphs into a neutral mask. "Strictly business related."

The abrupt shift in attitude almost makes me teeter. I grip the edge of the bar for support. "What just happened?"

"Nothing." His sharp tone leads me to believe I struck a nerve.

"Didn't feel like nothing," I counter.

If possible, Rhodes injects ice into his once sweltering gaze. "Good thing you won't have to feel it again."

I meet his glare with one of my own. "Don't do that."

"Do what?" He crosses his arms, the action putting his sculpted biceps on display.

"Deflect whenever the subject gets tough."

"Not sure what you mean."

I tip my face to the ceiling for a momentary reprieve. "Okay, listen. I think we got off to a rocky start."

"You think?" His condescending scoff isn't appreciated.

"Fine, I know we did. Happy?" I ask through gritted teeth.

"Far from it."

The urge to scream bubbles up my throat. "Then what're we both still doing here? Leave me to handle this place. Please."

Rhodes is already shaking his head. "Not gonna happen."

"And why not?"

Rather than answering, he flips to script on me. "What do you know about running a business? Do you have experience working in a bar or restaurant?"

I treat him to the same tactics. "Is this a job interview?"

He rolls his eyes. "I'm serious."

"And I'm not?"

Thunder vibrates from his rigid stance. "Trevor might've left his half to you, but that doesn't make you fit to fill his shoes."

The comment lands harsh and true, a verbal smack against me. My eyes water from the sting. But I refuse to wilt.

"Don't be mean," I spit. "You think this is easy for me? Trust me, asshole. If I could wish for anything, I'd want him here instead of me."

"Fuck." He spins away from me, palms resting on his hat.

The silence that follows is necessary. We're too emotionally charged. Too invested. Too stubborn.

I wait, chest rising and falling from the effort it takes not to crumble.

A stilted minute drags on before his voice cracks into the stillness. "You're right, and I'm sorry."

I cup my ear. "Care to repeat that?"

Rhodes faces me again, the fight seeping from him. "You're sassy too. Killer combo."

My finger trembles when I point at him. "Nope, don't even go there."

An apology is written across his stricken gaze. "Am I making you uncomfortable?"

"Just dizzy."

His brow furrows. "Huh?"

"Never mind." I wave my flippant snark away. We don't need to add more confusion. "But I need to make one thing clear. Open communication is important to me. We can't let stuff stew and fester. I don't want this to become a hostile environment."

He's nodding. "You're right. Again."

"That has a real fancy ring to it."

His chuckle is finger-licking good. "I'm sorry for being a dick."

"Work in progress, right?" I exhale, relief ripe in the breeze. "What's next?"

Rhodes glances over his shoulder, toward the far wall. "How about inventory? The beer and liquor are fine. Same with the frozen food. We just need to restock perishables. I can walk you through the order form."

I shrug and stand from the stool. "Sounds safe enough."

He grunts, his lips lifting. "With us? That remains to be seen."

chapter five

RHODES

I TIP THE BOTTLE TO POUR ANOTHER SIP INTO THE DIRT. "How's that?"

Silence whips between the overhead branches as Trevor's response. Not that I expected anything more. The real concern would be if I got a verbal reply.

That doesn't stop me from carrying on a one-sided conversation. "There's more where that came from."

I figured he could use a beer. Lord knows I needed to sit down and have one with him. On cue, I treat myself to a swig. Punchy hops flow with creamy malt. The cool liquid soothes a jagged edge cutting into my throat.

"This might be your best yet." I turn the bottle in my hands. "Smooth and rich. The sour bite is a nice touch."

Too bad the supply is very limited.

I brought two from the last batch Trevor fermented before passing. He planned to expand the bar into a full-fledged brewery. That was his most recent passion project. His enthusiasm couldn't be matched, and it shows in the finished products. But now, he won't get the chance to make it happen.

A cramp seizes in my gut. "Don't worry, man. I'll find a way."

I'm gathering the nerve to replicate his favorite recipes. That's a task I'm not quite ready to tackle yet. But one day. More likely is hiring a few brewers to turn his last dream into reality.

Beer bubbles into the soil when I give him more to taste.

Call me sentimental or wasteful, but he deserves to enjoy the fruits of his labor. Wherever he is.

"Damn," I chuckle. "I'm getting spiritual over your death. Never thought I'd see the day."

Wind rustles through the leaves again.

I lift my bottle to the sky. "Cheers to that."

Fuck, I'm losing it. Or already lost it, if I'm being honest. That's the most logical explanation as to why I'm talking to Trevor's grave and acting like he can hear me. I'm dousing the soil with beer in an attempt to make amends. This is what mourners do, or so I heard. Another helpful tip from my single therapy session.

My gaze lowers to the overturned earth, still fresh from the burial. Grass and weeds are beginning to sprout through the surface. There's a small wet spot from where I've been serving him, as if he can actually drink.

"All right, I've definitely lost it." My chuckle is little more than a rasp. "It's the thought that counts, right? I wasn't about to drink your fine IPA alone."

More than that, a visit is long overdue. Especially after the disaster with Rylee yesterday. Just recalling my behavior makes me cringe. I hang my head with a muffled curse.

"It was bad, man. Your sister hates me. Not that I blame her."

Another sinking sensation hits me when I imagine the horrified expression screwing up her pretty face. She was disgusted. I felt like the biggest hypocrite, drooling over her stacked rack and endless curves. That wasn't even the worst of it. For whatever reason, that woman gets under my skin. I can't seem to back off and let go without it turning into a battle.

The inscription of his tombstone snags my focus.

Trevor Patrick Creed
April 14, 1993 – September 3, 2022
Beloved son, brother, and uncle
"Never forget where you came from. That's how you get to where you're going next."

That last line strikes deep. It's something Trevor would often say. Don't be afraid to retrace steps already taken. A well-worn path keeps us humble.

Our roots nurture us. That gnarled foundation encourages us to grow. Experience pushes us forward. Challenges disrupt the journey, but those lessons are necessary hurdles. It's true that nothing worth having is easy to get. But that doesn't mean we have to make it difficult for others.

Pressure clamps around my torso as I allow that sentiment to sink in. I'm making his sister's life miserable. That's a real testament to me, seeing as Rylee is already in a permanent state of despair. The lump that lodges in my throat is heavy with guilt. I tilt the bottle for Trevor while guzzling from my own. Liquid courage is required to admit the truth.

Stubborn pride sticks to the roof of my mouth. Another gulp for good measure. "We don't get along. At all. It's probably my fault. Entirely. I'm being a dick, but I can't seem to quit."

Relief hangs in the balance, just waiting for approval. That wasn't so hard. The laugh I expel into the afternoon air is steeped in sarcasm.

I bend my leg, draping an arm over my propped knee. "She drives me crazy, Trev. I don't know what it is about her. We couldn't even agree on ordering fruits and veggies yesterday."

Silence acknowledges my efforts to repent. Even the branches are quiet.

"Not good enough, huh? Would it help to know that I feel really fucking bad about it?" I might be struggling with Trevor's death, but Rylee is suffering. She lost her brother, and I argued with her about broccoli. Such petty bullshit.

My regrets are piling up. Confessions too. And here I am, seeking answers from a source who can't speak. The stillness is almost mocking at this point.

I shift on the ground. My ass is half asleep, but there's plenty left to say. "Did you think this through? Because I gotta admit, pairing us together might just ruin the bar."

Failure smacks me with a mental picture of locking the doors for the last time. The image turns my stomach. Nothing would be worse than letting him down. Certainly not admitting that I'm wrong. There's a simple solution. It just pains me to voice it.

"Should I walk away? Rylee is capable of running the place. You left Bent Pedal in her name for a reason. If we can't get along, I'll just be a silent partner." Acceptance is tough to choke down, but this isn't about me. Far from it. "Then we would go our separate ways. That's probably best for the business, all things considered."

A pause for nothing more than doubt to slip in.

"Fuck, man. I'll be honest. Walking away doesn't sit right with me. The bar… it's become like a home. You know that. I'm too attached, huh?"

Further stillness scoffs at me.

"Do you want me to leave her be?" I glare into the distance, trying to ignore the fire building behind my eyes. "Is some sort of sign too much to ask for?"

The wind picks up at that moment. A subtle floral scent stirs within the crisp autumn breeze. I'm not too proud to take the hint.

What's left of his beer gets dumped down the makeshift hatch. I polish mine off as well. My joints creak as I climb to my feet. I brush grass and dirt from my jeans, ending on a stretch. A blunt stiffness alerts me to just how long I'd been sprawled on the hard ground. But then, the soft tread from someone approaching distracts me, my sore muscles momentarily forgotten.

When I turn, the breath gets trapped in my windpipe. A strangled cough shortly follows. I'm not sure what I'd been expecting, but it certainly wasn't this. That brew must've been stronger than I thought. My focus bounces from Trevor's grave to the sky, not sure where to look to find the responsible instigator.

Talk about a divine revelation.

Rylee lifts a hand to shield the sun. Maybe she doesn't believe who she's seeing either. I almost scrub at my eyes to make sure this isn't a hallucination. But she's walking closer, narrowing the gap separating us with a hesitant pace.

"What're you doing here?" The blurted stupidity is out of my mouth before I can rein it in. I scrub at my jaw while masking a cringe. "Fuck. Sorry. It's just a strange coincidence."

Rylee doesn't bother with a response. It's not like I deserve one after that intro. Besides, I'm too captivated by the refreshing visual she presents in this otherwise grim scenery. Any attempt to engage in a meaningful conversation would be embarrassing at best.

Instead, I shamelessly take my fill of her.

The freckles dusting her cheeks are highlighted by the sun. There's a glow bathing her in golden warmth. Her hair appears redder than usual, as if the strands are burning hot. Damn, she's beautiful.

And glaring at me like I'm her enemy.

"This is… weird." I dip my chin, squeezing my eyes shut. "It's weird, right?"

Especially after I asked for a sign. But she doesn't need to know that.

"It's only weird if you make it weird," she clips.

"Definitely not my intention," I mumble. "Just good timing, I guess."

"That's one way to look at it." Her rigid stance is a guard against me, preparing for the worst. She's probably still pissed about my dickish display yesterday.

"Do you come here often?" Sweet Jesus, there's something wrong with me. I wish I'd drank more beer so there'd at least be an excuse for the shit spilling from me.

Rylee blinks, most likely trying to make sense of me. "At least once or twice since I moved back."

"It's my first time." Maybe that will earn me some pity points, or explain why I'm a blubbering idiot.

"Well, I'm sure he appreciates it." She nods at the empty beers leaning against his gravestone. "Another sweet gesture."

I shrug. "Trevor didn't get to try this batch before…"

"What is it?" She stares at the bottles. There isn't a label to identify the unique blend.

"An IPA. He made this one a bit sour." I scoop them off the ground as if that will help.

"Wait, he brewed it?" There's wonder in her voice.

"Yeah." I pause when her stunned expression doesn't clear. "You didn't know?"

Rylee shakes her head. "He told me about brewing, but it was just a passing comment. I had no idea he was actually doing it, or that there were beers ready. Doesn't the process take forever?"

"Not really, but that depends on the type. This one was probably fermenting for about six weeks. His last blend," I murmur.

Her bottom lip trembles while she glances at his resting place. "Oh."

A realization smacks me. "Shit, I should've saved some for you."

Rylee sniffles, doing her best to conceal any stray tears. "Don't be silly. You didn't know I was coming."

"There's more. Two dozen or so."

"Next time," she whispers. Then she checks her watch. "I just stopped by for a quick hello before I have to pick up Gage from school."

If I read between the lines she's drawing, it would be written in bold to get gone. She wants to be alone, understandably. But I'm willing to believe we're both here for a reason.

That should be addressed before I go. Even if it's just to myself.

"Similar thinking, once again. I was about to leave and get Payton."

A thought seems to occur to her. "Where do you live?"

"Richemont," I smirk when her eyes blow wide. The south-western suburb of Minneapolis has a certain reputation.

Rylee whistles. "Someone is fancy, and far from home."

"Just thirty minutes."

"I bet this feels like an entirely different world." She waves a hand at our surroundings.

"How little you must think of me." Not that I've been helping.

She snorts. "That would require me to think of you in the first place."

"Damn," I grunt. "Totally walked into that one."

A real smile—although wobbly—brightens her features. "You did."

Just like that, I feel the strain lift an inch. Maybe this is doable. It's heading in that direction. I can stick my neck out for the sake of peace and prosperity.

"Do you have plans for the rest of the day?"

Suspicion immediately tightens her expression. "Why?"

"We could meet at a park in an hour. Somewhere in the middle. I'm sure Payton will get along great with Gage." Our kids can play as a buffer. They'll make this transition onto even ground a bit smoother.

Rylee studies me, picking at my layers of armor. "But we don't get along."

"That needs to change." I allow her to witness my un-guarded desperation, raw and difficult as it might be. "We're running a business together. You're my partner where the bar is concerned. I need to start acting like it."

She's quiet in her contemplation. It's not easy to watch the conflict flicker across her gaze. "Okay."

"Okay? Just like that?" Shock rings true, unmistakable in my voice. "I figured it would be a bigger—"

"It will be. I'll give you a chance at a truce," she amends. "Don't make me regret it."

The pressure returns, but this is different. My regrets from earlier resurface. It's on me to mend our fences. I'm the one with something to prove, and I won't give her any reason to doubt me. Not again.

I feel that acknowledgement shift some of the tension between my shoulder blades. We have the same goal, but I'd been too stuck in my rut. From this point forward, we'll put aside our differences and fight together for our business.

This is the beginning of a real deal between partners. But above all else, this is what Trevor would want.

I offer her my hand to shake, which she accepts. "You have my word, Firefly."

chapter six

Rylee

GAGE YANKS AT MY ARM FOR THE FOURTH TIME. THE FREAKING joint is about to pop from the socket. His excitement is infectious, though. That's why I find myself laughing with ease. It's happening more often lately, which almost allows me to believe there's an exit route from the shadows.

"Oh, oh. Look! There's Rhodes. Why is he alone? Where's his kid with the boy's name?"

I suck in my lips, trapping a megawatt grin. "Payton."

"Uh-huh, yep. We're gonna race."

"How do you know?" They haven't met, unless I missed a playdate.

He scoffs, as if I missed an entire explanation. "That's just what kids do. We like to go fast."

"Okay, I'll be rooting for you." I lift a closed fist for him to bump.

My son doesn't leave me hanging, ending the action with a loud explosion. "M'kay. You better watch me win."

"Wouldn't miss it," I vow.

His insistent tugging resumes. "Come on, Mom. Rhodes is lonely on the bench."

My focus shifts to where Gage is pointing. The man of my recent aggravation—and attraction—is lounging casually, legs splayed wide as if he owns the entire seat. Heat infuses my cheeks while I treat myself to a slow perusal. He didn't change clothes from earlier. The faded jeans and plain T-shirt are still molded to his brawn. An unbuttoned flannel has entered the mix. His colorful tattoos are now unfortunately hidden from view. Oh, and I can't forget the cherry on top. That dang backward hat will be my undoing.

Two very honorable mentions instantly pop into my brain.

The first is that Rhodes has no right to look that freaking sexy at a playground. Second, there is a pack of feral cougars swarming in his direct vicinity. They've probably sniffed out my number one notice as well.

Can't say I blame them, but that guy is taken. I stumble to an abrupt pause. Wait, that might not be accurate. We haven't discussed Payton's mother, or Gage's father for that matter. The subject never came up between our glaring contests and self-imposed ego stroking. But we're moving on from that. I think.

"Mommmmmm," Gage complains in an exaggerated fashion. He gains the attention of several park goers, Rhodes included.

I offer him a wave when our gazes clash before addressing my son. "Yes, puddin' pop?"

His button nose wrinkles. "What's a puddin' pop?"

A groan rife with disbelief rips from me. "Oh, my sweet child. I've done you a great disservice."

"Huh?"

"Never mind." I swat that off. "But you haven't properly lived without tasting a puddin' pop, kiddo."

Gage does a thorough sweep of the grounds. "Can we get one here?"

"Maybe." This park is stacked with the latest and greatest equipment and attractions, at least from an initial glance. It must be a recent build, or freshly renovated. "If they don't sell ice cream, we can grab some from the store."

"Okay." He shrugs. "Can we hurry now? You've been moving like a snail."

"Was not," I retort.

"Totally were, Mom. I've been pulling you along."

"Guess I got distracted," I mumble.

"By what?"

"Nobody." I quickly realize my mistake. "Nothing. I mean, nothing. Whoopsie. My head is in the clouds."

He peeks skyward. "How does that happen? I don't wanna lose my head to the clouds."

"You won't, sweetie. It's just an expression."

His small hand wipes across his brow. "Phew."

I snatch him in a hug before he can resist. "Gosh, you're too cute."

"Eww, Mom." Gage struggles against my hold, which I like to pretend is all for show. My little buddy needs to love hugs forever. After a few beats, he relents and sags into me. His arms even wrap around my waist to return the embrace.

"Love you," I whisper into his hair.

He sighs, nuzzling closer. "Love you too."

I set him free, and he doesn't waste a second before dashing toward Rhodes. My enthusiasm to reach him is slightly more contained. Their conversation is animated and mostly one-sided.

Gage is busy talking his ear off. "Where's Payton? We've gotta race."

Rhodes smirks at the motor mouth. "She's drawing with chalk. See that not-so-little girl over there?"

My son's eyes slide to where he's motioning. "Uh-huh."

"Want me to call her over and introduce you two?"

"Nope. I've got this." Without another word, Gage leaves us in his dust.

I giggle at his brave antics. The sound is loose and free and snags the focus of a certain someone. My pulse jumps into a sprint. His stare is warm, yet gentle. The early October evening offers a chilled breeze against my fair-skinned blush. Somehow, I still feel like I'm overheating. This calls for an icebreaker.

Once we're close enough, I nudge his shoe with mine.

"Hey, Daddy." I almost retch the instant I aim the term at him.

Based on Rhodes' cringe, he's not feeling the title from me either. He stays firmly planted in his seat. "Um, hi?"

Talk about the ultimate backfire.

"Not endearing, huh? I was trying it on for size." Ever since he started calling me Firefly—the reason why still remains a mystery—I've been searching for an adequate nickname to give him.

"Nope, that's not for me." He tacks on a gag for good measure. "But I won't lie. I've been curious, so thanks for giving it a shot."

"Noted, and you're welcome for the valiant effort." I take a bow.

"Maybe when Payton is older. I can't compartmentalize at this stage."

"Oh," I chirp and wag my brows. "Daddy isn't officially off the table?"

Rhodes shudders. "No, I can't. It's creeping me out. Please don't repeat it unless you want me to puke."

A devious laugh escapes me, extra throaty and loud. "The leverage you just carelessly tossed at me is going straight to the vault."

His brown eyes twinkle with our shared amusement. "You're in a good mood."

"Why wouldn't I be?" And once again, I immediately want to rephrase the context.

Understanding dawns in his kind expression. "It's okay to be happy."

"Is it?" Guilt is already clawing at me, desperate to shroud any semblance of joy.

"Of course," he insists in a tone that demands follow-through. "Trevor would hate to see you upset, especially every hour of the day. You know that."

"I guess." But that doesn't stop the sting from attacking my vision. I avert my blurry gaze, willing the freaking tears away. A traitorous drop dribbles out regardless.

"Ah, Firefly. Don't cry." Rhodes straightens from his relaxed pose and reaches for my hand.

Something about his words is a soothing balm. Just this small gesture from him offers more comfort than I've felt in a month. It makes the fiery rush spill from my eyes faster.

I swipe at the tears wetting my cheeks. "Ugh, this is silly."

"Definitely not." He tows me in until our knees bump. From his seated position, I'm on full display in front of him.

I tuck my chin to escape his concerned scrutiny. "Stop staring at me. You're giving me a complex."

"But you're sad, and I don't want you to be."

Flames lick at my eyes when I focus on the clouds above. "I'm fine."

His grunt calls my bluff. "I would disagree."

I pin him with a watery glare. "Well, too freaking bad. You're not the one crying."

He smirks at my bite of snark. "But you're not the only one."

My gaze follows to where he's pointing out several examples. "They're children. That's what they do. I don't have a scraped knee as an excuse."

"No, what you have is far worse." His stare is too invasive.

A shiver rolls through me despite the fire beneath my skin. I feel exposed, flayed open to my guts and glory. The urge to cower and look away weighs down my lashes. But there's another instinct rising to the surface that keeps me steady.

With his sole focus digging under my layers, I feel seen in a way that I'm unfamiliar with. My wounded spirit flutters. I realize that I don't care if he sees those jagged edges slicing at me. These flaws are mine. I'm not afraid to show my grief. It's how I'll choose to move forward that scares me.

Rhodes shatters our silence, psychic that he is. "It will get easier."

My throat is suddenly parched. "How do you know?"

"I just do."

"That's not very convincing."

"Do you have another suggestion?" He pauses for a breath, waiting for my argument. Another soft squeeze meets my palm before he releases me. "Have you tried talking to someone?"

"Like a professional?"

His nod is paired with a wince, most likely concerned about how I'll react. The stigma behind seeking mental health support still very much exists for many. But he doesn't have to worry about that with me.

I blow out a noisy exhale. "Yeah, I'd already been meeting with a therapist on a semi-regular basis. She saw me twice in the week before I moved here. I can schedule a tele-session with her whenever needed."

"Good." His Adam's apple dips with a thick swallow. "I'm glad you have someone."

The way he says that gives me pause. Awareness prickles along my scalp, lifting the hair on my arms.

"Do you?" I gulp at my own nerves. "Have someone, I mean."

Rhodes smiles, but the expression is limp at best. "There are people I can lean on. I tried a psychologist, but bearing my soul to a stranger isn't for me."

"I get that. You have to be comfortable with the person."

His gaze roves over me again. "My thoughts exactly."

"Thanks for this, whatever it was. I really didn't mean to cry. Especially here." I glance over my shoulder, at our very public surroundings. What a glorious place to have a sob fest.

"It will get easier," he repeats.

I glance over to my main source of sunshine. Gage is doodling beside Payton, their heads bent together. It's the picture of childhood bliss. That image alone fills my leaky cup to half full. "Yeah, I think it will."

"One day at a time. At any point along the journey, you can

always come to me. I'm a non-neutral party willing to offer un-solicited advice and extremely biased opinions."

I laugh. There's no trapping it. "What could be better?"

His chuckle carries several notes of humor. "See? We're al-ready on the way."

"We?"

Rhodes snorts. "Yes, we. We're in this together from now on. You're stuck with me, Firefly. For his sake, but also for ours. That's the direction we'll choose. Don't feel bad for laughing. Express yourself freely. It's okay to be all right. Live happier for him."

The thrill I get from him joining forces with me is embar-rassing. It's sad to acknowledge just how starved I am for af-fection. Even the strictly platonic kind from my brother's best friend.

He must recognize the signs of distress once my pregnant pause reaches infancy. His concern scours my face with precise scrutiny. "What's the blank stare for?"

I blink to clear the dust from my lashes. "This just isn't what I was expecting from our truce."

"There's no reason for either of us to throw in the towel. This isn't a battle we need to fight. We're on the same team." His gaze bores into mine, almost pleading. "Right?"

"Right, and very insightful," I muse.

He winks, the gloomy mood breaking from above us. "How 'bout that, huh? I'm full of more than bullshit."

"Let's not be too hasty." I nudge his leg with my own.

After all, we're barely balancing on stable ground. But I al-ready feel a bond blooming. Some residual grip left behind from Trevor maybe. Whatever it is, I can see us maintaining the peace.

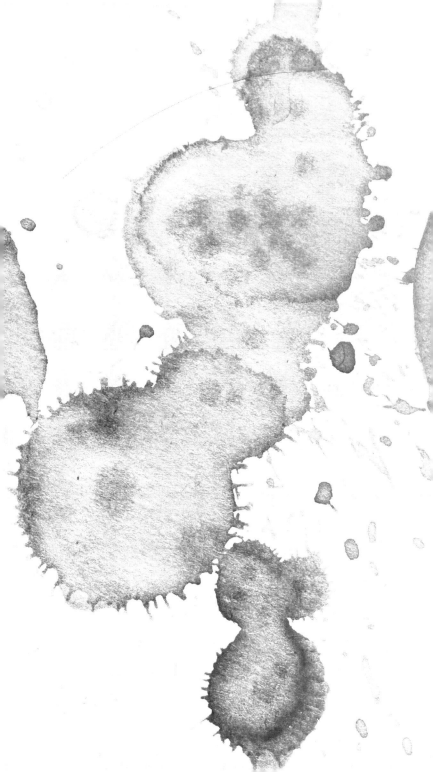

chapter seven

Rylee

THE LULL SNOOZING BETWEEN US IS PLEASANT. IDLE CHATTER from fellow park goers offers a welcome background hum of white noise. Unfiltered glee and energy perfumes the already buoyant atmosphere. I'm tempted to keep my heels plastered to this paved slab until the sun goes down. A peek straight ahead finds Rhodes at ease as well. My assumption—or desperation to meet in the middle—might just come to fruition.

My focus drifts to Gage again. He's still occupied without a care elsewhere. It's been just the two of us for years. When we moved to Knox Creek, our duo doubled overnight thanks to my parents. The hole where Trevor belongs is wide and gaping, but his memory seals our circle. There might be room for more. Eventually. I allow my attention to return straight ahead, and immediately snort at myself. Talk about being hasty.

That's when I notice our very rapt—and envious—audience. The cougars from earlier have multiplied into a flock of ruffled feathers. Two women are openly staring at us from across the basketball court. Another pair have their eyes locked on us while whispering. A sideways glance reveals similar results. It seems every direction has at least one lady eager to replace me.

I almost wave at a fellow redhead. The look she gives me

in return is nothing short of scathing. If glares could burn, I'd be up in smoke. So much for sisterhood.

My lips twist to one side while I run a quick risk assessment. These hens appear willing and able to do whatever is necessary for a chance at the lone cock. "Do you bring Payton to this park a lot, Plato?"

Rhodes furrows his brow. "Plato?"

"He's a famous philosopher who is also very insightful. Forget it." I flick my wrist, dismissing yet another failed attempt. "But do you come here often?"

"Now you're just stealing my lines. I know we're sharing the bar, but let's not get lazy." A smooth grin reveals a cleft in his chin that I hadn't previously noticed. The divot is buried under thick scruff, but I can't unsee it.

I nearly sway on my feet. "Give me a break. I'm off kilter."

"Wanna sit?" He pats the empty spot beside him.

"It's not reserved for your harem?" But I plop down onto the bench without further concern for my wellbeing. A few brows were undoubtedly raised that I've been lurking in front of him this entire time.

Rhodes twists on the seat to face me. "The fuck?"

I make a non-discreet motion to the slobbering onlookers. They have no shame and I'm merely following suit. "You have a fan club."

He does a fast sweep of the grounds, ending with a grimace. "That's being generous."

An unladylike snort rocks me backward. The metal bench squeaks from my abrupt shift. "Puh-lease. It's like you're famous or something. Am I invading their sacred territory? Intruding on a protocol? Do I need to wait in line?"

His scowl deepens. "I don't recognize any of them."

"They've never met you?"

"Not that I'm aware of."

"But they're acting possessive." Pretty sure the brunette on my left is foaming at the mouth.

Rhodes brushes off their behavior with a shrug. *"Just ignore them."*

"How are you okay with this? They're making me uncomfortable." My voice is a muted whisper. I'd hate to give them a motive.

His raspy chuckle blows my cover straight off. *"It's not that bad. You're acting like they're going to Hulk smash at any moment. Besides, I'm used to it."*

"You shouldn't have to get used to this." I hitch a thumb behind us, no longer concerned with ruffling feathers.

He makes a noncommittal noise while glaring into the distance. *"Comes with the territory. I've had seven years of practice."*

"It's a wonder how you've remained single." Although, to be fair, I'm not certain he is.

His head tilts left to right. *"I like my women a little less…"*

"Desperate?"

"Sure." Humor bursts from between his pressed lips. *"We can go with that."*

Disbelief still grinds my gears. I almost envy their brass lady balls. *"It's always like this?"*

His smirk is slanted in smug satisfaction. *"More or less. I'm immune at this point."*

A striking realization dawns over me. *"Oh, I get it. You love when they cluck over you. Probably gets your giblets hard."*

"Absolutely not." His vehement rejection vibrates with conviction.

"Really?"

His stare turns hard when our gazes lock. *"You don't believe me?"*

I don't reply just yet. Instead, I take a beat to measure his varied responses since I broached this subject. If he's not interested in these admirers, he won't mind if I test that theory with my own variable. I can set the stage and chase off these wishful thinkers.

The fact he took my hand a few minutes ago gives me the courage to be bold. I rest my palm over his in a practiced maneuver motion. To those spying on the sidelines, this might appear to be a natural occurrence. My breathing stalls as I wait for him to react.

Rhodes startles, but doesn't pull away. "What're you doing?"

"Staking a fake claim on you."

"Why?"

"Isn't it obvious?" I do a purposeful scan of those in our direct vicinity.

His curiosity tracks mine. My experiment will either diffuse this mating season situation or create a catastrophe. Most are instantly dissuaded and accept defeat with little more than a frown. Their prowl begins anew. Surrender isn't easy for everyone, though. A few stragglers remain, but they don't file a formal complaint. It's easy to ignore them while finishing my visual sweep.

Then I swivel my assessment to Rhodes. After the initial jolt, he doesn't appear the least bit bothered. On the contrary, he threads his fingers through mine. The interwoven clasp takes this flippant gesture to an intimate level. My belly leaps at the warmth spreading from between our joined hands. It feels nice. Better than a casual display initiated to divert interest. But we're just playing a bit of pretend.

I flash him a smile. "Not bad, huh?"

"Guess you'll have to come to the park with us more often." Rhodes winks, alerting me that he's following along with the farce.

Which should calm the erratic tempo beating from my chest. "I'll think about it."

"Ah, come on." He gives my palm a squeeze. "We make a great team."

The thump in my pulse lunges into a gallop. I once again blame my severe lack of male company. Rhodes is my business partner. That's it. The reminder shouldn't be necessary, but here we are.

My earlier assumption about his single status swerves from the back burner. "Can I ask you a question?"

"Sure." There's only a pinch of hesitation in his tone.

"It might be too personal. Feel free to opt out if that's the case."

He rolls his eyes. "I'm not sensitive. What's up?"

I gulp down the logic urging me to steer clear. "Where is Payton's mom?"

His neutral expression doesn't reveal a trace of upset. "Your guess is as good as mine. She's not involved."

"That's vague and ominous." And too familiar.

"For good reason." His eyes skip off mine, cutting off further prodding. "How about Gage's dad?"

Nausea instantly replaces the giddy flutters in my stomach. Gage's father—sperm donor is more appropriate—has the ability to make me physically ill, even with half the country separating us. I'd prefer to incinerate all memory of him, much like he set fire to my faith in human decency. But turnabout is only fair.

Lucky for me, I have an ironclad excuse to barely skim the surface.

"Well, I've signed a ton of paperwork that states we can't legally discuss him in relation to me or my son. So…" I pretend to button my lips while fighting projectile vomit.

Rhodes mirrors my gesture. "Damn, Firefly. Your circumstances might be more brutal than mine."

I release a sigh steeped in drama best left unsaid. That's not a competition I want to win, but he's probably right. "Maybe we'll gather the nerve to exchange our horror stories someday."

Before he can reply, conspiring whispers of the non-contempt variety swarm us. Gage and Payton are gathered in a conspicuous huddle right in front of us. How they got this close without me noticing further proves the previous topic should be avoided. Permanently.

Giggles erupt from their collaboration. My gaze narrows into a squint. It's obvious these two are up to something. Payton nods and breaks apart from the suspicious formation. I brace myself as she steps toward me, clearly elected to take the lead in whatever this is.

"You're Gage's mom, right?" Her question is a lyrical chirp, rhetorical as it might be.

I peek over at my son, who's taken a sudden interest in tying his shoes. "Yep, that's me. You can call me Ms. Creed or Rylee... or Gage's mom. I'll answer to any of those. Is your name Payton?"

"It is!" She beams, showing off her gap-toothed grin. The Tooth Fairy has been busy with this one.

"Such a lovely name for a young lady. It's very nice to meet you." I glance at Rhodes, who's stifling a laugh with his fist.

"You're pretty. Like really pretty." She blinks at me with pure innocence before turning those doe eyes to her father. "Isn't Rylee super pretty, Daddy?"

Now it's my turn to muffle an obnoxious cackle. With my lips sealed tight, I realize just how wrong my earlier attempt had been. Amusing, yes. But definitely a mistake.

A delayed concern overshadows my humor. The term could be tainted for him. I'm almost afraid to look, preferring to remain blissfully ignorant. But the guy looks cool and calm, with no signs of distress or cracking up. He must recover faster than me.

Gage and Payton share a quizzical shrug. I shake off the inside joke before they can ask. That flub isn't worth dissecting while more important matters are being discussed. I bat my lashes at Rhodes, waiting for his verdict.

His chocolate stare locks on mine. "She's stunning."

My breath catches. It shouldn't be a shock that he's set on knocking me sideways. I'm jostled from the misplaced romantic bubble by Payton's giggles. She's returned to the huddle stance with Gage. The whispers and flailing continue soon after.

"We're in trouble now," he whispers from the corner of his mouth.

I cross my ankles and recline against the hard seat. "Let them have fun."

"Famous last words," he mumbles.

Gage straightens, scrawny shoulders rolled back. "Payton is my girlfriend."

Rhodes' eyes bulge. "What?"

Payton's smile could replace the sun. "Gage wants to be my boyfriend."

Her dad struggles to form a response, jaw hanging slack. He's not so cool and calm anymore.

I let my own giggle roam free. "Oh, yeah. We're in so much trouble."

Rhodes looks to me for advice, or a way to defuse this premature dating situation. Something seems to occur to him, the wheels spinning wildly behind his gaze. He pins Payton with a protective father mean mug that could make me quake in my boots. "Henry is already your boyfriend."

She flips her hair. "I can have two."

That barely registers. I'm too busy studying Gage. "Yeah, let's talk about this. Don't you already have a girlfriend?"

"I have six girlfriends." Pride sings from his voice.

I gape at him. "Excuse me?"

He proceeds to prattle off their names, ending with a pleased grin. "But I want to marry Payton the most."

Rhodes chokes on nothing but shock. "Marry?"

I make a slicing motion to Gage. "We've talked about this."

My son's focus slides to the bristling body beside me. "Uh-oh. Are you gonna get me with a shotgun?"

"The fu—fudge?" Rhodes is glaring at me.

I hang my head with a groan. "It's just something I told him once when he was caught flirting. The dad wasn't impressed that his little girl was blowing kisses and looking lovesick. I was kidding. Obviously."

"That was funny," Gage laughs from his belly.

"Okay, whatever." Rhodes slashes the air. "You aren't getting married."

Payton stomps her foot. "Are too. We're in love."

"You're really not," he retorts.

She rolls her eyes. "But that's no fair. You're gonna marry Rylee."

"Oh, no. We aren't getting married," I insist.

Gage squishes his lips into a pout. "But you're holding hands."

I lower my gaze to confirm that we are, in fact, still holding hands. Rhodes drops me like a hot potato. The kids double over in a fit of laughter. Apparently, our spoof is more believable than I thought. Especially to a pair of second graders.

Rhodes grips the back of his neck. "We were, uh, practicing."

Payton wrinkles her nose. "For what?"

His expression blanches in a panic I feel deep in my gut. It seems my partner in crime isn't too stellar on the fly. He has to go and prove me wrong, of course. "Our staff meeting on Friday."

My mental brakes squeal in protest. "Whoa, whoa. Our what now?"

His eyes shift to mine, a wince already pinching his expression. "I didn't get a chance to tell you."

I guarantee disappointment is seeping from my pores. "Why wasn't I involved in setting the date?"

He wrenches on his hat, spinning the bill to face forward and shadow his eyes. "That's my fault."

"Is there a planning process I missed?"

"No."

I reel in the blast of accusations ready to fire in his direction. No good will come from fighting in front of our kids, but that doesn't mean I have to keep quiet. "What if I couldn't be there on Friday?"

His mouth opens and closes like a broken, soundless record.

At least he has the decency to appear apologetic. "We would've rescheduled."

"We shouldn't have to."

He rakes a hand through his hair. "I was trying to be proactive."

"By leaving me out completely?"

"It isn't like that." His eyes flint with steel.

More than anything, his oversight hurts my already bruised spirit. "This isn't good for our truce, Bozo."

Gage snickers, dipping toward Payton's ear. "She called him a clown."

"They're totally in love," she whisper-shouts.

I do my best to ignore them, refocusing on my so-called equal in this arrangement. "What's happening at this meeting?"

"That's for us to decide."

"Oh, we're a team again?" Maybe I'm blowing this out of proportion, but being excluded from my business—*Trevor's business*—doesn't feel great.

"Firefly—"

I hold up a finger. "Nope, don't even."

Rhodes chuckles, but the sound is a mockery. "Hold on. You're actually angry? I was trying to make the transition easier for you."

"Which would have been appreciated if you'd asked, or told me ahead of time." I peek over at our kids, finding them tuned into our conversation. "We'll discuss this later."

"Oooooh, my mom is super mad at your dad." Gage clasps a palm over his mouth to trap another giggle.

Payton leans in, as if she's missing out on juicy details. "Why?"

He shrugs. "I dunno, but she's using the mad voice. Maybe he isn't listening to her. That's why she gets fussy at me."

And now I feel like a terrible mother. Freaking perfect.

Heat springs to my eyes in a fiery blast. Just when I think

the tears have dried up for the day. I've hit my limit twice over, and this is the final curtain.

Blood rushes to my head when I stand in a hurry. "It's time to go, Gage. Say bye to Payton and Rhodes."

My son frowns but doesn't argue. His wave to my former bench mate is sheepish, but gains momentum once Rhodes reciprocates. That gives him the courage to hug his favorite girl-friend with extra enthusiasm. The precious moment only makes my upset multiply. A sob hiccups in my throat as I lower my watery gaze. I'm ripping him away early because I can't maintain a mood for more than five minutes. Although, this isn't entirely my fault.

Before running off, I hold out a fist for Payton to bump. "Great meeting you, kiddo. Thanks for playing with Gage. I'm sure we'll see you soon."

She smiles wide, not at all dimmed by the adult nonsense clogging the air. "M'kay. See ya!"

Strong fingers grip my elbow, pausing my hasty retreat. "Rylee, wait. We need to talk about this."

"And we will." I'm a stiff board against him, my eyes glued forward toward escape.

"When?"

I tug myself free from his hold. "At *your* staff meeting. I'll be sure to arrive early. I'd hate to miss anything."

chapter eight

RHODES

WITH A SHARP PIVOT, I SPIN ON MY HEEL AND STALK TO THE opposite wall. The fast clip against the floor syncs with the rapid thud in my chest. I check my watch again. It's almost half past nine. Two minutes have ticked by much slower than my relentless pacing.

The morning sun is still rising, streaming through the front windows in a golden cascade. It does little to brighten my mood. Each glimmer reflects a second I've wasted.

Rylee said she'd arrive early. That's a broad frame of time. Maybe it was her intention to leave me guessing. Mission accomplished. I wasn't about to let her arrive without me waiting.

Muffled curses spew from my sealed lips. Why I care so much has boggled my brain into scrambled mush. This isn't me. Far from it. I honestly can't grasp what the fuck has gotten into me.

Other than the obvious, of course.

The guilt of being the cause of Rylee's tears has plagued my every waking moment since she left the park. I've been at fault for countless crying spells. Enough to be immune to glassy eyes and wobbly bottom lips. But for some reason, hers hits on a different level. Maybe I'm manifesting some protective instincts from Trevor. A spasm in my chest warns me to repair the damage before it's too late. Lord knows he'd be madder than a caged lion to discover I made his little sister cry. The stupidest part, or maybe most ironic, is that I don't have the foggiest idea why she got upset.

But that ignorance certainly won't grant me any favors.

The door creaks open as I'm about to begin another lap. I slam to an immediate halt to watch Rylee enter the bar. My heart jumps straight into my dry throat, which in turn makes me feel like a bigger shmuck. That's not even the worst of it.

Words I've rehearsed for days die a quick death on my tongue. I nearly crash to my knees, ready to beg for mercy.

She damn near glows with the sunshine as a backdrop. Her mouthwatering curves are wrapped tight in a green dress. The clingy fabric was designed to make a sane man lose his mind, or commit a felony. Probably both, if the instant shot of lust that surges into my veins is any indication. Just thinking about other guys being served this visual delight ignites a burning rage. It's unfamiliar and uncomfortable, effectively tipping my scale closer to losing common sense. That doesn't mean I quit gorging myself on her, though.

Some complicated twist holds her hair hostage. The style is too… severe for her bouncy personality. I have the urge to pluck out every last pin until those glossy waves spill over my fingers. That would certainly get me a knee to the family jewels. A shudder churns the premature nausea in my gut.

It's best to avoid the temptation for now. That doesn't mean I can't set my sights elsewhere.

Rylee's plump lips are stained a deep red. A delectable—albeit indifferent—pout is pursed in my direction. I can't scrounge up an ounce of remorse with that pucker aimed at me. That's when I notice the briefcase slung over her shoulder. We have business to handle. She looks the polished part while I've spun myself into disheveled slop, too busy blazing a trail into the stamped concrete.

"I fucked up," is how I decide to kick things off.

"With what?" Her tone is too polite under the circumstances.

That gives me pause, suspicion narrowing my eyes into a squint. *"The meeting."*

"Is it canceled?"

"No.

Rylee struts into the otherwise empty space and drops her bag on a stool. When she turns to face me, her posture is loose and relaxed. The picture of poised professional doesn't falter. *"Then what's wrong?"*

My responding blink is sluggish. This isn't how I expected our conversation to go. *"I should've consulted you before scheduling it."*

With an airy swat, she waves me off. *"It's fine."*

I feel my brows take an upward hike. *"That's… news to me. You didn't seem fine with it on Tuesday."*

She smiles, which only deepens my confusion. The expression is faker than a winter tan. *"I've had time to think about it. You were trying to do a nice thing by setting this meeting up. It came across as a jab at first, but I don't think that was your intention."*

"It wasn't."

"See? I get it now. You're the boss, at least until I get a better handle on running the bar. No hard feelings. There's probably a foolproof system you've relied on for years. I stomped into your routine as a newbie, assuming I'd fit right in. That's on me." Her logic is sound, yet I don't fully believe it's authentic.

"This is a partnership. We're in this together, remember?" I'm beginning to suspect she's forgotten most of what we discussed earlier this week. Or she's choosing to block it out. The latter is more likely.

Rylee's nod is measured, too formal. *"Our relationship doesn't extend beyond these walls. Strictly professional. Period."*

I scratch at the overgrown scruff on my jaw. *"That doesn't mean you have to be so…"*

Stiff. Cold. Bored. Dozens of descriptors stab at my skull.

None of them are flattering. The last thing I need to do is offend her further.

She waits for me to string a simple sentence together. When I'm still faltering moments later, she takes pity on me. Kind of. "So…?"

"Whatever this is." I thrust an arm at her façade.

"Do you have a problem with how I'm acting?"

"No, but it's clear you have a problem with me."

"I'm not sure what's giving you that impression." Her plastic mask doesn't slip.

An ache spreads behind my sternum. This isn't the same woman I've started to get to know.

But that's the problem. I don't really know Rylee Creed beyond our limited interactions this past week. Still, there's a noticeable difference in her demeanor.

If I'm at fault for this abrupt flip, then it's my job to steer us back on track. "What's wrong, Firefly?"

The nickname barely gets a reaction. Rylee clucks her tongue but otherwise remains in Stepford character. "Other than the usual?"

"Yes," I snap. Regret immediately punches me. I rake a hand through my hair, sending the strands into further disarray. "Fuck, this isn't you."

Her laugh is phonier than the rest. "How would you know?"

My stare locks onto her flat features. "Is this really how it's going to be between us?"

"Do you prefer when we fight at every turn?" The syrup in her tone is just begging to stick me in a jam.

I scoff. "Obviously not."

"Then we agree. This is for the best."

"Is it?" Maybe I'm the only one disturbed by carrying on in an overly proper dynamic.

She smooths a palm over her flawless dress. "Yes, I let emotion get involved before. That's a mistake I won't make again."

My experience with women might consist of meaningless

flings and one-nighters, but even I can smell bullshit ripe in the air. "We're more than business partners. Trevor made sure of that."

Her gaze dips to a random spot on the floor. "I apologize if I've crossed lines, or given you the wrong idea. We need to maintain boundaries for the sake of our company."

I glance from left to right, up and down, all the while wondering if I've somehow lapsed into a stupor. "Are you trying to get back at me for scheduling the meeting without you?"

"Get back at you?" She levels me with a flinty stare. "You're making this a much bigger deal than it actually is."

"Can you blame me? You're acting like a completely different person."

"I've never been vengeful," Rylee quips.

"Noted, but that doesn't explain the drastic change."

She expels a windy sigh, but the farce doesn't crack from her expression. "If you must know, I'm embarrassed about the other day. It was a major overreaction on my part. You don't need my permission to schedule a meeting. From now on, I'll abide by the same practices."

Rules and regulations aren't strangers to me, but this version of Rylee is. "That's not how to run a successful partnership. We should be a cohesive unit."

"In that case, there shouldn't be any further misunderstandings. This is a learning curve for me. If you grant me some patience, I'll extend you the same courtesy. Smooth sailing, captain." She tacks on an exaggerated salute as if this entire situation isn't already sideways.

Who in the hell is this cardboard cutout and what did she do with my unpredictable firefly? Not that Rylee is mine. Dammit, there I go again.

I absently wonder if this woman was dropped in my path to drive me straight to madness. It's only logical, considering I'm on the verge freaking the fuck out.

The fuel to propel this conversation onward gets trapped in

my lungs. Something she said earlier circles round to the forefront. "I'm not your boss. We have equal say. You have just as much right to rule the roost as me."

"And once I gather my bearings, I'll be more than happy to do so. For now, it's clear you have a set way of running things. I won't interfere while you're training me in. After that, you can return to your regular schedule."

I furrow my brow. "What do you mean?"

"Bent Pedal isn't your only business, right? I'm sure you have other places to be."

The assumption is valid. I do, in fact, have six other buildings I could stand to visit more frequently. But those companies don't hold the same personal value. They also don't require the same level of attention from me. After I hand them a check, my presence isn't expected. That investment model extends across the board except where this bar is concerned.

"I'm afraid you're not getting rid of me. This is my home base, more or less." I rock back on my heels while scanning the comfortable environment I helped create.

A muscle twitches in her cheek. "Super."

"And to think, I almost let the bar go to waste." I've lowered myself to aggravation tactics. Chivalry and grace are taking a backseat.

"You don't need to remind me."

"Yet you're giving me full control."

Her glare almost has me pumping my fist. "Yeah, right. Let's just move forward with you in the driver's seat. Indefinitely."

My former guilt splinters, hardening into stony resolve. I'm done playing pretend. "Whatever blows your skirt up, Firefly."

She rolls her eyes, a sign of her usual fire glinting through the surface. "I'll give you a hint, caveman. It certainly won't be you."

The stab is a gory wound to my ego. "Your loss."

Rylee wrinkles her freckled nose. "I doubt it."

"How little you must think of me." Which strikes far lower

than the last time I used that line. My muscles twitch while I wait for her to snatch the thread.

"There you go again, assuming I'm thinking of you at all." Ah, she doesn't disappoint.

The fact she remembers is more telling than closed captioning. Her plastic mask doesn't slip completely, but the knot in my gut goes slack. I celebrate with a victorious smirk all the same. Our banter is a comfort I didn't want to admit I've missed. But here we are.

I tug my bottom lip between my teeth. "You're not curious about what's hidden beneath my layers?"

Her eyes flit to the tattoos exposed on my forearms. And the gulp she tries to hide doesn't escape me. "Hard pass."

chapter nine

RHODES

BEFORE I CAN THOROUGHLY INCINERATE RYLEE'S FROSTY EXTERIOR, the door flings open with a crash. Casey and Adam—both cocksure bartenders—saunter in like they own the place. The overconfident pair simultaneously slam to a stop. My upper lip curls with awareness. I know exactly what's drawn them up short. It's like watching two pubescent teens drooling over their first porno.

Nope, scratch that. This is worse.

I'd almost laugh at their humiliating display if it wasn't for Rylee's outward relief. The strain in her shoulders droops with an audible exhale. She glides forward to greet them, a friendly smile on her ruby lips. Her hand is outstretched for their meaty clutches to devour. If I were a lesser man, I'd interfere with possessive peacocking. As it stands, I'm barely concealing the fumes from streaming out.

The real glue sticking me in place is that these two don't threaten me in the least. I'll give them three minutes before pulling the plug. Maybe five if history repeats and they blow it for themselves.

"Holy shit," Casey breathes. "You're smokin' hot."

Adam lets a wolf whistle loose. "This job just got sexier."

Real discreet, not to mention eloquent. Secondhand embarrassment ribs me on their behalf. Rylee doesn't seem to mind the obnoxious compliments, though. A blush instantly races along her slender neck. The reaction is available for all to see thanks to her pinned hair.

Casey doesn't bother hiding the fact that he's staring at her tits. "Are you a new hire?"

"Please say yes." Adam clasps his palms in a pleading gesture.

"I'm actually Trevor's sister, and your boss." Rylee sounds disappointed, but I'm assuming it's aimed at their behavior.

Casey bites his fist. "Ah, damn. That took a dark turn."

"Yep." She pops her lips. "I'm off-limits. Sorry, boys."

Meanwhile, I'm grinning like a mated loon. My chest puffs out in primal delight. Her blatant dismissal is more satisfying than Irish whiskey straight from the distillery. How fucked in the head am I? It's probably worse that I don't care.

Adam snatches her hand, tugging her closer than socially appropriate. She begins to pull away when he dips to kiss her knuckles. "How can I change your mind?"

The refined gentleman persona is wasted on him. He's practically transparent. As fucking if. I snort loud enough for them to hear.

Three sets of eyes swing toward me. Rylee's bland indifference is back in action. The guys wear matching scowls as if I pissed in their beer. Adam is the first to recover. Casey isn't too far behind. Neither one makes a move to leave her side.

Adam sends me a limp wave. "Yo, Walsh. Glad the gang is getting back together."

"Likewise," I deadpan.

"Can't say I hated getting paid to sit on my ass, though." Casey elbows his equally douchey counterpart.

"Yeah, bro. That was balls deep. But I've missed my ladies." Adam punches his hips forward in a thrusting motion.

Good Lord, these two are beyond words. I almost forgot just how lewd and crude they are. I'd kick them to the curb if it weren't for their aforementioned loyal customers. They put on multiple flair performances every shift. Those tricks draw a crowd, which pads our pockets. I can't complain too much about that. The constant ego-stroking it gives them is another matter entirely.

As if reading my thoughts, Adam and Casey begin reminiscing on their greatest achievements. None are appropriate to share aloud, let alone with their bosses in earshot. But Rylee appears content listening to them wax idiotic. Maybe she's picturing them falling down an escalator. That's probably just me.

We're saved from further panty raiding tales when the remaining crew begins trickling in. There are six servers, four bartenders, three cooks, and two dishwashers on staff. One after another, our team makes her acquaintance. I stew in the shadows, just waiting for the welcome parade to end.

She's full of smiles and laughs for them. Whenever her attention shifts to me, the rigid veneer is plastered on. The heat of her frustration strikes a match to the distance separating us. I retire to the background, determined to give her space. She'll cool off after they boost her spirits.

Tendrils of their conversations reach me. The girls gush over her dress while the dudes appreciate how she looks in it. I find a spot against the wall to watch the reunion unfold. Nobody rushes over to join my pity party. If anything, they're probably stunned to see me out of the office. More often than not, I'm buried underneath the paperwork that keeps us afloat. A tightness tugs at my chest. Maybe it's time for a change.

Trevor was the favorite front man. His free spirit and magnetic personality sucked people in like a gravitational force. It seems his sister carries the same infectious traits. She's the center of attention, surrounded by those drawn into her orbit. My firefly thrives in these conditions. Temptation stirs in my gut. Pleasure would certainly find me if I got close enough to her infectious energy. But I'm resigned to stay put.

Finally, Jeremy strolls over to my darkened domain. The quiet cook shares my preference for the sidelines. We often bonded in silence during the lags in service.

"Heya, boss." He parks himself on the wall beside me.

I nod at him in greeting. "Good to see you, man. Thanks for coming in."

"Wouldn't miss it." As our kitchen's head honcho, he's probably eager for the grind to get back on track.

My smirk is forced. "Sorry it took this long."

"Nah, I understand. Is there a date yet?"

"That's next on the agenda." I hope, at least.

It depends on when Rylee will be receptive to discussing details with me. As of now, I'm thinking next year. That's definitely not what Jeremy wants to hear.

"She's gonna fit right in," he drawls.

My gaze seeks Rylee like a tracking device. I bristle at the sight of her behind the bar with Adam. He's testing the limits of her personal space again. The difference is she doesn't appear to be in a hurry to break away. Blood rushes hotter than lava beneath my skin. I curl my hands into fists as the scene unspools like a nightmare.

The sleaze has her positioned in front of him, tucked far too close. He's holding a wooden bottle used to practice tricks. It spins wildly in his palm while he whispers something in her ear. Rylee giggles, her focus rapt on whatever flair sequence he's explaining. Those unfamiliar instincts from earlier pound against my temple. What a fucking ploy.

I push off the wall with my sights set on a very specific target. "Excuse me. I gotta take care of something."

Jeremy chuckles. "Yeah, boss. Put an end to that."

With pleasure.

My shoes slap against the floor as I mow down the area between us. "Give it a rest, trickster. She's married."

"What?" The cozy couple flings disbelief at me in unified outrage.

"To the job," I tack on to appease the masses. Mostly the redhead set to cut me with her glare.

But the deed is done. Adam slinks off to avoid my wrath.

No doubt it will take him less than five minutes to find another unsuspecting victim of his scheme. I pay him no mind. My pulse hammers as I reach the bar, white knuckles gripping the edge.

After Rylee has more than adequately flayed me open with her stare, she sashays her fine ass over to me. I brace for impact—verbal or otherwise. The flames licking at her heels strongly suggest she won't disappoint. Only an inch dares to separate us when she stomps to a halt.

"What in the hell was that?" She spits the question through gritted teeth.

I slide my attention to the crew, finding most of them already distracted with their own conversations. That's a small relief within this shitstorm I've stirred up. It's best they don't witness the bosses bickering, or fucking. The latter might be too optimistic. I guess we'll see how this goes.

"Returning the favor," I hedge.

"How?"

I cross my arms to avoid direct damage from her fury. "Adam was pawing all over you. Figured I'd help you ditch him."

Her mouth drops. "Wait. Are you comparing this to the park?"

"Well, yeah. I thought that was obvious." It's not. I'm just reaching for a shovel to scoop my way out of this mess.

"Very different," she quips.

"Not from where I was standing."

Her eyes narrow into slits. "Did you stop to think that I might like his attention?"

"Not even for a second."

"Typical," she scoffs.

"How so?"

"You can't see beyond your bruised ego."

I rumble out a chuckle at that. "My ego is stroked on the regular, but thanks for your concern."

"But not by me. You couldn't handle me giving them attention. Wow, you're threatened. Intimidated."

"He's your employee."

She scoffs and pops out a curvy hip. "I didn't say I was going to marry the guy. It's just nice to feel wanted for a change."

Is she joking? Men openly gawk at her with their jaws slack. Me included. "You're okay leading him on?"

"Don't be a dick. It was harmless flirting."

Now I'm wondering if Rylee needs her eyes checked. His gaze rarely left her tits and ass. In fact, he's probably still leering from the corner he snuck off to hide in. I should've gotten rid of him when I had the chance. One problem at a time.

I prowl forward, caging her between the bar and my dishonorable intentions. "You need someone to flirt with?"

She teeters for balance, slim fingers fisting in my shirt. The drum that booms underneath is her doing. I was correct about her energy seeping into me. It's fast-acting and addictive. My veins practically beg for another hit.

Rylee's eyes search mine, the green swirling with secret desires only I can satisfy. Our labored breaths move in sync, our chests rising and falling to the same erratic tempo. My gaze is fastened on hers as I fight for control. This isn't supposed to happen, but the way she molds against me demands I reconsider. She gulps and her exhale paints my parted lips.

Just when I think Rylee is going to give the green light, she ducks under my arm and evades the inevitable. I nearly sway from the loss. My palm blindly slaps onto a nearby stool as I watch her retreat.

She doesn't go far, but keeps her back to me. "Strictly professional, remember?"

"My memory is pretty foggy, to be honest."

"I'm not interested." But the wobble in her voice betrays her.

"No?"

"No." Rylee whirls to face me. The icy shield is erected once again, but it's useless against the fire in her stance. "I would appreciate it if you kept your possessive streak on a leash."

"Possessive?" I scoff at the word choice, accurate as it might be. "Try protective."

She quirks a brow. "Whatever blows your skirt up."

I barely trap a groan. My dick gets hard from that mouthy sass making an appearance. Rylee might deny it, but I'm pretty certain we're soulmates. It's only a matter of time before she gives me permission to prove it.

"Still pretending you're not interested?"

"Not pretending," she chirps. "But moving on. Do you have a plan, or are we done for the day?"

I feel like this is a trap, but there isn't anywhere safe to step without getting snared. "This was mostly about you meeting the staff. Introductions are done, thanks to your initiative. They already know the drill. Nothing much has changed other than—"

"Me," she provides. The hurt in her tone causes me to flinch. "I know the score. We're good."

"Firefly—" I stop short when she skewers me with a fierce scowl.

"It's fine. I just have to find my place."

Which is nowhere near Adam. My lap probably isn't on the list either. That would be a sure way to keep her safe, though.

"The crew already adores you. Just be present."

Her stare glides to the front window. "When are we opening?"

"That's up to you." I refuse to be the sole decision maker, whether she agrees or not.

Her eyes flash, exposing the smolder buried beneath. She snuffs out the flames with a slow exhale. "You're the boss."

"Not of you."

"Might as well be," she grumbles. "I'm going to be your freaking shadow until further notice."

The thought of Rylee stuck to me like glue is too appealing. As if I need more blood pumping directly to my cock.

I grip the back of my neck to release some pressure. "When would you like us to reopen?"

"The group and I got to talking," she begins.

"I'm well aware." Maybe I became an invisible shadow after an hour of fuming in silence.

She huffs. "Let me finish, huh?"

"Please," I motion her onward. "Continue."

"As I was saying, Amber mentioned that the three-year anniversary is approaching soon. Next Wednesday, I think? We thought that would make the event extra special."

"That's a great idea." And one I hadn't previously considered. The only dates I care to remember revolve around Payton.

She squints at me. "We'll be ready in less than a week?"

"Yeah, for sure."

"Okay…" She doesn't sound convinced.

"Can I get you a drink to celebrate?" Or a boost onto the counter, spread wide for me as a feast. Somehow, I don't think she'd appreciate me making a meal out of her. Yet. My confidence refuses to assume there won't be a when.

"Gonna need a raincheck, bucko." She turns to wiggle her fingers at the douchebag duo. "I already have plans."

I follow her gaze, steam already billowing from my ears. "With Adam and Casey?"

Her attention returns to me, eyes narrowed into fine points. "Is that a problem?"

I'm about to straddle a fine line. "That depends on what you're doing."

Rylee blows out a harsh breath. "Not that it's any of your business, but I'm having lunch with friends from high school. I figured Adam and Casey could tag along."

"Why?"

"Why not?"

"You met them." I jut my chin at the pair currently laughing at their own jokes.

She shrugs off my reasoning. "They're a solid source of entertainment."

"That's one way to describe it." I'd go with torture, but that's just me. "So, you're bringing them dates. Where's yours?"

Rylee begins backing away. "I'm about to find out."

chapter ten

Rylee

QUINN SLAMS HER GLASS ONTO THE TABLE, SENDING BEER SLOSHING over the rim. She doesn't pay the mess any mind. Her focus doesn't waver from me, zoomed in almost too close. "Let me get this straight. You surrendered? Just like that?"

I blink at the blonde bombshell I've known since kindergarten. "This is about more than selfish pride."

"Could be about both," she mumbles.

"It isn't worth the fight. I just want what's best for the bar."

Heidi, my other long-standing bestie, slurps at her frozen margarita. "Shouldn't he want the same thing?"

I sip my Bellini with a bit more poise. "He does."

Quinn furrows her brow. "Then why did you have to fold?"

"We don't get along," I explain with a sigh.

"Ah, and you took it upon yourself to bend over." Heidi clucks her tongue in blatant disappointment.

"That's one way to look at it," I mutter.

"You're doing the right thing. Trevor would be proud of you." Quinn's smile is sweet but sad. She once had a short romantic stint with my brother, much to my dismay. The only silver lining is that they ended things on decent terms.

Moisture floods my vision with a sting. The freaking waterworks rarely cease unless I'm arguing with Rhodes. For whatever reason, he's the only one that can keep my spirits up—despite enraging me at the same time.

I squint at the lofted ceiling, willing the tears to stay tucked in. "Thanks. I like to think so too."

"He would." Heidi rests her palm over mine, offering a gentle squeeze. "That brute was always looking out for you, even now. You're home. He brought you back to where you should've been all along."

The battle against my tears is a losing one. I swipe at my wet cheeks while nodding. "Yeah, he did that."

Quinn flicks her wrist. "So, forget the incidentals. We're together at our favorite restaurant. There are two extremely sexy—although obnoxious—men vying for our attention. This is a win-win situation."

I have to agree with her logic, skewed though it might be. We glance over to where Adam and Casey are downing shots at the bar. Their raucous cheering carries across the otherwise tame establishment. It's only noon after all.

Like I said to Rhodes, they provide solid entertainment. I smile just recalling my parting blow to him. He was getting a bit too cocky for my taste.

"Who has you grinning like a loose goose in heat?" Heidi wiggles her eyebrows.

Bile tickles my throat. "Ewww."

She makes a noncommittal noise. "Not my best, but it's early. Let my wit simmer while you spill."

"My not-boss needs to be brought down a peg or five."

Quinn's pretty face screws up into a pinch. "Not-boss?"

"Rhodes claims he isn't my boss, but that doesn't stop him from getting bossy with me." Although to be fair, there are moments I like it. Kind of.

She smacks her lips. "That sounds pretty hot. No wonder you surrendered to him. Let him boss all over you, Rye."

Heidi releases a wistful sigh. "Remember the Hot Boss on TikTok?"

Quinn copies the dreamy sound. "How could I ever forget?"

"He quit working at that store, right?" Heidi's mouth puckers into a pout. "I wonder what he's doing now."

"I think he's modeling," I mumble absently.

Bubbles and peach puree paint my tongue while I quench my thirst. This place makes a delicious Bellini. I make a mental note to check if Bent Pedal has this on the cocktail menu—and if not, to put it on there myself. We can't properly brunch without it.

That's when I realize the abrupt silence. My friends exchange a wide-eyed glance. The entire restaurant seems to go quiet and still. A glance over my shoulder confirms that no one in close proximity is eavesdropping.

Quinn is the first to recover from swallowing her tongue. "Hot Boss is a model? Like for real?"

"Where?" Heidi grabs her phone, preparing to run a thorough Google search.

Their astonished expressions are too rich. Humor erupts from me in a cackled stream. I'm not even embarrassed that I snort. It feels fan-freaking-tastic to giggle without restraint.

I fan my watery eyes. "He's been on several romance novels."

"Shut the front door," Quinn blurts.

Heidi stabs the table with her finger. "I need the titles. Stat."

Amusement still dances in my chest. "Look on his socials. He's good about sharing."

"Wow," she breathes. "This is brand new information."

"I know what I'm doing tonight," Quinn nudges her with a wink.

"Same, girl. Same." Heidi shakes herself from the lustful clutches. "Anywho, back to your not-boss."

I purposefully ignore the zing that travels along my spine. "What about him?"

She seems to consider the wide realm of possibilities. Can't say I blame her. "You two don't get along. Isn't that bad for business?"

The sour gurgle in my stomach is becoming too familiar. "Our little feud won't reach that point. If he pulls any stupid shit, I'll ask my dad to get involved."

Which I plan to avoid until absolutely necessary.

I'm capable of managing Rhodes on my own, but I'm not willing to risk my brother's bar. Besides, Bent Pedal has become a family matter since Trevor's passing. My parents won't risk the place going down in flames.

Quinn hums in agreement. "It's mighty nice to have a lawyer as your father."

"Especially when an entitled scumbag tries to take advantage of you." Heidi curls her hands into fists, ready to rain blows on a specific someone. A similar reaction arises whenever Gage's sperm donor is mentioned.

I almost heave just recalling the spin cycle that man chucked me in. "Precisely. But I'm hopeful that my situation with Rhodes won't require legal repercussions."

"Better not, or he's gonna be facing our wrath too." Heidi smacks her fist onto an open palm.

"Okay, She-Hulk." Quinn stage-whispers to me, "Better keep an eye on this one. She's gone savage."

Warmth spreads through my chest. "I appreciate the support, even if it's just in jest. You ladies are my rocks."

Heidi's bottom lip trembles, the hostility from moments ago vanishing. "We're always here for you, Rye. I will say, it's much more convenient now that you're back in Knox Creek."

Quinn beams at me, lashes fluttering to mask the pooling moisture. "I would've flown my bitch ass to South Carolina just to cuss out that rotten pile of trash."

"And I love you for it," I coo. But the revolving reference to that asshole is putting a serious damper on my spirits.

Heidi must sense my desperation for a topic change. "Who is this not-boss guy exactly?"

The strain banded around my torso goes slack. "He's an

investor, I guess. Seems legit. Trevor trusted him. They were close enough to own a bar together."

"But where's the dirt? I need some juice with this tequila." She scoots to the edge of her seat.

"About Rhodes? He was friends with Trevor. His daughter is adorable. Her mother isn't in the picture. They live in Richemont. I don't know much more than that." Except for the fact he looks crazy attractive in a backward hat.

"What's his last name?" Quinn makes a rolling motion.

"Walsh."

My friends simultaneously choke on their drinks. Quinn nearly hacks up a lung while Heidi mops dribbled margarita off her chin. Our fellow patrons steal peeks at us to see what all the fuss is about. Meanwhile, I'm left gaping at their extreme overreactions.

"Did you say Rhodes Walsh?" Heidi's voice is a comical croak.

"Yeah?" My gaze bounces between them. "What's the big deal?"

"Rhodes Walsh, that's who."

"I'm lost," I mutter.

"But your shock value is on point this afternoon." Quinn thwacks her chest, still recovering from her coughing fit.

My exhale is forced. "Do you know him or something?"

Heidi rolls her eyes. "Along with everyone else in the Midwest and surrounding areas."

Confusion becomes a dense cloud. "I'm definitely missing something."

"Seriously?" Quinn gapes at me. "You've never heard of Rhodes Walsh?"

"Other than as my reluctant business partner? Not so much."

Heidi makes the gesture of her head exploding. "Um, he's a local celebrity. Made a huge chunk of change in his early twenties from several very wise investments. Pretty sure he's filthy rich, especially by Minnesota standards. And his enterprise is just getting started."

I take a brief reprieve to let the news sink in. That explains how he could afford to pay the staff for a month off without batting an eyelash. I assumed he had money, but not to this extent. It's no wonder we argue on a constant loop. The pang of loss inside my chest is misplaced. Me and wealthy men don't mix.

"Well, that's… something." More articulate phrasing escapes me.

It feels like my tongue is tied seven different ways. But I need not worry. My friend is on a roll.

Heidi leans in, eyes twinkling with glee. "The best part? He's chronically single, which makes him even more desirable."

Quinn fans herself, resting a floppy palm over her forehead. "He's on those lists for most eligible bachelors under thirty. Women go nuts for him. And I don't blame them. He's a hottie."

And that explains why we had hordes of admirers at the park. I was smart to establish boundaries, albeit inconsistent and belated. But the mystery of why he's spending so much time at Bent Pedal remains. If what they're claiming is true, Rhodes is most definitely needed elsewhere.

I rub my temples that are suddenly throbbing. "This is a lot to take in."

"You didn't recognize him?" Heidi shakes her head as if she can't believe it.

"No…?"

Quinn's eyes are still saucer-sized. "How is that possible?"

Oh, let me count the ways. "I don't make a habit of scouring the tabloids for notorious playboys."

She squints at me. "But you have all the details on the Hot Boss."

A laugh bursts forward. "Uh, yeah. I'm almost ashamed you two didn't. You're welcome, and happy reading."

They serve me different versions of gratitude, both mumbled and disgruntled. Heidi polishes off her drink and quickly signals for another. Quinn follows suit. I'm on the one-and-done track, waving off their attempts to convince me otherwise.

Heidi props an elbow on the table. "Rhodes Walsh is a different story entirely. He's practically in your backyard."

Quinn makes a noise of agreement. "You stayed away for too long, Rye. I blame South Carolina for this oversight."

"Would you like me to introduce you?" If either one dates him, this inconvenient attraction will surely snuff out. The gurgle in my belly calls my bluff. It might be better to avoid him altogether.

She sighs, slumping low in her seat. "It'll just be a waste of time. He's not shy about his relationships, or lack thereof. Rumors about romantic entanglements are debunked almost instantly. His little girl is the love of his life."

My heart trips over itself. Damn, that's some single mom catnip. "I'm sure he gets plenty of company far from prying eyes."

Heidi wags a finger at me. "Don't try to sully his charm. None of those temporary floozies make an impact. The way he looks at his daughter can't be beat. I want a man to light up like that for me."

I'll admit to swooning, unless Rhodes is the one to ask. That's the only excuse I've got for mumbling a breathy, "Uh-huh."

"I think someone has a crush," Quinn teases.

My focus swivels between them until I realize they're both staring at me. "What? No, I don't."

"Don't try to lie. You wanna bang the rich daddy." She rocks her hips to an erotic beat.

I slap a palm over my mouth to stave off the vomit. "Please don't call him that."

"But he's a daddy." The seductive tone Heidi uses serves to further curdle my lunch.

"Not to me," I gag.

A sharp whistle severs the naughty route of this disturbing

conversation. Our attention is effectively redirected to the disruption. Adam is signaling to us from across the room.

Casey cups a palm around his mouth. "Pool table is open, ladies. Hustle up."

Heidi quirks a brow. "Do we still want to play?"

"Probably not. We're an odd number." Quinn doesn't sound all that upset about it.

I reach for my wallet. "Count me out. I'm the fifth wheel."

Heidi stills my attempt to pay. "Absolutely not. It's quality bonding hour."

"Which we've done twice over," I reply with a tap to my watch.

Another shrill alert cracks into the idle chatter. Patience doesn't appear to be a virtue for Casey. "Come on, babes. Don't keep us waiting."

"You can either be heads." Adam bobs a palm back and forth on his groin.

"Or tails." Casey is busy shaking his ass.

"Ladies' choice," Adam adds.

Heidi pinches her lips. "Wow, that's a toughie."

My entire body is shaking with laughter. "Good luck with that."

"You're really leaving?" Quinn bites her inner cheek.

"I should get going anyway. Gage will be done with school soon." My butt is already halfway off the seat.

Heidi has yet to release me. "Are you sure?"

"Positive. My threshold for the unexpected has just about maxed out." I shoo them away before my mentally drained state can bleed through the surface. "Go have fun. I expect to hear a filthy retelling later."

Quinn winks at me. "With those two buffoons? It's bound to be a circus."

chapter eleven

RHODES

I TAP MY THUMB ON THE STEERING WHEEL IN MUTED CELEBRATION when the car line crawls forward an inch. Why this version of torture wasn't included in the parenting manual is beyond me. A warning would've been nice. At the very least, I could use a thorough explanation as to why the school district believes this is a useful waste of our time.

But it's not just the waiting game that spikes my irritation. Well, that's not entirely true either. I focus on the resounding radio silence I've received since the staff meeting. Rylee has definitely kept me waiting. On purpose or not is the ongoing conflict. Four days without a peep is bound to make a man suspicious. Or desperate for answers.

With nothing else to do, I allow my mind to wander down this well-beaten path. At the very least, I figured she would reach out about the bar. Bent Pedal is set and staged to open tomorrow. It's safe to assume she's been working behind my back on the finer preparations. That much is obvious whenever I've stopped by to investigate. A feminine touch lingered on each prop and decoration. The place looks like a viral social media post.

Not that I can fault Rylee's lone wolf tactics after our most recent altercation. There's no doubt that she's bound and determined to keep her distance. Although to be fair, I haven't tried very hard to contact her. She's taking great lengths to avoid me while I'm cocking off with a thumb up my ass. A single voicemail doesn't compare to the mounting desperation itching beneath my skin.

Once again, I'm spiraling into unfamiliar territory. The woman is a dynamite stick lit to blow my balls into smithereens. To my knowledge, and the scraps worth committing to memory, this is the first time I've had to chase a woman. If that's what I'm even doing. Either way, it's… refreshing.

Which further proves that my wheelhouse is severely lacking when it comes to Rylee Creed. The damn thing might as well be constructed from tissue paper with the way she punches holes into my logic. That doesn't mean I'm going to shy away. Fuck that. Acceptance is an important part of the process.

If she thinks I'm not willing to make an effort, she's poorly mistaken. My own determination solidifies as I crawl forward in this mother trucking car line. I'll earn Rylee's affections until she's passing out praise like free peppermints at the host stand.

The back door flings open, scattering my mental ramblings in the breeze. "Hi, Daddy!"

"Hey, Bumblebee. How was school?" I watch in the rearview as Payton tosses her bag on the seat and hops in.

She gets herself buckled in before returning my grin. "Fine."

I'm already headed for the exit without a backward glance, all too eager to ditch the parking lot. "What'd you learn today?"

"Nothing."

"How is that possible?"

"I dunno."

This script is nearly threadbare. It only takes a second for me to scrounge up my next prompt. "Did you practice math?"

Her features scrunch. "I think so."

"How about reading?"

"Uh-huh." Payton stares out the window, finding the clouds more entertaining.

I can take a hint. "What did you eat for lunch?"

Her gaze skips back to me. "Pizza."

"Was it yummy?"

She's nodding with her entire body. "Super yummy."

"Were you outside for recess?"

"Yep. I pushed Lizzie on the tire swing."

"Wow, they still have those?" I wink at her in the mirror.

She shakes a skinny finger at me. "You know it's my favorite, Daddy."

Warmth spreads through my chest from the cheesy grin she's wearing. "I'm just teasing, Bumblebee. What else happened at recess?"

Payton kicks her legs, narrowly missing the back of my seat. "Henry wanted a turn to swing with me, but I told him our fire is burning out."

I furrow my brow. "Your… fire?"

"Uh-huh. He's still my boyfriend, but I feel more fire with Gage." She prattles this off in a flippant manner, as if we're discussing the weather.

Meanwhile, my pulse begins to go haywire. I'm not sure I can handle another boyfriend discussion this soon. "You feel a *fire?*"

"Yeaaaahhhhh." She makes sure to pump that word full of bedazzled snark. That sparkle machine will forever haunt me. "That's why we're gonna get married. I told you."

And this is the point I want to stuff my ears with cotton. Or bang my head on the steering wheel. Maybe both. This slope can get slippery real quick.

I pivot while turning onto the main drag through town. "Do you have homework?"

Payton puckers her features like she just sucked on a lemon. I chuckle in victory. Bet that doused this supposed fire.

"Maybe," she mumbles after a brief delay.

"Is it in your folder?"

"No."

"Why not?"

Her sheepish expression could win an award for Best Stalling Tactic. "I forgot."

"Payton." I hang a scolding note on her name, but it's mostly in jest.

Her sigh is loud and long. "I know, I know. I gotta be more memorable."

That gets a laugh from me. "You're plenty memorable, but you have to remember better."

She shrugs. "Same thing."

Not really, but this conversation has a short shelf life and we've reached its expiration. I have years to teach her the importance of being a responsible student. My daughter must be in agreement. She shifts her focus to study the street and stores passing by.

"Where are we going, Daddy?"

Options flicker through my drifting thoughts. "What would you like to do, kiddo?"

"I wanna play with Gage." Zero hesitation.

My gut clenches while the dead-end obsessions from earlier host a reunion. Definitely not reversing down that road. "Maybe another time."

"But why not now?"

"Gage and his mom are busy." It's a safe enough assumption. If only Payton could be convinced that easily. "With what?"

"I'm not sure." Let's hope honesty doesn't bite me in the ass.

"Then how do you know they're busy?"

Maybe I should've considered a fib. "I just do."

"Can't you just call her and ask?"

"I'm driving." And not ready to face the music, or her sending me straight to voicemail.

"But you don't even hafta hold the phone. It rings through that speaker thing above your head."

"It's distracting. I need to concentrate."

"Then send a text. That takes like two seconds."

If only it was that simple. "I can't text and drive."

Payton flails her arm in a wild circle. "There's a stop sign. That means you gotta stop."

"I'm still not supposed to send a text."

She releases a string of nonsensical grumbles. "Fine. Whatever."

"Hey," I chide. "Don't be a party pooper."

"Every party needs to have a pooper, Daddy." She recites the phrase I taught her with ease.

"You're very smart, Bumblebee."

Her mood rebounds with a chirped, "I'm a genius."

"And humble," I chuckle.

"What's humble mean?"

This will also require me to define sarcasm. Again. "I just meant you're kind to yourself."

"Well, duh. I got the kindness from you. It's in the jeans pants you gave me." She never forgets, or misses a beat.

"Ah, see? You can remember well."

"Only when I wanna."

"You should want to do your homework." This comes from the guy who fed more than a few assignments to his imaginary dog.

"Homework is a party pooper."

I try not to laugh, but it's a losing battle. "Did you eat sassy soup for lunch?"

"No, Daddy! I ate pizza. You're not a good listener."

"Are you sure?"

"Yes." Delight bubbles in her voice.

"I don't know. You're acting kinda sassy."

"Am not." She tries to fight it, but a smile twitches her lips.

That sparks an idea. "Should we call Grandma and see what she thinks about your sass? I bet Grampa would recognize it. Maybe they'll drive down for a visit."

My parents live about three hours north near Duluth. The distance doesn't stop us from seeing them often enough. Although, if my mom had her way, we'd move in right next door.

"No!" But she's giggling. "Nana will bust me for being a stinker."

"Oh, is that what she says?"

"Uh-huh." Something seems to occur to her. "How come we can call Nana, but not Rylee and Gage?"

Damn, I'm totally busted. "Uh, talking to grandma about your sass isn't distracting."

Payton rolls her eyes with dramatic animation. "Is too."

There isn't an excuse fitting for my farce. "You're right. We shouldn't call anyone."

Her mouth pops open. "I didn't say that."

"Pretty much. Now, what would you like—"

She suddenly jerks forward as far as her seatbelt allows. "Slug bug!"

I gasp with feigned shock. "What? Where?"

Her excitement bounces the entire truck, putting the shocks and alignment to test. "You missed it, but I didn't. How many points do I have, Daddy?"

That's a good question. It's been years of keeping the score. We started this game when she was three and have yet to hit ten. The relics are harder to find these days.

"Seven?" The guess is as good as any.

She claps with a giddy squeal. "I was gonna say six, but seven is better."

"You're going to win."

"I kn-ow," she sings. "I'm the best at finding slug bugs."

That's when I hit a four-way stop. Indecision plagues me with a dizzying strain. Left would bring us to Bent Pedal. To the right is our direct route home. Straight ahead leads to Payton's favorite restaurant. If we want a real shot at bumping into Rylee and Gage, that would be the direction to take. I'm at a crossroads in every sense of the word.

"Daddy and Rylee sitting in a tree. K-I-S-S-I-N-G. First comes love. Then comes marriage. Then comes a baby in a baby carriage."

Shock loops around my throat with a tight squeeze. I can

barely suck in air through the cocktail straw my windpipe has become. "Why are you singing that, Bumblebee?"

Payton giggles. "You know why, Daddy."

"I really don't," I mutter to myself. Any romanticized notions are currently being blocked from memory.

Her perfect hearing picks up on my denial, of course. "You love Rylee. That's why you held her hand and said she's super duper pretty. She's gonna be my mommy."

Black spots dance in front of my vision. I might be insanely attracted to that woman, but that doesn't mean we're skipping off into the sunset to live happily ever after. Far fucking from it. We barely tolerate one another.

But my daughter isn't done. "I can't wait for us to be a family."

And now it feels like my chest is caving in. There's a reason I'm extremely cautious when it comes to relationships. The reminder isn't necessary, but I'm smacked with a hearty dose all the same. The last thing I want to do is feed into this fairy tale Payton is writing for me.

With my decision made, I press down on the accelerator. My heart thrums to a furious tempo as I cruise through the intersection. It only takes a minute for Payton to discover which path I picked.

"We're going to The Tavern for dinner?" She squeaks and smacks her lips. "I'm gonna get buttered noodles and garlic bread."

"Whatever you want," I croon.

"Does that mean we ask Gage and Rylee to meet us?" Payton holds up her crossed fingers for me to see.

"Here we go again," I mumble.

"Go where?"

A muffled curse shapes my lips. I need to internalize better. "We're going on a date, Bumblebee."

"Really?" She sounds skeptical.

"Yep. Just you and me."

She thumps her head on the seat. "Yuck, Daddy! That's gross."

"Too bad. You're stuck with me."

Payton brightens at a speed that raises suspicion. "Can I get dessert?"

I expel my trapped breath with a sigh. "Only if you order it with extra cherries."

chapter twelve

Rylee

A GIDDY THRILL SKIPS IN MY STOMACH AS ANOTHER SATISFIED customer fills out his credit card slip. He hasn't stopped smiling since stepping foot inside. That's been the case for most of the folks I've had the pleasure of serving today.

The man tips an imaginary hat in my direction. "Thanks again, Rylee. Real glad you're carrying on Trevor's legacy. He loved this bar. Hell, we all do."

A unified chorus of applause booms from the dwindling lunch crowd. Infectious joy pulses through the energized atmosphere. People appear equal parts pleased and relieved to return to their local watering hole. I think my brother would be proud.

Strong hands grip my shoulders from behind. "And that's how we kick off a comeback."

"Puke and rally! We're never down for long." Casey pumps his fist in the air.

I feel my lips twitch despite the less-than-appetizing visual. "That was really fun."

The comfort of accomplishment swaddles me in a rewarding embrace. My background in marketing and advertising came in handy while staging the scene. In my previous jobs, I didn't get to witness the gratifying payoff for my labor. It's no wonder Trevor rarely took a day off. I could get hooked onto this natural high after a single shift.

"Great job, boss." The fingers still teasing at the knots in my muscles drop away. "Couldn't have done it without you."

"It was a team effort." I twirl to face Adam, palm raised flat for a slap.

He follows through with the high-five. The guy doesn't seem like the type to leave a lady hanging. "Hell yes. You're gonna be stuck behind the bar with us from now on. Three isn't a crowd for us."

"We had a lot of business, right?" It seemed busy from where I was slinging drinks.

"For sure. The regulars didn't disappoint. There were a bunch of new faces too."

"Is it always like this?" I mimic a roller coaster climbing and falling with the rush.

Adam's gaze scours the space. "More or less. Gives us a chance to recoup and restock. But it's never an empty house. We have loyal locals who are always willing to warm a seat."

I offer a smile to the stragglers who remain firmly planted at two o'clock in the afternoon. "They're not in a hurry to leave."

"Nah, not a surprise. They'll probably still be here for dinner."

That gets a jolt of shock from me. "Really?"

He nods, something resembling affection brightening his features. "It's more than a bar for them, you know? This is where friends gather, mistakes are made, differences are reconciled, reality is escaped, bathrooms are repurposed, orgasms are granted—"

I squish a finger over his lips. "All right, I get the picture."

His chuckle is devious. "Anyway, it's a safe haven. They missed their routine, whatever that entails."

A deep sense of belonging thrums through my veins. That's eerily similar to how Rhodes described Bent Pedal to me. Turns out he was right, not that I would dispute this particular claim. It's obvious the bar is special. The proof lingers within every relaxed pose and easy grin.

Speaking of the surly grump, Rhodes has made it a deafening point to avoid me. We haven't spoken since his chilled greeting upon arrival. That distance suits me and my reinforced determination just fine. It's for the best that we maintain professional boundaries.

But I still find my attention drifting to him whenever the mood strikes. As it turns out, that happens more often than I'd prefer to acknowledge. Much like this moment.

Unlike Casey's nausea-inducing terminology, the mere sight of this man has my appetite returning tenfold. Rhodes delivers a mouthwatering display with a white dress shirt and black slacks. Even fully dressed, his brawn can't be concealed. The material folds to his sculpted contours in effortless glory. His mussed hair and scruffy jaw don't escape my notice either. I could devour him for every meal.

Our paths hadn't crossed since the staff meeting last week. An entire month couldn't prepare me to withstand his temptation, much less five measly days. The breathy exhale I release is pathetic at best.

That's when Rhodes catches me ogling him. His chocolate depths hold no warmth for me as our gazes clash and hold. I can almost feel his static shield zap me. Damn, his noticeable withdrawal still stings. Humorless laughter puffs from my pursed lips. If that isn't sideways hypocrisy, I don't know what is.

"Ah, that's why I can't crack into your honey hole." Adam's arm bumps my ribs in a gentle nudge.

I register his words with a feigned gag. "That mouth of yours is the main reason."

He dips down until his lips nearly brush my ear. "You wouldn't complain after experiencing the pleasure this mouth can—"

Something shatters behind us. I jolt upright, narrowly missing Adam's nose with my elbow. He leaps backward with an arm blocking further attempts at damage. That'll teach him to respect my personal space.

Then I recall the noise. It came from the general direction I last spotted Rhodes. A quick glance confirms my suspicions. He's clearing off a table that was recently vacated. It seems excessive force is required to dump beer bottles into the trash. The fire in his eyes isn't focused on the cleaning duty. Those brown flames are attempting to set me ablaze. Yet he makes no move to approach me. His exposed forearms ripple with what I imagine to be barely restrained fury.

I rip my attention off him with a muttered curse. The need for distraction barrels to the forefront. My eyes search for a worthy task, fingers already twitching in anticipation.

Adam squints at my antsy pants. "Restless already?"

"Idle hands aren't my specialty," I mumble.

Especially when there's a broody grouch breathing down my neck. He has the uncanny ability to stoke my arousal from across the room. Very inconveniently, I might add. The heat expanding in my lower belly is sorely misguided and gets shoved to the back burner. I grab a rag and begin scrubbing the glossy counter.

Casey appears out of seemingly nowhere. "Take advantage of the break while we have one."

I pause my useless attempt at redirection. "What do you mean?"

His gaze almost twinkles under the overhead lights. "Just wait, boss. The weekend is mayhem."

Adam nods in agreement. "It was smart to ease us in on a Wednesday."

The possibility of a more intensive trial run makes me dizzy. I wipe fake sweat from my brow. "Good thing I had two veterans flanking me."

The dynamic duo takes a well-deserved bow. Casey and Adam spent the last three hours buried in the trenches with me. They weren't frazzled in the least. Meanwhile, I stumbled my way through mixing basic cocktails.

Casey licks his lips. "I'll make sure you're standing all night long, boss. Unless you prefer a slight bend at the waist."

"Freaking shameless," I grumble.

"That's why you pay me the big bucks," he hoots while thrusting his hips.

A stunning brunette slides off her stool, starry eyes aimed at Casey. "Bye, handsome."

He clutches at his chest. "No, you just got here."

"Gotta get to work." She blows him a kiss.

Casey jumps to snatch the smooch from midair and tucks it in his pocket. "How about I get your number first?"

"How about I keep you guessing until next time?"

"You should know my patience has the depth of a puddle."

She snorts. "That's appealing."

His fingers pluck a cherry from the garnish station. "Do you need some incentive?"

Her eyes track the dangled offering. "Is that all you've got?"

"There's plenty more where this came from," he croons while blindly grasping for a pineapple chunk.

The brunette leans across the bar and snags both pieces of fruit between her teeth. "Juicy."

Casey staggers sideways. "You have no idea."

"Until next time, cherry picker." Then she spins on her sky-high stiletto and strides to the exit.

We watch her leave, hips accentuated with an exaggerated sashay. Secondhand confidence thrums beneath my skin. I can appreciate a woman's curves and her seductive strategy in using them.

Once the door slams behind her, a dense silence settles again. The urge to stay busy prods at me worse than before. I feel like a spare part, which only serves to increase my jitters. There's plenty to do, but I'm not sure where to start.

A few tables are still occupied by so-called squatters. Casey makes a lap on the inside track of the bar to check on the three sitting in our jurisdiction. Adam begins reorganizing the supplies we thoroughly depleted. One of them could probably go home early, but that's a decision for Rhodes to make. He already cut the servers off the floor. They're busy rolling silverware in a corner booth.

I blow out a double dose of insecurity. Welcome to the afternoon lull indeed. But a little slack in service won't dampen my spirits. Besides, I don't need to worry about entertainment with these two on the clock.

"There goes my smile," Casey slouches against the cooler after finishing his loop. His adoring fans must have officially left the building.

Adam smacks his arm. "More like your erection. Looks like you're having blue balls for lunch."

"Nah, I'm still solid in that department." Casey grips himself through his jeans.

I turn away with a groan. "You two are terrible."

Casey scoffs. "You mispronounced charming and irresistible."

"That doesn't translate for me." I giggle at his wounded expression.

But his crooked smile rebounds in the next beat. "Let your guard down and see what happens."

"The boss is off-limits, remember?" I wiggle my fingers for emphasis.

He crosses his arms while treating himself to a slow once-over. "Incorrigible flirting is allowed, right?"

"Just don't forget she's married," Adam says.

I roll my eyes. "Yeah, to the job."

Casey rubs his palms together. "In that case, we need to hone your skills."

The possibilities run wild in my imagination. "I'm afraid to ask what that involves."

"Just some basic flair tricks." Adam snags a nearby liquor bottle, giving it a spin.

Casey snaps his fingers. "And the sexy cocktails."

"Yeah, bro. Good call." Adam claps him on the shoulder.

I quirk my brow. Of those two options, drink recipes are a higher priority. Although, I'm not entirely sure I want to know the mixes they consider sexy.

My gaze bounces between them. "What do you suggest?"

Casey appears dumbstruck with wide eyes and a slack jaw. "You're asking us?"

"Well, yeah. I'm not a bartender."

Adam grunts. "Could've fooled me. You kept pace with us."

Casey bobs his head. "Best shift I can remember in a long time. The booze was flowing faster than the Mississippi. We're a dream team."

Pressure brews behind my eyes. Turns out, these playboy nincompoops aren't half bad for the damaged soul. But they don't need to see me cry.

Instead, I force out a scoff. "You flatter me."

"We'll do a lot more than that." Adam isn't shy about checking out my ample breasts.

Give 'em an inch, and they'll take a footlong. "Yes, honing my skills for the bartender role. Let's get back to that."

Casey glances at Adam before answering. "If you're giving us control, then we're making magic."

I take a moment to study their giddy expressions. "Why do I get the feeling I'm going to regret this?"

Adam tries to sober his glee, but the cheesy grin won't be tamed. "Don't worry. It's only uncomfortable at first."

Suspicion narrows my vision into a squint. "Are we still talking about making cocktails?"

"Without the tail." Casey folds in half with a gruff belly laugh.

With my palms lifted straight out, I begin backing away. "This was a bad idea."

"We're just fucking with you. C'mere, boss." Adam beckons me forward.

"Don't be shy. It's just a Dick Sucker." Casey snags a bottle of pear vodka from the shelf.

Adam searches the liquor selection. "Mountain Dew Me and Leg Spreader are a must."

Casey's features sparkle with mischief. "Oh, and Slippery Panties. Juicy Screw is popular too."

His partner in crime slaps their palms together. "Screaming Orgasm is a classic."

My brain trips over naughty innuendos blended with salacious deeds. No wonder this pair strives to upload a lewd reputation. If anyone overheard this conversation, they'd assume I was taking a trip to Pound Town.

"All right, boss." Casey turns to me, fingers steepled in front of his grin. "I'm ready to be your test dummy. What do you wanna pour down my throat first?"

"Oh, jeez. I dunno. The choices are quite appealing," I mumble absently. "How about—"

A loud crash interrupts our mixology preparations. I peek behind our station to see a chair toppled on its side. Rhodes stands beside the innocent victim, making no move to correct the injustice. His chest is rising and falling to a fuming rate.

I blink at the scene. "You good over there?"

His eyes become little more than a furious glare. "Just peachy."

Bullshit is ripe in the air. I wrinkle my nose from the perceived fumes. "Sure about that?"

"It slipped." Rhodes still doesn't pick the chair up off the floor. Instead, he proceeds to crush a soda can in his fist.

My eyebrows wing upward. "Maybe you should take a break from… whatever it is you're doing."

"That's not the problem."

"But there's a problem to address." At least we're making some progress.

"Why don't you tell me?" He wrenches the condiment caddy off the table. The pepper shaker and mustard go flying. Yellow splatters out in streaks to stain the concrete. It appears as if Rhodes is compiling a playlist that sounds an awful lot like irrational jealousy. He can listen to the tracks on repeat while continuing to lose his composure.

"I'm not the one making a mess." My gaze remains steady on his excessive disturbance.

"Sure about that?" His tone is mocking while he repeats my earlier phrase.

The urge to ask if we've reverted to kindergarten dances on my tongue.

Before I get the chance, Rhodes begins throwing empty beer bottles into the trash again. What he lacks in finesse, he gains with impeccable aim. Glass shatters on impact, but he just tosses another. I shake my head at his caveman performance. When he doesn't comment, even though his icy stare is boring into mine, I toss my hands up.

"Is that really necessary?"

"I could ask you the same thing," he deadpans.

What in the fudge cake is he going on about now? I glance over my shoulder to find Casey and Adam both staring at my ass. Ah, right.

I snap my fingers an inch from their dazed drooling. "Boys, knock it off. I'm not a member of your harem."

Casey's goofy smile belongs in a cartoon. "You're certainly not."

"Give it a rest, yeah?" That's meant for all three testosterone junkies in my direct vicinity.

Adam chuckles and begins collecting ingredients. "I have just the thing to smooth this situation over."

Once again, I'm almost afraid to ask. "And what might that be?"

"Guaranteed to relieve unresolved tension in the workplace." His gaze skips to a certain spot behind us before refocusing on me. "It's called Sex with the Bartender."

chapter thirteen

RHODES

JEREMY SHIFTS HIS STANCE ON THE WALL BESIDE ME. "BUSINESS AS usual."

I narrow my eyes on the late evening crowd. "Something like that."

If the dependable cook notices my sour mood, he doesn't comment. "It's like we never left."

"Never should have," I grunt.

"Nobody faults you for that."

"Wouldn't blame them."

"Don't be too hard on yourself," he mutters. "That shit will eat at you, man."

A hollow scoff escapes me. "Too late."

His head dips with a slow shake, silently admonishing me. The scene is becoming routine. Jeremy steps from the kitchen for a quick break and finds me holding up the wall. Not sure why he bothers trying to pry decent conversation from me. I'm shit company.

A calm breeze skitters across the vast space spread before me. Sunday night doesn't compete with its weekend predecessors. For that, I find myself eternally grateful. I haven't recovered from our grand reopening, let alone the past two days. There's a sinking sensation in my gut that suggests it's only going to get worse.

I've been more irritable than usual. Payton is the only one who can drag me out of my foul attitude. My frustration melts in the palm of her hand, leaving me as a docile puddle. But she's not here, so my fragile balance in her presence is completely off-kilter. That uneven slant is currently aimed at a particular redhead mixing drinks.

Jeremy follows the sharp edges in my glare to where Rylee is in her element. A knowing smirk crooks his lips. I ignore his quiet assessment, until he insists on voicing it aloud.

"She's doing well." The flippant observation goes without saying.

A little too well. But I don't share my petty feedback. Instead, I nod along with his praise. "Crew loves her."

"Customers too."

Another reminder I don't need. The dim lighting does little to conceal the scene right in front of me. A guy just snagged the only available stool in Rylee's section. She's very popular with the patrons, especially our male clientele. I can't fault them for being drawn to her. That's precisely why I find myself stuck in a similar spot each shift she's on the clock.

I've taken on a new role as head bouncer. Although, the only one I'm protecting is capable of handling herself. The gnawing in my denial demands to be fed. Our truce is jaded and stilted. I haven't exchanged more than a handful of strained words with her this past week. Not that I deserve more from her. Still, it wouldn't hurt her to acknowledge my existence every now and then.

I settle for a compliment that won't grate on my nerves. "She's catching on quick."

Rylee is happier than I've seen her. The grief that shrouds her features isn't as persistent once she enters Bent Pedal. Or those snapping jaws are easier to manage. I'm sure she feels connected to her brother just being in the building. Most of us do.

"Glad she found her place," Jeremy offers with a nod.

So am I, even if the terms aren't in my favor. I might as

well be a fly on the wall for as little care she pays me. She barely glances my way while everyone else gets a blinding smile. The fact she's smiling at all is a victory. I just wish I was responsible for her joy. Selfish as fuck, but here I am.

"Adam and Casey are taking good care of her." By some miracle, my tone remains even.

He scoffs. "Not from where I'm standing."

I glance over at him. "They can't cause too much damage."

His laugh holds no amusement. "That's one way of putting it."

The reflex to storm off and find a quieter corner scratches at my feet. "She hasn't shown much interest in anything else."

"Have you given her a choice?"

That gives me pause. Our job roles are in constant conflict. She was supposed to be my shadow, but her shifts are mostly spent behind the bar. I guess that's her comfort zone. Too bad I don't find anything comfortable about watching her flirting with other guys, especially when I'm watching it on repeat.

I drag a hand through my hair. "Rylee isn't interested in what I can teach her."

The noise he emits makes my assumption sound foolish. "Might want to check again, yeah?"

In a rare occurrence, the woman in question flicks her attention to where I stalk the darkness. I'm a creeper in the shadows, keeping my sole focus locked on her under the guise of protection. The former me—the one from before Rylee strutted into Bent Pedal that fateful Saturday afternoon—would be appalled to see just how far I've fallen down this territorial hole. Maybe that should make me reconsider this crooked path I'm stumbling along. But no, my sights are set.

"I'll consider broaching the subject with her again."

Now humor sparks in Jeremy's gaze. "I bet you will."

That's when another man approaches Rylee's portion of the bar. I curl my hands into fists as she turns to greet him. The uncontrollable, foreign urge to stake a permanent claim rushes to my rigid stance. There's a caged beast prowling just beneath the surface. I want to pummel every asshole who dares to steal a glance at her, not to mention testing the limits of personal space.

The customer already teases that line minutes after parking his ass on a stool.

"He'd be glad to see you lookin' after her." Jeremy's finger points to the ceiling, a hint of a grin gracing his lips.

"Appreciate that, man." I'd like to believe the same, but I don't let myself think too hard about it.

Trevor might approve of the extreme measures I'm taking to keep an eye on his sister, but he probably wouldn't appreciate my ulterior motives. He certainly wouldn't be pleased to discover just how depraved my desires flow.

Rylee Creed will be mine. Seems only fair since she fondles my balls in a vise on a daily basis. It's far more than that, though. I want her. Badly. In the permanent sense that doesn't fade.

Tonight is no different. I can feel the tension about to snap and I'm powerless to stop it. The chase is on. She just doesn't know it yet, or her resolve won't allow our truth to seep through the cracks.

I'm coming for you, Firefly.

The douche canoe currently salivating over Rylee decides to initiate that plan earlier than I anticipated. I glare at his hand resting on her arm as if my fury can burn him. It's in this moment that I recognize my error. Rylee is already mine, and he's touching her.

His fingers drift across her wrist like a lover's caress or something reserved for mutual attraction. Far more intimate than a friendly gesture, that's for damn sure. She must agree and begins pulling away. The asshole doesn't take the hint. His palm slides forward to erase the distance she just created.

My sneaking suspicion from earlier makes a resounding reappearance. That drop in my stomach quickly rebounds and I go freakishly still. I should look the other way and leave her be, but that's not an option. If I'm going down in flames, she's going to be the one striking the match. This might be the point I deliver us to the fiery pits of destiny. I'll welcome the burn.

"Fucking relentless," I grumble.

"And there's your cue," he chuckles.

"Not sure that's wise." But I'm ready to launch a not-so-stealthy attack.

"Since when is that our concern?" Jeremy straightens from his post. "Better get back to the kitchen. I'll leave you to it."

It seems that's the permission I've been waiting for.

In the next beat, I'm striding across the room with our previous conflicts chasing me. Only a few were related to my supposed jealousy. That's her accusation, but I haven't done much to dispute the theory.

Although, in my defense, I quit intervening with Adam and Casey. Rylee made it abundantly clear that they were on the same level as her obnoxious cousins. But this fuckboy is a stranger in my house. I'll be damned if some random Joe Schmo skirts in under the radar.

As if hearing my thoughts, he bends forward to whisper something in her ear. She blushes in response to whatever he said. I imagine the worst possible content. That only serves to push me faster.

Thunder roars in my ears with every step it takes to get to Rylee's side. People leap from my collision course, but I pay them no mind. Red stains my vision as he shifts to grab her again. That's when I arrive at the scene.

Rylee startles at my sudden presence. "Um, hi?"

"Hey, Firefly. You okay?" I attempt a measured tone, but gravel coats each syllable.

The smooth flesh between her eyebrows puckers. "Why wouldn't I be?"

That's the point I direct my glare to the man who's still leaning too close. He doesn't seem the least bit concerned with my interruption. Instead, while Rylee's eyes are trained on me, his are feasting on her tits. That solidifies this wayward scheme. A storm crashes over my features and I barely contain a feral growl.

My attention returns to the one who matters. "Is this guy bothering you?"

"What?" His petulant bark is drowned out by the pounding in my chest.

Rylee appears to connect the dots. A scowl replaces the mild confusion on her pretty face. "I've got this under control, noble knight."

That very well might be the case, but I've already taken the nosedive. "Can we talk?"

"About?"

"It's private." I'm done pretending to be logical.

She rolls her eyes. "That's convenient."

"Doesn't make it any less true." That's not a lie. There's plenty we need to discuss.

Dumbass knocks on the counter. "Listen, man—"

I lift a finger to cut him off. "This doesn't involve you."

"The fuck it doesn't. I was just about to ask this fine-ass lady for another round." He shakes his empty glass.

"She's busy," I reply.

"No, I'm not." She elbows me out of the way. "I'm trying to do my job, which is more than I can say for you."

Her rejection is aimed directly at me. That pill is bitter to swallow, but I won't let that deter me. I plant my feet with purpose.

She scowls at me. "You're just going to stand there?"

"Yes."

"Why did I think we could remain civil?"

The weasel whistles like a cartoon wolf. "Damn, woman. You've got a sharp tongue. I know just what to do with it."

Rylee blinks at him, most likely weighing her options. "Let's focus on what you're drinking."

"Are you on the menu?" He wags his brows.

I'm beginning to think this jack-off will dig his own ditch, but I've already come this far. Meanwhile, Rylee is struggling to swallow the bile pooling in her throat. An assumption, yet the odds are heavily in my favor.

"Ready to close out?" I'm already halfway to the register. Might as well grab his tab while I'm here.

"Thanks for the offer, but I'm not going anywhere just yet. Rylee is keeping me entertained. I have a feeling I'll be here all night." He winks at her.

And my patience is officially depleted. I paste on a pitiful frown. Purely for his benefit, of course. "Bad news, man. Rylee is coming with me. There's something very important I need to tell her. Just between business partners. You understand, right?"

"Liar," she mumbles. The fact she doesn't put up much more of a fuss is a win for me.

Dudebro glances between us, ending on his intended target. "Well, in that case, I better give you my number."

Did someone ask for the last straw? This guy just tossed it down. My blood sets to a boil as I wait for her to tell him off. But Rylee doesn't do that. She doesn't do much at all other than look stunning.

What else is new?

Not dissuaded in the slightest, he whips a pen from his pocket like it's 1999. Then he proceeds to jot down his digits on a cocktail napkin.

I swipe the sorry excuse for paper from him before he can finish scrawling. "She's not gonna call you."

He juts his narrow chin at me. "How do you know?"

"Because she doesn't have your number." I make a dramatic display of ripping the napkin into unrecognizable shreds.

A hush seems to fall over the bar. My eyes slide to Rylee. She's stabbing me with a green-eyed glare. I'm definitely going to wrestle her wrath for the barbaric display, but the deed is done.

In my humble—although idiotic—opinion, this intervention has been a raving success.

"You're unbelievable, Tarzan," Rylee hisses. She spins on her heel and stalks off before I can fully digest that she's gone.

"And you're welcome," I call to her retreating form.

Then I turn back to the guy responsible for this entire fiasco. Okay, maybe that isn't fair. We can share the blame.

Until he opens his mouth. *"Way to go, bro. You scared her off."*

"I'd apologize, but I'm not sorry. Now, if you'll excuse me, I better go take the edge off for her. Have a great rest of your night." It's only polite seeing as I certainly will, chasing a certain firefly.

chapter fourteen

RHODES

RYLEE DOESN'T GO FAR. FOR THAT, I'M THANKFUL. I'M ALSO grateful that she chose to confine herself in our office. She's pacing the small space when I catch up to her. The sight of her hot and bothered strokes my arousal with a sure fist. I stroll into her temporary haven as if welcomed. My intrusion makes her abruptly stop the flustered stomping.

Green fire flashes in Rylee's gaze as she whirls on me. "You can't even give me five minutes alone?"

"Like you didn't expect me to follow." I shut the door behind me. Nobody needs to hear what's about to happen between us.

Her slitted glare manages to narrow, a retort waiting to flay me. "I don't expect anything from you."

If I were a weaker man, I might flinch. The last two months have provided me with thicker skin than the crocodile layers I already don like armor.

I cross to the desk in the corner and park my ass on the edge, giving her the illusion of distance. "That's real good, Firefly. Then you'll never be disappointed."

Rylee sidesteps that flippant comment. Instead, she thrusts out an arm to signal at the bar beyond our barricade. "What the hell was that?"

My shrug is lazy, but inside I'm cranked to boil over again. "He was hassling you."

Her huff disagrees. "He really wasn't."

"I saw you pull away and he kept coming. That doesn't bother you?"

Smoke crackles in her gaze. "I had the situation handled."

"You did, but I was tired of him stealing liberties. He wasn't the only one either."

"That's none of your concern."

"You're wrong, Firefly." I stand from my makeshift seat but keep my feet firmly planted. "Suddenly I'm finding that you're of great concern to me."

"As my not-boss?"

I shake my head to clear the sticky cobwebs. "Not-boss?"

"You're not my boss, right?"

"Right," I agree with dense hesitation. This feels like one of her infamous traps.

"But you sure as shit like bossing me around. That's how you've been acting since we met." She does a twirling motion down my splayed stance, as if that's precisely what I've been doing.

"You think this is bossy?"

She snorts. "You don't?"

My chuckle is dark shadows stalking the brightness. "Nah, baby. I can do far worse. This is me being playful in comparison."

Her eyes widen as she digests that crumb. She once again chooses to skirt around the muddy tracks I created. It would be a real shame if we got stuck in the dirt together. "Oh, I'm your baby now?"

"You're a lot of things."

Rylee combs a few fingers through her hair. She left the reddish waves free today, cascading around her shoulders. Another thing of hers I appreciate. Although, when it comes to her, there are countless actions and mannerisms I can worship.

"I feel like you're talking in circles," she says after her next exhale.

An easy smirk slants my lips. She's not wrong. That's her influence on me. I can't stop my brain from revolving around her.

Not that I'm ready to admit the newfound weakness. *"It doesn't matter if I'm straight or corrupt, that douche doesn't deserve to touch you."*

"Says who?" Her bottom lip wobbles, but the fury in her eyes is scathing. *"And don't you dare use my brother as an excuse."*

It's horrible to admit that's where my mind was heading. The warning is appreciated, considering that would shift the tide to drown me. The defensive—albeit shitty—retort dies in my throat.

I turn away from her, fisting a hand in my hair. Fuck, this woman drives me to behave like a beast. When I regain possession of my composure, I find her stare waiting for me.

"You wanna hear me say it?" The silence that follows is answer enough. *"Fine. I'm telling you he's not good enough."*

She rolls her eyes. *"Let me guess, this the part where you tell me nobody is good enough."*

I step forward, just a foot. *"Damn straight."*

"Unfortunately for your alpha ego, you can't tell me who to date."

"Wanna bet?"

The flames dancing in her eyes dare me to eliminate more space between us. *"Yes."*

"Prepare to declare me the winner. I'm about to claim my victory prize." I prowl closer to erase more denial separating us.

Rylee's focus is zeroed in on my measured approach. *"What're you doing?"*

I won't take what she doesn't freely offer, but that doesn't mean I can't stoke the embers until those fiery coals burn us both. *"What does it look like I'm doing?"*

She drops a fist on her cocked hip. *"If I knew the answer, I wouldn't bother with the question."*

Her hostility is thick enough to chew on. Why that tightens my nuts is a mystery. But the reason reveals itself in the next breath.

It's the heat in her eyes. She might be mad, flinging hate

like rubber bands, but there's more to it. Maybe it upsets her that she likes fighting with me. Lord knows I get off on this shit.

I pause in my steady gain toward her. "Would you like me to apologize?"

She sputters and almost appears taken aback by my abrupt swerve. "Are you actually sorry?"

"No." I don't even have to think about it. "There isn't a stitch of remorse when it comes to protecting you. Not then. Not now. And certainly not ever."

"It's not your job to protect me."

"What if I want it to be?"

Her eyes search mine. After several beats, she gulps audibly. "You shouldn't."

"And why is that?"

Her next blink is weighted with indecision. Then the spell is broken.

Rylee moves to make another escape. At this point, it might become a habit. Maybe she isn't ready to admit the inevitable. Her heels click on the floor with each swift step until she's at the door. In contrast, my stride is a silent prowl.

Without a backward glance to see where I stand, she delivers a parting blow. "I'm done with this conversation."

I slap a palm on the wood, halting her hasty exit. "We're hashing this out, once and for all."

She curls her fingers on the knob but doesn't attempt a twist to open it. "You're not going to let me leave?"

"Afraid I can't do that, Firefly."

Her eyes peek over at me, hovering within reach. "And why not?"

I lean in until my nose brushes her temple in a gentle sweep. "We're not finished. Not even close."

"That would suggest something started between us to begin with."

"Need me to prove that's very much the case?"

The room smells stale, just waiting for us to infuse the air with lust and reckless decisions. That's our cue to let this bottled passion between us free. If only she would allow it.

"You're off your freaking rocker, smooth talker." She twists slightly until we're facing one another.

This position has our chests almost meeting, especially when I inch forward. "For you? Absolutely. But otherwise? Nah, you're wrong. I'm finally making sense."

It might be my imagination, but a vein in her neck throbs. "How do you figure?"

I debate whether broaching this subject is wise, especially under our fragile conditions, but she already mentioned him earlier. "Your brother kept us apart for a reason."

"Why might that be?" Rylee doesn't sound convinced, but she doesn't disprove my theory either.

"He knew I wouldn't be able to keep my hands off you."

"You're doing a pretty decent job right now." She takes a pointed look at my palm resting flat on the door.

My other hangs idly at my side on standby. "I'm testing my restraint."

"And how is that working out for you?"

I shift to cage her in between my bent arms. "Why don't you tell me?"

Rylee could easily ditch this bubble I've made for us. There's no force holding her captive. The fact that she's staying put is telling. I'm not alone in this madness.

An exotic fragrance I can't name infiltrates my senses. The floral scent is fresh and strange and exhilarating. That's what this woman is to me. I have an overwhelming inkling that she's barely scratching the surface.

Her lashes flutter when I treat myself to a deep inhale. "What're you doing?"

"I'm not doing anything. *We're* about to get this over with." The emphasis is necessary, and it's about damn time. Two weeks is an eternity while refraining from the ultimate temptation.

"Wow, that sounds like a chore we're forced to endure."

Her gaze dips to my lips, but only for a quick jolt. "Did I miss the planning phase again?"

I almost kiss her right then and there, just to silence the nonsense she insists on spewing. "Trust me, Firefly. That's a mistake I won't repeat."

"Yet you've trapped me in the office and claim this so-called resolution is a tedious task. I was doing just fine behind the bar until you rudely bulldozed all over me."

My wince is sincere. I take it one step further and straighten from my predatory stance. The handful of inches now wedged between us is like the Grand Canyon. "That wasn't my intention."

"Then what was?"

"Getting you alone."

She seems startled by my honesty. Her slack jaw snaps shut a moment later. "To get this over with? What does that even mean?"

"To avoid any further confusion, the only thing we're getting over is the business-only boundaries. That's a chore we've both endured. And while we're on the subject." I dip low until our lips almost become intimately acquainted. "In case you missed my earlier conviction, I'm not okay with other men touching you."

Her body quakes, fighting to go limp against mine. "Too bad that's not a choice for you to make."

I trail a finger along her arm. A thrill shoots through me when goosebumps erupt in my wake. "Are you sure about that?"

The sparks in those green flames billow toward me. "Has anyone ever called you a brute?"

I snort for the sake of entertainment. "No, this is new for me. You're the only one who pokes my inner bear. He's been hibernating until you walked into the bar."

"Oh," she breathes. "That's almost sweet."

"You still mad at me?" I drift my thumb along the blush staining her freckled cheek.

"Yes." She pokes my chest with her finger. "It's going to take more than a few half-baked lines to smooth things over."

"That shouldn't be a problem. My groveling game is strong." I'm familiar with reaping forgiveness thanks to Payton.

Rylee's expression hardens. "I won't accept a bunch of money tossed at me either."

"Huh?"

Her eyes skitter off mine. "Never mind."

But I'm stuck on her comment like a stage-five clinger. "Did I do something else to offend you?"

She glances at a fake watch on her wrist. "How much time do you have?"

The demand in her tone strongly suggests I stop pulling at this thread. I'm aware that my reaction was extreme, but I can't seem to rein in the baser instincts when it comes to her. That doesn't mean I won't pull away at the first signs of her distress. Until then, I'll break through this restraint for both of us.

"We can do this all night," I reply after the slight lull.

"It's not important compared to the guard dog routine you put on." A drop from her chin further cuts our connection.

With a thumb notched in her dimpled cleft and a soft tug, I sever her avoidance. "I'm sorry, but I won't sit on my ass and watch other men touch what's—"

She presses a finger over my lips. "Don't finish that sentence."

"But—"

"Unless you want me to storm out, just stay on the amends path."

"All right," I grumble. "I apologize."

"But only because your brutish behavior upset me."

"The last thing I want to do is upset you," I admit honestly. "For whatever reason, the urge to pummel any man in your section is extremely difficult for me to resist. It's territorial as fuck, I know. You just bring out this need to defend and rescue. I've never felt this way before."

She wrinkles her brow, as if she doesn't believe me. "I don't need you to save me."

A harsh breath expels from my flattened lips. "You're so damn strong, Firefly. I wasn't trying to suggest otherwise. If that's how it came across, I'm truly sorry. All I meant to do was protect you."

"Along with your masculine pride," she grumbles.

"Will you give me a chance to prove I'm better than a neanderthal?"

"Maybe." That's better than I deserve.

Through a clenched jaw, I reach for a compromise. "I'll do my best to let you handle your customers however you see fit."

Her gaze narrows on my attempt at a solution. "I imagine that's going to be hard for you."

"Trust me, Firefly. I'm capable of controlling myself, especially for your benefit and comfort. The hardest part about this situation is my dick."

Her eyes go wide when she feels the evidence for herself. "Uh, do you have a whiskey bottle in your pocket?"

"Something like that," I chuckle.

Rylee shifts against the door, effectively nudging my cock. "That's... impressive."

The reflex to pound my chest thrums through my veins. But when push comes to shove, she needs more than prideful arrogance from me. I gaze into her eyes, willing her to see just how far my feelings flow. "You're not just my business partner. We need to get over our differences. Together. You with me?"

"How do you propose we do that? Bang it out quick?" She laughs until her attention lingers on my stoic expression. "You want to screw me into compliance?"

"I probably wouldn't use that exact phrasing, but... sure, let's go with that."

She sputters, her disbelief puffing against my lips. "You're serious?"

"It couldn't hurt," I prod.

"Well, that depends." Her gaze lowers to the noticeable bulge behind my zipper.

I smirk, getting the urge to kiss her again. "You flatter me."

"By the looks of it, you flatter yourself."

Since she's already stroking my courage, I have the confidence to guide us into the abyss. "Would it be so bad if you let me take care of you?"

"Yes."

"Why?"

An internal debate flickers in her green depths. "Maybe just once."

A gruff chuckle escapes me. I'll let her believe that for now. "What the lady wants—"

"She gets with no strings attached." The slim brow she quirks dares me to argue.

Instead, I crash my mouth onto hers with a feral growl. Rylee mewls in response, lifting her arms to thread around my shoulders. Our lips part in unison, tongues gliding out in a seamless introduction.

First impressions can determine compatibility within moments. And this kiss? Hot fucking damn. This kiss proves just how deprived I've been. Rylee sucks on my bottom lip as I nip at her top one. It feels instinctual. The flow is natural, as if we've been playing tonsil hockey together for years. Our immediate connection is intense, I don't let my mind get too stuck on the fine print.

My thoughts scatter completely when she yanks on my hair to haul me closer. Need bursts behind my shuttered eyelids. Mint and combustible chemistry are swapped between us. The impact makes my knees weak. Then Rylee begins jostling her legs.

When I glance down, she's trying to kick off her boots. My eyes pong back to hers while warmth spreads through my chest. I'm not sure what I was expecting when I followed her in here, but it certainly wasn't a full meal. Not that I'm complaining to discover she's in this with me.

Her restless movements continue. "These were a bad choice."

"Allow me." I lower to my knees and remove them for her with a gentle tug. The clunky soles hit the floor with a thud when I chuck them aside. Next, my palms drift along her thighs until my fingers reach the waistband of her leggings. "May I?"

"By all means." Rylee arches her lower half to assist me.

The stretchy material cooperates easily enough. I lower her pants and thong as a package deal. Then she's exposed for me to eat.

Still kneeling, I glance up at her. "Are you wet for me?"

"Yes."

"Not shy, huh?"

"Have I ever been?" She threads her fingers into my hair, giving me a hearty yank.

"Nope, I like that you call me on my shit." My mouth is inches from her slit, saliva pooling for a bite.

"We don't have time for that." She tugs at my shirt impatiently.

"There's always time for dessert before dinner."

"Not when we're at work. What if someone comes looking for us?"

"Let 'em try."

"They might knock," Rylee clips.

"Are you seriously worried about our staff while I'm admiring your pussy?"

"No, but they could very well interrupt us before we even get started." She makes a valid point.

"Such a shame." I glide my fingers through her wetness, swirling a calloused pad around her clit.

She whines at the ceiling. "Save the remorse, cowboy. Quit teasing and saddle up."

I give her slippery folds a lingering look before rising to my feet. When I'm certain her eyes are on mine, I pop the appetizer into my mouth. A groan trips from me as her tangy nectar bathes my tongue. Rylee's pupils dilate as she watches me feast on her taste. Then she bats my hand away and attacks with vigor.

Her lips latch onto mine while pure male satisfaction surges in my veins. My tongue slides along hers, sharing the essence. A starved noise rumbles from her throat. It's a hunger I'm familiar with. She makes me ravenous enough to beg. I'm about to get fed my first solid meal in longer than I care to recall.

Rylee rips at my belt, attacking my jeans next. Once the denim is pooling around my hips, she reaches inside for my cock. A breathy gasp escapes her when she finds me hard and aching.

I nearly go blind as her fist grips me. "That's what you do to me, Firefly. Without even touching."

"Damn, I'm good." There's a smug edge to her voice that's well-earned. "Is this my reward?"

Liquid heat fills my groan while she strokes me. "Yeah, baby. Allow me to thank you properly."

I have her hoisted in my arms in one second flat. She automatically lifts her bare legs to wrap around my waist as I press her back against the door. I feel her ankles cross at my ass. Every fluid move she makes is a declaration that we're in this together. Our eyes collide and lock. The energy in the room seems to thrum, like an emptiness about to be filled. I'll gladly do the honors.

My dick nudges her entrance in greeting. "I'd prefer to see you naked and spread out, but this will have to do."

Her blunt nails dig into my biceps. "Gosh, what a sacrifice for you."

"That sass," I groan. "You're so damn sexy just spitting nails at me."

"Prove it," she taunts.

I'm welcomed into her slick warmth with a thrust. Another forward drive gets me halfway. A third stroke sends my cock to the hilt. Flames blaze under my skin when she accepts all of me without further resistance. A mutual sigh streams between us.

Rylee's features go slack. She blinks in rapid succession as if wading through a fog. I study the flush rushing to her cheeks. Then my mouth closes over her parted lips. The shock wears off and she's quick to reciprocate. Our tongues clash while I withdraw and sink in again. She adjusts to my intrusion, wiggling her hips against mine. The staccato in my pulse matches the clench from her inner muscles.

"Holy shit," she purrs.

"That good, huh?"

Rylee bangs her head against the door. Her labored exhales mirror mine. "This doesn't mean I like you."

I pull out to the tip, then feed her my length in one slide. "You don't like this?"

"Too early to say," she spouts on a whimper.

The incentive to prove my worth finds a faster gear. I slam my dick into her core, forward and back, to a relentless rhythm. My balls begin to tighten after a few measly pumps. There's not a chance this ends before she's adequately sated.

With that in mind, I return my mouth to hers for a thorough claiming. We've waited long enough to officially seal the deal. Her lips spreading beneath mine seem to agree. Our teeth gnash in an attempt to gain traction while circling the drain.

She rips her mouth from mine. "Don't stop."

"Wasn't planning to." I increase the pace for good measure.

"More," she demands.

My hips hammer forward and pause. "Wanna try that again?"

"Please," she begs. "Please, please."

"That's my girl."

"I still don't like you," she insists.

"Let those beautiful lips keep spilling lies. Your pussy tells the truth. The rest of you will come around soon enough." I grip her thighs in a tight hold. This position leaves me in charge, but she puts forth her best effort to participate.

Rylee tilts her hips and rocks into me. The angle allows me to slide deeper. "Yes, yes. Just like that."

"Oh, you do like me." I nip at the exposed column of her throat.

She cranes her neck to grant me better access. "Just your penis. The rest can take a hike."

"You don't like my tongue?" I trace a path from her pulsing vein to her earlobe.

She trembles in my hold. Her fluttering pulse vibrates against the trail I lick there. My licks laving trail. "No, it's kinda slimy."

"How about my lips?" I pull her sensitive skin into my mouth. "And my teeth?"

Her pussy clenches around me when I bite down ever so slightly. "N-nope."

"How about my hands?" I palm her breast, tweaking a pebbled nipple through her shirt and bra.

"They're too meaty." Her words suggest a complaint, yet she thrusts her chest into me.

"Oh?" I drift a so-called meaty mitt down to clutch her ass. "Do you like my fingers groping you here?"

She chews on her bottom lip to trap the truth from tumbling out. "I dunno."

My grip on her provides leverage to slap our hips together at a furious tempo. Her actions scream far louder than the brittle words. She clings on tighter with each powerful thrust. Rylee's thighs grip my waist, refusing to sacrifice an inch. I'd never leave her depths if I could get away with it.

My gaze feasts on her passion. I covet the sheen that shines across her brow, marking our mutual enthusiasm. The bliss reflecting in her eyes clutches me in comfort. Her beauty steals my breath and I struggle for my next words. Sex hasn't been a verbal sparring match for me. Until her. That comes as no surprise with every other string she's pulling.

"You have no idea," I murmur.

She blinks from the daze. "About?"

"Just how crazy you make me."

Her pelvis rolls against mine. "I'm getting a pretty big hint."

My dick slides into her awaiting heat. "Do you like me yet?"

"Only certain parts," she breathes.

I accept the challenge, brushing a delicate touch across her puckered hole. "Like when I do this?"

She jerks from the brief preview. "Oh, sweet Jesus."

"Firefly," I growl into her throat. "When I claim this ass as mine, there won't be anything sweet about it."

"So confident that I'll agree to that." The bubbly anticipation in her tone does little to dissuade me. Same goes for the vise her pussy becomes.

I flex my hips to grind us together. Meanwhile, my pinky does another pass along that not-so-sweet spot. "Won't you?"

"Dirty boy," she chides.

"You like me and my filthy intentions." After a final sweep, I remove the temptation before I push too far.

"Maybe," she relents.

"Now we're making progress." To accompany my victory, I kick the steady motions into a higher gear. Our skin smacks together with each harsh entry.

"Dammit," she cries. "I was supposed to stay away from you."

"Yeah?" I smile into the crook of her neck. "How's that working out for you?"

She spanks my shoulder. "Maybe I'm just testing my restraints."

My lungs burn while I pour more energy into making her shatter. "Sorry to be the one to tell you, but those restraints are blown to unrecognizable pieces."

"Yeah, by your monster cock."

"Fuck, that snarky streak will be my undoing. You love this, baby?" I thrust hard, making sure she feels all of me.

"Like was already a stretch," she moans. "We're far from love."

"Guess I need to try harder." I piston my hips to a seductive tempo.

When Rylee's head lolls to the side, that's my cue. My thumb dips to where we're joined in search of her clit. She squeals and bucks against me when I've hit the target destination. A smirk grows from the stroke to my ego.

"I think you like this a lot."

"So fucking cocky," she mewls. The pleasure spilling from her doesn't sound the least bit upset.

"Let's see if you like screaming my name while I make you come."

Rylee has no idea what's coming for her, but she will. My muscles bellow in protest when I search for a faster speed. I pet her clit with lavish strokes while she bounces against the door. If anyone is standing on the other side, I bet they're catching quite a show watching the hinges rattle.

Those thoughts splinter when the telltale pressure builds into an upcoming explosion. A far too delayed realization almost stops my frenzied pumps. "Am I safe to come inside you?"

Her head is already thrashing in approval. "Yes, don't you dare pull out. I'm on the pill."

The fact she wants everything I'm desperate to offer sends me stumbling to the ledge. I increase the friction against her clit while my hips become a blur of chasing relief. We get swept up in the storm of our own making.

"Oh, oh. Almost there…" Rylee squeezes her eyes shut and clamps down in preparation.

"Say my name," I command.

"Rhodes, Rhodes, Rhodes," she chants.

My cheek presses against hers while I bend to whisper in her ear. "Drench my cock, baby."

"With pleasure." And she does just that.

Her scream rips from the very depths of her pleasure. The ripple from her orgasm triggers mine. My pace falters as tingles spread. Rylee's body latches tight to mine while relief swaddles her. She's a trembling puddle in my grip. If I wasn't propping her upright, she would topple sideways. I pull from her seizing core only to plow forward one last time. Then I'm thrown into the mercy of euphoria.

My cock throbs as I spill inside of her. It almost feels like my teeth go numb. I jerk against her beyond control. Endorphins flood my bloodstream while I struggle to see straight. My motions become sloppy, and I surrender to the blistering sensations engulfing me.

Rylee's fingers claw at me while she remains lost in the throes of passion. I attempt to steer us from the clouds with slow strokes. My lips pepper kisses to her temple, drifting to her cheek and jaw. Her skin sticks to mine from our joint efforts. There's a post-coital glow wafting from every pore.

Warmth blankets me in relaxation. The strain between us seeps out with each labored breath. After what feels like an hour, I manage to regain proper functioning. I hold tight to the woman responsible for the most intense climax of my life. Rylee doesn't protest about being clutched against me. Aftershocks twitch our entangled limbs.

I stroke my fingers through her damp hair. "Do you like me now?"

"I'll admit no such thing, but maybe…" Rylee finds the strength to lift her head off my chest. Her eyelids are heavy, barely open halfway. She clears her throat to finish what she started. "Maybe we could give the truce another shot."

chapter fifteen

Rylee

THE RICH AROMA OF A HOME-COOKED MEAL SATURATES THE AIR. I treat myself to a greedy inhale while striding into the kitchen. Pot roast in the slow cooker is one of my specialties. It's a savory comfort food that's quick, simple, and delicious. Not to mention good for the soul. Especially in autumn.

But the biggest selling point of this recipe is that Gage loves it. That kid can be pickier than, well… a seven-year-old.

A thought occurs to me after lifting the lid and giving a quick stir. Cabernet will pair well with the tender meat. I'm about to grab a bottle just as pounding footsteps barrel down the hallway. If we didn't live on the first floor, the landlord would be forwarding noise complaints on the daily.

"Mom, mama, mommy, momma," Gage chants while racing into the room. "Is dinner ready?"

I laugh at his antics. "Not quite. Gramma and Grampa aren't here yet."

He groans and slumps in half. "Oh. My. Gosh. I'm starving."

"You just had a snack," I remind him.

"That was forever ago. I'm super hungry. Can you hear my tummy? It's angry." He sticks his stomach in my direction.

I kneel and beckon him toward me. Once he's within reach, I press my ear to his belly. An exaggerated gasp is my initial response. "Holy moly, kiddo. You sound hangry."

Gage's eyes are wide with wonder. "What's hangry?"

"It's hungry and angry mixed together."

"Oh!" He bounces on his toes. "That's what I meant. I'm hangry. Will you feed me?"

"Soon."

"Like when?"

I glance at the clock. "Ten minutes."

"But Mommmmm," he complains. His impatience vanishes in an instant, replaced by giddy excitement. "Wanna watch me do a trick?"

"Of course." I'd agree to just about anything when he flashes that beaming grin at me.

Gage proceeds to do one of his semi-famous acrobatic sequences. The routine begins with some wild hand gestures that lead to him collapsing on the floor. His body becomes a blur as he twists into a roundoff cartwheel and ends with a sideways kick. Then he leaps to his feet and takes a bow.

Pride puffs out his skinny chest. "Wasn't that so cool?"

"Very creative, sweetie. I'm impressed. Where'd you learn that?"

"Kid City. I can't wait to have my own YouTube channel. It's gonna be awesome possum sauce!" He pumps his little fist in premature victory.

"Uh-huh," I mumble absently.

My muscles twinge when I rise to my feet. The extra-sexular activities with Rhodes yesterday left a lasting impression. There's a hidden heat still tingling beneath my skin too. Freaking not-boss and his monster—

I give those inappropriate musings the shaft. This is so not the moment to digress into our against-the-office-door tryst.

Gage continues chattering about his grand channel plans. That's the point that I go in search of a distraction. This is an ongoing discussion we tend to get stuck in more often lately. It's a situation I attempt to avoid rather than disappoint him.

The wine rack catches my eye. There's a stack of napkins that could go on the table. Maybe the toilet paper in our main bathroom needs to be restocked before guests arrive. I'm edging that way when his voice stops me short.

"My followers are gonna be called Gage's Ragers. It's almost like Rage Gage. I think Uncle Trevor would like that. Right, Mom?"

A sob instantly gets caught in my throat. I choke on the ball of emotion. Oh, sweet syrup on a sundae. This kid knows just what to say. Sniffles erupt from my stinging nose while I try to blink the moisture from my vision.

My son notices, of course. He trots to my front, peering up at me. "Why are you sad?"

"I'm not. These are fake tears." I frantically wipe at my eyes to hide the evidence.

His adorable features curl into a corkscrew. "Nuh-uh. You're crying."

"Y-yeah, you're right," I blubber. More droplets trickle down my cheeks. "I've been a bit blue. That's just… normal."

This is another difficult subject we stumble across. The craters in this sodden road deliver pain I could do without. My cracked spirit weeps at the reminder. I'd rather argue about YouTube.

"But you were getting happy again." Gage's observation startles me.

I shake off the shock, blowing out a slow breath. "What do you mean?"

"When Uncle Trevor left, you got really sad. You cried so much. It made my heart soggy." His bottom lip wobbles, sending my own into a quivering fit. "But Rhodes makes you smile and laugh. I like it when you're happy."

"Ohhh, my little lover boy. You're the cutest. C'mere." I lower on a bent knee and beckon him into my arms.

Gage lunges at me for a tight hug. "Don't be sad, Mom. M'kay?"

"Okay, Schmutz."

"And Mom?"

I give him another squeeze. "Yes, kiddo?"

He pushes from my embrace. "I'm not little."

That gets a laugh from me, even if it's crispy at the edges. Then I size him up and paste on a wide-eyed expression. "When did you get so big?"

His tiny biceps flex under my motherly perusal. "I'm seven, Mom. You know that."

I palm my forehead. "It just happens so fast."

He nods in understanding. "That's what my teacher says about her lunch break. I wish recess was longer too."

Now my shoulders shake with amusement. Those reasoning skills are a real gem. "Yep, time could really slow down. I swear you were a baby last week."

His nose wrinkles. "No way! I'm not a baby."

I ruffle his hair. "It's just a figure of speech."

He blinks at me. "I don't get it."

"That's for the best. What's important is that you're not little or a baby."

"Duh," he huffs. "I just told you that."

I pull him in for a quick hug, smacking a kiss on his cheek. "Don't ever lose those smarts."

"Not gonna. Lexi loves it when I put on my thinking cap." Gage mimics the act of doing just that.

"Who's Lexi?"

"My girlfriend." This child has the gall to sound exasperated.

"You didn't mention her before," I murmur.

"We just started dating."

"But you already have other… girls who are your friends."

If he notices my clever phrasing, he chooses to blow right past it. "Yep, I have eight girlfriends."

"Eight?" My voice rises to a shrill pitch. "I thought it was six?"

The playboy in training wiggles his brows. "Eight."

"Wow," I breathe. "Who's raising you?"

"You are." He seems all too pleased about that fact.

It melts my disbelief into gooey mush. "That was rhetorical, which means it wasn't meant to be a real question."

"Then why did you ask me?"

"For… fun?"

The confusion vacates his features, leaving youthful glee in its wake. "I like fun!"

"Guess what?" I lean in to whisper, "So do I."

"That's why we're relatable. I'm gonna play with Sue and George. Lemme know when I can eat." Then he spins on his socked feet and dashes from the room.

I stare after him, another laugh bubbling from my belly. Gosh, five minutes with that kid is a better boost for the soul than a month's worth of pot roast. Speaking of, I need to turn down the heat on the cooker.

Once I've flicked the dial to low, I admire the thousand square feet that's ours for the next year. Or what I can see from this vantage point. My gaze wanders the stone counters and walk-thru kitchen. The visual tour leads to the lounge area that's visible through a cutout in the wall. That's where we spend relaxing evenings curled up on the couch. From there, I steal a glimpse of the hall that leads to our bedrooms. The dining table is nestled in a windowed nook just off the kitchen. Sunlight bathes the curved space, brightening the cozy seating arrangement.

The view of Main Street from this spot might be my favorite part. I grew up in Knox Creek and missed this sleepy small town something fierce. We're a short block from where the rural hustle meets country bustle. The sight alone fills me with familiar warmth.

Memories already paint the apartment walls in a vibrant display. There's something special in every nook and cranny. Over the past month, we've transformed the lonely shell into a home. It's not perfect, but this place will do until I can afford to buy us a house.

A notification pings on my phone, knocking me from the

lapse of productivity. My heart leaps while picturing a text from Rhodes, which is ridiculous. One orgasm—unforgettable or not—doesn't mean I immediately swerve onto Lover's Lane. I agreed to a truce. Nothing more.

With that brief detour settled, I glance at my screen to see a message from the security app our apartment complex uses. Gone are the days of simple buzzers. Now we get a pop-up notice whenever someone pushes our name in the resident display.

My bare feet slap across the wooden floorboards as I walk to the entryway. It's at the mouth of the family den space, which is the center point of our home.

I flip the deadbolt, open the door, and spread my arms wide. "Hey, family!"

Momma doesn't hesitate to rush forward. She wraps me in a tight hug, adding a kiss to my cheek. "How's my baby?"

"Good, thanks." I nuzzle into her toasty embrace.

She clucks her tongue. "I meant Gage. Where is that boy?"

"Jeez, Momma. Thanks for the love."

"Just teasing, dear." She boops my nose, a habit I've inherited from her.

"Uh-huh, sure. I know you only agreed to schlep all this way was to see your grandson."

"Yes, the five miles separating us is daunting." She presses a palm to her forehead in mock travesty.

Not that she drove. My father created a passenger seat princess with this one. Which reminds me…

"Where's Dad?" I peek over the threshold.

"Coming," he calls from around the lobby corner. "Got caught up talking to one of your neighbors."

I nod, well acquainted with his infectious personality that sucks strangers in from all sides. "Was it Bill?"

"And Ray," he adds.

"Ah, are they heading out for bingo?" The two older guys have a strong tradition on Monday nights. I often see them leaving when we're arriving.

"Seems that way."

"Maybe you'll join them next time." I'd love to see my dad find his groove again.

He shrugs his broad shoulders. "The invitation stands."

My mother pats his smooth jaw. "It would do you some good to get out more."

"And leave my lady behind?" His gaze glitters while he stares at her.

She scoffs. "Am I not invited?"

"Might be a gentleman's club," he muses.

"I'm sure they wouldn't turn you away," I laugh. "Now come in. We don't have to hover in the foyer."

My mom inspects our apartment like she does with each visit. "You've done more decorating."

"Don't give me too much credit." I spy her focus zeroed in on a painting Gage crafted the other day.

"Is the artist joining us this evening, or is he at the gallery?" Her lips twitch at her own humor.

"He's playing with Sue and George in his room."

"Friends from school?"

"Huh?" Then I realize why she's asking. "Oh, no. They're toy dinosaurs he got last week. He named them after—"

"Sue and George," my dad fills in.

"Our neighbors? How sweet." Momma presses a palm to her chest. "They'll be tickled pink to hear that."

"Maybe you'll get to meet their stunt doubles, or he's about to ditch them in a second flat. Gage," I call. "Gramma and Grampa are here."

Thunder echoes from the hall with his rapid approach. If that isn't enough, he releases a squeal that shakes my eardrums. "Finnnaaaaallllyyyyyy!"

My mom braces herself a breath before he crashes into her legs. "I've missed my sweet boy."

"What took you soooooo long?" My son stomps his feet like a toddler.

I fling my eyebrows to the ceiling. "Excuse you. Want to try that intro again, kiddo?"

"Sorry," he mumbles. His properly reprimanded attitude fades when he swivels his focus to my mom. "I'm just super hangry, Gramma. My tummy is in control of my marbles."

The wrinkles on her forehead deepen. "I'm not sure I understand, Gagey."

"Me need food." He squishes his stomach as if there's a mouth between the skin folds.

Momma titters at his silly display. "Oh, heavens. You didn't need to wait for us."

He turns a pointed stare on me. "Momma said we had to."

I boop his nose. "Because we did. We're eating as a family."

"And on that note." Dad motions toward the table. "No more delays. Let's dig in."

"Yesssss!" Gage is the first to his chair.

Three stragglers follow behind at a more reasonable pace. I swerve to the kitchen for the pot roast while my parents take their seats. Everything else is already set. Gage is one beat away from banging his spoon on his bowl. That's my cue to serve him first.

"Now, be careful. It's—"

"Hot, hot, hot." He spits out the steaming mouthful and fans his tongue. "Why didn't you warn me?

"Just tried," I croon. "You were too busy stuffing your face."

Which is precisely what he's doing with a slice of crunchy bread. "Shewww grewwwdfff."

"I'll take that as a compliment." Even though all I did was stick the loaf in the oven for ten minutes.

My mom blows on her incoming bite. "Thanks for cooking. This smells fantastic."

"Thanks, and you know I don't mind." It's somewhat of a passion project combined with a coping mechanism. I find the task soothing in its flawed predictability.

Pleased noises rumble from our quad pod as we chow down.

The blend of spices compliments the meat and potatoes flaw-lessly. A sweet nibble reaches me from the carrots. My tastebuds sing my own praises.

A delayed thought occurs to me. "I forgot about the wine. A cabernet would pair well. Would you like a glass?"

Momma bypasses my suggestion with a sneaky grin. "We stopped by Bent Pedal over the weekend."

I frown. "When I wasn't there?"

She fiddles with her napkin, dabbing her spotless lips. "I'll be sure to check your schedule before our next visit."

"Okay." I glance at my mom before studying Dad.

A sneaking suspicion tumbles in my belly. For whatever rea-son—be it denial, acceptance, or avoidance—our moods have improved dramatically in the last two weeks. I'm not alone in no-ticing the change. My parents exchange soft smiles, still creased in grief, but lighter all the same. Something is definitely brew-ing in the gravy.

"How are you getting along with Rhodes Walsh?" The way she casually drops his name raises my hackles.

I choke on a hunk of celery. Apparently, we're diving straight into not-so-subtle dinner conversation. She's looking for a lit-tle extra sauce for her roast. It's not like I'm capable of denying her this simple pleasure. That doesn't mean I need to purge all the salicous details, though. Just the thought makes me sweat.

Once I'm sure the strain has evacuated my voice, I go for short and easy. "Fine, why?"

"He was there when we dropped in. Very helpful young man. Kind and considerate. I can see why Trevor was good friends with him." She scoots toward me until our sides are pressed together. "And he's quite dreamy, isn't he?"

Heat rushes up my neck. "I wouldn't go that far."

Her scoff is an invasion of my secrets. "Please, dear. I might be old, but I'm not blind."

"Mother," I scold.

My dad mumbles around his recent mouthful. "And I might be chopped liver, but I'm still sitting here."

"Oh, pish-posh." She swats him on the arm. "I'm merely curious to hear what Rylee thinks about her business partner."

I snort into my bowl. "Yeah, and I have a twenty-five-inch waist."

Before she can respond to my snark, Gage pokes his nose into our delightful chat. "Rhodes makes Mom smile."

That's putting it mildly. I've caught myself grinning for no reason other than thoughts of him. "He's... growing on me."

"See? She loves him." My son sounds far too smug.

"No, Schmutz. Love is only for family." That's a safe explanation that should appease the masses.

"And crushes," he giggles between his fingers.

"If you're a kid with eight girlfriends." I blow him a kiss, earning me another laugh.

"Nuh-uh. Grown-ups have crushes too. There's a fire between you and Rhodes. Payton told me."

My amusement sobers. "A... fire?"

His nod is an entire body motion. The chair creaks with his enthusiasm. "Yes-huh. That means you like each other a lot. Your love is probably burning really hot. We can ask Payton. She knows more about that mushy stuff."

"He's just my um, business partner. Strictly professional. No romantic mushy stuff whatsoever." The lie is salty, and quickly ruining my meal.

I was lying to Rhodes, of course. I do like him. More than I should, after that jealous debacle yesterday. He might as well have peed on me while his ego rocket prepared for blastoff. Even with that disgusting visual, I can't categorize his actions as horrifying. His intentions came from a decent place. Maybe. It's difficult to completely disregard him.

And now I'm rationalizing his egotistical behavior.

In all honestly, I was flattered. I've never had a man defend my honor—other than my dad and Trevor. Maybe that makes me deranged or desperate or weak. Probably all three and then some. But instead of a negative tag, his intrusion made me feel strong and supported. Like someone who isn't family cares enough to stick up for me. As if I'm not alone.

That justification settles in with a thud. Yeah, I'm definitely losing it.

"Oh, this is better than my wildest imagination." Momma's eyes positively gleam while inspecting the internal debate I'm waging.

"About that wine," I'm halfway out of my seat when her next question halts all movement.

"Rhodes has a daughter, right?" Her gaze ping-pongs to my son. "Isn't she about your age, Gagey?"

"Uh-huh. Payton is seven too. She's my girlfriend. I wanna marry her."

She coos at him waxing poetic. "How precious. I bet you'd enjoy spending time with her over MEA."

His freckled nose wrinkles. "What's Emeah?"

"M-E-A," I laugh. "It's a conference for teachers, but that means you get a fall break. There are only two more days of school this week."

Gage stands so abruptly that his chair crashes to the floor. "Woohoo! Freedom. What're we gonna do, Mom?"

"I have a few ideas. But first, please sit and finish dinner."

He settles to do just that. "Can Payton come too?"

"And Rhodes can tag along. What a great idea, sweetie." Momma leans across the table to cradle his cheek.

My son preens under her praises. "Thanks! I'm a smarty pants."

Meanwhile, I pin her with a squint. "Oh, you're playing dirty with this scheming."

She shoots me a wink with all the extra sauce. "It's about time you notice. Welcome to the club, daughter dearest."

chapter sixteen

RHODES

THE ORCHARD GROUNDS ARE VAST. THAT'S MY INITIAL OBSERVATION after we enter the gate. Wide acres of green grass and rows of colorful trees sprawl in every direction. Autumn makes itself known with the vibrant red, yellow, and orange swinging from the leafy branches. Corn stalks stretch tall toward the cloudless sky. Childish laughter rules the roost in this place, the way it ought to be. Candy-coated sugar and endless energy crackle in the air.

Payton and Gage don't hesitate to join in the fun. The pair hold hands while skipping around a section of pumpkins. They appear to be in an intense deliberation. If I crane my ears, I catch something about a beauty pageant and judging. Apparently, five minutes on the scene is all they need to declare a winner.

Maybe they're in a hurry to move along. There appears to be an entire day's worth of fun to be had.

Wide, flat fields are sectioned off for different activities. I spy a makeshift block for a farmer's market. Booths and stands frame a separate portion, featuring games and food, and a wooden stage is set up off to one side. Two teens are currently entertaining a small audience with cheesy jokes. This is our first trip to Jack's Apple Shack, and I suddenly find myself wondering why we haven't been sooner.

I smile while watching the kids debate over which pumpkin should claim victory.

Rylee hums beside me. "You're quiet. More than usual."

A sideways glance finds her studying me. "Still adjusting."

"To what?"

"The fact that you invited me."

"Gage really wanted to see Payton. Unfortunately for me, you're a package deal." She forces her tone to sound disappointed.

"I can leave." A thumb gets hitched over my shoulder. "Melinda can take my spot."

She tilts her head while squinting at me. "Melinda?"

"Payton's nanny."

Something steely flashes in her gaze. The softness in her demeanor hardens right along with it. "Ah, right. Is she on call twenty-four-seven?"

I dig my boot into the gravel path. "She lives with us, so I guess?"

"Must be nice." Now her voice holds a true edge.

"Your parents help out with Gage a lot, right? I bet they love having you close. Mine live about three hours away."

Rylee's laugh is forced. "Yeah, the past month has been a breeze compared to the last seven years."

I pause with a slew of questions dancing on my tongue. Her life before returning to Minnesota remains a mystery. Maybe that's on purpose. I'm not sure how far to push, or if I should even ask. This restored truce between us is fragile at best.

"Do you want to talk about it?" My lame attempt at a compromise tastes sour.

"My struggles in South Carolina? Sure, let me purge the word vomit all over this lovely warm morning." She scoffs, tacking on an eye roll for good measure. "I'd rather forget."

"Why didn't you move back sooner?"

Her wince is a strike against me. "It's complicated."

If anyone understands that phrase, it's me. *"Maybe one day, I'll trade mine for yours."*

"Your what?"

"Complications. What we'd rather forget. We might have more in common than you think."

The brittle exterior masking her vibrant splendor wavers slightly. *"To be determined."*

Something Jeremy mentioned about the bad shit eating at me rings true in this moment. *"It might be good for us. We can start slow, when you're ready."*

She seems to mull it over. Then amusement tugs at her mouth. *"You don't strike me as the type."*

"To do what?"

"Ease in." A rosy hue splotches her cheeks.

I feel the tension seep from my shoulders. *"Certain situations call for a… gentle entry."*

She grants me a devious grin. *"Just the tip of a pinky? I'd hate to sprain my… feelings going balls to the wall straight from the gate."*

If she wants to pull my chain, I'll give her nine inches to yank. *"Could you handle the whole thing?"*

We haven't even discussed the office bang, but our simultaneous orgasms make an appearance in every sultry grin she sends my way. The sexy redhead knows exactly what she does to me. But the influence seems mutual. That makes me feel marginally better.

Rylee pulls her bottom lip between her teeth. *"I don't spook easily, but I prefer big surprises in moderation. Do whatever you'd like with that information."*

Along with the innuendos.

At this point, I'm not sure if we're discussing how to handle the skeletons in our closets or our next fuck. *"What would you like from me?"*

"I'm open to suggestions." Her eyes skitter to a random spot far from mine. Whatever she finds near the stack of haybales

makes her frown deepen. The awkward lag that sneaks into our exchange ruins the flirty moment. "Or we could move on like it never happened."

Confusion clogs the flow of our dialogue. Something feels… off. We haven't recovered since I mentioned Melinda. "Is everything okay? Between us, I mean."

"Sure," she clips.

"You expect me to believe that?"

She glances at Gage and Payton, who are busy climbing up a metal cow in the playground area. Maybe she was serious about feeling obligated to include me. "Believe whatever you want. That's not my issue."

"But you admit there's an issue?"

Rylee crosses her arms. "We've resolved most of it. Assuming you can keep the beast in his cage when other men approach me, that is."

That's not in the realm of possibilities, but she doesn't want to hear that. It's in my best interest to steer us off subject. "Do you regret sleeping with me?"

"I should. It was a severe lapse in judgment."

"That's not an answer."

"False," she snips. "It's just not the one you want."

"I want you to tell me the truth," I urge.

A chilly breeze swirls across the open space. She shivers and burrows into the thick scarf wrapped around her neck. There's a sudden—not to mention highly inappropriate—urge to use the wool as makeshift cuffs while she's squirming beneath me. Another frigid gust chases those lustful fantasies into the ether.

Rylee's teeth chatter ever so slightly. The thin long-sleeve shirt she's wearing does little to stave off the blast. It might be mild and sunny and unseasonably warm, but it's still mid-October. I fight the ingrained instinct to snuggle her close for warmth. She probably wouldn't appreciate me snatching a liberty right about now.

As if reading my intentions, she twists the opposite way

when another gust strikes. "We're here together having a lovely time, right? What could possibly be wrong?"

I squint, scrutinizing her flinty avoidance. "There's more to it. You're acting strange. When you look at me, it's different now."

"After you got a personal guided tour of my vagina? That's shocking." Her sarcasm is transparent.

I peer through the deflection tactic with a grunt. "Before that, Firefly."

"Oh, you mean when I was respecting our professional boundaries?" She quirks a brow.

My chuckle is husky, ripe for the shucking. "Those lines were drawn with the purpose of being crossed."

"Speak for yourself."

A snort pushes from my flared nostrils. "Right. Let's keep pretending you're fine and dandy."

I wasn't under any illusions that our… dynamic wouldn't shift after sex. That label trips me for a beat. Definitions just create more complications. Rylee can barely hold my gaze as it is.

"Do you expect me to beg and roll over after getting a taste of the monster in your pants? Good luck, Chuck. I've already told you I'm not part of the harem." She flicks her wrist outward in the general direction of the farmer's market.

That's when I notice the lingering stares from several women. My gut clenches. Is Rylee jealous? Doubtful. But not completely out of the question.

Before I can pry further, rapid-fire chatter crashes into our bubble.

"I get to go first." Gage stomps his foot.

Payton shakes her head, sending her dark hair flying. "No, I do."

"Nah-uh. I won paper-rock-scissors. That was the deal."

My daughter curls her upper lip. "You cheated!"

"Did not!"

"Did so. Ladies are supposed to go first."

Rylee clears her throat, gaining their attention. "What're you two arguing about?"

Gage steps forward, sticking his tongue out at Payton along the way. "I have something to show you."

"It's not that cool," Payton grumbles.

He ignores her, waving his arms frantically at us. "Mom! Rhodes! Watch me, 'kay? I'm gonna do a trick."

I give him a thumbs-up. "Go ahead, buddy."

Rylee creates imaginary binoculars with her fingers and peers through the holes. "Okay, I see you."

Gage begins punching and kicking the air in what I assume is meant to be a martial arts routine. His mom keeps her focus rapt on every choppy move. The smile she shines on him is pure parental pride. His performance hits a peak where he becomes a windwheel of motion. As suddenly as it started, he stops and bows.

Rylee claps beside me. "Great job, Gagey. Those ninjas didn't stand a chance."

Payton has been watching this epic battle go down from the sidelines. Her eyes flip to me as she starts bouncing on her toes. "Daddy, it's my turn. Watch me, okay? Don't look away for a second."

"Glad I'm not alone in this," Rylee mumbles from the side of her mouth.

My gaze is trained on Payton as she twirls and spins like a pint-size ballerina. "This is normal then?"

She makes a noise in confirmation. "I guess they're all actors at this age."

My daughter finishes her recital with several sloppy hops that kick up dust. I give her a rowdy round of applause. Rylee whistles between her teeth, gaining curious stares from people with functional hearing. The kids blow kisses to their adoring fans. With the spotlight still on them, they begin bickering about who's faster.

"Race you to the buckets," Gage spouts to his competition.

Payton is already running in that direction. "I'm gonna beat you."

"No fair! You got a head start." But he dashes off after her without further complaint.

"Ah, to be young again." The amusement in Rylee's voice is a welcome reprieve.

I accept the easy escape from our previous downward spiral. The hot seat was beginning to burn my ass. A thrum from a guitar catches my desperate search for a distraction. Familiar chords soon follow.

The jokester teens have been replaced by a guy singing solo. His acoustic rendition of "Glycerine" serenades us from across the field. "Great choice."

"Very fitting," she murmurs. "Trevor was a sucker for the stage."

"Did he do celebrity impressions?" I was an unfortunate bystander for a few attempts. If that's even what he was trying to do. My buddy was many things, but his impersonation skills needed improvement.

She laughs, but her tone carries a wistful tune. "Those were reserved for his inner circle. He preferred plucking on his guitar. Sometimes he would sing too."

"Ah, that makes sense." A missing piece slides into place. "He suggested having an open mic night at the bar. It was mostly him filling the slots."

"Always the performer. I bet he soaked in the five minutes of fame and glory." Her eyes are glassy as she sniffs.

"This town loves him."

Rylee rubs at the center of her chest. "That's why he never left. He set his sights on planting roots and made it happen. Somewhat, at least."

"The bar was a solid decision."

"I'm glad you took a chance on him."

A fond memory rises to the surface. "Would you think less of me if I admit that he took a chance on me first?"

"Puh-lease, panty snatcher. You have your moments, but you're not that bad." She elbows me in the ribs.

I follow her lead and surrender to temptation. With an arm looped around her shoulders, I tug her against my side. "Not like that, Firefly. I was a huge dork in college, and Trevor took me under his wing."

"You were a dork?" She scoffs and pushes off my chest to give me a salacious once-over. "Yeah, okay."

"Still am," I insist. "Number cruncher for life. Data and figures are my jam."

"A passion for numbers doesn't make you a dork," she explains. "It makes you even more attractive."

Talk about a stroke to the ego. "Is that a fact?"

"You're like a coochie crave combo, which is why you're not getting sympathy votes from me. Maybe they can be of service." She juts her chin at the vultures circling our area.

"I'm not interested in them."

"Why not?" Her breezy pitch sounds genuinely curious.

"My singular taste refuses to accept substitutions."

Rylee snaps her fingers. "Guess that sucks for the rest of us."

"Don't lump yourself in with the masses. You're an individual flavor meant to be savored."

"Oh?"

I pause, allowing my meaning to sink in. With a thumb curled in her belt loop, I haul her back against me. Then my lips lower to brush her ear. "It's been days, but I still feel your pussy squeezing my cock. Bare. I've never done that before."

Her eyes flare. "Oh."

"That's not something I'm about to replace. Ever." There's no mistaking the conviction in my voice, and I'm not just talking about sex.

"Um, wow." Rylee detaches from my hold to fan her face. "That's, um… wow."

"You have no idea how much it turns me on—"

She claps a palm over my mouth. "Okay, freaky geek. Let's calm down. We're at a family-friendly establishment."

"If people are listening, that's their fault."

"Our children are present," she insists.

I look over to the newfound buddies happily laughing and playing together. "They're too preoccupied with their balloon animals to care about what we're doing. Besides, I'm not asking you to get naked and jump on my lap."

"Might as well be." She wipes fake sweat from her brow.

"Am I getting you hot and bothered?"

"Will you quit pestering me if I admit it?" The heat in her gaze is plenty revealing.

"Maybe," I rasp.

Rylee straightens her stance. It's obvious to any onlooker that she's about to derail our conversation. "While we're on the subject of what happens at *work*"—she grins when I choke at her phrasing—"do you think Bent Pedal is surviving without us?"

I let her off the hook again. There will be more bait to dangle soon. "Worried already? They just opened the doors at eleven."

She shrugs. "It feels strange that we're both here. That means someone else is responsible for our bar."

When she calls it our bar, a thrum of pleasure pumps through me. "You make it sound like we're their parents leaving them home alone for the first time."

"Kinda feels that way."

"Casey and Adam have things under control."

"Do they?" She sounds skeptical.

"Believe it or not, they're quite capable."

"I'm not the one who seems to doubt them constantly."

"Only when it comes to you."

"Territorial caveman."

I wag a finger at her. "Protective not-boss."

She huffs. "You like that, huh?"

"Probably too much," I admit freely.

Rylee wiggles her fingers at Payton and Gage when they turn to check on us. Wide smiles and infectious cheers blend with the hyped-up atmosphere. After showing off their balloon creations, they return to the picnic table to make another craft. It seems the entertainment is nonstop.

A similar thought must be on her mind. "Have you ever done a group outing for the staff?"

"Not that I recall."

"Would you be interested in one?"

"That depends," I hedge. As previously stated, Trevor was always the frontman. Nobody would choose to spend their free time with me if given the choice.

"It doesn't have to be a full-blown retreat or anything. We could just rent a party room or something." An idea sparks behind her gaze and she claps. "Oh, how about WhirlyBall?"

I search my memory, but nothing clicks. "Never heard of it."

She smacks my chest in mock outrage. "You've been denied a real treat. Nothing is better than driving bumper cars in an enclosed court while clutching a plastic scoop and trying to score."

I try to picture it. The visual I create is hilarious. "That's an actual thing? I feel like you're pulling my leg."

She giggles and nudges me in the side. "It's real. Maybe not that common, but it definitely exists."

"Okay, you have my trust. Use it wisely." I wiggle my brows.

"You could just do a quick search and prove me right."

"Where's the fun in that?"

"Exactly!" Rylee playfully punches my arm. All these subtle touches are about to add up to one sensual stroke. "We'll have a blast. I think it will be good for the staff to do something together as a group."

I'm nodding along, totally buying in, when a thought occurs to me. "But if we invite everyone to play, who's going to keep the bar open?"

"Damn, I didn't think about that." She taps her lips. "I could ask my parents. Bent Pedal is like their third child in an upside down, convoluted sense."

"That's definitely one way of looking at it. But even if they're willing, running the kitchen requires training."

Rylee's joy crumples at the edges. The sight is worse than a punch to the gut. "Could we cut food service for the hours we're gone? Or I could stay behind to sub in as cook."

I send her a flat stare. As if I'd allow that to happen. "Absolutely not, but we'll figure something out."

Her shoulders slump. "We can hold off until things calm down and—"

"Now is as good a time as any. Probably better, actually." I'll be damned before I see her excitement get snuffed out completely. "Trevor would love this."

Moisture immediately springs to her eyes. "Oh, stop. That's not… well, maybe. I want to connect with his people."

"You already have. This will make them stick to you like free shots at late night happy hour."

She snorts, the sound mulish—and sexy as fuck. "I guess that's a compliment."

"Would you prefer I circle back to—"

"Nope, probably not. Let's finish discussing this later." Her gaze searches the grounds. "Meanwhile, we could get a funnel cake."

"Before lunch?"

"For lunch," she corrects. "It's a family tradition of sorts."

"Who am I to intrude on a tradition?"

"I give you permission."

"Mom, you made a rhyme!" Gage suddenly appears at her side.

Payton also materializes from thin air. "Are we eating sugar pie?"

"Funnel cake," Rylee says.

My daughter blinks at her. "What's the difference?"

"Oh, you'll see." She motions toward the food stand and the dynamic duo takes off running.

Our matched stride is slower as we follow. Rylee is glancing from left to right at a noticeable interval. Her eyes finally grace mine. "Do you come to Knox Creek often?"

"When I'm at Bent Pedal."

She ribs me, tacking a huff on for good measure. "Other than that."

"Not really."

"People seem to know you." It's almost like she's hinting at something.

"Well," I scrub at the back of my neck. "It comes with the territory."

"Right," she drags out. "Want me to hold your hand to scare them off?"

"Would you?" Fuck, I sound desperate for a simple exchange of physical contact.

"Sure, big shot. I'll share the heat with you." She's referred to me with more names than I can recall, but this feels personal. And not in a good way.

That doesn't stop me from linking my fingers between hers. "Did you Google me?"

"Nope." She doesn't elaborate, not that I expect more.

"But you know about me."

Rylee flutters her long lashes in an animated fashion. "That's assuming I care to know anything at all."

"Brat," I growl into her cheek.

She giggles and shoves me away. "Quit it, brute. I'm about to eat my favorite meal of the season."

We order three funnel cakes without pause. The kiddos find a table and immediately start scarfing it down. Their so-called lunch is already demolished by the time we arrive on the scene. Rylee clucks her tongue at the mess, yet her smile conflicts with any assumed upset.

Her son shrugs. "I was hungry."

"The sugar pie is super yummy." Payton licks her lips, appearing a tad loopy.

"I'm glad you enjoyed it, kiddo." Rylee gets situated on the seat across from them.

I slide in beside her. Deep-fried dough and clogged arteries waft toward my nose. "Definitely smells worthy of a thousand calories."

She tips her head back with a throaty laugh. "You're adorable. Don't think about the caloric intake. Just enjoy it."

"Can we ride the train while you eat?" Gage points to the tracks that circle the benches we're at.

"Oh, oh! I wanna do that." Payton is already halfway to her feet.

Rylee glances at me. "Is that all right with you?"

"Sure. How much does it cost?"

"Nothing," she states like I should already know.

"Right, it's all included in the ten-dollar entry fee."

She winks. "Cheaper than the State Fair."

I wave the kiddos off on their next adventure. "Have fun, troubles. Don't make any extra."

Payton cocks her hip. "You're not funny, Daddy."

"Does that mean you're not funny either?" I tease. "We have the same genes."

"But I only got the best from you. And guess what? I'm not even wearing pants today. My funny jeans are safe at home." She spins on her heel and trots to where Gage is already waiting in line.

That's when I realize Rylee is in the midst of devouring her funnel cake. There's no other way to describe it. Refined tact and manners don't belong at this table. She shovels one forkful into her mouth, shortly followed by another. I'm not ashamed to admit my dick twitches in approval at the sight. Then she moans.

The seductive sound is meant for intimate moments shared between lovers. Perhaps that's how she feels about her meal. If that's the case, this is the first time I've been jealous of food. I should be more concerned about the arousal about to tent my jeans.

Rylee told me to cool it with the steam I was blasting her with earlier. Unfortunately, I can't seem to control myself where she's concerned. She's fucking irresistible.

When I glance over again, a rumble rolls off my chest. This woman isn't shy about exposing her desires. She doesn't hide her true self behind pounds of makeup and a fake personality. And she sure as shit doesn't hold back while eating her favorite carnival food.

She's a mess, and all the more beautiful for it. The truth is, I've never been more drawn to someone than I am right now. The breath damn near stalls in my lungs. Rylee Creed is the most stunning woman I've ever seen, even with powder sugar dusting her skin. The excess sugar just makes me want to lick her clean.

My stare must reach creeper status. Her chewing slows as she peers over at me. Concern pinches the space between her brows. Then she glances at my plate.

"You haven't touched yours."

Unadulterated lust clogs my throat. "I was busy."

"With what?"

"Staring at you."

"Wow, that's extremely honest."

"And you're extremely distracting." In the most appealing definition of the term. I never want her to leave my side.

Rylee shakes her head as if to clear the influx of sugar. "What's wrong?"

"You have a little something here." I wipe my face to show her where to swipe on hers.

She makes a valiant effort, but the residue remains. "Did I get it?"

I move into her space, ducking to her level. "May I?"

Her pupils blow wide at my proximity. "Sure."

I grip her chin between my thumb and index finger, then brush away the evidence. "There you go."

"My hero." She sags into me, making no move to escape my grip.

My gaze drifts from her hooded eyelids to her pouty lips. Every feature is slack while mine are chomping at the bit. "Can I kiss you?"

Rylee stiffens against me, but only for a moment. Whatever she finds in my expression puts her at ease. She quirks a brow. "Why would you want to do a swoony thing like that?"

"Because what I really want to do would lead to us getting arrested for public indecency, not to mention scar our children for life."

Her snort is more unladylike than her eating habits—and just as addictive. "I've missed that dirty mouth."

I inch closer, my grip on her never faltering. "How much?"

"Don't bother digging for compliments." Then she cups my jaw and pulls until our lips press together.

The kiss is chaste and fast, but heat still explodes in my veins. That's just what she does to me. When we break apart moments later, the breath wooshes from my lungs.

I curl a stray lock of her hair around my finger. "Strawberry blonde has become a recent obsession."

She studies the spiral motion. "Do you have any others?"

"Obsessions?" I don't take my eyes off her. Although, can't is more accurate.

"Yes," she purrs.

I stare at her, wondering how much is too much. I settle for, "Green."

She gets my meaning, of course. A deep blush blooms on her freckled cheeks. "Look at you being romantic."

My thumb follows a path along the rising warmth of her modesty. "I'll deny it if you tell anyone."

Rylee peeks up from under her lowered lashes. "Your secret is safe with me, Romeo."

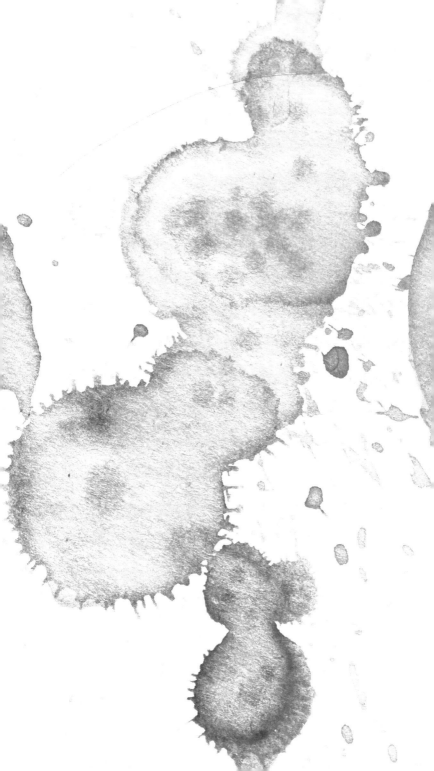

chapter seventeen

Rylee

ASEY AND ADAM STRUT ACROSS THE PARKING LOT TO WHERE we wait in the lobby. The carefree pair are the last to arrive at WhirlyBall. As it turns out, we were able to pull off this outlandish idea much faster than I could've planned. I casually mentioned a group outing yesterday—not expecting anything to happen for at least a month—but here we are.

The entire Bent Pedal team chose to join us. That's seventeen including Rhodes and me. Gage and Payton tagged along as well. They've been occupied in the arcade while we were waiting for everyone to arrive. Looks like that time is now.

Adam approaches Rhodes, who hasn't strayed far from my side. "Thanks for doing this, man."

"It wasn't me. Rylee is responsible for making our WhirlyBall dreams come true." He hitches a thumb at me.

I bump him with my hip. "Okay, Mr. Humble. You can take most of the credit."

"All I did was make a few calls to get the court booked."

"What about the replacement staff you hired for the afternoon?" Which I still can't comprehend.

"A buddy owed me a favor." He shrugs it off like finding coverage for a packed shift is no big deal.

"And let's not forget that you insisted on picking up the entire tab," I provide with an exaggerated flutter of my lashes.

"Which was no small feat," he grumbles.

Casey glances behind us toward the bar. "Does that include drinks?"

"Whatever you'd like." Rhodes motions toward the lounge area.

"That's the tits, bro." Adam lifts a palm flat for his boss to slap.

Rhodes seals the high-five with a chuckle. "You're welcome."

Those two wander off in search of alcoholic refreshments. A few follow them while the others circle around us for directions. I glance at Rhodes in all his backward hat glory. My traitorous lungs seize at the mouthwatering sight. It's becoming increasingly difficult to resist his charms.

Unaware of my internal debate, he makes a forward sweeping motion, as if granting me the floor to speak. The guy is giving me far too much credit. Not to mention power.

"We're on court three. Once our group has gathered in the attached party room, a WhirlyBall expert will be by shortly to explain the rules. Our reserved hour begins after we sign the waiver." I paste on a broad grin while reciting the spiel from the lady who checked us in.

Becky begins to jog in place. "What're we waiting for?"

The bubbly server starts a trend. Her fellow crewmates are quick to share in the anticipation. Even Jeremy, who rarely cracks a grin, appears eager to begin. I smile at their cohesive display. This is already going better than I could've predicted.

"You can head that way. I just need to herd the—"

"Mom, mama, mommy, mumma!" Gage comes barreling over from the claw machine. "Look what I won!"

I gasp when he thrusts a stuffed animal straight at my face. Once I recover my bearings, I take a moment to appraise his prize. "Oh, wow. What is that?"

He studies the strange creature with unconditional affection in his gaze. This kid is such a lover boy. "He's a prouble. Isn't he cute?"

That makes me laugh. "A prouble, huh? I didn't know those existed in the wild."

"Duh. We're like a whole pack. I can't be the only one," he mumbles.

Rhodes moves his focus from Gage to me. "What's a prouble?"

"It's a slip of the tongue." I giggle at his perplexed expression. "When Gage was being a stinker—"

"I had dessert before dinner," my son explains with far too much pride.

Rhodes nods and strokes his chin. "I've been guilty of snacking before a meal too."

Flames sizzle on my cheeks when I picture him sneaking a lick before ramming into the main course. My thoughts wander straight to filth thanks to the man on my left. A quick glance at him, and his smolder pinned on me, confirms the suspicions.

"Anyways," I continue. "In my flustered mom moment, I blurted out 'trouble' and 'problem' at the same time. That's when 'prouble' was born. It kinda stuck."

Gage cradles his toy, peppering the oversized head with kisses. "You're such a good prouble."

Rhodes dips until I feel him exhale against my ear. "I didn't think it was possible to be more attracted to you after the funnel cake, but I was wrong. Your random nonsense is so fucking sexy, Firefly. I can't wait to hear you combine more, harder, and faster when I'm thrusting deep again."

"You're bad," I murmur and tuck my chin.

"And you've only seen the tip of that kinked pole."

Thankfully, for the state of my withering composure, the lid on this inferno gets cracked in half. A victorious squeal pelts the air seconds before Payton runs toward us. She's clutching what looks like a unicorn crossed with a mermaid. Whoever provides the stuffed animals for that game has a warped imagination.

"Daddy, look! I won, I won!" She hops around in a blur, which doesn't help with the identification of her creature.

"Great job, Bumblebee. Is that a prouble too?"

Her prancing comes to an immediate halt. "No! This is Princess Fairy Violet Sparkle Twinkle Twist."

"Oh." He smacks his forehead. "That was my second guess."

"Silly, Daddy." She snuggles into his side.

That's when I notice her creative hairstyle. "What happened to your pigtails, cutie?"

Payton straightens to look up at me. "Huh?"

I motion to the mismatched set. "You're all crooked and bumpy."

"My dad did it. Don't I look super pretty?" Lofty praise complements her tone while she tugs at a section.

The man in question is wearing a sheepish cringe. "This is an improvement, believe it or not."

Payton edges closer to me and cups a palm to her mouth to whisper, "He tries his best."

The next exhale wheezes from me in a sputter. Oh, my poor heart. The sappy, neglected organ doesn't stand a chance. Damn him and his endless appeal.

Through the lovestruck kernels clogging my windpipe, I manage to suck in a pitiful breath. "And on that note, we better get going. They're waiting for us."

"Race you there," Payton says.

Gage doesn't hesitate. "I'm gonna beat you."

The constriction in my chest eases as I watch them go. "They get along very well."

"Almost like siblings." With a hand notched in my lower back, Rhodes guides me in the correct direction.

Which is appreciated, seeing as my legs have the consistency of jelly. I fight the urge to collapse against him. "I was going to say best friends. At least, until they get married."

He grunts. "That will get complicated with our situationship."

"Oh, we have a situationship?" My laugh is strained.

His brows fling upward. "Don't we?"

"It's a tad soon to give us a title, even a trendy one." My gaze drops when I find the carpet to be extremely interesting.

"You're looking at me funny again."

I gulp at the knot in my throat. "Really? That's… odd."

Probably because he's responsible for providing the best orgasm of my life. But he's also untouchable. As in, I cannot allow that to happen again. No matter how loud my kitty purrs when he's near. This is about my principles.

Before Quinn and Heidi dumped the tea, I didn't want to blur any lines for the sake of maintaining the peace. Now? He's a reminder of what I narrowly escaped mostly unscathed. That's probably not fair. Hell, I know it's not. But here we are.

Rhodes hums, the soft noise holding too much density. "We're going to trade secrets someday, Firefly. Mine for yours. Just not right now."

All eyes land on us when we step into the room. A man in WhirlyBall attire beckons us forward. "Ah, great. Everyone is here. I just need to review a few simple rules before setting you free."

We join the group huddled on chairs in the center. Adam and Casey are heckling each other about a girl they met in the lounge. The two other bartenders provide jeering commentary. Becky, Margo, and Elaine roll their eyes as a seamless unit. Harmony thrums in the atmosphere. I find myself wishing Trevor could witness this. A sideways glance at an empty seat leads me to believe he might be.

"All right, listen up. This will only take a minute." The guy waits for us to quiet down before diving into his protocol. "There are two colors—yellow and red. You can mix and match or choose teams. Whatever you'd like."

Hushed murmurs stir among our crew. It seems some are already dividing to conquer. I grin and peek over at Rhodes. He shoots me a thumbs-up and a wink in return.

"Since your party is larger than the number of cars, you'll have to rotate in and out. Only step onto the court when all the cars have come to a complete stop. Keep your belts buckled whenever you're in motion. Be fair and play safe. Don't use excessive force. Keep the language clean for the kiddos. Who, by the way, both squeaked in just above the height requirements. Well played, Mom and Dad." He gives us a round of applause. "That doesn't mean the adults should hammer the youngsters full force. Be gentle, okay? The scoops are used to handle the wiffle ball, not to whack your opponents."

Grumbled protests collide with that last note. Adam waves to get the guy's attention. "What if someone wants to put my balls in the scoop?"

"Oh, my gosh." I hide my flaming face between my palms. "Whose idea was it to invite him?"

"Don't be shy, boss lady," Adam cracks. "I'll give you a piece of the action."

"You're worse than the children," Rhodes admonishes. "Who have excellent selective hearing and only pay attention to the bad stuff. So, zip it."

Adam peers to the far wall where Gage and Payton appear distracted by stacking paper cups. "It's a fair question. The hottie at the bar said—"

"Not the time," I interrupt. Then I motion for the WhirlyBall pro to plow onward. "Excuse him."

"I appreciate the excitement. Please only use our equipment for its intended purpose. You want to scoop and score, but keep it on the court. Most importantly…" He pauses for dramatic effect. "Have fun!"

The group whoops and hollers while jumping to their feet. I'm a bit slower on the uptake, still reeling over the doofus who doesn't waste a chance to be inappropriate. "This should be interesting."

"It's definitely going to be something," Rhodes chuckles.

Jeremy leaves the group to stand beside us. "We decided the kids should play however long they want. That leaves eight cars. You two have been elected to participate in the first heat."

That gives me pause. This is about them having fun, not us. "Are you sure? I don't need to hog a spot. We can sit—"

"You've been specifically summoned. Unanimously."

"Lucky us," I mumble.

He sweeps an arm toward the door. "Good luck out there."

"We'll do our best." Rhodes' hand reclaims the spot at the base of my spine, leading me onto the court.

Two red cars sit unoccupied. The rest are claimed by eager beavers with their sights set on our approach. I cut a path to Gage to check that his belt is tight. Rhodes does the same with Payton. It seems they're both already strapped in with precision.

Adam whistles from across the sleek floorboards. "Don't worry, Mama Bear. We got your cub set."

Casey nods at his boss. "Same goes for you, Pops. The princess is tucked tight into her castle."

"That's reassuring," Rhodes grumbles.

"Don't get your pubes in a twist. The kids are off-limits." Casey waves his scoop at Gage and Payton.

My son mirrors the action. "I'm on Payton's team. We're gonna bump each other."

"You're my bumping buddy," she coos at him.

"Bump, bump, bump," Gage chants while slashing the air with his scoop.

Rhodes looks a tad ghostly around the gills. "Don't bump each other too hard, or too much."

"We won't," they reply in unison.

His swallow is thick. "Why do I have the sudden urge to vomit?"

"It'll pass when they're eighteen," I say. "Or maybe thirty."

His stricken appearance gains intensity as we get situated in our own cars. "My nerves are already shot and she's only seven."

"Enough stalling. The small ballers have themselves covered, but the big bosses? You two are free game." Adam's chuckle promises retribution.

For what? I'm not certain. "Are we on teams?"

"Sure." His devious smirk suggests otherwise.

Casey motions from his eyes to mine, keeping me in his sight. "We're coming for you hard, boss lady."

Adam grips the steering wheel with white knuckles. "I'll get her from the back."

An animalistic sound rumbles from my right. A peek at Rhodes exposes the culprit. He might as well be foaming at the mouth while glaring at the cocky instigators.

"Why don't you come after me instead?" He doesn't bother unclenching his teeth.

Casey scoffs. "Where's the fun in that?"

"You're about to find out."

I have a hunch that the beast is about to bust from his cage. "Remember, boys. This is for the children."

Casey scoffs. "Hell no. This is to boost morale."

I can't argue with that. And now I understand why they wanted us to be involved. We're the enemy target.

The other four on the court don't appear phased by their co-workers' taunts. From their lax expressions, they're ready to go with the flow. Divide and conquer indeed.

"Is it all of you against us?" I give a quick scan to detect any allies.

"I'll handle the lewd and crude combo." Rhodes hasn't taken his eyes off them.

Becky pops her gum. "I just wanna score."

"May I be of assistance?" Kevin smacks his lips at her.

She gives the young bartender a once-over. "Let's see what you've got."

"All right, WhirlyBallers. Are we set?" A voice booms from overhead speakers.

"Yes!" We reply as a whole.

"Then go, go, go!"

The cars power on with a mechanical thrum. Energy pulses from floor to ceiling. I slam on the accelerator and crank the wheel. It seems everyone does the same, zipping around in chaotic glee as laughter and competitive spirits pelt the air. A collision behind me steals my focus. Rhodes erects a territorial wall of testosterone and protective instincts. Casey and Adam do their best to hammer through his shield. Rubber bounces while metal skids, trying to gain traction. He doesn't give them an inch.

Their threats don't stand a chance of reaching fruition. Not even close. The moment they change course to stage an attack, he's there acting as my personal defense.

"I'm gonna ram you in the rear, boss lady." Casey whoops while attempting to skirt around my guard.

The snarl Rhodes unleashes might scare a bear. Casey and Adam barely notice the threat, though. Their unwavering focus is entirely on crashing into me. One goes left and the other shoots right, but Rhodes manages to cut them both off before they get within contact range.

"You don't need to worry about me, selfless knight."

"That's where you're wrong." He drives straight into their next approach. "I'll defend your honor until my last breath."

"Whoa, Casanova. Who am I to resist an offer like that?" I swerve off in the opposite direction.

The ball is on the floor for the snatching. A fast scan reveals everyone occupied elsewhere. Nobody appears to be concerned about scooping it up. They're too busy chasing each other. That works in my favor.

I drop my patrol and press harder on the pedal. Thunder enters my bloodstream while I lower the scoop. That's when someone rams into me from the side. My body lurches to the left on impact. It takes a second to regain my balance and locate the guilty driver.

Gage is already speeding away, waving his scoop in farewell. "Got you, Mom!"

Meanwhile, Payton snags the ball and launches it at the board. A buzzer confirms her score. "We did it!"

My son veers over to where she's stalled. They slap their

scoops together in victory. I gape at their strategic ploy. Those two hustled me. A backward glance shows the fray in a similar state of shock.

Then we erupt in roaring cheers.

I let a shrill whistle loose. *"Great job, Schmutz. You too, Payton."*

"Those smiles are infectious." Rhodes wears one of his own.

My lips are stretched to the aching point. *"I'll sacrifice the win for them."*

"Always." He leans over to cradle my cheek.

"You were right, boss lady. It's totally for the kids." Adam zooms off to assist Gage and Payton with their next play.

Casey is quick to follow. *"We're gonna beat the bosses."*

I glance over at Rhodes, who's already studying my profile. *"See? They have redeeming qualities."*

"Yes, teaming up with the children to win. How high and mighty."

"A little competition never hurt anyone. Catch me if you can!" I wink before ditching him in my dust.

Rhodes gains on me almost instantly. His husky response is a sultry touch tracing my spine, eliciting a shiver. *"Silly, Firefly. The chase started the second you walked into our bar."*

chapter eighteen

Rylee

"THEY'RE REALLY CLOSED." I STARE AT THE ABANDONED WEBSITE that's loaded on my phone.

"You didn't believe me?" Rhodes smirks while steering our ankle biters toward the grocery section.

Gage and Payton are engaged in a pretend sword fight. The lady seems to be besting the knight, based on her stealthy jabs. She's graceful while plotting her next move, searching for his weakness. My son is less covert in his approach. His actions are flashy and reckless. It's all about stage presence with that kid.

After an internal shake, I get myself back on track. My bottom lip juts out in a dramatic pout. "Nothing against you, but I didn't want to believe it. Vali-Hi is a relic."

A comforting touch settles on the small of my back. "Don't fret, Firefly. I'm on a rescue mission to revive this extravaganza."

"Oh, my. An extravaganza?" I clutch a palm to my fluttering chest. "Careful or my expectations will go through the roof."

Rhodes winks. "The better for me to exceed them."

"Cue the swoon, Suave." I almost sag into him for dramatic effect. That must be where Gage gets his knack for animated flair. "My faith in you is restored. Not that this wasn't already solid. Gotta keep you humble, though."

Hunger sparks in his coffee eyes. "Damn, you really have no clue."

I shiver from the heat in his voice. He's made similar

comments at least twice before. If he keeps up with these romantic gestures, I'll connect the dots pretty darn fast. This is already starting to feel like a whirlwind affair.

Which serves to remind me that I should be careful.

My gaze returns to the screen and our reason for this impromptu trip to the store. "I'm still trying to wrap my head around this news. It's really disappointing."

His determination to save the night leads us to the snack food aisle. "Maybe they'll reopen. Their social media page is filled with pleas and requests to get the place running again."

The fact that he's invested in their story eases the sting. Rhodes wanted to plan our next outing. Originally that included one of the last standing drive-in theaters in Minnesota. It's the only one that holds sentimental value. But the proof is glaring me straight in the face.

I ignore the rock that's dropped in my stomach. He has a backup plan, which began with picking us up at our house and taking a detour to Target. Now there's an empty basket hanging from his bent elbow. The next task is combing the candy selection for our favorite indulgences. It's obvious the guy has something special in his back pocket. I'm not referring to those tight buns either.

Another sharp jerk of my head sets me straight. Time to get a grip. His firm butt is off-limits.

My thumb swipes as I search for any crumb suggesting a rebound. "I hope this isn't the permanent end for them. My parents took us to Vali-Hi all the time when we were young. It turned into a hot spot for teenage summer nights too."

A secret grin crosses his lips. "Same here. Lots of good memories."

"What if we would've bumped into each other?" I toss him a saucy wink for deflection's sake. Totally innocent. The harmless gesture doesn't mean I'm going to sleep with him again.

"Trevor would've chased me off," Rhodes muses. Then

his features pinch in concentration. "Actually, he might've let me take a shot. I was a super dork, remember?"

"Sexy geek," I correct him. "My brother must've liked you. I'm sure he would've let you spread out beside me in the truck bed."

He squints in my direction while snagging a pack of licorice for our stash. "Did he allow random boys to sneak under his defenses often?"

"Never," I laugh. "He was extremely protective. Any attempt I made of getting frisky beneath the sleeping bag was squashed almost immediately."

"That's what I thought," he grunts.

Memories rise from the ashes of those challenging days. "Even when I was a senior in high school, my brother insisted on sabotaging my relationships. He would chaperone me under the guise of wanting to go wherever I planned. We fought like enemies, but I knew his intentions came from an honorable place. Especially now."

My brother was one of the greats. The phantom ache of his absence might never cease, but I don't want it to. That sibling bond won't break, which I'm eternally grateful for. Another burst of relief soon follows. It's becoming easier to talk about him without immediately bursting into agony. A smile even graces my mouth. I find a similar expression stamped on Rhodes.

"We were good friends. Still, I'm not sure he would give me his blessing to date you."

I add dill pickle chips and fruit snacks to our haul. "Good thing that's not what we're doing."

His chuckle is juicier than an entire box of Gushers. "Oh, this is a date."

"With children tagging along? How romantic." I wiggle my brows for emphasis.

"Are they not allowed to be present as noisy bystanders? They're halfway in love with each other. We must be rubbing off on them." He dares to lean in and give me a peck on the cheek.

Traitorous flutters erupt in my belly. *"Or maybe it's the other way around."*

Conspiring whispers tickle my ears. I turn to find Gage and Payton locked in a familiar huddle. Their focus is locked on us, giddy glee reflecting in their features. The tight-knit instigators barely raise my suspicions at this point.

That's when I take stock of our intertwined position. I'm practically plastered to Rhodes. My entire being goes up in flames as I scoot from his personal space. The shift is subtle, yet I practically have to force myself to comply. Freaking Rhodes and his magnetic charms.

I cough to release the steam curling off my tongue. *"What're you two chattering about?"*

More shouty whispers are exchanged between them. Gage murmurs, *"They're gonna get married."*

Payton squeaks. *"Does that mean they're gonna spread the love and have more babies?"*

A tiny shrug is visible from my son. *"I guess. That's what happens when a husband and wife have too much love inside them. It spreads to the mom's belly. That's where the baby grows."*

She gasps and pulls back to gawk at him. *"How do you know all this?"*

"YouTube." Concrete knowledge clangs from his voice, as if that's the most reliable news program on the planet.

Rhodes has the audacity to laugh. *"See, Firefly? It's totally a date."*

"That's what you get from their conversation?"

"I'm adopting their selective hearing methods. Besides, those two together are working in my favor."

"How convenient." A haughty brow gets quirked his way.

"It's better than focusing on my daughter being infatuated with your son."

"If it makes you feel any better, I think the feelings are mutual."

He turns and props himself against the nearest shelf. His slanted stance drops him into my direct vicinity. "I'm interested in your feelings."

"About our children plotting against us?"

"I'd say it's for our benefit."

"It's a bit early to be setting a wedding date, Casanova." I'm still trying to resurrect the boundaries between us, pitiful as the attempt might be.

Then he has to go and feast his coffee eyes on my curves like I'm the only flavor shot for him. Pretty sure he said as much at the orchard. "How's our truce?"

I gulp at the sudden dryness in my throat. "Still standing."

"This doesn't count as me throwing money at a problem, right?" His tone holds a cautious edge. A complex I'm responsible for giving him.

"No, it doesn't. There's no problem. We're doing this for the kids. It's different," I reply. He's different from—nope, not going there.

Rhodes stares into my eyes. "Don't go quiet on me. Your thoughts are a marching band, yet you won't let me hear the song."

"Are you saying I think really loud?"

"That's what you're choosing to get from my statement?" His gaze twinkles when he rephrases my earlier comment.

"Does that mean I can use selective hearing as an excuse?"

"You're stalling," he murmurs.

I lengthen my pause on purpose, letting the lull drag out longer than my brother's notorious beer belches. "Diversions are best served cold."

Rhodes snorts. "That's revenge, Firefly."

"There can be multiple dishes," I hedge.

A harsh tug on my shirt is a welcomed interruption. That is until my son speaks. "I doubt your doubt, Mom."

There are too many ways I can interpret his meaning. I settle for a classic, "Huh?"

"You're wrong about the fire."

I blink at him. "What fire?"

"The fire between you and Rhodes, remember? I told you it's burning really hot. Like super duper."

Now my jaw unhinges to hang slack. I snap it shut in the next breath. "We've talked about this, Schmutz. There's no fire."

He shakes his head. "I doubt your doubt."

"That doesn't make sense."

"It totally makes sense," Rhodes argues. "Payton explained the fire thing to me. I'm not on board when it comes to her and the boyfriends, but I'm good using it in this context."

I turn my shock onto him. "Whose side are you on?"

"Theirs."

"Figures," I mutter.

Rhodes grows bold when our rapt audience gets distracted by something extra sugary. His arm bands around my waist and he tugs me close. "Only a matter of time."

The breath in my lungs is held hostage while I wait on him to elaborate. I cave after less than a minute. "Until what?"

His nose is buried in my hair. In the following beat, I hear him inhale me. "You tell me what's stopping you from falling in love with me."

My lashes lower to conceal the desire I'm sure is reflected there. "Wow, someone is full of himself."

The laugh he gives me curls my toes. "Just wait until you see what I've arranged for our date."

"Oh, brother. I'm in trouble." I barely wince at my choice of subject. If anyone can understand my potential downfall, it would be him.

"Daddy!" Payton's loud and sudden presence has me

straightening fast enough to bash Rhodes' forehead with my temple.

"Holy sh—shitake mushrooms. That hurt." He clutches the inflicted area.

"Sorry," I mumble while rubbing my own wounded area. "Nice save, by the way."

"Thanks." He manages a tight smile.

"Um, hello?" His daughter taps her foot as if she's been waiting on us for hours.

Rhodes squints in her general direction. "What's up, Bumblebee?"

The adorable nickname melts the hurt right off me. This man is guaranteed to wreck me. I almost forget why I'm fighting so hard.

Gage makes his presence known by bumping into Payton's side. "Guess what, Mom?"

I wait for his beloved to stomp on his rude intrusion, but she just smiles like he's Tom Holland. That reference unravels my tongue. "Chicken butt."

"Mommmmm," he complains.

Laughter bubbles from me despite my throbbing head. "Why're you fussing? That's the right answer."

He rolls his eyes. "No, it's so wrong. Payton hasn't tried a puddin' pop."

"No way!" I gasp. "That's a travesty."

His perma-grin twists into a pucker. "Trava-whut?"

"It just means I can't believe it," I explain.

"But I'm telling the truth. She told me."

"Okay, I didn't nail that quite right."

"You can nail it right later," Rhodes rumbles dangerously close to the smash zone.

I peek up at him. "You didn't learn your lesson earlier?"

Something naughty flashes in his gaze. "Are you trying to keep me away?"

An impatient stomp comes from Gage. "Mom, what about the puddin' pops?"

I make a point of swinging my gaze to the man leading this so-called date. "Why're you asking me? I'm not in charge of this extravaganza."

Rhodes' chest very well might puff out to double the sculpted brawn. "It sounds like we need to grab puddin' pops."

Payton snuggles into his side, further transforming my resistance into useless slop. "Then we'll go home for the movie thing? I can't wait to see what you chose, Daddy."

Rhodes presses a finger to his lips. "That was meant to be a surprise."

Her adorable features screw into a crooked pinch. "But why? We live there. It's not a secret."

He laughs at her logic. "You'll see, Bumblebee."

"M'kay." Then her attention returns to Gage. "Where are the popsicles?"

"Puddin' pops," he pronounces with expert fluency.

"Sure. Whatever. To the freezer!" Payton shouts.

They lead the way with us following close behind. My nerves bubble in a rhythm that can't be silenced. This isn't like a regular trip to the drive-in. Not the experiences I've had at least.

"So," I drawl. "We're going to your house to watch movies?"

"Something like that." The phrase is becoming something of a signature for him.

"Ominous much?"

That freaking dimple makes a dashing appearance on his cheek. "Can't handle a little mystery?"

"Is it going to freak me out?"

He seems to consider something. "You don't spook easily, right?

"Not unless it's scary," I provide.

"Then there's nothing to worry about."

Gage and Payton grab the frozen treats for our collection. She beams with pride. "Our basket is super full."

"You're right." Rhodes groans while pretending to make an effort to heft the load higher. "On that note, do we have all we need?"

Gage bounces in place. "Can I help scan the stuff?"

Rhodes ruffles his hair. "Of course, buddy."

"Me too, Daddy?"

"Yes, Bumblebee. Don't worry. Both of you are my helpers."

"Do you have a favorite?" That comes from my son.

Only a slight flicker across his expression reveals his distress. "Nah, you're equally amazing in picking out snacks."

"Woot!" Gage spins in a circle. "We're the best."

"You're so hyper," Payton scoffs. It only takes her a second to join in the twirling.

"Less criticizing, more self-analyzing," her dad prompts.

The tykes exchange a glance full of confusion. Before they can delve into more questions, Rhodes strides off. The kiddos are quick to flank him. The sight is ovulation bait. I very well might drop an egg just gazing after them.

I'm in a daze as we make our way to an available self-checkout. That's why I'm delayed in jumping on the helpful wagon. Before I can offer to do anything other than stare off into space, he sends me a panty-killer smirk.

"I've got it handled."

And that seems to be the case, considering how well he's performing. All I can do is stand back and watch the magic unfold. Not to mention my ovaries going into overdrive.

Rhodes wearing a hat backward is the definition of sexy. What's even sexier is him meticulously packing groceries and refusing my help. He's done with the entire process in one minute flat. It's an applause-worthy display. Dammit, I very well might sleep with him again. I snort at my own incredulousness. Screw that. There's no might about it.

"Shall we continue onward on our adventure?" He sweeps an arm toward the exit.

Gage and Payton giggle in unison. My son is the one to respond. "I love adventures! Are we gonna fight pirates? Or maybe dragons? Oh, oh! What about sea monsters?"

Rhodes strokes his chin. "That might be tricky, but we can try to slay them all."

"Yes, that's awesome sauce!" Gage thrusts a fist into the air.

The man responsible for my son's glee glances at me over his broad shoulder. "Are you coming, Firefly?"

Gravel seems to line my throat, but that doesn't stop me from responding. "Nothing could stop me."

chapter nineteen

RHODES

WHEN I TURN INTO MY DRIVEWAY, RYLEE'S JAW HAS DROPPED to damn near touch her luscious tits. "Um, whoa. The gated community should've clued me in, but… whoa."

I can't stop the laughter that spews from me at her sputtering. "That good, huh?"

"You live here?" Her arms flail at the windshield and the luxury three-story bungalow that rests just beyond.

Another chuckle escapes as I scrub over my mouth. "I sure hope so, or the owners will be wondering who's visiting at this hour."

"There's a wraparound porch." Sheer glee trips from her voice.

"That's actually my favorite feature. The sunset view is tough to beat." It's easy to recall the first time I saw this place through her fresh scope. Similar astonishment had captured me then, as it still does now. The urge to pinch myself twitches my fingers.

Rylee gasps, ripping me from the reverie. "Oh, my gosh. Do you have two rocking chairs sitting out there somewhere?"

My nod is a slow dip. "They're on the rear side, facing west."

"Too bad it's already mostly dark. We missed the show," she mumbles. Little does she realize, that's vital for this plan to succeed.

Warmth spreads through my chest as I admire her freckles under the interior lights. "I guess you'll have to stop by again."

She peeks over her shoulder to where Gage and Payton are engaged in a cutthroat rock, paper, scissors battle. A soft smile curves her lips when she looks at me again. "I'm sure that can be arranged."

"Would the chances increase if you knew that the beach is a block away?"

"Is there a lake attached?"

"Obviously," I scoff. "We're pretty far from the ocean."

She rolls her eyes. "The chances we'll return for a stroll through the sand are guaranteed, even if it's too cold to swim."

"I like those odds."

The green in her eyes seems to sparkle like priceless emeralds. "Is this a dream?"

"Nah, Firefly. This is real." I slide an upturned palm across the center console to clasp hers.

Her reaction bodes well for me. I want her to fall in love with my home. Falling for the rest will soon follow.

She glances at our entwined fingers. "I got a tip that you were pretty filthy rich, but that's proving to be a massive understatement."

"Does it change your opinion of me?" I nod toward my expansive estate.

"No." But she won't look at me. Her expression is guarded, but not to the extreme she's harnessed before.

I trace her knuckle with my thumb. The gentle touch is meant to remind her that I'm just a regular guy holding the hand of the girl he's crazy about. "Well, don't inflate my status too much. I'm more filthy than anything."

"Sure, Mr. Money Banks."

The barb stings. It stands as harsh evidence leading to the barrier between us. There's definitely something she isn't telling me. Not that I have any right to criticize her reluctance, or expect more than I'm willing to share. My gut clenches when she straightens in her seat. We'll need to clear the air sooner rather than later.

"Are you with me in this?" I squeeze her fingers threaded in mine.

"Trying to be. It's… complicated." Rylee loosens her grip, seconds from breaking our connection.

And that's my cue to move things along before she pulls away completely. "Do you want a tour, or would you prefer a direct route to the surprise?"

"The surprise." Her exhale whooshes from her in what sounds like relief.

"What the lady wants, I hope to provide."

She nibbles on her bottom lip. "Spoiler alert, honey buns. That shopping trip by itself raised your appeal several notches. It can only go upward from here."

The strain eases off my rigid posture. Her quick praise—lofty and inaccurate though it might be—serves to kick the mood into a positive spin. It feels like the awkward tension has flown right out the window.

"Well, in that case, let's get this deal sealed and my ego score boosted into the stratosphere." It takes great effort to release her from my grasp. Then I shift the truck into reverse before pulling forward onto the paved path that frames the property.

Rylee's eyes me warily. "Where are we going?"

"To the backyard."

Her brows leap skyward as she gapes at the lush trees that are in complete autumn mode. Red, yellow, and orange leaves blend with the grass that's maintained its green hue. The vibrant landscape is a worthy distraction. Even the kids have paused their intense battle to appreciate the colors.

She shakes herself from the momentary daze. "And why do we need to drive there?"

"It's part of the surprise."

"I'm beginning to get suspicious."

Without taking my eyes off the road, I reclaim her hand in mine. "I'd be worried if you weren't."

The fence that surrounds the area behind our house slides open as we approach. Floodlights from the house and strategically sunken lamps illuminate the yard. I park with the tailgate facing the lower patio. That also puts the main event behind us and still hidden from view. Rylee is too busy studying the rest of the enclosed space.

"Sweet sugar syrup. This is all yours?" The awe in her voice might as well be a fist stroking my accomplishments.

"Not too bad, huh?" I probably sound cocky, but a man should be proud of his domain.

Rylee's blatant perusal of the structured layout is almost comical. "I probably should've considered a career in investments rather than advertising and marketing. Talk about a fail on my part."

"It's not always a sure thing. I got lucky. Several times," I admit that truth easily enough. Anyone can look up how I climbed to wealth.

"No kidding." She lets a low whistle loose. "How big is your lot?"

"Just over two acres. The house takes up most of it. All of this stuff occupies plenty too. I'd rather have this than a plain lawn. Less to mow." I wink at her.

"Wow." Her eyes land on a separated section of the grounds. "Is that what I think it is?"

"Probably. There are only so many objects that come in a similar shape and size."

Her nose is practically plastered to the window to get a better look. "Of course, you have a pool."

"It came with the rest."

She hums. "Another excellent selling feature."

"No argument here," I chuckle. Although to be fair, the whole package is worthy of an instant sale. The realtor didn't need to create a pitch before I was agreeing to sign on the dotted line.

"I bet summer is a blast at your house," Rylee muses.

"Payton doesn't complain." My gaze finds her in the rearview, but she's occupied with her fellow meddler. They deserve extra dessert tonight. "The pool is sealed up tight until next year, but I hope you'll join us for a swim then. In the meantime, there's an attached hot tub.

She sags in her seat with a loud sigh. "Oh, you're speaking my language. I might have to dip a toe in later."

I lean across the divider to brush my nose along her cheek. "You can do a lot more than that."

Her next swallow is an entity all on its own. "We'll see."

"Daddy, are you done schmoozing?"

I choke on my daughter's choice of phrasing. "Where'd you learn that word?"

"At school," she chirps.

"Who was schmoozing at school?"

"I dunno. A teacher said someone was with someone else and I like the way it sounds. Shmooozzzzing," she repeats while drawing out the syllables. "What does it mean?"

Gage thrusts his arm straight in the air. "Oh, I know!"

Rylee turns to squint at him. "You do?"

"Uh-huh. It's when you're talking too much and aren't listening to directions and the person has to repeat themselves and you get in trouble and forget to do your homework and the teacher makes you stay inside for recess." The kid manages to spit that out in one breath.

Payton blinks at his explanation before turning her gaze on me. "Is that right, Daddy? It doesn't sound right."

"I mean, all of that could happen if you're schmoozing too much." Seems plausible to me, anyway.

"Yeah, close enough," Rylee agrees.

My daughter accepts that answer with a sharp nod. "Okay, can we get out now? We're bored."

"Sure thing, Bumblebee." I give Rylee's fingers a farewell squeeze before letting go and stepping out to open Payton's door.

She's eager to escape, nearly flinging herself onto the gravel trail. "Watch out, Daddy! We're having a race."

I stumble to avoid a collision. "Since when?"

"Now! Go, go go." And she's gone.

My gaze shifts to where Rylee has released Gage from the back seat clutches. He darts off after Payton, his skinny legs becoming a blur. His mom whirls backward with exaggerated pinwheeling.

"Have fun, you two." She calls after their retreating forms.

"We will." Their tandem reply carries on a breeze as they run toward the trampoline.

"Gosh, you have everything. Gage won't want to leave. Ever."

That's a fairly favorable outcome considering his mom would also stick around. The old me—before Rylee—would balk and tear off in the opposite direction. But this version leans into the idea without hesitation. I've just been waiting for the right woman. One who just so happens to have a built-in best friend for my daughter. The comfort that floods my veins is quick to agree.

I step around the truck to meet her near the tailgate. "What about you?"

She turns to face me. "Huh?"

"Would you like to stay?" My tone is a gritty rasp.

"The night?"

I swoop down until my mouth hovers over hers. "Forever."

"Someone is awfully forward this evening." Yet she lifts her chin to receive my kiss.

For a brief moment, I get lost in her. She parts her lips on a soft exhale. Heat instantly rushes under my skin. If I don't put an end to this, I'll be tempted to call off the surprise and haul her upstairs. Our tongues barely touch before I'm straightening.

"Figured I should just go for it. Why waste time when I know what I want? Taking the risk is a new habit I've developed since meeting a certain redhead." I twirl a lock of her glossy hair around my finger.

Rylee sways into me. "Careful, or you'll make me feel special."

I just shake my head and mutter, "Still don't have a damn clue."

"Seems you're willing to give me another big hint." Her hips nudge mine to find me hard and eager.

"Which is extremely unfortunate under our current circumstances and company. I'm having nine inches of regret that we're not alone tonight."

"You're definitely filthy," Rylee laughs. Then she takes notice of the seating area on the patio. Strings of twinkling lights frame the space and set the mood. "That looks like a cozy spot to relax after a long day."

"Or in the bed." I hitch a thumb at the truck box.

"Why would we—wait a second." She spins on her heel to inspect the scene again. That's when she recognizes the equipment nestled in the center. "What's happening? Is that a projector?"

"Looks like it."

Rylee's narrowed stare swivels to me. "Are you playing coy?"

"Why would I do that?" Other than to get this exact reaction from her.

"I have no idea. You haven't downplayed a damn thing since we pulled into your driveway." She pauses, getting caught in thought for a second. "More like ever since we met."

And there's good reason for that.

Just as I'm opening my mouth to explain, Payton and Gage burst our bubble. My daughter squeals while discovering the secret I built for them. Rylee's son is more subdued while digesting the scene he previously ignored. To be fair, the trampoline is an attention hog.

"Is that for me, Daddy?" She points to the small theater campsite I created for them.

"And Gage," I counter.

"Really?" He stares at the mostly solid structure with instant love pouring from his expression. "Mom tried to make us a fort once, but it collapsed before we could get inside. Yours is so much better. This is freaking awesome!"

"Is this why you were being sneaky?" My daughter studies me like I'm an egg about to crack. She tried grilling me earlier after sneaking a few peeks with little success. "I knew something fishy was going on."

"You were right, Bumblebee." I did my best to be stealthy. It's not my strength.

"How cool! You made us a cave. This is way better than watching a movie on the couch," Payton says.

The kids shriek and dive into their fort fit for two that's stuffed with pillows, blankets, and oversized cushions. I set aside bowls for the candy we bought. There are a few random costumes I found—seeing as Halloween is right around the corner—that I thought they'd enjoy. Based on the decibels their shrieks are raised to, I'd say it's a raving success. Their joy fills my heart until the beating mass stretches to nearly bursting. I rub at my throbbing chest and realize Rylee is silent beside me.

"What do you think?" My knee bumps into her thigh, dragging her attention to me.

"Me?" Her tone is high as if she's shocked that I care.

"Your approval is important."

She flutters her lashes with enthusiasm. "As if that's honestly in question."

"Can't stroke my ego a little bit?" Or a lot, depending on her mood.

"It's… incredible." The awe in her voice mirrors the sentiment.

"I'm glad you think so."

"Look at them. They're so happy. I can't believe you went

through all this trouble." Rylee scans the setup I've put together again. "It might be excessive."

"Nah, I wanted to make it good for them."

A gust intrudes on our bubble, shoving a biting chill into the comfortable warmth. She shivers against the onslaught. I'm quick to drag her into me and reclaim our... fire. If we can't beat 'em, might as well join 'em.

Her body melts against mine, heat immediately billowing between us. "You did good, Prince Charming. Real good."

A muted groan slips from me as I wrap my arms around her waist. "Your reaction is better than theirs."

She rests her chin on my sternum. "How do you figure?"

I lower my forehead to kiss hers. "You look like you're gonna eat me up."

"Keep making swoony moves like this and I just might." She licks her lips as if I'm icing on her favorite cake.

With an offer like that, I might as well roll out the grand gesture I planned specifically for her and our date. I lower the tailgate to expose the futon mattress I slid in there this morning. Our own pillows and blankets are piled under a nearby tree.

Rylee's jaw goes slack for at least the third time. "How did I miss all this?"

"That's easy to do when you aren't searching for it." I wonder if she catches my secret meaning.

The spark in her eyes suggests so. "Has anyone ever called you romantic?"

A snort is an appropriate response. I tack on a curt, "Absolutely not."

"Maybe a reluctant version?"

"It's still a no." Any woman who's previously crossed my path would probably refer to me as cold and callous at best. "Except for you, Firefly."

"Now this is a dream," she breathes.

"Is that the only way you'll let yourself believe this is real?"

Rylee expels a sharp puff that resembles a laugh. "A dream come true?"

I nod against her. "We couldn't go to the drive-in, but that doesn't mean we can't make our own."

She sags further into me. "You went all out."

"And you're giving me too much credit. It just took time, which I gladly give to the cause. There's a flat, windowless section of the house that's just right for the viewing. I had the projector, but I've only used it inside."

"Do you have a movie theater room?"

I trap a laugh desperate to escape. "Not exactly."

Her eyes roll skyward. "That's a yes."

"It's more like a family cave." My fingers dig into her hips for a gentle squeeze.

"I love a cozy den space."

Which instantly brings forth a picture of us huddled together on a frosty winter night. "Me too. Ours will be better with you and Gage."

"There you go again," she sighs.

"Are you complaining?"

Rylee shakes her head, our cheeks brushing. "Not really."

I hug her tighter, our close proximity not quite enough. "What's holding you back?"

"Soon."

"That's fair," I concede.

"Dadddddddyyyyyyy." Payton's wail comes from deep within their fort.

I twist slightly so as to not blast Rylee with my reply. "What up, Bumblebee?"

She pokes out from the canopy flaps to huff in my direction. "Are you gonna start the movie or what? We're waiting."

"Someone's impatient," I call.

"Duh," she returns. "We have this super cool fort and nothing is on the fake screen."

"They have a point," Rylee croons.

"Whose side are you on?" I tease.

"The one where I get to be at the drive-in without leaving your backyard."

"Why didn't you say so sooner?" I wink and move to toss our supplies into the truck bed.

"You're ridiculously attractive right now," she purrs.

I pause in my pillow-fluffing mission to see unfiltered lust steaming from her sultry gaze. "Just right now?"

Rylee's lips twitch before she lets a crooked grin free. "Always, but I find you taking charge of mundane tasks extremely sexy."

It takes a solid minute for that to sink in. Just being there for her is flipping some sort of switch. Perhaps she just needs a man to rely on. Period. That's probably an even better way to approach her resistance.

I make an entire production of unrolling a sleeping bag and laying it flat. "Then allow me to handle whatever you need."

She bites her inner cheek, allowing a soft moan to fondle me. "Now you're just talking dirty."

The urge to get this woman wrapped in my arms makes the remaining process a breeze. Our private suite is complete after I finish arranging an excessive amount of cushions against the far end. I hop down to retrieve the snacks and remote controls. Rylee jogs over to the children and dishes out their chosen treats. I'm getting the system booted up when her return approach slows to a snail's pace.

"What's in there?" She nods to the storage building located on a corner of my property.

My gut pitches sideways. "It's a garage of sorts."

"Ominous again?"

"I'll show you next time." Maybe I'll be better prepared by then.

"Ah, yes. Along with the lake and sunset. We better reserve an entire day."

A rumble rolls up my throat. "I'll ask Melinda to watch the kids."

Our nanny's name seems to spark something in her mind. "Is she here now? Should we ask her to join us for the movie?"

"I gave her the night off. She's visiting her sister in St. Paul."

"Just the four of us then." Rylee makes that sound very appealing.

With a come-hither motion, I beckon her toward me. "That's what I want, Firefly."

"Firefly," she murmurs. "Are you ever going to tell me where that came from?"

I chew on my response for a beat. "Soon."

Her fingers walk up my chest and tug at my shirt collar. "Another thing to add to the list."

"It's getting rather long. We might need to tackle a few items."

"We just might." She hoists herself onto the open tailgate before I can offer to help.

I jump to join her, the metal groaning in protest. "Is everything to your liking?"

"You must be joking." She snorts, then sobers her disbelief at my stoic expression. "Yes, babe. Without a doubt. This is the greatest date in dating history, especially for me."

My mouth captures hers for a chaste peck. "That's all I wanted to hear."

"What did you choose?" She flicks a wrist at the screen.

"Well, Gage gave me a tall order."

"He does that," she laughs.

I scroll through the Netflix selections with one in mind. "How about this?"

Rylee's smile confirms my decision. "Let's see what the peanut gallery has to say. In three… two… one…"

Gage leaps forward from the confines of their fort. "Sea Beast is the best movie ever!"

Payton comes into view as well. "Ohhh, I love Red. She's such a pretty monster."

"Pretty?" Gage's offense is highlighted by the protector's glow. "She's like super deadly and totally cool. The way she blows the boat to bits with one fireball."

"Uh-huh, whatever. She's really strong, but also pretty."

The children bicker as we get situated on the mattress. I scoot backward until a solid surface greets me. Rylee is quick to plaster herself along my side. My arm loops around her to eliminate any unwanted space. Contentment is a wistful sigh we release in unison.

"This is nice, Rhodes." She pats my chest and snuggles in. I definitely approve.

I adjust against the cushions propping me upright. "Not a bad alternative to Vali-Hi, huh?"

Before she can respond, Payton's whisper reaches us. "If my dad marries your mom, does that mean she'll be my mom too?"

Gage swings his focus to where we're sprawled in the truck bed. His shrug is a solitary bounce. "I think so."

Payton gazes at Rylee like she's a lifetime supply of ice cream with extra whipped cream sprinkles. "That'd be cool."

His gaze lands on me, a similar puzzle getting sorted through. "Yeah, it would."

And just like that, the stakes are infinitely higher. It's not just about making a love match with Rylee. No, what's brewing between us is far more valuable. It involves all of us. If things go the way I'm imagining, we could be a family. The type our kids have gone without.

Rylee shivers and snuggles closer. "What're you thinking so hard about? You've gone stiff, and I'm not referring to the garden hose in your pants."

Amusement cracks the pressure radiating through my chest, but the significance remains. "I'm just happy you're here."

"Aww, such a charmer. I figured you were about to give me another strong dose of Romantic Rhodes."

"Soon, Firefly. Not sure you're ready for the rest quite yet."

Her breathing turns shallow, as if the weight of this moment just swept her up. "Soon."

But I give her a small spoonful to tie us over. "When you're ready, we'll exchange broken hearts and mend them together."

Rylee's eyes find mine as the opening credits begin to roll. "Oh?"

"Mine for yours," I whisper into her skin like a brand.

chapter twenty

Rylee

THE LONE CUSTOMER LEFT GUZZLING BEER AT THE RAIL POLISHES off his last call with a slurp. Sal slams his empty mug onto the counter with a resounding sense of finality. "All right, I get the message. You're kicking me out."

Casey crosses his arms and adopts a firm stare. At least, I think that's what he's going for. I swallow the laugh that tries to weasel its way up my throat. Sternness doesn't fit the face of this perpetual goofball. The expression looks like he smells a terrible fart.

"We've already let you stay fifteen minutes past close," he drawls. "I wanna go home."

There's no trapping my snort. "More like strut over to Roosters for some company."

Sal's features brighten at my mention of the other bar in town. The regular is loyal to a fault, but only to a certain hour, it seems. "That's right. They're open until two."

Casey wags his brows, all former pretense wiped from his face. "Where do you think I go after my closing shifts?"

"Thanks for the tip." Sal knocks on the wood.

"Same to you." Casey snags the cash he left behind.

Sal slides off his beloved stool and ambles toward the door, tossing us a wave over his shoulder. "Take care, Rylee. I'll see you down the block, Casey."

"Send my regards," I call to his retreating form.

And then there were two. Scratch that—three of us remain, but Rhodes is noticeably absent. He disappeared into the office thirty minutes ago and hasn't returned. I glance at the darkened corner, willing him to appear. Ever since his impromptu drive-in extravaganza, I've felt this clingy instinct tug in my chest. I'm choosing to enjoy him and his newfound romantic whims. Regret can find me later.

Casey follows my stare, which is no doubt filled with longing. "He's probably doing inventory or something boring. You wanna stock the cooler while I mop?"

A brow gets quirked in his direction. "I get the easy job?"

He shrugs. "You're the boss. I'm lucky you're willing to lighten my chore load at all."

Which gives me an idea.

"How about you head out instead?"

Casey's eyes nearly bug out. "And leave you to do everything?"

"It's not much. Go on," I urge. "Rhodes will do the rest with me."

"You sure?" But he's already rounding the corner to make a swift escape.

"We're taking off early tomorrow for Halloween, remember? Consider us even."

"Heck yeah. Those kiddos are gonna be stacked with candy." He rubs his palms together while walking backward to the door. "Trick or treat, boss lady. Tell Rhodes I hope he gets the latter."

"I'll see that he does."

Understanding dawns in his expression. "Oh, you're trying to get rid of me. Maybe we're not quite even after all."

I send him a look that's steeped in flat annoyance. "As if you're upset to be skipping out on cleaning."

"True story." Casey spins on his heels to take off in search of his next conquest. "There's extra bleach in the closet. Don't do anything I would do."

"No promises. Make sure to reset the lock behind you.

Tootles." I wiggle my fingers at him in farewell. Then I'm on a direct course to see what's keeping Rhodes occupied.

My heels click on the floor with each rushed step. There's a sizzle under my skin that's unfamiliar, but thrilling in the same beat. It's almost as if I'm walking a tightrope. Which direction I tumble depends on what I find inside.

The low rumble of his voice curls my toes once I'm within hearing range. I slow my approach when an internal conflict begs for logic. If he's busy, I shouldn't interrupt. My curiosity isn't easily satisfied, though. Fortunately for me, the door is open a crack to offer a skinny preview.

I squint to get a better view and see him straight ahead, sitting at the desk. He's cradling his forehead with one hand and clutching his phone in a white-knuckle grip with the other. It's after midnight, yet he's engrossed in what sounds to be a serious conversation. Talk of stocks and bonds and investment jargon flings so high over my head, it might as well be in orbit. Based on his clipped tone and the context, I'd guess this is a professional call—and it isn't going well.

Rhodes rakes several thick fingers through his already disheveled hair. After shooting a sharp retort down the line, he shifts his focus to the ceiling and glares at some unsuspecting spot. The warm brown swirls in turbulent chaos. Combined with his pinched features, it's even more obvious this isn't a casual chat.

His dress shirt is rumbled with the sleeves rolled to expose his tatted forearms. Someday in the very near future, I plan to trace his ink with my tongue. But the colorful designs are just the top layer. His ropey veins snake upward in a tantalizing trail. My mouth waters to lick those as well.

The thoughts alone make me lightheaded, and I clutch the knob in front of me for support. A telltale creak reveals my presence. The hinges groan even louder, making me wince. I'm busted.

His eyes snap forward to collide with mine. Time freezes

as I muffle a gasp. Dizziness is common a side effect whenever Rhodes Walsh is nearby. The oxygen grows dense in my lungs and I find it difficult to take a decent breath. I've been close to him the entire shift, yet he renders me immobile.

Awkward tension wages a fresh debate in my foggy mind. Do I stay or go? I part my lips to ask just that, assuming he will grant me a response. But a verbal acknowledgment isn't necessary.

The choice is made as the steely frustration melts from him in an instant. His smirk is adorably lopsided, almost as if he's relieved. As if just the sight of me puts him at ease. I'm allowing my imagination to run wild, but the hunger in his eyes spurs me onward.

A fantasy I didn't previously dare to let roam is suddenly on the loose. What would it be like to soothe his insatiable appetite while he has to maintain his composure? I guess there's only one way to find out.

Just then, a new rule occurs to me. It's too late for strictly business. In every sense of the concept. Pleasure has arrived to take control.

Rhodes must mistake the resolve on my features as impatience. His finger lifts to indicate that he needs a minute. If that isn't enough, he mouths something along the lines of being almost done.

The picture of his surprise when I take that as an invitation to cross the threshold and shed my nerves is worth hanging on the wall. We haven't done more than kiss since our sexcapades in this very space. A tingle spreads from my lower belly. I'd say we're overdue for the next round.

Nobody else is here, but locking the door is symbolic. His brows wing upward at the distinct click that ricochets across the otherwise silent room. Rhodes has made an abrupt turn onto the sweet and swoony scale in the last week. There's no reason I can't give saucy and sexy a try. Something that resembles suspicion narrows his gaze and trails my approach.

I offer a coy grin to alleviate any apprehension. When I speak, my tone is barely a hushed whisper. "You look stressed, not-boss. Is there a problem?"

His nod is a single jerk.

"Maybe I can be of assistance." There's a sultry purr in my voice that I don't recognize.

Other than an audible gulp, he doesn't protest. One word from him and I'd take a hike. This is far from my expertise or comfort zone. Kinks in general are beyond my grasp. My sex life has been plain vanilla without any swirls, but I have a feeling this man is going to add all sorts of flavors to my sundae. That's precisely why I gather the courage to try something new.

Rhodes flares his nostrils as I slink closer, my nail skipping along the edge of the desk. The phone is still pressed to his ear, but the voice on the other end is too muffled to comprehend. Whoever it is seems to be on a rambling roll. Their long-winded spouting works just fine for me.

When he's almost in reach, I bat my lashes at him in mock innocence. "Since you've been so generous with me, maybe I can return the favor. Would you like that?"

The chair squeaks when he shifts into a blatantly sprawled pose. If that's not an obvious invitation, I'm not sure what is. That doesn't mean I can't needle him a bit.

"Getting more comfortable? Must be a very important call."

The unknown individual—who has a masculine timbre—continues to drone on without pause. White knuckles grip the armrest while Rhodes bucks his hips at me.

Soft laughter puffs from me. "I take that as permission granted."

Then I'm sinking to the floor between his splayed thighs. The stamped concrete is cold beneath my knees, but the flames lashing from his riveted focus set my insides to a boil. My leggings offer minimal padding as I wedge myself farther into the gap he spread for me.

We still aren't touching… technically. I can feel the heat

through his clothes. My skin crackles at our nearness. His eagerness is visible in each subtle adjustment, but he doesn't steal my thunder.

Just before I'm about to make contact, I stick out my bottom lip in an exaggerated pout. My tone remains a velvet whisper. "Are you sure this is okay? I don't wanna get you in trouble."

The plastic case on his phone cracks. He doesn't seem to notice or care while that unwavering stare stays locked on me.

"Okay, Hulk. No need to smash things." I drift my palms along his thighs in an upward sweep. Muscles bunch and flex under my touch.

Rhodes barrels through my lazy introduction, clamping his legs against mine to capture me. Then his ankles cross at my ass to drag the point home.

I'm trapped and have a definite answer. The bulge behind his zipper beckons me. "Is this mine? Are you hard for me, big boy?"

He clenches his jaw, giving me another sharp nod.

"Should I try to relieve some of that pressure?" My fingers are already at the button of his jeans.

"Can we finish this another time?"

I almost startle at his booming rasp. It only takes a second for me to realize his question is directed to the unseen person on the line. My progress stalls while I wait for his verdict.

Rhodes clenches his eyes shut at whatever response he gets. "What a damn mess."

Doubt douses the embers of my bold actions. I consider giving him some privacy, but I'm still very much captured by his lower half.

His gaze returns to me in the next beat. I grin when he quits grinding his molars and releases the tension. Any signs of turmoil are extinguished. Desire reigns, an unfulfilled promised that demands to be kept.

"Messaged received," I murmur.

Muscles twinge in protest as I bend slightly to get a better position. Then I'm undoing his jeans, sliding the zipper down with extra care. The soft cotton from his boxer briefs does little to contain his arousal. There's already a wet spot on the material that betrays his desperation. I circle the stain on my route to setting him free from the stretchy confines. His resulting grunt is full of need.

Anticipation is a quake in my hand, but I try to hide the giddy tremor. He shifts while I reach in the trapdoor flap to release his dick. My palm is quick to curl around his exposed length. Another harsh breath whistles through his teeth when I give him a gentle squeeze. He's veiny and solid in my grip. His girth is thick, almost too large for my middle finger and thumb to connect. It's no wonder I was feeling him days later. My perusal leads to the reddish hue that's darkening his strained flesh.

"That looks painful. Are you aching for me?" A fiery flush burns my cheeks. I'm not sure where this sexy vixen has been hiding, but she's fabulous.

A choked sound has me glancing up from my inspection. He lifts his brows, silently prodding me along.

"Okay, okay. Spoil my fun," I joke.

His eyes roll to the ceiling as if asking for patience. I yank the denim gaped at his waist to offer him—and me—more room to roam. The faded material barely budges. He lifts his ass off the chair to assist me in the process. Then I return my fist to his shaft. He's steel encased in satin and mine for the pleasuring. A pearly bead appears from the slit when I rotate my wrist for an upward stroke. My gaze is latched on that iridescent appetizer.

"Let's wrap this up," he bites out. "It's getting late."

My downward motion is a starter course of its own as I wait for clarification.

"Then spit it out," Rhodes demands.

Now I definitely know he's not talking to me. I peek up at him from under my lowered lashes. "Want to hear a secret?"

He expels a noisy breath in response.

"Blowjobs aren't really my jam, but I'm kinda stoked to try it with you. Is that weird?"

"Fuck," he barks. Remorse immediately floods his features. "Right. My apologies. Continue, but make it fast. Other… projects require my attention."

My next breath is exhaled across his cock. "I think you deserve a reward for going above and beyond. The not-boss should get a bonus too."

His approval is a pleased rumble that boosts my confidence.

I wet my lips before pressing a soft kiss to his tip, sucking away the precum. A hint of salt mixed with intense craving paints my tongue. The punchy flavor is a heady combination. That makes me laugh, which is highly inconvenient.

"Please," he mumbles.

"Since you asked so nicely," I croon, "allow me to offer you some relief."

My mouth closes around his flared head with strong suction. Rhodes jolts from the abrupt change in pace. I'd giggle if my lips weren't stretched wide to accommodate his size. As a compromise, I hum around his length. Then he groans, long and low. The sound harmonizes with his fraying control. I pop off his shaft with a wet gasp.

"Shhh," I admonish. "You have to be quiet. Just relax and let me take care of you."

After a forced exhale, he sags into the chair. His willingness to comply and follow directions is extremely sexy. I don't hesitate to suck his dick into my mouth. I sink about halfway before bobbing back up. It's going to require a valiant performance to devour nine inches.

Somehow, he manages to grow thicker. The man is too blessed in the penis department. I slide down on his length with enough pull to form a tight seal. Drool is already escaping to lubricate my flow. Every ridge and notch I come across provides an intimate glimpse into this man. That soon becomes a desire to uncover him completely.

A throbbing pulse greets my tongue as I increase the suction. Rhodes' breathing turns shallow, which encourages me to go faster. It's still difficult to imagine taking his entire length, so I focus on another aspect instead. A moan bubbles from me while I picture him losing complete control. I hollow my cheeks and draw him in deep again. My motions are fluid and seamless as I bob up and down. The smooth rhythm feels effortless, like he belongs there. His answering huffs and puffs agree.

A peek up at Rhodes finds his eyes blazing and pointed directly at me. Carnal passion thrums in my veins, along with determination. My eyes water when I push the limit. Pride blossoms when I see that I'm almost there. That gives me the courage to open farther in an attempt to accept him in full. I choke on his length, but keep going. The challenge isn't solely mine.

Although, his composure game is strong. I've got his dick crammed down my throat and the man is still carrying on a conversation. My purpose solidifies. I want to make him break.

My hand slides along the fabric until I'm cupping his balls. Gentle pressure is all it takes. Nonsensical responses begin to spew from him. I find myself smiling into the next downward glide.

That's right, man meat. I'm committed to the cause.

"Ohhh, dammit. I'm gonna… need to… fuuuuck. I gotta call you back." His voice is strangled.

There's a pause, most likely a response from the other end. I smile into my next downward slide, My lips curve into a broader grin around his length. Victory is within reach and soon to be mine.

"Yeah, it's… an emergency. Some massive… bump in my plans. It just popped up. I need to handle the issue before… exploding."

Rhodes must toss the phone after that. It clatters on the desk seconds before his thick fingers are buried in my hair. He doesn't control my motions, just gets a grip as an anchor. I get a tad lightheaded just envisioning him relying on me to keep him grounded. His fists gather my strands to lift the strawberry blonde curtain away from my face. Maybe he just wants an un-obstructed view.

"You're naughtier than I gave you credit for, Firefly. That's one helluva power play. Did you want me to lose control? Does that turn you on?" Those strong digits tunnel deeper into my locks.

My scalp burns when Rhodes tightens his grip. He's going for my roots while I seal my lips against his. I withdrawal nice and slow, until just the tip remains. Then my tongue traces laps around his sensitive crown.

"Very clever sneaking in here," he mumbles. "And look at you. Fucking perfection."

I moan in agreement before gliding off his length. "That's exactly what I was aiming for."

His fingers give my head a massage while I suckle on his. "Well, you succeeded. I just hung up on a major investment deal. Might've tossed millions down the drain. But I'd do it all over again for a single lick from that wicked tongue."

I lave along his entire length, paying special attention to the thick vein on his underside. "Happy?"

"Like you wouldn't imagine. I've never put much faith into a higher power, but you might just make me a believer." Warmth transforms his fiery expression into tenderness flooding from his expression. There's something else in his gaze too, but it's too soon for that. "Almost positive you're heaven sent."

I'm kneeling between his thighs with his dick nudging my lips, but this might be the most romantic moment of my life. It's definitely too soon for that. "Would you like me to keep going?"

"If you'd be so inclined to prove this is real." His praise combined with the adoration shining from every pore motivates me to finish the job with polished execution.

"Afraid you're dreaming?"

Rhodes smirks. "Can't be too sure with you."

After dragging in a lungful of air, I lower my mouth to cover him again. I get caught in the cycled movements, listening to his accelerated breathing and grunts as cues. Some deeply in-grained thrill rises to the surface at listening to his satisfaction build. It's the most basic reinforcement and encourages me to double my efforts.

He collects my hair into one hand, then rests the other palm flat on my throat. His touch is delicate, just to feel me swallow-ing him. There's no pressure. Only awe. "You know what this does to me?"

Rather than answer, I repeat the motions. Once, twice, then thrice. His legs clamp me in a caged bond. Hooded eyelids ad-mire me while I bypass my gag reflex to suck him down to the hilt. I begin to squirm in earnest. How I'm getting turned on is a mystery. Then Rhodes bites off a string of expletives that end on a growled note. That sound spreads warmth through my core. I wrap my fingers around his base to join in the finale.

His thumb traces the joint of my spread jaw. "Gonna come soon, baby."

My acknowledgment is an extended hum. I have every in-tention of drinking every drop, but the fact he warned me is en-dearing. My lips connect with my hand to form a partnership in getting this done. Rhodes bellows at the feverish pace I set.

His telltale salty flavor suddenly blends with the pungent longing already on my tongue. The end is near. A final pump does the deed. Rhodes erupts with a roar, not holding anything back. I take it all with a greedy swallow. Then another for good measure.

He shudders against me. "Fuuuuck. That's so fucking good."

My belly swoops with his grunted curse. I slow the tempo to a lazy crawl before releasing him from my clutches. An ache blooms in my jaw, but I barely notice. Rhodes is a thoroughly blown mess. His eyelids droop into heavy drapes. The sight of him blissed out from my exertions sends me soaring.

"Holy shit," he exhales while collapsing into a relaxed

puddle sprawled in his chair. The beast is sated—for now. "That was unexpected."

I sit back on my heels and wipe the corners of my mouth. "You're welcome."

He wipes invisible sweat from his brow. "Any more tricks up your sleeve?"

The Halloween reference is appreciated and granted a saucy wink. "That was more of a treat."

"Was it ever. I'm ready to reciprocate." His blatant intentions lead him to lewdly ogle the space between my thighs. The man rebounds faster than a basketball pro.

Meanwhile, I shift on the floor while my knees scream from holding the bent position. "How about a drink first?"

"Still thirsty?" Rhodes nods at his cock, which hasn't deflated in the slightest.

"Parched." My cheeks blaze anew while I treat myself to another languid once-over. I can still feel him hot and hard in my mouth. "Three fingers of whiskey should get me warmed up."

chapter twenty-one

RHODES

I FEEL MY BROWS RISE AT RYLEE'S REQUEST. "YOU WANT WHISKEY?"
Laughter chimes from her. "Did you expect me to be craving something else?"

It does sting a tiny bit that she didn't ask me to rip off her pants and bury my face in her pussy. But I can handle easing into it. My teeth are still numb, which suggests I could probably use a longer recovery. In my orgasmic haze, I realize Rylee is still crouched on the floor.

"All right, let's get you a drink." I stand on shaky legs and offer her my hand.

She bats those seductive lashes at me while sliding her palm into mine. "Such a gentleman."

"Jeez, Firefly. Just how low are your standards?" With a gentle tug, I haul her upright.

She wobbles on her feet and tumbles into my chest. Her hips rock forward, finding me hard and hanging out to air dry. "You're steadily raising the bar each day, midnight flasher."

"This is entirely your fault." I put my dick away, which requires solid effort and several adjustments. The damn thing hasn't lost an inch with Rylee's pouty lips swollen and wet from sucking me off.

"As if you aren't extremely happy with my performance." She begins untangling knots created by my enthusiastic grip on her hair.

"Hottest fucking thing I've ever experienced." Which has given me the road to run with a fantasy of my own. I cradle her jaw and she immediately leans into my touch. That small gesture sends my blood pumping to dangerous levels. "You're getting the idea, huh?"

Her nod bumps along my hand. "All the clues are stacking up."

I brush my mouth against hers, swapping a quick exhale. "Let's celebrate with a drink."

"About time you soothe this parched throat." She pats the inflicted area.

My gaze lowers to her slender column, so delicate and brave. The same smooth expanse where my palm rested as she took me deep. If I wasn't already setting up camp in my jeans, that alone would pitch a mighty fine tent. She deserves one helluva drink after that.

"There's something here you might like." I force the lust from my lungs and turn toward the filing cabinet in the corner. In the top drawer hidden in the back, I find the inverted bottle that would make any scotch connoisseur cream themselves. "This ought to do the trick."

Rylee's eyes bug out when catching sight of the label. A gasp soon follows. Then she's shaking her head, palm lifted flat and straight to ward me off. "Holy shit, no way. I'm not drinking that."

A grunt admonishes her outright refusal. I'm offended on the scotch's behalf. "And why not? This is damn good whiskey."

She scoffs but doesn't remove her gaze from my proffered treasure. "I'm well aware, thank you very much. Macallan 25 has gotta be like two grand for a bottle."

"More like three, actually." Prickles attack my nape when she openly gawks at me.

"That's… too much money for booze. Sometimes I forget you're that rich." Her tone has taken a bitter turn that doesn't bode well for me.

"Is it terrible for a guy to treat himself to an extravagant gift? Although, that isn't why I bought it. I was trying to make myself feel better after Trevor's accident." And to drown the guilt that still sloshes in my gut.

Sympathy more than pity shines in her features. "All right, you're forgiven."

If only I could hear that from him as well. "Does that mean I can pour you three fingers?"

Rylee rejects me with a firm shake of her head. "Keep it for yourself. We can grab something else from behind the bar."

I make no move to leave. "What's your favorite drink?"

"That's random."

My shrug is lazy but purposeful. "Just realized I don't know much about you."

"Ditto," she coos wistfully.

"It's about time we change that, starting with your beverage of choice." I roll my wrist to get her talking.

"Iced tea, if we're talking before happy hour. But nothing beats an oaky scotch."

"You're really a whiskey girl?" I had an inkling based on her reaction to the Macallan, but assumptions seem to land me in trouble more often than not.

She laughs at whatever version of disbelief crosses my face. "You sound shocked."

"Not many have crossed my path. You're almost like a myth or a legend."

A snarky brow gets arched my way. "Or you just haven't met the right women."

"Touché." I tilt the sole possession in my secret stash toward her. "Have a drink with me?"

"That's special, just for you." A thought seems to occur to her. "Why you insist on storing such a rare treat in a lowly office is another concern entirely."

"If you cared about the scotch's wellbeing, you'd allow it to grace your lips."

"Now you're playing dirty." It's almost as if she knows what else is shoved up my sleeve.

"You'll be ruined for all others," I taunt.

She glances at the label. "That's what I'm afraid of."

My heart kicks faster. There's hope that she's referring to more than the liquor. "Don't overthink it. Aren't you curious why they call this the 'Rolls-Royce of Single Malts'? It's been matured in Sherry oak for no less than twenty-five years."

Rylee traps a moan between her pinched lips. "Sounds too good to be true."

"That's what I say about you, Firefly. Let's give my Macallan a new purpose. I can't think of a better occasion." Other than what lies ahead, but it's too soon to broach those possibilities.

"Really?" She rolls her eyes. "The blowjob wasn't that great."

"You're right, it was better." I hang my head in mock shame. "But this is the best bottle I've got. Forgive me?"

Her shoulder nudges mine. "I'll feel guilty."

"Why? You asked for whiskey."

"I usually settle for Jonny or Jack."

"Don't talk about other men, baby. It makes me jealous." I chuckle when she sticks her tongue out at me.

"Your top spot is secure, barbarian. They're just my weekend roster."

My thumb snags her lower lip, tracing the lingering swell. "I'm the only one who gets in this mouth from now on."

Rylee stares at me, green smoke rising in her unwavering focus. "Are you trying to stake an exclusive claim on me?"

"Yes."

"Good."

I stamp a kiss on her to seal the vow. "While we're on the subject, I've never shared this… private stash with anyone. Never wanted to, until you. Do me the honor?"

She's still on the fence, chomping that lower lip that's still carrying evidence of having been wrapped around my dick.

"Okay, fine. If you insist on wasting your ridiculously expensive scotch on me, I won't deny you."

"Nothing is a waste with you." I loop an arm around her waist and haul her against me. Magnetic chemistry thrums under my skin. Endearments climb along the lump in my throat, but I settle for simple and sticking to the mood. "You're so fucking sexy."

"Just wait until I have whiskey on my tongue." That further proves she's following me down this kinky path.

"We'll never get out of this office if you keep taunting me with your finer tastes."

Rylee trails her nose along my scruffy jaw, inhaling deep. "How long can we make that bottle last?"

"I'm about to find out." With her fingers laced in mine, I guide us out into the main room.

Nobody is here, which is a belated relief. I didn't consider the possibility that we'd have to kick the closing crew out. My hurried stride slows while I survey the scene. The place might be empty, but there's a mess left behind.

It's only now I realize how damn long I was on the phone. "What happened?"

"More like what didn't happen. I let Casey take off early, for obvious reasons. We'll have to clean after our nightcap." She cuddles into my side as we step behind the bar.

There's not much arguing with that, but it does serve to remind me. "You like it neat?"

"Of that? Absolutely." Rylee nods to the whiskey in my grip.

"Damn, that's hot." I snag a rocks glass on our path to the far end that's hidden from the front windows.

"Only one?" She furrows her brow as I set hers on the rail next to the scotch.

"I plan to sip mine from an interactive vessel. If she'll allow it." My hands skim the hem of her shirt, drifting under to caress the inviting softness of her torso. I lift the fabric slightly to make my intentions clearer. "May I?"

She lowers her gaze to where I'm stroking her stomach. Recognition widens her eyes, snapping that awareness to my awaiting smirk. "Wait. You want to do what exactly?"

"Will you let me drink my whiskey off you?"

"Like a body shot?" She raises her arms in silent permission.

"Sure, let's go with that. But I'll be having far more than one." I drag the cotton up and over her head, tossing the bundle over my shoulder. "And I intend to be less sloppy."

Just her black bra conceals her modesty. Goosebumps pebble her flesh as I trace the satin straps. "Have you done this before?"

"No." I unscrew the bottle and blindly drop the cap. Before I serve her, a nauseating visual assaults me. "Is this something you've done?"

"Almost," she murmurs.

"But?" I prod when she doesn't elaborate.

Crimson flushes on her freckled cheeks. "I couldn't go through with it."

I trace the blooming heat with my thumb. "And now?"

"You're different."

"That's right, baby. I'm very different for you." I pour precisely three fingers into her glass, as requested.

She inspects the portion with a glint of approval, yet makes no move to take it. "What am I supposed to do with that?"

"Get warmed up," I rasp.

"Alone?"

"Just to take the edge off."

"This isn't what I had in mind when you suggested celebrating with expensive whiskey." She glances down at her mostly bare upper half.

"Would it make you feel better if I took my shirt off?"

"Yes." Zero hesitation.

"Allow me to put you more at ease." I reach behind me for

the collar of my shirt, wrenching it off with a single yank. My hair most likely resembles a static storm.

"Don't bother," she purrs when I attempt to tame the chaos. "You pull off disheveled very well."

My muscles flex under her thorough perusal. "Would you like to see more of my talents?"

Rylee doesn't appear to have heard me. "Where do you find the time to exercise to such an… extensive extent?"

I chuckle at her jumbled praise. "There's a gym at my house."

"Ohhhh, yeah. I bet there is." Her appraisal hasn't moved from my abs. She grows brazen and traces the defined grooves. "We should start offering laundry services."

"Huh?"

Her fingers dance across my torso. "People can scrub their dirty clothes on your washboard. It'll be great for business."

My gaze narrows into a skeptical squint. "You'd be okay with other women touching me?"

"Not even a little bit," she mumbles absently.

"That's what I thought." I shift to press against her, dipping my face until our foreheads kiss. "Are you still thirsty or would you prefer to skip straight to an orgasm?"

That gets her attention. Starry eyes lift to mine while she wraps her arms around my waist. "You make me very thirsty and horny. I'm a glutton for scotch-soaked orgasms."

Now we're talking the same language. I jut my chin at her untouched pour. "Your whiskey awaits."

Rylee lifts her glass, sniffing the rich aroma I know well. A moan breezes from her after that single whiff. "And when are you planning to have some? I figured we would share in this experience."

"Oh, don't worry. We'll share, all right. If all goes according to plan, it will be mutually stimulating. Not to mention engaging. I'm just deciding where to start." My thoughts are scattered. It's becoming increasingly difficult to stop my mind from wandering down a filthy path while faced with her irresistible curves.

"Maybe a sip of liquid courage will cure your indecisiveness." She waves her drink under my nose, as if I need additional incentive.

"Perhaps, but I'm suddenly feeling at a disadvantage." I graze my knuckles across her ample cleavage. The satin cups barely contain her, which gives me an idea.

"Would you like me to ditch the boulder holder?" She's already reaching behind her back.

"If you don't, I'll do it for you."

Her arms shift in what I assume is a search for the clasp. "The bossy side is coming out to play."

"Are you gonna be a good girl and listen?"

Before I can finish dishing out the bait, her tits spill free from their restrictive cage. Saliva immediately pools in my mouth. Supple flesh peaked with rosy tips beckons me. I'm already sweeping my hands along her sides, over the bumps of her ribs, on the path to clutch those luscious breasts. Just when I'm about to feel their weight, I flick my eyes up to gauge her reaction.

Rylee thrusts her chest forward. If that's not permission granted, the definition doesn't exist. But in the slim case of lingering doubt, she murmurs, "Yes."

Unadulterated lust pummels me as my palms overflow with her. It flips something deeply primal inside of me that this woman offers more than I can hold. I rub my thumbs across her pebbled nipples. She trembles against me when I pinch the needy points. In the next breath, I ease the sting with a gentle caress. A soft whimper stumbles from between her parted lips.

"More. Please," she whispers.

I release her to smack the wood surface. "Up you go."

That's the only warning she gets. My grip lowers to her ass, taking a brief pause to squeeze. Then I'm hoisting her onto the counter. Rylee squeaks from the unexpected lift and secures her legs around my hips. This position aligns her against my cock better than I could've wished. Awareness ignites her stare into a blaze, and she grinds against my shaft.

I seal my mouth over the eagerness about to fall from her lips. "Not yet, Firefly. Lean back on your elbows for me."

She complies without hesitation. A quirked brow silently seeks my approval.

"That's my good girl." My fingers roam along her reclined torso before snagging the whiskey she once again abandoned. "You'll be needing this."

"Thank you." She adjusts to prop herself on one side in order to hold the glass.

"You're the one who deserves thanks. The visual you present beats any fantasy." Without removing her from my sight, I grasp for the bottle.

"Is that what this is?" Rylee watches me over the crystal rim, still refusing to take the first sip.

"Very much so." My spank bank has always been explicit by nature, but even more so since she entered my life. "I hope to act out many more with you."

She rubs her thigh against mine. "That can be arranged."

And with our future sexploits paved, I scour her exposed upper half for makeshift trenches and dips. When she shifts again, a hollow forms above her collarbone. A pleased rumble ripples through me at the discovery. Might as well start from the top and work my way down.

"Try to hold still so I don't make a mess." The grit in my voice betrays my desperation to be quenched.

With steady patience I don't truly possess, I dribble scotch into the shallow groove. Rylee's gasp morphs into a husky wheeze. My girl is feeling the heat with me. As I'm leaning in, I catch her finally taking a swig from her glass.

Her responding hum wraps a fist around my arousal and offers a practiced stroke. Before I can get distracted by her erotic noises, I slurp the whiskey from her skin. The smoky shot immediately sets a fire in my blood.

One taste feeds the fever that's pacing beneath the surface. My restraint snaps and I'm carelessly splashing my next mouthful into the concave at her chest. I sip from her like she's my only form of sustenance. A guttural growl soon rips from me in agreement. After that, I become a man undone in the presence of his ultimate temptation.

I rest my cheek on her stomach and pour scotch down the valley between her breasts. My tongue licks a line along the remnants. Not a drip to be missed. Whiskey douses her nipples, leaking in every direction for me to suckle.

"You're wasting it." Rylee's words sound like a complaint, but her tone demands more.

"Nah, baby. I'm savoring each drop."

"Does it taste better this way?" Her own scotch is set aside. She's seemingly intoxicated enough just by the sight of me drinking off her.

"You tell me." I swoop down to kiss her, my tongue seeking hers to share the complex malt.

She moans into my mouth while lifting to get closer. Our bare chests stick together, the slippery friction setting off sparks in my bloodstream. I band an arm around her back and deepen the kiss. The smooth whiskey slides along our desire to feed to flames. I break apart from her mouth with a groan.

"You annihilate me, Firefly. Forget the scotch. I'm already drunk off you, but I'm far from finished."

Next is the slope of her belly, which trickles into her navel. I straighten to chart my descent and become captivated. Her eyes are glazed while she sputters underneath me. My labored breaths match hers. Between the alcohol content and Rylee's addictive allure, I'm clobbered by fiendish yearning. There's an urgency to conquer. The force gains momentum, twitching my limbs. But it seems I'm not the only one.

"More, Rhodes." She swivels against the wooden surface. "Don't stop. Please."

The mission to combine Macallan 25 and Rylee into a personal blend resumes. I drift the bottle lower, skimming the flat expanse between her hips. She's so damn lush and enticing. My tongue nearly lolls out for a swipe. The limits blur as I drag the bottle along the edge of her leggings. I hook a finger under the elastic while my imagination runs rampant.

"These are coming off," I state with authority.

Rylee lifts her ass off the bar. "By all means, disrobe me."

"The better to eat you out." I step back and peel the stretchy material down her legs.

Her shoes hit the floor with simultaneous thuds, followed closely by the whoosh from her discarded pants. "I didn't want to assume, but I'm glad you practice similar foreplay priorities."

"Yet you stopped me last time."

She pushes upright to glare at me. "That was once in a rushed fuck situation. I don't typically deny myself freely offered orgasms."

"Another thing we have in common." I wink while setting my sights on her lacy thong. "Are you attached to these?"

A noncommittal noise puffs from her lips. "Not particularly."

"Good." I strip the scrap from her with a whisked sweep. "They're a souvenir for me."

"Something to remember me by?" Her haughty tone sinks to the hilt of my dick.

I stuff the skimpy fabric into my pocket. "Nah, Firefly. To start a collection."

"You say that as if I'll allow you to constantly snatch my undies."

"Won't you?" My finger traces her bared folds. "Someone is already wet for me."

She flops onto the counter with a drawn-out sigh. "You're

a dirty talker, huh? Let me bask in your feasting habits before I commit to future panty raiding endeavors."

"Such little faith," I rasp. With Rylee spread and exposed to me, I resume my downward trek with the bottle.

A squeak jolts through her when the glass touches her pubic bone. "What're you doing?"

I pause in my descent, drifting the ridged mouth just above her mound. "Do you trust me?"

"Yes." Her throat bobs with a heavy gulp.

"You told me to relax and let me take care of you. Let me return the favor." I drag the whiskey lower until the top almost dips into her slit.

Her hand shoots forward and claps onto my arm, stalling any progress. "Are you about to do what I think you're about to do?"

"Probably."

A flush burns up her chest and neck. "Wh-oah… why?"

My focus is riveted on the ridged glass barely skimming her sensitive flesh. "I'm going to mix my two favorite flavors."

"No, don't you dare. You'll ruin the scotch." Her protest is a harsh smack against my very motivated intentions.

"Ruin it?" I scoff. "More like enhance it."

"Sweet words for a man who's about to desecrate a rare and treasured commodity."

"Just the tip," I tell her. "A garnish for the rim."

Her exhale sputters. "You're serious?"

"I wouldn't joke about such provocative measures. This will quite literally bottle your essence."

Rylee might be struck speechless because only silence answers me. I test her resistance to the idea by sliding the bottle along her slick center. When I bump her clit, she lurches off the bar with a moan.

"Does it burn?"

She shakes her head. "No."

"Does it feel good?"

"Umm, maybe. Yeah? I mean… that last swipe did." Her stammering sends me soaring.

I repeat the motions until her hips are swiveling to match my tempo. The bottle glides through her slippery pussy with ease. That makes the choice to travel onto kinkier territory feel like a reflex.

"Just the tip," I remind her while nudging at her entrance.

Rylee remains frozen, almost concerningly so. I'm not sure she's even breathing. My focus is a laser as the grooved glass slips inside. It's only an inch, maybe less. Somehow it seems infinite. Or maybe that's just her trust in me to deliver this fantasy.

I watch the top disappear. Almost instantly, I pull back. Her eyes widen when the solid object returns to her core. A cycle begins as I withdraw and insert the ridged mouth again. My wrist spins to add an extra twist or two.

"This is so dirty," Rylee breathes.

"Fucking delectable." I'm transfixed by the sight. My mind has always been filthy, but I've never felt comfortable enough with a woman to let the naughty parts out to play. "Does that feel good for you?"

"Yes," she admits on her next exhale.

"Welcome to the depraved side, Firefly. I'll gladly be your guide until the end of our days."

As if another alternative exists. There's no chance I can unsee this. If Rylee wasn't stuck with me before, she sure as shit is now.

I pull back and drag the bottle through her folds. The glass glides along her slick heat without a hitch. She rocks forward with each swipe, demanding more. I give her three thorough passes before dipping into her center again.

"Did my vagina hypnotize you? Would that mean you're vaginatized?"

"Huh?" It takes a momentous effect to shift my gaze off

her pussy. I blink her expectant features into focus. "Did you say something about your vagina?"

She giggles at my dumbstruck expression. "You're just staring at me down there like the sight is mesmerizing. Or maybe it's cliterizing."

"Why are you making up words?"

Her bottom lip gets trapped between her teeth. "Seems fitting for the occasion."

Since she mentioned it, I flick her clit with my thumb. My calloused pad rubs in lazy circles while I give the bottle a final twist. She collapses onto the bar with a choked stutter. I pull the properly garnished whiskey from her while increasing the speed of my swipes. With her spine arched, she begins to babble at the ceiling.

"Yeah, keep talking nonsense while I bathe my tongue in nirvana." I don't slow my assault on her while tipping the scotch to my mouth.

She's there on the rim, just as I'd hoped. The raunchy invention drenches my lifelong drought. Her tangy honey blended with rich smoky tones hit the spot I didn't realize was missing. I swish the sip and gargle for good measure.

A wide grin spreads once I swallow. "It's official."

Rylee hikes her brows, lust clouding her eyes from my continuous strokes to her clit. "You're upset the whiskey is tainted?"

"Nope. I've just experienced true tastebud euphoria." I pause her climb to orgasm and thrust my arms to the side. My head tips back in gratitude as the potent flavor revitalizes me. The relief pumping through my veins is stronger than I ever felt. Then I lower my gaze to the promised land spread for me. "Want a taste?"

"See what all the fuss is about?" She crooks her finger to beckon me in.

After curling a palm under her nape, I yank her against me. Her clammy skin burns a brand into mine. The impact stuns me still for half a second. Then I slam my lips to hers without further delay.

Rylee's tongue swipes my lower lip, seeking permission I'm all too greedy to grant. I shove my hand into the static between us to finish what I started. She bucks her hips when I find her swollen clit. The noises spewing from her suggest she's already flying toward the cliff.

I'm standing with her splayed thighs cinched around me. Her nails claw at my shoulders while I massage her neck that's still in my grasp. Still, we crush our bodies to align as one. There's not an inch separating us as we fight to get closer. All the while, my fingers continue thrumming her to climax. She's grinding against me, gaining the friction needed to tip over the edge.

Suddenly, Rylee goes rigid in my hold. She shatters against me and trembles in my arms. Her cries pelt my lips while I clutch her tighter. The climax washes over her with a jerk, followed by several more. My touch slows while easing her back to reality.

Once the afterglow sweeps in to replace the orgasmic punch, Rylee sags against my chest. "Wow, I wasn't expecting that to be so… intense."

I chuckle into her hair. "Me either."

"That was something else entirely. You've got some naughty tricks up your sleeve, partner."

I smack my lips. "Best damn thing I've put in my mouth. Whiskey is ruined for me. I'll need you as a flavor shot from now on."

"Happy to accommodate," she purrs. Then a fresh blush blooms on her cheeks. Rylee covers her face with her palms, muffling a groan. "I can't believe you stuck a three-thousand-dollar bottle of whiskey into my cooch."

"Three grand? Nah, baby." I grunt and nod at the item in mention. "You just made that rich shit priceless."

"How do you manage to make even that sound romantic?"

"It's a gift. Which reminds me…" I let the next phase taper off for maximum impact.

"There's more?" She sounds shocked.

Silly, Firefly.

A smirk crosses my mouth while I begin to adjust our position. I guide her to scoot backward until she's completely sprawled on the bar. Just her bent knees dangle over the edge. After draping her legs over my arms, I bend forward and prepare to bury my face in her pussy.

I exhale across her exposed flesh, my grin spreading when she chews on nonsensical curses. "And now you'll give me a proper drink to chase this whiskey."

chapter twenty-two

Rylee

MAIN STREET HAS BEEN TRANSFORMED INTO SPOOKY GOBLINVILLE for the annual parade. Anoka might be known as the Halloween capital, but Knox Creek isn't too shabby. Orange and black explode from every surface in haunted excess. Green is sprinkled into the mix, along with purple, to complete the candy-coated theme. Decorations by the dozens adorn every store front. Skeletons, pumpkins, and ghosts are visible for a mile in each direction.

Bent Pedal is very much included in the festivities. Our bar is straight ahead from where we're lumped in the horde of spectators. Cobwebs and paint cover the windows, obstructing my view of the interior. Casey assured me they had the crowd under control. It helps that Rhodes—once again—magically provided alternate staff for the occasion.

That doesn't necessarily ease my worry.

The man himself leans over to intrude on my thoughts. "Everything is fine over there."

"I know," is my mumbled reply.

"But do you actually believe it?"

"Yes," I huff. "But it's very busy. My concern isn't unwarranted."

Rhodes tucks some hair behind my ear to give him better whispering access. "Your attachment to our bar is very attractive."

"It's purely sentimental, and has little to do with you." I'm a liar, of course.

All I can seem to think about when glancing across the street is what we've done together within those walls. My inner muscles clench on nothing but air, missing a certain long and solid appendage from a specific someone. His tongue and fingers aren't bad either. Then there's the tip of the bottle he slid up, down, around, and in to blend my taste with the whiskey. Fire singes my cheeks just picturing the blunt object entering me. Lord have mercy. I might never recover.

"You're thinking about it again, aren't you?" His gravelly rasp exhales across my neck.

A sideways peek finds his chocolate gaze trying to melt me. Another burst of flames attacks my face. I can't seem to stop blushing whenever he looks at me in that secretive way. "Gah, will you get out of my head?"

"Not gonna happen," he scoffs. "You're incredibly easy to read."

"Then quit staring at me." I force my eyes to stick forward.

Rhodes chuckles. "That's even less likely, Firefly."

Determination thrums in my veins for both of us. It's ridiculous to feel this giddy over a guy. Especially one I've just started to date. If that's what we're even doing. The scene I currently find myself in provides indisputable evidence to support that status.

I'm sitting on the sidewalk in a folding chair among the throng of other parade goers. Rhodes is parked in a matching seat beside me. The armrests overlap to dispute any suspicion that we aren't together. If that's not enough, our children are also glued at the hip a few feet in front of us. Gage and Payton squeal in sugar-hyped delight while the high school's marching band begins to pass on the road. They're playing "Monster Mash" and stomping their feet in sync with the beat.

My son suddenly winces and claps a palm over his face. "Owwwwwie."

Overprotective-mom-mode kicks in and I'm immediately on my feet. "What's wrong?"

"Something is poking my eyeball."

"Let me see." I grip his chin to begin a thorough examination.

He peels his hand away to let me inspect the damage. "Do I need surgery?"

"No, it looks okay. Must've been some dirt and a bug."

"Okay, good. This is my winking eye." He demonstrates for Payton, lavishing her with several flirty blinks that are far too adorable.

She giggles and taps the tip of his nose. "You're so cute. I'm glad you're my boyfriend."

He preens under her affections. "Me too. You're my favorite girlfriend ever."

"Oh, my goodness." I touch my forehead and pretend to faint. The sight of them fawning over each other is just too much.

Rhodes groans behind me. "We're in such big trouble."

I send him an extra droopy frown over my shoulder. "Yep, we might as well break this off before it gets too serious. Sorry, honey. Our kids fell in love first."

He scowls at me. "Not funny."

"We can't get in the way of their fairy tale." I reclaim my seat after an obnoxious twirl fit for a palace ball.

"The hell we can't. They'll be siblings by the year's end if I have any say in the matter. That'll shift their dynamic to favor ours real quick."

A laugh bubbles in my throat, but the cheery sound fizzles flat when he doesn't share in my amusement. "You're hilarious."

"Don't remember telling a joke, but thanks." His smug expression further proves he's stomping into delirious territory.

After an extended pause, I manage to uncoil my tongue. "Um, anyway… I'm glad our kids get along."

"Like brother and sister." Rhodes is stomping on the accelerator and not letting me off at the nearest exit.

I twist in my chair to fully face him. "Are you really trying to insinuate we'll get married in a month or two?"

"Can't you picture it?" He snatches my hand, lacing our fingers together. "We're combustible together. Practically inseparable already."

It takes several seconds for my brain to compute this scenario into reality. "You're pushing commitment issues on me?"

"Seems that way."

"Uh, wow. I'm not familiar with this version of the script."

His thumb strokes over my knuckle. "Get used to it, baby. You've never met a man like me. Never will again."

"Are you an alien?"

"I'm a fucking unicorn with his horn pointed at you, and only you."

My gaze doesn't waver, just waiting for the instant he recedes back to his broody self. "Who are you and what did you do with the guy I butted heads with not too long ago?"

"He decided it's far more advantageous to bump uglies instead." The body double wags his brows.

I pinch the bridge of my nose. "You're ridiculous."

"You mispronounced charming and romantic."

"I think we're speaking a different language." Or I need a new dictionary for this warped dimension.

But the truth somersaults in my belly. Rhodes makes me feel good. Freaking fantastic, really. Our connection is effortless, even when we were fighting. And that's when it hits me. I'm... happy. My heart is racing in renewed faith. That didn't seem possible after Trevor's death. Guilt quickly slinks under the radar, snuffing out my uplifted spirits. Pressure builds behind my eyes soon after.

Rhodes stiffens beside me. "What just happened?"

I drop my watery gaze. "A reminder."

"Of?"

"My brother went crazy for Halloween," I say instead.

Understanding cracks across his stern expression. "Trevor would want you to have double the fun on his behalf."

I sniffle, keeping my stare averted. "How can you be so sure?"

The backs of his fingers skim my jaw, eliciting a trail of goosebumps. "How can you not?"

"Mom, look!" Gage thrusts his arms at me. Black scribbles mark his skin.

"You drew on yourself?"

He huffs with childish exasperation. "No, I made tattoos for my costume."

The cogs in my brain misfire. "But you're dressing as Optimus Prime. The sleeves will cover all that fancy artwork."

Gage shakes his head. "I changed my mind."

"Talk about last minute," I mumble. Then I paste on a wide smile. "Who are you going as, Schmutz?"

"Uncle Trevor." His tiny chest puffs with pride.

Meanwhile, my throat seals shut over the emotional onslaught. I find it hard to breathe, sucking in a ragged gasp. "That's… perfect."

He's nodding with his entire body. "Uh-huh. I'm gonna wear his leather jacket that Gramma gave me. People can call me Rage Gage. It'll be awesome!"

Payton waves a red marker. "Want me to add a heart?"

"Oooooh, that'd be super cool." My son hops to his previous spot next to her.

A gentle squeeze lands on my shoulder. "You okay?"

Rather than look at Rhodes, my eyes shift to the sky. Evening is just encroaching on the day. Fluffy clouds loom overhead as a few stray tears trickle down my cheeks. Somehow, I manage to whisper through the wreckage lodged in my windpipe. "Double the fun, huh? Okay, I get the message."

"See? He lives on." Rhodes nods at Gage.

I wipe at the droplets before my ears get drenched, still searching the endless blue above. "Yeah, he does."

"Want to hear a story about Trevor?"

"Always." I lower my gaze to meet his.

"I had a fear of needles as a kid. Followed me into early adulthood. That's when Trevor told me that if I don't conquer my weaknesses, those weaknesses will conquer me."

"Does that ever sound familiar. Brave to a fault," I mumble.

"So, I let him drag me to a tattoo parlor. That same afternoon, Trevor convinced me to get my first one." He points to a nondescript sequence on his forearm.

I squint to get a better look, just about falling off my chair. "Wait, is that—?"

Rhodes grunts at my reaction. "A complex calculus equation? Yes, it sure is."

"Freaky geek," I mumble under my breath. "That's dedication to the subject."

"Still think I'm sexy?" He chuckles in an insecure way that's very uncharacteristic for him.

"Extremely. The math tattoos get me very hot." I fan my face despite the chilly temperature.

"It's safe to say I got over my fear after that. I have a bit of an addiction." He gestures at the colorful designs that his clothes don't cover.

"I've heard that can happen," I muse. "Did you lose count yet?"

He shrugs. "There must be at least a dozen, but a few bleed into one another. The piece here"—he taps his left upper arm—"is a work in progress."

"I'd love to get a closer look at them." My loyal flush rises to the surface again.

"And I'd love to show you." He swoops in for a stealthy kiss. "Do you have any tattoos?"

"Just one. Here." I point to the date inked on my inner wrist in typewriter font.

"Ah, Gage's birthday?" Rhodes traces the numbers with his thumb.

"I'm super unique, huh?"

"Very much so." His tone noticeably drops several octaves.

Gosh, this guy can flip me on an axis faster than a carnival ride. I'm almost thankful for the icy gust that smacks at my blush. When a second wind blows in, I duck my face into my thick scarf. Then I notice Rhodes staring at it.

"You like this?" I tug at the loose weave.

His nod is slow, almost calculating. "I was admiring it at the orchard as well."

"Would you like me to knit you one?"

He blinks from whatever stupor caught him. "You can knit?"

"And crochet. My grandma taught me when I was little."

The sound he makes is too sensual for this topic. "Maybe I'll tie that wool around your wrists to test the stitches."

"What the—?" It's my turn to gawk and blink while heat prickles my cheeks. These are the times that fair skin is a nuisance. I'm ripe and rosy on a constant basis around this man.

"Is that too much?" He has the uncanny ability to wrench me from a wallowing pit one minute and deposit me into the gutter in the next.

"You want to restrain me? Like… bondage?"

Rhodes scrubs at the stubble coating his jaw. "Not really. Well, maybe. Just to try it out. Mostly to give the impression you're under my control."

My face flushes hotter. "That's… uh, not something I've done before."

"Me either."

I'm sure my eyes are still bugged. This isn't a discussion we should broach in public. "Do you ever not think about… screwing around?"

His gaze follows mine to where our kids are standing in front of us near the curb. They're adequately entertained by the floats passing by. A witch is tossing handfuls of tootsie rolls from her cauldron and Gage and Payton are clamoring for them in a crowd of other kids. They couldn't care less about what we're talking about. The dirty talker beside me must reach the same conclusion.

Rhodes returns his unwavering focus to me. "Honestly, sex never did much for me aside from the momentary relief. I'd just go through the motions for the fuck of it. But since you came into my life? I'm a damn deviant. The intimacy between us has changed me, Firefly."

I gulp to avoid choking on my spit. "Has anyone ever told you that you're really intense?"

His dimple pops when he smirks. "Only in business. Never pleasure."

"You're making me feel special again, stud muffin." I'm nothing if not skilled at cutting the tension. Another breeze would be sen-freaking-sational right now.

"There's so much I want to share with you. We can explore and experience together." A shadow suddenly crosses his expression, one I recognize from when our paths initially collided. "But I have stuff to tell you first."

"I'm listening," I urge.

"Not now. We'll save that for later."

"Really?"

Rhodes furrows his brow at my deadpanned tone. "What?"

"You're just going to leave me hanging?"

His exhale ghosts across my temple. "Only when orgasms aren't involved."

I manage to pin him with a shrewd glare despite the shiver he stokes. "Don't try to distract me. My vagina has formed a personal attachment to that word thanks to you."

"If you're expecting me to apologize, we'll be here well after the last glitter bomb floats by. I'd hate for the kids to miss out on trick or treating." He nods to Payton and Gage. The pair is currently boasting about how much candy they're going to collect once darkness falls.

As if I'd be responsible for spoiling their fun. "Just promise we'll move beyond this… void."

His sigh is heavy with worry. "We will."

We have a date tomorrow night—one I'm willing to officially claim as such. There's this pressure building in my chest, but I'm not sure why. It's not like his opinion will change of me. My dirty laundry isn't that filthy. I highly doubt anything he's going to unload will have a shattering impact.

The strain he's carrying on his drawn features suggests otherwise.

My palm clasps his in a comforting hold. "Is it a big deal?"

Rhodes rubs at his chest. "Probably not. I have a bad habit of harboring secrets."

"That makes two of us," I tease. "Mine for yours, right?"

"You've got yourself a deal, Firefly."

chapter twenty-three

RHODES

RYLEE HUMS BESIDE ME IN WHAT I IMAGINE TO BE CONTENTMENT. The rocking chair creaks when she leans forward against an incoming breeze. Moments ago, she polished off a precious bottle of Trevor's beer. That soothed a few frazzled edges—mine included. A wool hat and fluffy scarf stave off the evening chill. With her legs folded on the seat, she looks at home on my porch. Then she smiles. The expression is nothing short of peaceful.

It weaves a calmness to blanket my nerves. "You like it here, Firefly?"

"Very much so." Her gaze hasn't wandered far from the horizon where the sun is slowly descending.

I force my fixation to stray from her, but only for a brief reflection to gather my bearings. The darkening sky is an adequate distraction. Almost. A dry scoff calls my bluff. But I command my focus to stay trained on the scenery all the same.

Bright streaks of purple and orange overshadow the crisp blue. If I squint, the lake is almost visible from our perch. There's a private road that leads directly to the beach. Maybe I should've brought her to sit in the sand. The unobstructed view of the sunset over the water is tough to beat. Depending on how the next hour goes, we could stroll to the shore.

Doubt hammers against my temple. I'm overthinking

every damn minute. This doesn't have to be a struggle. We're past the worst of it. The shadows have started to fade from her features, replaced by light. We're healing. Together. At least, I like to hope she sees me as a positive influence. Or I'm just fooling myself.

Then a recognizable flicker skips in midair. The sight makes me freeze, as if my breath might disrupt the powers at play. Several more sparks appear near the first.

Rylee gasps, her hand blindly flinging sideways to grip my arm. "Oh, my gosh. Are those what I think they are?"

"Fireflies," I murmur.

She watches the tiny flashes with awe. "This is a nice surprise. It's not even dark yet."

"Yeah, we don't see them too often this time of year."

Her hum agrees with the seasonal shortage. "Want to hear a secret?"

"You're doing the honors of kicking off our trade?"

"Might as well."

I motion her onward. "By all means, spill your guts."

"Whoa, it's just about lightning bugs," she clarifies. "Lower your expectations."

"Anything you have to tell me deserves my full concentration."

Rylee exhales a foggy breath. "There you go again, trying to romance my pants off."

"I better try harder. You're still fully clothed." The pang in my chest loses its hollow edge.

"Insatiable," she grumbles. But the lopsided grin she tries to hide reveals her jest.

"That's special for you." Which is further proof she's the only cure for my relationship aversion.

As if hearing my internal commitment, she turns to stare at me. The beginning of dusk paints her face in vibrant streaks. Silence stretches into a lull that I begin to assume might lead us straight between the sheets. Then she blinks from whatever daze I managed to catch her in.

The chair rocks as she shifts to face the yard. "Okay, as I was saying…"

"You want to take your pants off," I provide helpfully.

"Um, no. But solid effort. My secret is that I've always thought these little beauties were under-appreciated. They're special, you know? Subtle, but bright. Just floating along, doing their own thing, and breaking apart the gloom. Those short bursts remind me that hope remains even when all else feels lost. Only itsy-bitsy glimmers, but they're still visible." She shakes her head, an amused noise puffing steam from her. "Listen to me prattling on about insects. I've just always been fascinated by them."

"Couldn't agree more."

Red splotches bloom on her cheeks when she realizes I'm staring at her, not the bugs. "Jeez, you're laying it on thick."

"Tell me to stop," I murmur.

She tucks her face against her shoulder, those green eyes lifting to mine. A choice seems to tip the scale behind her gaze. Suddenly, Rylee is off her seat and crossing the foot of space separating us. There's no hesitation as she climbs onto my lap. Heat like I've never felt surges under my skin in a feverish rush. I band my arms around her huddled form to siphon more. Her addictive floral scent invades my senses until she's everywhere. The comfort she presses against me smooths some jagged edge I didn't realize was torn. That she sought me out in this very moment is indescribable. There isn't an accurate definition of what this woman does to me.

Once she's situated sideways on my thighs, her chilled nose traces a line up to my ear. "No."

I palm her ass, giving a squeeze for good measure. "Kinda figured that out on my own."

Her breath warms my jaw. "I almost stopped believing."

"In what?"

"This." She snuggles into me for emphasis. "A visceral connection. Is that cheesy?"

"Nah, Firefly. That's exactly how I would describe us." I can feel her smile against my skin.

"Why do you call me Firefly?"

A pinch radiates outward from my sternum. "When I saw you at the funeral, I couldn't help but notice the similarity. It stuck with me."

Her snort is loud in our otherwise quiet surroundings. "I'm not sure whether to be offended or flattered that you just compared me to a bug."

"That's not what I meant. You're a beacon in the bleakest instances. A light fighting in the dark, refusing to be snuffed out."

She makes a satisfied sound. "Okay, that's better. Keep talking."

After a chuckle, I fulfill her wishes. "Those short bursts of hope you mentioned earlier? That's how you made me feel. Like you could chase away the shadows."

Rylee adjusts until her chest meets mine and our gazes collide. "That might be the sweetest thing I've ever heard."

"Comes from in here." I tap the spot over my heart.

"Gosh, you're really upping the swoon stakes."

"You're the one who put a crack in the dam. I can't be held responsible for what comes pouring out. Beware of a flood."

She nuzzles into the crook of my neck. "I'll gladly drown in your adoring sentiments."

My humor sobers. "I should've joined you."

"When?"

"In the rain, at Trevor's funeral. It haunts me. I can't stop thinking about that moment." Regret plagues me now, even with her warmth replacing my icy detachment.

Her laugh is brittle. "Gosh, I was a mess."

"Past tense?" Might as well attempt to salvage the banter that feeds my soul.

"Jerk." She shoves my shoulder, her giggle a spring bloom sprouting from frozen ground.

"Guilty."

"As if," Rylee scoffs. "You're a good guy, Rhodes. Way out of my league."

That gets a grunt from me. "Says who?"

"Me."

"Well, damn. How do I get an invite?"

Her eyes roll skyward. "As if you want to slum it with us lowly common folk."

I notch a bent knuckle under her chin, lifting until our lips brush. "Quit pretending you're anything less than extraordinary, Firefly. Your league is the only one that matters."

"Okay," she mumbles with stars in her gaze. "I can't compete with that."

The porch lamp automatically switches on, bathing our private moment in a yellow glow. It serves to remind me of the time. One of us needs to leap across the void first. It might as well be me. Besides, I'm the one spinning my wheels to nowhere.

It requires courage I don't possess to lift Rylee off my lap. Once she's steady, I stand from my chair. My own reluctance makes the swift motion more like a sluggish drag. "There's something I want to show you."

She eyes me warily. "Please don't tell me there's another room in your house. I lost count after ten. Why do you need five bedrooms?"

"Plans for family expansion." I wink at her.

"Oh, my." She tucks her chin, but there's no hiding her blush.

My palm slides into the dip at her spine. "It's in the storage building."

She bounces on her feet with far more enthusiasm than me. "Another mystery to be solved."

We trek across the dewy lawn with the last strands of sunlight guiding us. My pulse is a staccato boom as we approach the structure cloaked in revelation. I type the code into the keypad, my hand turning the knob once the green symbol flashes. Rylee crosses the threshold when I step aside to let her enter ahead of me. My fingers blindly search for the switch panel just inside. Rows of fluorescent bulbs buzz to life overhead. It takes several moments for my eyes to adjust.

The wide room smells like motor oil and dusty memories. Abandoned passion floats in the stale air. My eyes drift across the open space to admire what used to boost my adrenaline. Snowmobiles, a variety of all-terrain vehicles, and two massive sailplanes are stacked on industrial shelves along the wall. Storage containers on another. The pontoon and speed boat occupy a bit more real estate. My corvette is parked in the center, already tucked in for the colder seasons.

Rylee's whistle echoes off the metal panels. "Um, wow. This is… quite the collection. The Macallan 25 no longer holds much shock value."

It's the inevitable that has my focus trailing to the far corner. "I'm certain this will."

She skirts around me to get a better look. Her stride is already hesitant, but she slams to an abrupt halt when chrome and custom paint glint ominously. "You have a motorcycle?"

Remorse glues my throat shut. I manage a jerky nod.

When she turns to me, tears already glisten in her eyes. Rylee claps a palm over her gaping mouth. "Did Trevor pressure you into this too?"

"The other way around actually," I rasp.

"Huh?"

"I already had a bike when we met. Traded in my car the week before leaving for college to save on gas."

Rylee's brows fling upward. "That really goes against the dorky visual I'd created for you in my head. How did the ladies keep their hands off you?"

My chuckle lacks humor. "I was shy? Not interested in

sleeping around. The only time I hooked up with a girl at a party led to Payton's conception, which is another tale entirely."

"Yeah, let's put a pin in that and finish this chapter first." Pain strikes her features in a wince.

"I was with Trevor when he bought his chopper." Which is nothing more than a mangled mistake after the accident took its toll.

"Were you there that night?" She doesn't have to elaborate while reading my train of thought.

"We'd been at Bent Pedal when a biker group pulled into town. They were on a run to Iowa. Trevor wanted to join them and tried to get me saddled as well. But it was late. I went home after the bar closed. He ragged on me for being responsible. My priorities were too straight. We hadn't done many long rides together since Payton was born. Then he was gone." My heart plummets, the beat spinning out of control. "If I'd tagged along, maybe I could've prevented him from hitting that sinkhole and swerving off the highway."

Each piece I strip from the story is an eggshell to walk across. I wait with fucking bated breath for the crack that will crush them all and she'll storm out. But I shouldn't expect the worst, not with Rylee.

Her eyes are glassy as she blinks in earnest. "Don't blame yourself for his choices. It was a freak accident. You couldn't have changed the outcome."

"Kinda easier said than believed." The desolation in my tone only yanks me lower.

"Hey." Her palm rests on my forearm, a gentle support not to be taken for granted. "I wasn't there, but I'm sure you tried to talk some sense into him before he left."

"I could've done more."

Rylee quirks a brow. "Like what?"

"Taken his keys." I kick at the concrete. It would be more satisfying if rocks went skidding across the floor along with my petulance.

She snorts. "Oh, yeah. That would've gone over well. Stop beating yourself up, babe. You had no control over the situation. My brother was a stubborn ass with a reckless streak larger than you and I can fathom, let alone try to tame."

"But I wasn't there with him."

Her grip gives me a reassuring squeeze. "Neither was I. What could you have done riding beside him? No matter what you did or didn't do, he made the decision to be careless."

And that's the bitter truth. There's not a damn thing I can do other than accept that my best friend brushed me off. That advice might've saved his life. Instead, his pride cost him the ultimate price.

"I wasn't able to protect him. Maybe that's why I have this instinctual desire to keep you safe." My smile is limp.

Rylee sways into me. "Oh, Rhodes. That's incredibly heroic, and explains your extreme methods."

"Not the word I would use," I grumble.

"Do you prefer brutish behavior? Territorial and possessive? Maybe just plain ol' jealousy?" She flutters her lashes fast enough to blow me away.

"Can those be combined into one option?"

"I'll make an exception for you."

The perpetual ache in my chest eases under her encouragement. "For some reason, I thought you'd be upset with me."

She recoils. "Why?"

"Because I got him interested in motorcycles."

Her forehead crinkles. "No, you didn't. Trevor was obsessed with bikes long before you came around. He had all sorts of daredevil tendencies. My parents always shut that down, but I knew the minute he got the chance he'd go wild."

"Smart folks," I mumble.

"Yeah, if only our concern was enough to save him from himself. His tolerance for danger scared us." She sniffs and glances at my Harley. "We were right to be afraid."

I snake an arm around Rylee's shoulders and draw her

against me. Turbulent guilt propels a wave to crash over me. "I should've stopped him."

She pulls away to meet my eyes. Hers are watery again. "You couldn't have. Trust me, I've had this discussion with my parents on repeat over the years. Eventually, those fearless habits were going to catch up to him. No matter what we did to steer him in the opposite direction."

"But I was *there*." It's nearly impossible to force the words past the lump in my throat.

"And he didn't listen." The smile she gives me trembles at the edges. "I just remembered something. Trevor told me about this friend of his who was boring to ride with because he obeyed the speed limit. It must've been you."

That's when I get choked up. Heat burns my eyes. The pressure in my chest returns with punishing force. A garbled noise rips from me as I turn my gaze to the ceiling. "I'll take that as a compliment."

"As you should."

I shift my focus back to her. "You have no idea how much that means to me."

Rylee nods in understanding. "See? You helped him. Even if he didn't let the lesson sink in."

"Am I overreacting?"

She shakes her head. "There's no such thing when it comes to grief. Everyone responds differently to loss. Death is final. The end. But it's impossible to just move on. In a tragedy, we don't get closure. We'll never get the answers to solve our pain. Instead, we find ways to cope and heal. He's gone physically, but we keep his spirit alive. Isn't that what you told me?"

"Something like that." I manage a smirk. "Thanks for letting me lean on you."

"We're in this together, right?"

"Yep, you're stuck with me." I have plans to make it official sooner rather than later.

The glint in her stare suggests she approves. "As a non-neutral party?"

"I won't hesitate to spread my bias over you."

Her laugh is the sweetest song. "I'm glad our truce is solid."

Relief pours from my lips as I bend to kiss her. My harsh exhale rushes across her upturned jaw. "Fuuuuck, Firefly. Me too. I'm so damn grateful for you."

"Same." Rylee pats my left pec. "You're a much more comfortable support system than my teletherapy sessions. Oh, speaking of. I'm not trying to invalidate what you're thinking or feeling, but I do want to absolve your guilt. It isn't your fault."

"I probably needed to hear that. My own demons get the best of me every now and then." I tap my temple.

"One day at a time."

My strain loosens at the familiar phrase. "It will get easier. I've been carrying this baggage too long."

"Healing is hard. I read the police report. That was brutal, and probably a mistake." Her gaze slinks to a crack in the cement.

Bile rises up my throat just recalling the detailed records. "Damn, I wish I could've shielded you from seeing that."

"Motorcycles are dangerous, but they don't have to be. My brother wasn't wearing a helmet." Her bottom lip quivers. "I'm so angry at him for risking his life, which makes me feel awful."

I have Rylee enveloped in my arms before the first tear leaks down her cheek. Broken sobs are muffled against my chest. She clutches my shirt in white-knuckled fists while guttural anguish screams from her. The cotton is already drenched where she has her face buried. Her entire body racks with agony while mine spills in fiery trails. Our hearts thrash to a synced beat, reverberating like heavy peals of thunder. My grip on her never falters.

We cry for him, but also for us. The ones left behind to collect the shattered pieces and attempt to reassemble the brittle shards into something whole. Our crippled spirits obsess on an endless loop about that critical moment. That single second we can't undo, but it's changed us irrevocably. If only I'd forced him to stay behind with me. If only Rylee had been in town to talk some sense into him. If only we'd had the power to convince him. If only the pavement was smooth. If only he'd protected himself. If only…

These scenarios play until the frayed script is nearly consuming. The damage is done. We're still here.

Rylee clings to me while the memories dump over us in suffocating succession. My lungs are on fire as her shudders escalate. We share in this misery, but maybe one day it will hurt less. As if on cue, the sorrow streams from my eyes to cleanse denial from the road. Passage for acceptance arrives soon after. Her grasp on me shifts to hug my waist. I rub a palm along her back while the other clings tight to her hip. Time ebbs and flows as we hold on to one another through the storm.

Eventually, the downpour slows to a steady trickle. Rylee hiccups a breath as her wet lashes peel open. A waterfall of emotions splash across her features. Relief seems to settle at last while the current subsides.

She sniffs and lifts her red-rimmed eyes to mine. "Will you do me a favor?"

"Whatever you want, just name it." With the exception of me letting her go.

"Can you take me for a ride?"

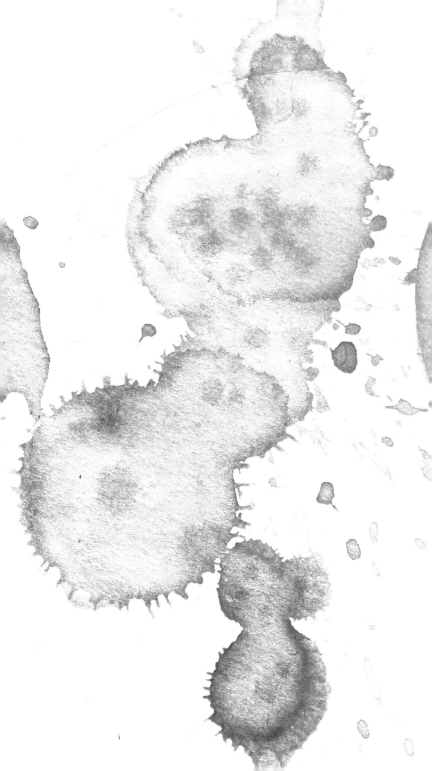

chapter twenty-four

Rylee

THE CRAMP IN MY STOMACH HASN'T SETTLED SINCE I BLURTED the words. My request hangs in the grief clogged between us. Rhodes appears frozen. I don't think he's taken a breath. Another minute drags on when the restlessness begins to gnaw at me.

"As closure. It might be good for both of us." I explain my reasoning in a hushed whisper.

"That's kind of a big ask, Firefly." His posture sags with a rough exhale. "And it's probably not a good idea."

"Why?"

Rhodes clasps the back of his neck until the flesh blooms red. "I haven't been on a bike since Trevor's accident. Barely had the balls to start the engine a few weeks ago."

A wince pinches my features. But determination reigns. "I've never been on one at all. Ever."

His brows dip into a perplexed crease. "And you trust me to drive with you on the back?"

Disbelief is ripe in the musty air. This feels like a pivotal moment. Just one of many we've exchanged in the last hour.

"I wouldn't ask otherwise." A pang ricochets off my breastbone as I stare at him. "I also wouldn't ask anyone else."

He blows out a heavy breath, as if my faith in him is a major privilege. "Wow, I wasn't expecting that."

"This"—I motion to my face that's tight with swelling and probably a wide array of splotches—"was cathartic, but I think we need to push a bit more. For the sake of healing."

"I don't want to deny you," he mumbles.

"But?" I prompt after his extended pause.

"What if you get hurt? I couldn't handle that." The pain in his voice has me second-guessing this impulsive agenda.

That kernel of doubt drops to the pit of my stomach. "Okay, let's forget it."

A tortured groan rips from him as he glares at the ceiling. "Fuck, you're disappointed."

"That's better than you being uncomfortable. Like you said, it's probably not a good idea."

"But a short ride might be okay. Just to test your theory."

Agreement squeaks past my pressed lips. "We don't have to go far. You can just take me down the driveway."

An idea seems to flash across his tense expression. "How about the beach?"

"Now? It looks dark outside." I glance out the small window, noting the pitch blackness through the glass.

"The stars are brightest from there."

"Don't tease me with a great view if I don't get to see it."

"All right, Firefly. If that's what you want." He's leaving the decision in my control, which I appreciate more than whipped cream topping a milkshake.

I'm already nodding. "For some reason, this feels like the right decision."

Rhodes doesn't respond to that. He's busy grabbing leather jackets off hooks on the wall. Helmets too. Those get slung on the Harley's handlebars. His gaze drops to my mid-calf boots. "Couldn't have chosen better footwear if you planned this."

"Thanks." I click my heels together.

Next, he passes me a jacket. "You'll swim in it, but that's better than nothing."

I slip on the protective shield. Motor oil and baked sunshine blend with thousands of miles traveled to waft off the sturdy material. The sleeves hang empty past my hands while the bottom trim nearly touches my knees. "Fits great."

His eyes heat into molten flames. "Didn't think you could get sexier. You swallowed in my leather might be better than you swallowing me."

"I find that hard to believe."

An animalistic growl disputes my claim. He's on me in the following beat. His fists grip the parted sides of the baggy garment to haul me against him. Our lips collide in a feverish rush. Flames immediately blaze beneath my skin. I rise on the balls of my feet to get closer, slinging my arms around his neck.

Rhodes groans into my mouth when I slide my tongue along his. Mint and reckless abandon slip into our desire for one another. The stubble on his jaw scrapes me with a delicious friction that curls my toes. With a slight tilt, I angle further for more of the burn. His palms drift lower to clutch my ass and yank me in tighter. He's hard against my soft belly. I squirm to get that ridge pressed deeper.

Just when I'm about to seek a surface to bang this out quick, Rhodes is loosening the cinch he's caught me in. His hands peel off my butt and begin to roam. I feel a tug at my thighs. After a final swipe along his bottom lip, I break our kiss to investigate. He's fiddling with something between us. Then the zipper glides up to conceal me.

His smirk is smug at the trussed-up picture I undoubtedly make. "It'll be cold in the wind."

"I'm pretty toasty at this exact moment."

"And I'd prefer to keep you that way." He plops a helmet on my head and buckles the strap under my chin.

"It's starting to feel real," I murmur. The somersaults in my stomach agree.

"Are you sure about this?"

"I trust you." I'll repeat it until he believes me.

"Damn, that does something to me." Restrained pride jerks his head in a single nod. "I'll keep you safe."

A hot sting blurs my vision. "You already are."

"Does that mean you accept my hidden groveling?"

I blink the moisture from my lashes. "You've been groveling?"

Rhodes snorts. "If you're questioning me, clearly not."

"What're you groveling for?"

"The first few weeks." That's all I get from him.

"Okay…?"

"I was an ass."

Amusement tickles my chest. "Oh, are you just coming to terms with that?"

"No. That's why I've been groveling in disguise."

"That's not a thing." Or I'm just super removed from that dating game.

"It is. I've been making moves on the sly, so you didn't freak out."

"Why would I freak out?"

He shrugs. "There's something you're not telling me, and it stood in our way. I figure you'll share whatever it is when you're ready. In the meantime, it seems like you've forgiven me. Or given me the benefit of the doubt. Either way, the not-so-obvious groveling paid off."

The reminder snatches the air from my lungs with a muted wheeze. "I'll tell you. Soon. Just don't be upset about what I can't share."

"I have zero plans to get upset with you. Ever."

That's a bold lie he can't keep, but I'm willing to humor the farce. "Promise?"

"Forever and always."

It's too soon for such a serious sentiment, but I'm too emotionally wrung out to care. "Now what?"

"Hang tight." Then he jogs to where we came in.

After flipping the deadbolt to lock the building, he pushes a button on the electrical panel. A loud whir grinds into the still-ness as the garage door opens. Cool air blasts against the flush on my cheeks. My earlier suspicions are confirmed—it's com-pletely dark outside.

A paved path is visible from the floodlights. Once the gears stop lifting, silence descends again. It's quiet enough to hear crickets chirp to the tempo of resolutions for a happier tomorrow.

My heart hammers as he returns to my side. "Hi."

Rhodes smiles, his dimple popping out for me to drool over. "Ready?"

"As I'll ever be."

"Hey." His fingers clutch mine. "We don't need to do this."

"Yes, we do."

"Then saddle up, Firefly." He nods to the bike.

My gait is stilted as I creep toward the chrome beast. "It's a beautiful motorcycle. An imfamous Harley Davidson at that. Very sleek and sparkly. Is it a girl?"

Rhodes scoffs in obvious offense. "It is now."

"Oh, there's a seat for me." A sour gurgle churns in my stomach. "Do you entertain a lot of company on late-night cruises?"

His grin catches my jealousy. "Just Payton."

My brows shoot skyward. "She rides with you?"

"I'm very careful." He slides on his own helmet with those words.

"Of course, you are." That puts me at greater ease.

He does the honors of getting on first. His leg swings over, the kickstand springs upward, and he plants his feet to balance. "C'mere, baby."

My knees wobble from the endearment in his gravelly tim-bre. I manage to clamber on behind him without tumbling right back off. "And I hold onto you, right?"

"Like a python." He reaches for my arms and loops them tight around his waist.

My butt scoots forward until I'm plastered to his back. "This is cozy."

"Don't let go."

I nod, knocking our helmets together. "Got it, boss."

His torso bounces from a gruff chuckle under my grasp. "Fuck, you're too much."

Just when I think we're about to peel out, Rhodes turns slightly in his seat. That panty-melting smirk is still in place. He brings two fingers to his lips, then presses the calloused pads against my mouth for a makeshift kiss.

I get a little lightheaded. "Gosh, that was romantic."

He winks. "Who knew, huh?"

Definitely not me. I'm still half-convinced he's an alien who invaded Rhodes with Prince Charming swoon. A unicorn with his mighty horn pointed at me isn't a terrible alternative either. While I'm still caught in a trance, he lowers a plastic visor over my face.

"I didn't even realize that was there."

"Extra precautions. All set?"

My grip around him returns to snake-like standards. "Let's do this."

"Gonna be extra loud to clear out the cobwebs." That's the last warning he gives me.

I'm stiff against him when he cranks the throttle. The punch of noise could shatter an eardrum. "Holy shit!"

But my shock is gobbled by the roaring engine. Even through the guard of my helmet, the sound sets my teeth on edge. My entire body quakes when he revs the motor again. The loud rumble is deafening, drowning out the pounding in my veins. He repeats the motion once more and my brain just about misfires. It's almost a relief to not think for a second. I allow the experience to wash over me. The vibration beneath me is intense, and not unpleasant. My eyes almost cross at the sensation. Then we're moving and I'm trembling for an entirely different reason.

Rhodes steers the bike outside. My eyes burn from the sudden darkness, even with the lights guiding our way. The garage door begins to close after we clear the threshold. Either the spring-loaded contraption is magic, or he has an opener in his pocket. That's not important.

Even with the visor shielding my face, cold sneaks in through the cracks. But the chill doesn't bother me. I'm not sure what I was expecting for my maiden voyage on a motorcycle, but it certainly wasn't this peaceful. Rhodes is reliable and responsible. His solid presence keeps me grounded. There's nothing to fear. The chaos in my pulse returns to a calm thump. An almost blissful numbness captures me while I snuggle in for the duration.

It's less of a ride and more of a crawl. He drives slowly along what I assume is a private road. Houses frame one side of the street. The structures are massive and imposing, much like the man in charge of our safe arrival. Trees and foliage thin out on the right to provide a preview of the lake. No other traffic passes us on the short journey. The Harley creeps to a stop at the front of the empty lot. My ears ring when he turns off the engine. I work my jaw back and forth to regain the feeling I didn't know was lost. There's a twinge in my arms and it's tough to release him from my clutches. A giggle breezes from me. The bike took me for a ride.

Rhodes lowers the kickstand before dismounting. "This is the place."

I climb off my perch with far less grace. My legs resemble jelly and require several squats to cooperate. "That was like three minutes."

He unbuckles my helmet before removing his, slinging them on the handlebars. "We could've walked if you wanted to be suctioned against me longer."

"Maybe next time."

A groan steeped in pleasure ripples from him seconds before

he plants a noisy smooch on me. "I love it when you talk about the future with me included."

The abrupt affection sends me reeling. "Um, wow."

"What?"

"You're just not afraid of commitment. At all. It's… refreshing, I guess."

"This is new for me too. I'm embracing the changes you bring forth." Then he makes a forward sweeping motion. "Shall we?"

That's when I take in our surroundings. Only a single streetlamp glows from the corner. Pavement butts up to sand. The moon glints off the water's glassy surface. That's about all I can see. I take another scan of the desolate area. "Is it okay that we're here so late?"

Rhodes links our fingers together and guides me toward the shore. "Sure, Firefly. This spot isn't open for public access. It's all ours."

"Be careful, or I'll get used to exclusive treatment."

"I hope you do." He finds an adequate spot for us to sit and tugs me down onto the sand.

"You want to spoil me?"

"Yes, if you'll allow it." There he goes again, making me blush.

Thankfully, the pitch black hides the heat on my face. A cool gust kicks across the lake and I tip my chin. The clear sky fills my vision with a glittering blanket of stars. "I should've looked up first. This is the money maker."

"Didn't I tell you? Best view I've ever seen."

When I peek over at Rhodes, his gaze is firmly fastened on me. "You're not even looking at the stars."

"I know."

Cue the belly swoop. I bite my bottom lip to trap the gushy mush from dumping in his lap. If I'm not careful, I'll chase him off. Rather than be a pessimistic pooper, I return my focus skyward. There's a force I can't explain floating in the shadows.

That elemental shift hugs my wounded spirit in a comforting way that brings tears to my eyes.

"Do you think he's up there?"

Rhodes hums while draping an arm around my shoulders and tugging me into his side. "Without a doubt."

"You're very certain." But the smile I send him is relieved that he feels the influence.

"I'm also certain that thanking those lucky stars will never be enough."

I rest my head in the crook of his neck. "For what?"

"Bringing you and Gage to Payton and me."

Emotion wedges my throat shut as I burrow into his stubbled skin. The burn in my nose almost feels natural after the night we've had. "You're going to make me cry talking like that."

"Happy tears, I hope."

"Very happy." A single droplet escapes to zigzag down my cheek and drips somewhere on his shirt. "I'm so very happy we found you and your sweet girl."

Silence cocoons us while we let those raw confessions heal our broken edges. Crickets chirp to serenade the lull. Intermittent plops and splashes come from the water, providing a soft soundtrack in the distance. The fresh air gives me the courage to reveal my harshest truths.

But that doesn't mean there isn't an insistent ache spreading through me. A long exhale pushes me past the pressure. "I met Vince midway through my senior year in college. That's Gage's biological father, by the way."

Rhodes seems startled that I'm just diving straight in. His wide eyes slide to mine. "Okay."

"I didn't know much about him aside from the basics. We had a class together, so he wasn't a total stranger. That might be why he singled me out as a no-strings target. It was one night. No big deal. We went our separate ways. Simple, right?"

"This sounds terribly familiar," he murmurs.

I straighten from our cuddled position and pat his chest.

"Yeah, real original. I'm sure you've heard a similar version at least once or twice."

"Or lived it."

I wince on his behalf. "Okay, even worse. You'll get your turn in a second. Just let me spit this out."

"Ladies first." He makes a gesture for me to continue.

"Such a gentleman. You're a rare breed, as it turns out. Vince was the opposite. Same goes for the rest of my pitiful relationship history. No wonder my brother was ultra-protective."

Even in the dark, I see a muscle tick in his jaw. "You can skip over the parts where you were intimately acquainted with other men."

"Gah, sorry. I'm nervous. It's not a pretty story." My hands tremble and I shake out the jitters.

Rhodes engulfs my palms with his. "Just talk to me. You trust me, right?"

"Explicitly." Then a thought occurs to me. "That being said, I shouldn't share their family name. I signed a nondisclosure. Besides, you might recognize it from mingling in… similar circles."

"Wait. Is this why you were resistant to fall in love with me?"

"I appreciate your humor in this moment." My eyes roll for sarcastic flair. "But yes, I held the stigma against you. Unfairly, I might add. Please don't be upset."

His frown suggests he wants to argue. "This guy's mistakes ended up doing me a favor, even if you lumped me in with him at the beginning."

"That's mighty noble of you."

He grunts. "Yeah, I'm a true white knight."

"The best I've had the pleasure of consorting with."

The groan he releases is pained. "Please, Firefly. Get to the point."

My cheeks go up in flames. "I'm usually not this flustered. Okay, so… Vince lost his shit when I told him I was pregnant.

The dude was usually cool, calm, and collected. Un-freaking-flappable. Suddenly, he was frazzled."

"Sure you don't want to tell me his last name? I'd like to pay this asshole a visit."

"Which is precisely what I want to avoid. Just listen," I insist.

"No promises." Yet he pretends to button his lips. Such a dad move, and it's stupid sexy coming from Rhodes Walsh.

An audible inhale gets me back on track. "I didn't understand the significance of his behavior until a week or so later. Someone from their legal team contacted me about obtaining a paternity test. No problem. I understood and complied. Once the results came back, things got more… complicated. As it turns out, Vince was betrothed to a very unlucky lady and this whoopsie would cause all sorts of hiccups. But that wasn't my issue. He should've taken better precautions, or not done the deed with anyone who wasn't his fiancée. It takes two to tango and all that."

"What a piece of shit," Rhodes spits.

"That's my favorite nickname for him now too." Bile rises in my throat just recalling their demands. I gulp at the urge to vomit. "The blackmail started when I refused to terminate my pregnancy. Their family is wealthy beyond measure. They're even high up in politics. Vince was being groomed to become a state representative. A child out of wedlock that early in the game would ruin his chances. I couldn't care less about his selfish aspirations. Let them do their worst, right? There wasn't much they could manipulate, aside from threatening my college degree. Too bad for them, my professors weren't the type to accept bribes. I was going to have my baby with or without Vince's involvement or permission."

He makes a gruff sound in confirmation. "As you should."

"That didn't mean he was done trying to convince me. Vince and his family used money to solve problems. Turns out, I became a very large one for them. That's where my snarky comment came from. Not that you would throw cash at me like they did. Again, that was a horrible insinuation on my part."

"I get it," he grunts.

"Right, sorry again. This is really strange to repeat out loud. Not to mention, it sucks to dredge up. I've never shared this story with anyone."

Rhodes squeezes my fingers that are still linked with his. "You don't have to if it makes you uncomfortable."

I stare at our joined hands, getting lost in the past. "Just one and done. Then I can go back to not thinking about him."

"Nothing would make me happier than to wipe him from your memory, along with every other man who came before me."

A dry scoff slices from my pursed lips. "As I was saying, it went from worse to insufferable. Once Gage was born, their hatred for me multiplied. They didn't want Vince's name listed on the birth certificate, but I once again refused their demands. It's not like I was going to leave it blank. My son has a father. Vince just refuses to acknowledge him. In return, his family became relentless in their pursuit to ruin me. But I didn't have a socialite reputation to destroy. My future job prospects were in Minnesota, since I had every intention of moving home at the first available opportunity. That was good for me because it limited their options for payback for the heinous crime I'd supposedly committed. I'll spare you the brutal details, but we were locked in a custody battle for years. That was their trump card and they played it ruthlessly. They kept me trapped in South Carolina for all that time."

Rhodes glares at the starry sky while chewing on a few choice words. "No wonder you wanted nothing to do with me or my bank account."

I suck in a sharp breath. "For the record, I never expected anything from them. Not a single penny. They had to shovel out child support to keep up appearances, but it felt tainted. I created an account for Gage and only used the funds in emergencies.

Other than that, I tried to shield the blows from him. He needed me to stay strong. I'd never quit fighting for him."

"You're so damn brave, Firefly." His rasp sends a pleasant chill along my spine.

My body automatically sways into him, knowing he's there if I need him. That allows the rest to flow. "All I wanted from them was for Gage to know his father. I held onto this glimmer of hope that Vince would eventually want to meet him. But that wasn't on their agenda. They used my son to gain leverage, which truly hurt me. Gage is a blessing. A priceless gift to cherish and love unconditionally, but they treated him like a pawn. We reached a point where I knew something had to give. I couldn't handle their constant hatred, especially aimed at my son. That's when my dad reached his limit. He's a lawyer, not sure if you knew that."

He nods. "His firm is solid. I'm shocked he didn't get involved sooner."

"You and him both. I thought it was a conflict of interest. It's technically not, but I didn't want Vince and his family to have a reason to go after mine. It was best to just fight my own battle. Well, until I couldn't anymore. Frank Creed doesn't take any shit for his regular clients, let alone when his flesh and blood is at stake. He has a partner at the firm who specializes in custody cases. I can't remember the legal terms, but she pretty much threatened to sue them for ruining my life."

Rhodes scrubs at his jaw. "Extortion? Defamation? Fraud?"

"Umm, sure." I wave the options off. "It doesn't matter. This past spring, we permanently cut ties. It certainly helped that they didn't make an effort to meet Gage, not even once. That didn't look stellar for them and their false accusations. Vince relinquished his parental rights. His family dumped a small fortune in a trust fund for Gage. I never have to see them again. The end."

He hugs me tight to his chest and stamps a kiss on my forehead. "Shit, Firefly. That's fucked up."

"And just the gist. It was torture, and I often felt like

throwing in the towel, but I didn't let them win. Gage was attached to my hip through thick and thin. That's all I cared about. It might've felt like a hopeless situation at times, but at least I had my son. All they have to hold is their money and empty hearts. He's worth everything, and I didn't back down." Just saying it aloud fills me with renewed optimism. The past seven years were dark and sullied, but we waded through to reach a brighter future where home has always been waiting.

"You're an incredible mom. He's fortunate to have you."

The strain loosens from between my shoulder blades. "I'm the fortunate one, and we have each other. Gage fills me with purpose. He motivates me to be a better person. That's what kept me going. Every decision I make is with him in mind."

"Couldn't have said it better myself."

"Thanks for listening." I blow out a heavy breath. "That was actually beneficial. I feel lighter somehow."

Rhodes sets a whistle free. "You've been hauling quite a load. For what it's worth, I was right. My sordid tale is a lot less courageous, but we share a few key components."

"It's not a competition, especially not one I want to win. The stakes are too high." I shudder as my heart clenches from pain far from forgotten.

His lips brush my temple. "I can't pretend to understand what you suffered through. Those bastards deserve to pay more than money for your grievances. If you say the word, I'll use every influence in my possession to destroy them."

It's probably deranged that I get a thrill from his threats against them. "I know you would. The fact that you'd come to my defense is just… remarkable. It's a support I treasure and won't take for granted. But to tell you the truth, I'd prefer to put the struggles behind me and move forward."

"All right." He exhales a ragged breath. "Mine for yours, right? Although, you'll be sadly underwhelmed by this trade."

"Not a competition," I repeat.

"Which bodes well for me. The juiciest piece is that I

hooked up with Payton's birth mother at a party, as I previously mentioned."

"I'm so happy for you," I mutter.

Rhodes chuckles. "Glad I'm not the only jealous one. So, I met Becky that night and didn't see her again until approximately nine months later. She entered my house, sat on the couch, and proceeded to grant me full custody of our baby girl. You can imagine my shock. That's not something I ever expected to happen. It's also not something I could've prepared for, seeing as I had no clue she was ever pregnant. Pretty sure my pulse is still elevated from that friendly chat. But I took one look at Payton and fell in love. No hesitation. Not a single regret. I didn't even need the results from the paternity test to prove she was mine. From that moment on, my daughter became my entire world. That's about it. Fairly cut and dry. I haven't spoken to Becky since that afternoon."

"Wow, you got off easy." I straighten from my slumped position against him. "That's… really interesting. I figured the newborn drop and dash was reserved for controversial talk shows and soap operas. Holy shit, I'm being insensitive. Still raw, I think. But that stuff actually happens?"

"To the likes of me. Apparently, she didn't want to deal with me during the pregnancy. That fucking hurts. Am I a bad guy, Firefly?" His gaze is solemn and imploring, nearly cracking my sternum in half.

"I'm sure it's nothing against you personally."

"That's hard for me to believe. However, she gave me Payton. I can't be upset about that."

Warmth spreads through me at the conviction in his voice. "Exactly. Becky must've thought you were halfway decent. Why else would she trust you with her baby? Gosh, I can't imagine relinquishing my parental rights to a person I slept with once."

"Me either, but she really didn't want kids. I hate to picture what the outcome could've been if it weren't for her strong personal beliefs on terminating a pregnancy."

Heat pricks my eyes. I'm bound to be dehydrated by now. "Not everyone is cut out to be a parent. That's her choice. In my opinion, she made the best decision for Payton."

His mouth twitches with the start of a smirk. "Thanks. I appreciate the vote of confidence."

"Please believe it. You're a wonderful father, Rhodes. Other than Papa Frank, you outshine the masses. And my dad would be quick to agree. He sings your praises."

"Needed to hear that. I'll never give you a reason to doubt me." With a downward swoop, he seals the vow with a kiss against my lips.

"This has been an enlightening conversation," I note.

"Welcome to my seedy past," he drawls.

"We sure know how to pick 'em."

"That's behind us. I'd say those mistakes brought us to where we were meant to be."

The giddy flutters are bound to send me straight to the stars at this point. I rest my cheek on a bent knee, giving me a mouthwatering visual of the man beside me. "I think I like you a lot, babe."

Rhodes laughs, this time from deep in his gut. The throaty sound drops into a sultry octave that I feel in my core. "Well, that's a damn relief. It would've sucked if this attraction was one-sided."

"Nope, I'm officially smitten with you. I guess this means we're dating?" The rise in my tone betrays me and leaves the unknown hanging.

"I'm about to take you to my bed. No other woman has been between those sheets. What do you think about that?"

I gulp. "Uh, that sounds pretty serious."

Rhodes incinerates me with his smolder. "You're mine, Firefly. No question about it."

chapter twenty-five

RHODES

RYLEE'S KNEE BOUNCES IN AN OPPOSING RHYTHM TO THE COUNTRY song belting from the radio. Her gaze swivels from the passenger window over to me. From there, she takes a visual detour into the backseat for a peek at our kids. Payton and Gage are adequately distracted by the huge pile of books they borrowed for the weekend from the libraries at their respective schools. If all goes well, they might attend the same one next fall.

I bite my lip to stave off a groan. There's no need to draw attention—especially of the inappropriate nature—from the aforementioned kids stuck in the truck with us. When I glance to the left, Rylee's stare is feasting on me like a five-course meal. That sends a throb behind my zipper.

"Thanks for agreeing to tag along." I'm proud to admit that my tone remains level.

"As if there was an alternative."

"You could've denied me." My fingers curl on the steering wheel at the thought of her not being beside me right now.

"And you could've told me it was your birthday sooner." For whatever reason, she turns her voice down to a whisper.

I reach across the center console to grasp her hand. "Last night wasn't enough notice?"

"More like the crack of dawn when you finally let me rest." A blush rises on her freckled cheeks.

My chuckle rumbles across the enclosed space. "Let's not

pretend you're innocent. I recall you being just as game for a little midnight wrestling."

"It's your fault I'm insatiable," she grumbles.

"Do you not expect me to accept blame for that? With enthusiasm, I might add. It's invigorating to discover just how smitten my Firefly is." I bring our connected palms to my mouth, peppering her knuckles in kisses.

Rylee flutters her lashes at me. "Which is precisely how I found myself in this predicament."

"I'll give you a nine-inch predicament later."

"Daddy?"

I choke on my pooling drool. Thanks to I-35 being deserted, I can steal fast glances in the rearview. "Yes, Bumblebee?"

Payton beams at me. Then she tilts her head to admire the braid hanging over her shoulder for what seems like the seventeenth time. Her eyes shift to Rylee—the one responsible for the complicated style—and her smile stretches wider. "What's a predictablement?"

A wince catalogs the shame across my features while I search for an answer… or a delay. "A predicament?"

"That's what I said."

Rylee giggles, dipping her chin in a failed attempt to hide the amusement.

I squeeze her fingers still clasped in mine. "Would you care to do the honors?"

Her mouth forms a small circle. "Oh, no. I'd never take the privilege from you. Enjoy those nine inches of regret your foot just shoved into your mouth."

My focus narrows on the freeway ahead and the miles we have yet to travel. "A predicament is like being in a pickle."

Rylee snorts, which morphs into a hacking fit. She whacks her chest with a palm. Her watery eyes swing to me. "That's what you came up with?"

Heat prickles along my nape. I grace her with a sheepish

expression to match. "It's the best I could conjure on the spot. Besides, I'm not wrong."

She sputters another laugh. "Conjure? Forget the alien and unicorn. You might be a warlock."

"I'll be whatever you want me to be, Firefly. Just get me out of this pickle."

Meanwhile, my daughter is thoroughly perplexed. "Pickles? Those are sour, Daddy. Why are you gonna put Rylee in a pickle?"

"It's my birthday," I mumble absently. Seems as good of an excuse as any.

Rylee pulls her lips between her teeth. "This keeps getting better."

"Not sure I wanna eat a pickle," Payton chirps. "Maybe I'd like getting in a pickle. But that's weird."

Gage shifts his focus from the book in his lap to the chatty troublemaker strapped in beside him. "Pickles are just cucumbers in a jar."

Her jaw hangs open as she gawks at him. "Really?"

"Yep. There's a whole process. My teacher told me. I think it's science." He shrugs.

Payton's mouth is still dropped open. "Wow, science is cool. I wanna put cucumbers in a jar. Maybe I would eat those pickles. Do you like pickles, Gage?"

He nods eagerly, the force enough that I don't need visual confirmation. "Uh-huh. They're crunchy. I take big bites."

My daughter is quiet for a moment. "That sounds kinda fun."

"Oh, oh! Pickle is a funny name for private parts. My penis could be called a pickle. It's almost the same. Penis and pickle. Right, Mom?"

I nearly swerve off the road, releasing Rylee's hand to get straightened out. "Sweet Jes—cheese and rice."

Her next exhale is a whoosh. It seems as if she's struggling to collect her thoughts. That's something we definitely have in common. "Uh, that's not… maybe we should change the subject."

"Please. Anything but this," I spit.

She snorts. "You're the one who got us into a pickle predicament."

"Daddy, do I have a pickle private part?" Payton's voice is sweeter than pure sugar.

I almost bash my forehead on the steering wheel. "Oh, fudge frack. This is traumatizing."

Rylee's knee resumes its erratic bouncing. "It was your idea to invite us."

"No regrets," I croak.

"Sure about that?" She doesn't evoke much confidence.

I regain my composure and reclaim her palm against mine. "Yes. Not a single doubt. I want you by my side for every embarrassing moment. That's where you belong. Gage has a permanent spot there too. Even if he freely talks about his pen—nope, never mind. We're dropping it."

From my peripheral, I watch her chest rise and fall with a deep breath. "You accept him easily."

"Of course, baby. He's part of our package deal. Four is better than two." And there's plenty of room to grow.

Payton catches my attention again. "But, Daddy. What about my pickle privates?"

Gage makes a noise that resembles confusion. "Aren't you a girl?"

"Duh," she scoffs.

"I don't think you have a penis," he giggles.

"But I want a pickle."

"Sweetie," Rylee says while turning in her seat to address Payton. "Girls and boys have different private parts."

"I know." My daughter's exhale is resigned. "Nana told me, since I don't have a mom to explain that girly stuff."

My flinch is from the backhanded slap I often feel in our situation. It's fucking unfair. "I try."

Now Rylee gives me a reassuring squeeze at our linked fingers. "You do an amazing job."

I glare at the interstate through the windshield. "This topic is rough. I thought we were dropping it?"

"This is a good learning and teaching moment." Her grip on me softens before she shifts her focus to Payton again. "If you ever have questions, I'm here for you."

Payton gasps. "Really?"

"Of course, sweetie. Whatever you're wondering about. It could be makeup, dresses, boy cooties, running a business, math homework, baiting a hook, monster trucks, or private parts. That last one can be when it's just the two of us. No boys allowed. Just us girls, okay?" Rylee reaches to pat her knee, or something along those lines.

It's difficult for me to see. Through their heartfelt exchange, I'm trying not to bawl. I blink in rapid succession to wash away the heat. Minimal traffic aside, I still need to deliver us safely to Duluth.

"Okay," my daughter sighs after a brief pause. "I'd like that. A super lot."

"Me too," Rylee croons.

Payton's attention drifts to Gage. "Your mom is awesome."

"Yeah, she's the best." He better be preening with pride.

"Will you share her with me? I want her to be my mom."

"Sure," Gage replies. "But only if I get your dad."

"Like a trade?"

"Um, no. Like we'd be a family. Together. Then we'd have both parents." He claps with a squeak.

Payton joins in the celebration. The backseat is a soundtrack for childhood dreams coming true. "Oh, yes! I wanna be a family. That's even better than a trade. Let's get my dad to marry your mom."

"What a great idea! It's a deal." Pretty sure Gage thrusts a hand to her side for a shake.

"Mine for yours," I mumble under my breath.

Rylee's wide eyes find mine. "This is getting serious."

My thumb rubs along hers. "Does it scare you?"

She chomps on her bottom lip. The three seconds she takes for consideration is worse than fire ants on my balls. "No, I'm not scared at all."

"That's good, Firefly." I lift her fingers to my lips. "Damn good."

Rylee gulps, the small action louder than my pounding heart. The air swells until drawing breath is a chore. If I wasn't driving, I might be tempted to get down on one knee right here and now. I could pull onto the shoulder. There's no ring, but I could find a substitute.

Thunder drums in my ears at the very real possibility. It should concern me that I'm about to flip on the blinker. Comfort finds me instead. I'm not the coward I used to be. This woman has changed me. Irrevocably. She's the only one who could. I can prove just how much.

"Wanna read my shark diarrhea?" Gage effectively bursts the bubble with that offer.

Payton makes a disgusted sound. "Ewww, no way. That's gross."

"Why? It's about their life in the ocean. Wanna see?" It looks as if he tries to pass her something.

The pressure in my chest lifts when I chuckle. "Must be a made-up story. I don't think sharks get diarrhea."

Rylee is laughing so hard that there are tears on her cheeks. "Wait a minute. You have a book about shark… diarrhea?"

"Uh-huh, look." He holds the cover for her to appraise.

She swallows her next giggle. "That's a shark *diary*. Not diarrhea."

Gage grunts. "I don't get it. What's a diary?"

"It's like a journal or notebook. You write in it," Rylee explains.

"Oh, oh," my daughter cuts in. "I have one of those to practice my writing and doodles."

Rylee sends her a smile. "Yeah, a diary can be used for whatever you want. This book is a shark giving you its personal story."

Her son clucks his tongue in response. "Okay, I get it now. Diarrhea wasn't the right word. I didn't see any pictures of poop on the pages."

Payton seems to agree if her squeal is anything to go by. "That's cool. I wanna read the diary."

After a few moments of silence, Rylee's leg resumes the frantic jiggling. "Are we almost there?"

I drop our interlaced palms on her thigh. "Aren't the kids supposed to ask that?"

She puffs out her cheeks before releasing a loud exhale. "I'm… nervous. You should've given me more than a few hours to prepare."

"I figured the spontaneous route would be romantic."

"For a road trip on your birthday," she deadpans.

"How else would I get you to visit my parents this soon?" Although, I would've hauled her there weeks ago if it wasn't a three-hour drive. "Not to mention, you might've found an excuse to stay at the bar."

"It could've been planned rather than rushed. I didn't buy you a present." Rylee sounds the most upset about that.

"You're the best gift." I seal the conviction with a kiss on her inner wrist.

She tries to hide a grin, but her mouth curls at the edges. "You're just saying that because I didn't get you a real one."

"This is as real as it gets, Firefly."

"What if your parents hate me?" Rylee sucks air between her teeth as if the thought is physically painful.

I scoff. "They're going to love you."

"How do you know?"

Because I do. A glance in the rearview mirror reflects our captive audience. The moment isn't quite ripe. Payton and Gage would certainly add to the excitement, but they also bring expectations. I can't be hasty with our hearts. When I confess my love and loyalty to Rylee, I want to be certain she isn't pressured into returning the feelings.

"It runs in the family." I jerk my head in Payton's general direction.

But Rylee's focus is on me. "Gage and my parents love you too."

Emotion wells in my chest again. I almost rescind my hesitation from moments before. But our time will come. Soon. "Thank you, by the way. For what you said to Payton."

"We're a package, right? You can talk to Gage when he discovers... corn." She shudders and gags. "In the meantime, he can ask about why his cob gets hard at random intervals. Those are awkward conversations for me."

Memories of my own youth rise, bringing forward a pained laugh. Those natural occurrences and urges can be strange. "I can handle that."

"Oooooh, are we having corn on the cob for dinner?" Payton's innocent question cracks into our parental minefield.

Once again, the comedic relief is greatly appreciated. My gaze darts to the navigation display. "Eight minutes."

And not a moment too soon.

"Is this where you grew up?" Rylee's awe is a breathy exhale as she gazes out the window. "This street is stunning. Very picturesque."

Just arriving in the sleepy neighborhood lifts any tension I might've been harboring. I take a moment to appreciate the trees lining both sides of Kingston Avenue. Some are still vibrant with autumn leaves. "Yep, born and raised in Duluth. My parents bought this house before I started kindergarten. They haven't moved since."

Payton's patience is nearing its limit just in time. "How much long-er? Nana and Papa told you to hurry. We've been in the truck for a whole day."

"It's only been three hours," I correct.

"But can you go faster? They'll be super happy to see me. It's been for-ev-er." She draws out the word with a cheery tune.

"Do they wanna meet me?" Gage's enthusiasm rises to the occasion.

"Uh-huh. I've told them all about my very best friend."

"What? I thought you were my girlfriend," Gage grumbles.

A hiss escapes me, and I cringe. Poor buddy. The sting of being caught in the friend zone is legit.

"Not anymore. Our parents are in loooooove, remember? Next comes marriage. Then comes a baby, but they already have us. You'll be my brother." Payton begins reciting the childish rhyme.

He goes still, which is uncharacteristic. "I'll have a sister?"

"That's me!"

Rylee bends forward until her hair creates a strawberry blonde curtain. "I don't even know your favorite color and these two are sending wedding invites."

"It's blue, and we can curb their interference at any point. Just say the word."

Her green eyes sparkle in my direction. "How are you not freaking out about this?"

"When it feels right, there's no reason to panic." I pull into the driveway before any further meddling or meltdowns can ensue. "And we're here."

She appears to shed the shock from our kids' latest scheming to gawk at the view. "Oh, my gosh. This house is adorable."

I do a visual sweep of the two-story home while a fond smile sprouts on my lips. Comfort surrounds me in a familial embrace. The white siding is pristine and contrasted by black shutters. Flower boxes overflowing with big round sunflowers, bright verbenas, and orange-purple daisies rest beneath the four large windows on the first floor, giving the yard a beautiful pop of autumn joy. More blooms are arranged in the gardens my mother prides herself on. An attached garage stores outdoor toys and their sedan.

"It's full of memories."

"I can't wait to hear them, especially the embarrassing ones." She wags her brows.

"Be warned. There are some doozies."

My parents are crossing the lawn before I've shifted the truck into park. Rylee steps out to help Gage while I do the same with Payton. The kids dash to where Mom and Dad are hovering on the grassy edge. I hang back, allowing them to get spoiled with attention. Both pairs. There's a bite in the air, but the temperature is still in the fifties. Warm enough to stand out-side for a conversation without getting cold.

Payton doesn't bother with pleasantries. "Did you miss me?"

Mom crouches to fold the buzzing bumblebee into her arms. "Every second. It's been too long since your last visit."

She returns the affection, adding a noisy smooch onto my mother's cheek. "I told Daddy to drive faster."

"Safety is important," I call from my spot near the truck.

Rylee sidles up beside me, bumping her hip into mine. "You took good care of us."

My palm finds purchase on her ass, hidden from the others. "That's never gonna change."

"Better not." She's slipped on the leather jacket I bought her last week after our motorcycle ride.

"You look hotter than a biker fantasy," I growl. "Nope, fuck that. Sexier than my entire spank bank collection."

She lightly smacks my chest. "Quit. Your parents and our kids are right there."

"Yes, and their attention is directed elsewhere."

The welcome wagon continues on its quest when Dad pro-duces two peppermints from his pocket. "Who wants a treat?"

Gage and Payton can barely contain themselves. He leaps forward while she ducks under Dad's arm for a better angle. A collision occurs, resulting in no injuries. They're both victorious by reaching his proffered stash at the same second.

I glance sideways when Rylee laughs. "What's funny?"

"My dad always carries peppermints in his pockets. Gage is a huge fan."

"How coincidental," I murmur.

"Extremely," she replies while the scene plays on.

The kids are gratefully chomping on their candy when my mom turns her gaze onto Gage. "And aren't you a handsome fella?"

He beams at the praise. "Hi! I'm Gage. It's nice to meet you."

Mom almost appears taken aback. "Oh, my. You're very polite."

"Thanks so much." He rocks on his heels.

"You're most welcome. Please call me Nana, and he"—she motions to Dad—"is Papa."

Gage squints at them. "You're not super old like Gramma and Grampa."

She clutches her chest and giggles. Fucking. Giggles. "That's quite the compliment. No wonder Payton wants to marry you."

He stops munching. "Huh?"

"Nana," my daughter complains. Her puckered expression denies the accusation, as if she didn't just spout the marriage claim yesterday. "That's done. We have a new deal."

Mom lifts her brows in interest. "Is that so?"

Payton nods. "Gage's mommy is Daddy's girlfriend. It's kinda complicated."

My mother's gaze shifts to me, yet she addresses those in her direct vicinity. "Seems pretty simple to me."

Rylee squirms under the presumed scrutiny. "We'll be engaged by sunset at this rate."

I dip to whisper in her ear. "Would that be so bad?"

It's mid-afternoon. That gives me five or six hours before dusk settles. The magic I can accomplish in that amount of time might surprise everyone. There I go again, thinking with my—

"Does the happy couple have something to share with the rest of us?" That comes from my dad, the one who is usually reserved and aligned with me on the sidelines. "Or is my son suddenly shy?"

I smirk at his rare form. "Prying suits you."

"Ah, the art of deflection. You got that from me." He winks.

Payton thrusts an arm in the air, waving it wildly. "Oh! I got the jean stuff from Daddy to wear. See?"

My parents exchange a laugh while she spins in a circle. Mom pats her head in an affectionate way that spreads warmth through my chest. "That's true, pumpkin. Your dad gave you the best pieces of him. It seems he found two more to share that big heart with too."

Payton's features screw up. "I didn't know his heart was too big. Does he need to go to the doctor?"

Mom smiles down at her. "It's just an expression, or figure of speech. Remember we talked about what that is?"

She snubs the concrete with her toe. "Kinda? It's not like really real, just something you say."

"Correct. Your daddy's heart isn't bigger than normal in actual size. I meant there's more space inside of him for love to grow."

Payton blinks at her. "Do I have lotsa extra space too?"

"Of course," she assures.

"What about me?" Gage turns to Rylee. "Do we have the bigger hearts in our jeans?"

"Yes, Schmutz. There's plenty of love for us to spread."

"But I'm wearing gym pants." He tugs at the stretchy fabric, then a thought seems to occur to him. His wide eyes bounce from his mom to me and back again. "Wait. You're gonna spread the love with Payton's dad? Does that mean you're gonna have more babies?"

Rylee wheezes from her spot beside me. "No, no. This is… not the moment to discuss babies."

"All right, things are escalating quickly. We haven't been properly introduced and love is already heavy in the air." Dad chuckles and strides toward us. "I'm Stan."

She steps forward to accept his proffered hand. "Rylee. Thanks for having us."

"The pleasure is ours. That beauty is Linda, my wife." He nods at Mom, who appears to be waiting until later to approach.

"Apologies about my adorable son spouting whatever crosses his mind. We"—she motions to me—"haven't discussed the future in such detail."

"And we look forward to what might come. Always great

to see you, son." He grips my shoulder before retreating to the lawn.

Gage is bouncing on his shoes like there are springs in the soles. "Do you have pickles?"

"I almost forgot about those," Payton cries. "We wanna eat pickles."

My dad nods his approval. "It's a healthy snack."

"Did you know pickles are cucumbers in jars?" Gage pipes in.

"That's good knowledge," Dad replies.

"It's science." The kid offers a toothy grin.

"Do you have any pickles that aren't super sour?" This comes from Payton.

Dad scrubs at his jaw. "I can peek in the fridge."

"Let's go check," the duo shouts their urgency in unison before racing for the front door.

I watch the kids leap up the porch stairs while waving to my dad. "Thanks for managing their craving. Guess they're hungry."

"Got it!" He tosses a thumbs-up over his shoulder.

The entire time, Mom hasn't taken her gaze from Rylee. She finally approaches and gives her a warm smile. "Your son is wonderful. His behavior speaks very highly of you. More than that, the way my son looks at you is a treasure to behold."

Rylee glances over to where I'm already staring at her. "Oh?"

My mom hums. "I wasn't sure we'd see the day."

Mom is suddenly in front of me, her hand lifting to pat my cheek. "How's the birthday boy?"

"Pretending to be twenty-five," I joke.

"With age comes wisdom and experience." Her gaze slides to the woman on my right. "I'm very happy you're here, Rylee. It's lovely to finally make your acquaintance."

Rylee's smile is relaxed and right at home. "Likewise, Linda. Thanks for extending the invitation to include Gage and me."

Mom *tsks*. "Oh, my heavens. Of course, dear. You're always

welcome here. It feels like we've been anticipating this occasion far longer than you've known each other."

"That's very kind. I have a similar sense, which might sound strange."

"Not in the least." My mother doesn't hesitate to envelop Rylee in a hug. "Thank you."

Her arms automatically rise to return the embrace. "For what?"

"My boy is smiling with stars in his eyes." Mom sniffs while straightening from their huddled position. "That's a luxury to cherish. You have no idea what that means to me, and how much I've wished for you."

"Jeez, Linda. You're gonna make me cry." Rylee fans her face.

And she's not the only one. The sight of them molding a bond with such natural ease does something to me. These two have been essential in shaping me into the man I am today. In very different ways. Witnessing this exchange is… paramount. Overwhelming, too.

My mom gasps while looking at me. "What's this? Are your eyes wet? Mine must be deceiving me."

"No," I grumble and swipe at the evidence. "Just dust from the wind."

Rylee quirks a brow. "There's no breeze."

"Thanks for calling me out, Firefly." I trace her upturned jaw with my nose.

She sways into me. "No problem, babe."

My mother sighs, pleased to intrude on our bubble. "How precious."

"Mom," I chide.

"Right. Okay, that's enough mush. We better check on those three pickle eaters. It's too quiet." She gestures for us to get moving along the path.

I slide Rylee's palm into mine and lead the way. The instant we step inside, warmth and belonging enters my lungs. Mom ushers us straight into the kitchen. Payton, Gage, and my father are already there. Suspicion slows my pace until I see the ice cream cake sitting on the table in all its frozen glory.

My mouth waters at the sight. "You went to Dairy Queen?"

"Of course." Mom grins wide at her success. "It's only your favorite."

"Noted," Rylee murmurs from beside me.

After lighting the candles—all thirty of them—they serenade me with a pitchy rendition of "Happy Birthday". Payton belts out a few questionable high notes. Gage goes low, dropping to his knees for theatrical flair. Rylee is all smiles while singing along. And my parents… they look relieved and complete. Like this is the pivotal scene they've been waiting for. It brings heat to my eyes all over again.

We sit and the cake gets sliced. The pieces are way too big, but nobody complains. Silence descends as we dive in. Creamy vanilla, rich fudge, and the signature crumble melt on my tastebuds. Joy fills my gut along with a buzz from the sugar. A glance around the table proves that the numbers are finally balanced. Last year, we were two short. That's no longer an issue. This is a great fucking day.

Mom cracks into the quiet by clearing her throat. "Your father and I were chatting before you arrived."

My lips curve around the fork still buried from my last bite. "Uh-oh. That never pans out well for me. Should I be concerned?"

She wags her finger at me. "Very funny. Now, as I was saying, we could use some quality time with the children. You two should enjoy an evening out. Just adults."

Rylee shakes her head. "We should celebrate together."

My mom titters. "Pish-posh, as Mary Poppins would say. That's why we had cake before dinner."

"Dessert is the best meal," Gage says.

"Yummy in my tummy," Payton agrees.

"See? They're already having a great time with us. Feel free to show yourselves out. Our treat." Dad lifts his chin to the hallway.

Rylee laughs in that uncomfortable tune of hers. "Oh, you're kicking us out?"

"We insist." My mother uses a tone that leaves no room for argument.

I reach for Rylee's hand beneath the table. "It's up to you, Firefly."

She worries her bottom lip. "Me? This is your special day."

"Seems it could be ours," I murmur.

A blush stains her freckled skin. "How can I resist an offer like that?"

"You don't," Mom interjects. Her eyes twinkle in the kitchen lights. "Go spread the birthday love all over downtown."

I squeeze Rylee's fingers in mine. "With pleasure."

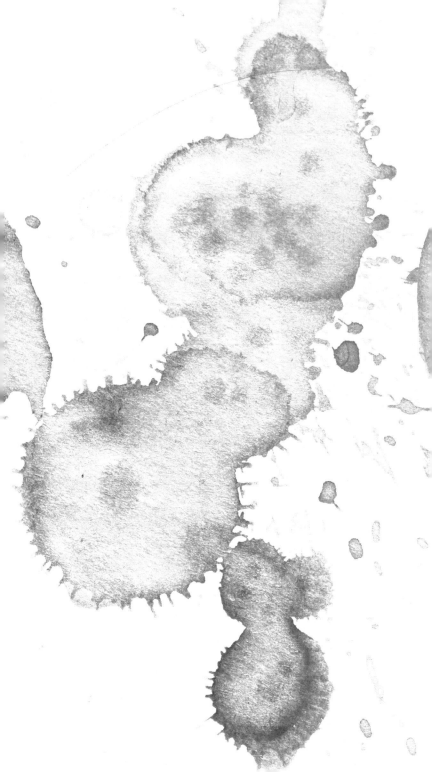

chapter twenty-seven

Rylee

"I T WASN'T A FLUKE," I INSIST. TO PROVE MY TALENTS, I PLUCK another cherry from the bowl. The candied fruit bathes my tongue in sugar. I don't bother trapping a moan when juicy syrup bursts from the bite.

Rhodes leans on his stool until his forehead bumps my temple. "You're making it sound like that garnish is the best fucking thing you've put in your mouth."

"Maybe it is." I lift a brow while twirling the stem between my fingers.

He slams his mouth onto mine. His tongue stabs at the seam of my lips, forcing me to open for him. I do, on a breathy whine, and bury my fingers in his hair. Blisters might be forming on my skin with how hot he makes me. There's just enough alcohol in my system that straddling his lap seems like the next logical move. Just as I'm lifting my ass from the leather seat, he wrenches from me with a tortured groan.

"Fuck that sugary shit, Firefly. Your pussy on the rim of my whiskey can't be beat." Rhodes flares his nostrils. The snort that follows is unsatisfied.

It takes me a moment to catch my breath. "Agree to disagree."

His eyes flash. A muscle leaps in his jaw when he clenches

down. Combined with the mused strands sticking straight up on end, his expression looks feral. "You need another taste?"

"Probably."

He bites his bottom lip until the flesh turns white. "That's the first thing you'll get when we're home tomorrow."

I get a thrill from him coining the bar as our home. The concept makes sense since we're practically inseparable within those walls. Before that notion can fog my focus, the task and game at hand resurface. I pop the stem into my mouth while his focus is rapt on me. Three seconds is all I require. With a palm curled around his nape, I wrench on him until only an exhale separates us. Then I shove the knotted victory into his mouth.

"Still a fluke?" A spark shoots across my feverish skin when Rhodes falters.

He pulls the stem from between his teeth and inspects my tongue tying. "Impressive."

I toss some hair behind my shoulder. "And you doubted me."

"Nah, I just wanted a trophy."

"The dozen pairs of panties you've collected aren't enough?"

"I'll never get enough. You're too fucking sexy," he growls into my neck.

Arousal spikes in my blood when he licks a fiery path to taste me. "It's your turn."

Rhodes pulls away and props a bent elbow on the bar. "We're still playing?"

I touch my nose with my tongue—a trick I exposed as truth in a previous round. "Absolutely. I'm learning so much about you."

We've been at Loose Goose—a rowdy sports pub in downtown Duluth—for a few hours. The birthday celebration has been a spine-tingling success so far if I do say so myself. I came up with the idea to play a game to pass the time. It also doesn't hurt to learn more about each other, considering the relationship road we're speeding down. Two Truths and a Lie seemed appropriate.

Our random facts fill in some blanks, but it's mostly fun to rile Rhodes up. He's not the only one to get hot and bothered, though. The atmosphere was already charged the instant we walked in the door. Electric static zaps harder with each non-sensical fact or fiction. Soon, I might need to step outside or I'm liable to combust.

Rhodes tips his beer bottle to take a drink, never taking his eyes off me. *"I'm horny. My cock is about to punch a hole through my jeans to reach your pussy. I want you to ride my face."*

"Oh, my." I fan my flaming cheeks. *"Are those all true?"*

"They are," he confirms.

"That's not how the game works," I chide.

His fingers tug on a stray curl brushing my jawline. *"I'm changing the rules, Firefly."*

"You're on your own, birthday boy." I hold up three fingers. *"This one time in Minneapolis, I kept petting a police horse's face even after the officer told me to stop. That same night, I fell down an escalator that was going up. I'm a virgin. Take your best guess."*

That dashing dimple appears behind his scruff. *"If you're a virgin, I'm Prince fucking Charming."*

I flutter my lashes. *"Will you take me to the ball?"*

Rhodes plants a kiss on my puckered pout. *"Hold that thought, baby. I gotta piss."*

A snort blows from me. *"How eloquent."*

"You don't love me for my manners." He stands from his stool.

"And now you're being presumptuous." Although, my blush betrays me.

As does his throaty chuckle. *"Be right back. Don't move."*

The instant his broad shadow recedes from my personal space, another much smaller one intrudes. Based on the muffled grumbles, this interruption is a man. I remain still. According to all the nature documentaries, predators prefer a chase. The same habits are typically true for barflies. If I don't move, they'll lose interest.

"Hey, foxy vixen."

Or maybe not. That doesn't mean I turn. The empty glass in my grip is more fascinating.

"Lookin' a tad lonely. Want some, uh… company?" His slurred speech matches the ripe stench wafting from him.

My nose wrinkles on impact. *"Nope, I'm fine. Thanks anyway."*

"Yeah, you are. I want a piece of what you're serving." The stranger stumbles closer until he hovers too close for comfort.

I study the ballsy boozer through a pinched expression. *"You're barking up the wrong tree, dude."*

"Woof, woof." He hiccups and almost topples sideways, but the counter stops his fall.

The scene is all too familiar. *"Can I help you get an Uber? Or do you prefer Lyft?"*

His gaze is unfocused. *"I dunno, can you?"*

"That doesn't make sense."

"You don't make sense. Why're your clothes"—he belches—*"still on?"*

A sudden storm cloud crackles with fury behind me. I don't need to turn to know that Rhodes has returned from the potty. My thumb hitches at him while I address the stubborn lush with cotton in his ears. *"He's mine, which means I'm his. I wouldn't recommend testing that theory."*

The guy shifts his focus from my boobs to the rock-solid hunk of muscle currently giving him a death glare. His eyes widen. *"Oh, shit. Where'd you come from?"*

"Back off, asshole." Rhodes crosses his arms. Muscles bulge and strain the seams on his shirt from the flexed position. *"Before I make you."*

It takes a pregnant pause for the message to be received. Then he lifts his palms in surrender while retreating with backward steps. *"Didn't mean any offense."*

Rhodes grunts. "Don't stare at my woman's tits—or *any* part of her—and we won't have a problem."

The interloper disappears into the crowd without another glance.

I giggle once the supposed threat vanishes from sight. "Someone is extra… territorial tonight."

Rhodes pins a scowl where the intruder was last spotted. "Not just tonight. Most know to keep their distance from who belongs to me."

My humor sobers into a glare. "Careful, or you'll stomp on my independence."

His features soften when he looks at me. "I belong to you, so it's only fair."

I let my tense expression fall loose as well. "Gonna tattoo my name on your ass?"

"Already have a design sketched."

"Puh-lease," I huff.

"You're driving me crazy." Rhodes extends a hand toward me. "C'mere, Firefly."

"Where are we going?" Even as I question him, my palm slides into his.

"To the fucking ball." He nods in the general direction where people are bumping and grinding to a seductive tempo.

My brows spike upward. "You want to dance?"

"With you? Very much so."

Then we're on the move. He leads me through the throng with relative ease. Most leap from his intended path to avoid a collision. I can't blame them, seeing as this man is a dominant force to be reckoned with. The power and strength he exudes just scream danger and destruction. But those thoughts evaporate when he spins me until my back is flush with his front.

I melt into him as bodies swarm and circle to create an intimate bubble for us. A thrum pulses through me in sync with the heavy beat. Sweat already dots my flesh as we begin to move.

Rhodes buries his face in my hair. Even with the music blasted to shattering volumes, I can hear him breathe me in.

We become a fluid motion while hypnotic tremors pound across the floor. His fingers dig into my waist, forcing my movements to mirror his. Steam builds between us. I snake my tongue out to trace the shell of his ear. He tightens his grip on me, punching forward on the next note. Jelly floods me and I sag into his capable hands. A palm flattens across my pelvis, rocking us along the soundwaves.

When the song changes to a sultry rhythm, I roll my hips into him. "Holy shit. Is that a whiskey bottle in your pocket?"

Rhodes grinds that steely girth into me. "Nah, I'm just real fucking happy to see you."

My ass cradles his hardness while I shimmy backward. "Maybe we should do something about that."

His breath is hot against my neck. "Careful, or I'll fuck you on this floor."

A shiver courses through me. My nipples pebble to brush against silk and lace. Deft thumbs instinctively pluck at the needy tips. I rest my head against him while allowing the stimulation to pleasure me. Rhodes makes me feel wild. Untamed. Like any second, I'll go off the rails into a spontaneous orgasm. That might be the three drinks talking. I've had just enough to lower my inhibitions. A bang in a bathroom stall suddenly seems like an excellent idea. Maybe one more song.

I lift my arms to loop around him, then clasp my fingers against his nape. "You're a really good dancer."

Rhodes peppers kisses to the expanse of exposed skin within his reach. Goosebumps prickle me when he suckles the dip at my inner elbow. "That was gonna be my next truth."

"Give me one more and a lie," I urge.

"You only get honesty from me."

A smile paints my lips. "Tell me the truth then."

"I want my ring on your finger," he rasps. Then his palms

rove to splay wide over my abdomen. "And my baby in your belly."

Desperate need pumps in my veins and I moan. "Why does that sound appealing? The idea gets me really excited."

Rhodes cinches me in a reverse hug. "Because you love me."

I spin in his arms. My lips part to deliver confirmation when a vibration from my back pocket stops me, and then the spell is broken. "One second. This could be important."

"The fuck?" His brows furrow along with mine at Adam's name flashing on the screen.

I swipe to accept, ducking my head in an attempt to hear. Crackles echo from the speaker. "Hello?"

"Hey, boss lady. Am I interrupting?" Adam's tone sounds uncharacteristically concerned. It must be from the loud noise screaming down the line.

My legs are still following the fast tempo, not ready to forfeit. "Yes. This better be important."

"We had to close the bar early," he shouts.

It's enough to wrench me from the early clutches of denial. I pull the phone away to check the time. "It's not even ten o'clock."

"The bar is busted up pretty good. Just the front, though."

"What did you say?" I stab a finger into my opposite ear to block out the deafening music.

"There's a storm," Adam bellows. "A tree got struck by lightning and split. The windows facing the street are shattered. Our sign fell too. You should probably cut your trip early. Apologies to the birthday boss."

"No, no, no." Heat stings my eyes as everything morphs into a blur. My motions come to an abrupt halt.

Rhodes grips my shoulders, providing me with a much-needed anchor. "What's wrong?"

"We need to go home." I lift my watery gaze to his. "Bent Pedal needs us."

chapter twenty-eight

RHODES

"A LRIGHTY, THAT SHOULD DO IT FROM MY END." THE SALES rep from Pane in the Glass scribbles a final note and tucks his pen out of sight.

Rylee's lips part, but it takes several seconds for any sound to form. "You're already done?"

"This type of job is simple." His eyes slide to mine. "You call and we install. Not much more to it."

Her focus lands on me as well. Red hair whips in the chilled breeze as she gathers her voice. "Did you pay him extra?"

Heat rises under my collar from her intense scrutiny. Similar questions have pelted me since we arrived on the scene. A cleanup unit already passed through to collect the broken shards and debris. Another crew sealed the holes with tarps as a short-term solution. The insurance agent left a few minutes before the glass guy arrived.

I pull her tighter into my side. "For thicker windows, yes. These will be better than before. Next time there's a bad storm, we won't have to worry. We discussed that earlier."

"You know what I mean," she murmurs.

My gaze burns into her. Lush green begs me for mercy. Guilt grows thick and swoops in like smoke to engulf me. Pressure immediately clamps my lungs and my breathing becomes difficult. I'm not sure what Rylee expects me to admit while she's still fighting the urge to cry. That persistent tremble in her bottom lip will be my undoing. It's only natural to solve this disaster quickly, seamlessly, and without further incident. Especially when her emotional stability is at risk.

A throat clears from beside me. "Are we square?"

I rip my stare from Rylee to acknowledge the man who's gone above and beyond. "Yes, everything is set."

The woman who clutches my heart in her fist nods. "You've been very helpful. This was unexpected and obviously devastating. It's comforting to know we can reopen sooner rather than later."

"Then that's my cue, y'all. The install folks will handle things from here. You should see them by tomorrow afternoon. Thanks for doing business. Take care now." The guy gives us a wave before ambling to his car.

I raise my hand in farewell. "We appreciate you making us a priority on such short notice. Be sure to stop by for a complimentary drink next week. You've got a friend in Bent Pedal."

He just chuckles while sliding into the front seat. We stand frozen—similar to the past hour—and watch him drive off. There isn't much else for us to do. Our own thoughts and concerns fill the gaps, wondering where the next step leads.

Rylee's hand is firmly tucked into mine as we survey the damage once again. Adam had sent pictures after his call last night. The images prepared us, but the physical proof is hard to choke on. Bent Pedal has seen brighter mornings. Icy wind whips at my face, but I barely notice. Her upset pummels me worse than any weather conditions. The silence becomes a dense presence. I can practically hear her uncertainty sobbing for answers.

"What did you do, Rhodes?" Wet lashes blink up at me.

The sight nearly cracks my resolve. I want to tell her what I did isn't enough. That's not what she needs to support her, though. "Just sped up the process."

It usually takes several days for an assessor to appraise the wreckage. A few more after that to build a quote. It could take weeks before contracted companies make contact about the bid. Fuck that wait.

Money talks and I spared no expense to cut corners and snip the red tape.

She worries the inside of her cheek until I'm certain the flesh is raw. "How much did that cost?"

"Don't worry, Firefly. I'll get reimbursed."

A fierce gust chooses that moment to warn us of worse conditions fast approaching. Rylee's rosy cheeks burrow into the wool scarf wrapped around her neck. "We could've waited for the insurance check."

"Sure, but that would've extended your suffering."

"I'm not suffering." Yet she swipes angrily at a fallen tear.

With an arm around her waist, I pull until she's hugging my front. "It's gonna be okay. This could've been much worse. Nobody was hurt."

Rylee nods against my chest. "Yes, that's a blessing."

I rub a palm along her back. "Two bay windows aren't bad, all things considered."

"That's awfully optimistic of you." She sighs, the sound heavy. "Even if I grumbled a bit, I'm glad you were willing to cover the repair costs while insurance gets sorted."

"That way, we can get the building restored immediately," I shrug.

"I'm too desperate to turn down the offer, but not too far gone to accept without contingencies."

"There are no terms to our agreement. It's done."

"But I own half this place," she whines. "That means I *owe* you."

The strain in my muscles ebb and wane with her pressed against me. I allow that relief to reassure me, but doubt has long since vacated the premises. Especially where Rylee Creed is concerned.

"Trust me, Firefly. You've already compensated me. Too much, probably. When you found me, I was alone in this bar.

I'd been wallowing in guilt, pity, and grief. That might've been my lowest. Other than Payton, I shut everyone out. You dragged me from the shadows. Just arguing with you saved me from spiraling. The renewed purpose you instilled allowed me to thrive. I've found acceptance, forgiveness, and closure because of you. Together, we'll pave our future. If you'll have me that long."

Rylee allows a lull to find us. When she replies, there's a smile in her voice. "Jeez, Mr. Romantic. You always have the right thing to say. Even in this dire moment. You know I love you, right? That's about all I've got to top your speech."

"It's not a competition," I tease. Then I tuck a bent knuckle under her chin and lift it gently. My words are vowed across her lips. "I love you."

She lets her eyelids slide shut as the words wash over her. "That's nice."

I drift my thumb along the curve of her cheek. "See? We'll be okay. Love is stronger than anything."

"You're a very wise man," she breathes.

"That's probably why you fell so fast for me." I bend to touch her forehead with mine.

"Just one of many reasons. Those nine inches that are always happy to see me certainly doesn't hurt."

Before I can respond, the wind whips at us in a fury. Plastic rustles and smacks from the force. The sparkle fades from Rylee's expression and she straightens against me. My own joy receives a somber edge.

Her gaze trails to the tarps that are plastered over much of Bent Pedal. "Will they hold?"

"I don't see why not. It's industrial quality and there are at least three layers."

She quirks a brow. "Did you pay extra for that too?"

"Just part of the deal."

Her exhale brings us back to the predicament we're literally facing. "I don't want to be sad, but this is… tough."

I'm quick to cradle her in my arms again. "What can I do to ease the burden?"

"You've already done plenty. Everything, practically. Are your parents disappointed we had to go home early?" Even facing our business in ruin—albeit very temporarily—she's concerned about others.

"They're just fine. Same with Payton and Gage. Your parents too. This is just a trial to test us. We'll become more resilient because of it."

"I thought we'd finally crossed a bridge, you know? This feels like several steps backward." She drops her gaze to hide the collecting moisture.

I study the tremble in her bottom lip with a curse. "It's just a minor blip, baby. The windows will be fixed tomorrow."

"But in the meantime?"

"We wait out the next storm." Which based on the clouds, is approaching in a hurry.

"My heart hurts." Her free palm lifts to clutch her chest.

I kiss her temple. "I'm sorry, Firefly. So fucking sorry."

Rylee's grip on me tightens. "There's nothing to apologize for. You didn't cause the lightning to strike and wreak havoc."

"I know, but you've been through enough already."

She stares at the remnants of crushed fragments littered on the sidewalk. Her focus shifts to rest on a specific absence. The spot where Bent Pedal's sign usually hangs is darker than the surrounding brick. It's obvious there's something missing.

"Do you think it's a hint?" Her voice is soft against the incoming gusts.

"We can look at this one of two ways."

"What do you mean?" Now her tone is stilted in hesitation.

"So, I have an idea. Feel free to say no," I rush to include.

Rylee's breath falters. "You're freaking me out."

"It's not bad," I chuckle.

"The fact you're not spitting it out isn't reassuring."

A cramp seizes my gut, but I won't cower. "I just figured

since the sign already has to be replaced, we could make a change. How does Trevor's Bent Pedal sound?"

She gasps, a trembling palm lifting to cover the shock. "That's... perfect."

"Yeah?"

In the next beat, she's plastering herself against me. I return the embrace, my fingers locked tight against the small of her back. Rylee's lips are too busy peppering me with glee to answer. I tilt my head until our mouths connect, tongues eagerly gliding out to join the celebration.

Heat replaces any trace of chill when I murmur, "This isn't the end. It's just the beginning, Firefly."

She smiles into our kiss. "Didn't we already have one of those?"

"Who's to say there can't be another?"

As if proving my claim, a loud clap of thunder booms from above. Only seconds pass before the sky releases the first drops of rain. We tip our heads in unison to accept the message.

"I think he agrees with us," Rylee giggles.

My gaze slides to her. "Yeah, he does."

She shrieks when the cold drops begin to cascade in a torrent. "Holy crap, it's really coming down."

"Come on. Let's go in. It's too cold."

"Just a minute." Her grin is aimed at me before she looks to the sky. Then she spreads her arms wide.

I'm struck silent by the sight of her getting soaked to the bone. The scene is eerily reminiscent, but I won't let history repeat itself. A different version—the one I saw in my mind at the funeral—plays again. I thread our fingers together and begin to spin us in a slow circle.

Rylee's hair is plastered in a dark sheet, but her green eyes have never appeared brighter. "What're you doing?"

"Something I've thought about since I first saw you."

Her lips spread into pure joy. "Dancing in the rain?"

"And it's just the beginning," I repeat.

chapter twenty-nine

Rylee

MY LAUGHTER IS A SQUEAL AGAINST THE DOWNPOUR WHEN Rhodes bends and tosses me over his shoulder. I bounce against him as he rushes into Bent Pedal to escape the storm. Silence welcomes us once the door slams shut. Only the wet slaps of his boots on concrete echo off the walls.

Another giggle streams through my smile. "Where are you taking me?"

Rhodes stops in his tracks. "Right here, if you'll let me."

I lift my head from the delectable view of his denim-clad ass. The empty bar is all I see, although a bit sideways and distorted. My brain struggles to process in this upside-down position. Too much blood rushing north. His palms drift along my legs before giving me a light spank. Shock jolts me as I begin to suspect his intentions.

The thrill that follows puckers my nipples. "As if we haven't christened this place enough already."

Rhodes lowers me, guiding my body to rub along his until I'm wobbling on my feet. "I'll never get enough of you."

"The feeling is very mutual," I mumble against his lips.

"Besides, when will we have another chance in broad daylight?"

Not that we can see the sun shining through the tarps. But it's about the illusion and what we choose to do with it. Which, based on where he's dropped me off, is a table that's front and center.

"Gonna put you on a pedestal. Everyone can watch while I make you scream for me."

I shiver from the thought, but also my soaked attire in its entirety. "Fortunately, I'm already dripping and making a mess."

He frowns as stray droplets trickle from my jacket sleeves. "Give me one second."

"One," I call to his retreating form.

He smirks at me over his shoulder. "Okay, maybe a few more."

I giggle as he races around the counter and ducks behind a shelf. When he reappears, there's a fluffy towel in his grip. My gaze tracks him as he crosses the distance separating us.

"Not just for dishes, huh?"

"It's new. Promise." His tone drops with conviction.

My focus follows his every move as he tosses the towel onto the table beside me. "I wouldn't have complained."

"Then you won't care if I remove these wet clothes."

"Please do," I whisper.

Rhodes is quick to strip me bare. Each article of sodden fabric lands on the floor with a defined splat. My jeans prove to be a challenge that requires cooperation. I press my palms onto the table while he yanks at the stubborn material. Synchronized relief expels from us once my legs are free from the restrictive obstacle. The rest is simple. Then I'm standing naked in the middle of our bar.

Flames lash at me from his eyes. As his smolder lingers, he must notice the tiny bumps skittering across my exposed flesh. Rhodes grabs the towel and swaddles my nippy form in the cotton. "Are you too cold?"

I take a moment to consider. There's a noticeable warmth thrumming under my skin, chasing away the bitter chill. "It's okay."

"Do you need me to keep you warm? I don't want you to

get sick. We can share body heat." He's already shrugging off his coat.

"I'll have a fire roaring soon."

His brow dips. "Where?"

"In my loins." I gesture at the area in mention.

"Damn, that's sexy."

"You're gonna have to stoke me." I thrust my pelvis forward.

Rhodes goes still, an idea swirling in his gaze. "Trust me with something?"

"Anything. Explicitly," I remind him.

He bends to retrieve my panties. With careful movements, he begins to loop the stretchy material around my wrists. That's when I realize he's only using one opening. That's a strategy I don't understand. But this is a foreign concept, to begin with.

The restraint is loose and barely there. I suppose it's the visual perception again. Even I can admit that the black lace against my pale skin is alluring. His fingers continue the motions. The rapid actions appear effortless, framed in practiced grace. He's already told me before that trying this would be new for him. That doesn't stop the jealousy from bubbling to the surface. The petulance must stream across my features.

Rhodes dusts my lips with a kiss. "I'm good with knots."

Once he's done, I pull at the makeshift handcuffs for dramatic effect. "I'm bound for you."

"To me," he corrects. "And I'll never let you go."

I shiver. "Big words."

Something flickers across his expression. "I'll prove myself until you believe me. Now, let's get you spread and properly pleasured."

Without further warning, he hoists me onto the table. Creaks and groans protest the sudden weight. I absently wonder just how sturdy the craftsmanship is. Those ponderings flee as Rhodes encourages me to recline flat on my back. The cool surface brings forth another shiver, effectively puckering my nipples. He doesn't hesitate to suckle the pebbled points in rapid succession. Warmth surges while he pulls me deep into his mouth. Before I can even squirm, he detaches with a wet pop.

His attentive gaze searches the space. Whatever he finds puts a satisfied gleam in his eye. "Lift your arms for me."

I stretch over my head as instructed. Rhodes glides his palms along my extended pose until reaching my connected hands. There's a subtle tugging at my wrists and I glance up to watch his adjustments. A section of the panties is now attached to the table somehow.

"What—?" I'm not even sure what I'm asking.

He gets me, though. "Those purse hooks were a great addition."

My clasped palms dangle over the ledge to accommodate the short tether. I tug to test the hold, not making much progress. "Indeed."

"It's just the illusion, right? You can get out."

I offer a slow nod in confirmation. "But I don't want to."

"No, you don't." Relief is ripe in his voice. "Just relax for me."

I do, allowing my body to go limp on the hard surface. His hands drift down, along with his mouth. Lips brush the sensitive skin at my inner elbow. Calloused pads drift along the curve at my shoulder before delving lower. His mouth finds my tilted jawline and treats me to several nips. Then expert fingers pinch my nipples before wet warmth eases the sting.

Then he's kissing me. Since my arms are out of commission, all I can do is accept his lips on mine. The sparks strike instantly. Our tongues clash in a tangle that makes me dizzy. My torso arches automatically to deepen the connection. I hiss when cold fabric grazes my bare skin.

Rhodes jerks upright. "Shit, sorry."

There's an empty pang in my core that's begging to be filled. I rub my thighs together to soothe the ache. Those subtle movements catch his attention. He admires my restrained position with a predatory gleam. My need burns hotter.

His gaze feasts on me until I feel more appetizing than a steak dinner. Maybe with some extra ribs and shrimp on the side. The hunger growls in those chocolate depths, promising me dessert. He stares while I squirm, our willpower at war. I'm the one to surrender, walking my toes up his jeans to tap at the button and zipper that's still very much intact.

"Maybe you should strip too."

"What the lady wants, I deliver." His hands lift to do my bidding.

"That's right, babe. Take it all off."

And he does. Rhodes sheds his soggy outfit in what appears to be a single fluid motion, as if I'll award bonus points for speed. And maybe I will. Drool pools in my mouth at the tent pitching his boxers. Those dark eyes remained locked on me without fail. His palms glide down my calves to grip my ankles. With gentle manipulation, he bends my knees to get me propped to his liking. When my feet are flat on the table, I'm left open and on display. But he's far from finished. Rhodes skims my inner thighs and pries me wider, a starved rumble rolling off his chest.

"Fuck, Firefly. You're drenched for me." His touch glides from clit to core.

I can feel how slick I am based on that single swipe. As if that isn't already telling, the wetness taunts my ears and stings my cheeks with a blush. He pulls his finger away and holds it up to the light. There's a definite shine. His satisfaction is a smirk wrapped around that digit as he samples my flavor. The groan that wrenches from him is that of a man savoring his favorite meal. I tremble with that audible stimulation. Another quake ripples when he kneels between my splayed legs.

"I couldn't have picked a better platter to eat you on," he rasps.

My eyes trail down to where he rests on his haunches. In a crouch, he's aligned at the same height where my core is perched. His hands grip my hips and tug until I'm nearly hanging off the edge. The resistance at my wrists reminds me that I can only go so far. He must come to a similar realization, leaving me where I hover.

Words fail me when Rhodes exhales across my slit. That persistent twinge in my lower belly demands to be sated. "Ditching your threads better be the only thing you're planning on rushing through."

His smirk is pure filth that curls my toes. "You'll come twice on my tongue before I make deep, passionate love to you."

Air is clogged in my lungs, and I croak. Multiple orgasms were a myth for me until this selfless giver barged into my life. I don't dare question him now that I've received the proof. Although, getting Rhodes riled up is one hell of a way to pass the time.

I allow a grin of my own to curve my lips. "Will your patience allow for that?"

His eyes flash. "You doubt me?"

Tingles are already spreading while I watch him dip his mouth inches from my core. "It just wouldn't surprise me if—"

The remaining words are stolen when he buries his face in me. Rhodes doesn't bother with another small taste or snack to sample my goods. His tongue is already lashing at me with furious swipes. This can't even be considered eating. It's too untamed. The only way to describe his actions is *devouring*. Tingles and fire erupt, attempting to spear me in half. With a throaty moan I feel inside of me, Rhodes stuffs his mouth with my fast-acting arousal. Each swallow claims more of me. Soon, he'll consume me completely.

There's no stopping the orgasm from ripping me apart. I don't have a spare instant to prepare. It's rushed and brutal—and too fucking good.

"Holy shit. Yes, y-es! There," I cry. My body convulses on the wood surface as I shatter into unrecognizable pieces.

Shockwaves slam into me. I'm lost to the clench of spasms. But Rhodes doesn't slow or pause, even as I attempt to wriggle away. His hands clamp the tops of my thighs to keep me locked against him.

"I need a moment," I plead.

He chuckles into my folds, still feasting without relent. The vibration of amusement sends sparks shooting across my hypersensitive flesh. His lips suckle, adding pressure I don't need.

Another climax barrels through me without warning. I bow into the waves crashing over me. A cramp stabs at my flexed muscles while molten relief pumps into me. The pleasure shoots me to the ceiling, even though I'm still stuck on the table. I collapse with a wheeze and my vision swims.

It's only then I notice that Rhodes hasn't stopped. A desperate tweak seizes my core. There's no sign he's coming up for air while I gasp for more of it. His eyes are fastened on mine, the command unmistakable.

Sweat prickles at my hairline as I attempt to wade through the fog. "Not a third."

His mouth stays buried deep as he denies my request. "Yes, baby. You'll give me another. Then you can rest."

I scream as his tongue lashes my sensitive clit. The knots at my hands pull tight. It would be easy for me to escape, but I find the limits of this captive state to be a thrill. It's invigorating to imagine myself under his control. This is a challenge I want to conquer. Maybe he thrives on listening to me fall apart from his unrelenting efforts.

Smoke and lust layer my voice. "Please have mercy."

"Give me what I want," he growls into my pulsing center.

"I can't," I whimper.

"Yes," he demands.

Then he's done non-negotiating. His face is buried in me with the next frantic breath. A low throb instantly awakens in my core.

It doesn't take long. Or maybe I've never come down from the clouds. Either way, a few licks against my swollen clit have me soaring again. The sounds Rhodes makes are ravenous. Even now, he can't get enough of me. I become a puddle against the wood beneath me. Only then does he release a pleased groan, as if his goal is finally met.

"You'll make me numb," I cry after the twitches fade.

He stands, much to my relief. "Nah, Firefly. I got you so charged that you'll go off from a single tap."

The brief reprieve allows me to recover from the third. I whimper when he shucks his boxers. Rhodes palms his length, fisting the generous girth easily. Before I can beg, he's angling that thick length toward my entrance. A long moan spills from my slack jaw, the sound getting louder with each inch he feeds me.

He props himself over me to lavish my nipples with attention. Sparks shoot across my flesh as he suckles hard at the needy points. "You've got one more saved for me, yeah?"

I'm nodding, the gesture sloppy. "Uh-huh."

And I'm not lying. Tingles were lying in wait, eager to spread the last ounce of pleasure I can commit. Rhodes begins to move, thrusting in and out at a measured pace. While his cock teases the clamp from my inner muscles, his lips drift toward mine. Our mouths meld and bond with a shared exhale. I arch into him, his damp skin sticking to me. Heat builds until I'm panting into him. My tongue roves along his in a feverish tempo. That desire increases his strokes into me, forcing my body to resume the chase for release.

Then Rhodes straightens and slips his palms under my ass to lift me off the surface. I wrap my legs around his waist, crossing my ankles against his back for added friction. The shift is about the extent of my range, and all I can manage in my wrung-out form.

The frenzy in our pace slams to a halt. He's buried deep, yet grinds to get impossibly closer. His finger drifts along my slit to where I'm clenched around him. He uses that digit to circle where we're joined. The touch is light and tender, yet extremely erotic. Then he gives voice to the illicit sensation.

"You're full of me," he groans. "Look how you stretch to accept my cock. You're spread to the limit."

"Feels incredible," I breathe in return.

His finger makes another lap, pressing into where we meet. "Fucking beautiful. Are you ready to let me put a baby in your belly?"

"That's not how the song goes," I chide.

Rhodes squints at me while withdrawing from my heat. "Since when are we following lyrics?"

"First comes love," I wheeze when he slams into me.

He retreats and punches in again. "We've got that handled."

"Then comes marriage." A whimper scrambles out when my sensitive bits thrum from his renewed efforts. Through my heavy lids, I notice he's about to speak. My tongue is quick to unravel, allowing me to interrupt. "And don't you dare propose while you're balls deep."

His lips press into a firm line. "Best finish this then."

I rock my pelvis into him. "By all means, go ahead."

Rhodes reclaims his grip on my thighs. "You're mine."

"Only yours," I insist.

"Reach those stars, Firefly. Catch them in both tied fists."

Then he's done being patient and collected. His rhythm is punishing, meant to hurdle me off the peak. A purposeful pressure finds my clit. Between his thumb and dick, I'm a goner. The combination steers me straight to the edge. My trapped wrists keep me anchored as I thrash. I'm a glutton, demanding more and faster. Eventually, I don't even recognize the words coming from my mouth.

A soundless scream trembles off my lips. I crest and leap while the trembles take hold. My pleasure shoots straight to the sky. An inferno blasts through my veins when I feel Rhodes go still against me. A guttural noise rips from him. We get submerged into ecstasy together, as one.

Static steals my sight for several moments. The afterglow

swoops in as Rhodes collapses on top of me. Our labored breathing creaks the table beneath our shared weight.

"I'll never be the same," I breathe.

He nuzzles my boobs. "Me either."

"What happens next?"

"I should probably release you from the thong trap." Rhodes does just that, freeing the lace from the hook.

"And then?" I watch as he unwinds the fabric from my wrists.

"We see where this road takes us," he murmurs against my lips.

My fingers tremble when I sweep some stray hair off his sticky forehead. "And let love guide us each step of the way."

chapter thirty

Rylee

GAGE IS BOUNCING BESIDE ME AS I FREE PAYTON FROM THE backseat. She springs out onto the sidewalk with the same unleashed excitement as my son did moments before. If it weren't for child locks, these two would require duct tape.

Bent Pedal stands tall and proud in front of us. The exterior appears fully restored. I wouldn't have guessed repairs were necessary if I hadn't witnessed the damage. The only thing missing is our sign, which is on order. Then we'll truly give my brother his legacy. In the meantime, we're returning to business as usual.

The kids race ahead to the entrance. Payton and Gage have a rare Monday off due to a teacher workshop. Apparently, their districts are on a similar schedule. Rhodes insisted they tag along, and I wasn't going to argue. There's plenty to keep them occupied for at least an hour or two. My parents plan to swing by for lunch and will take them off our hands.

I laugh at their endless energy. "What's the hurry?"

"There's something we gotta do," Payton says.

"Like what? Nobody's here yet. Customers have to wait until noon. Your dad is meeting us, but I don't see his truck."

"But we need to go," Gage insists.

And they do, disappearing from sight while I'm still locking the car. I'm right behind them, stepping through the door that they left wide open. My forward progress screeches to a standstill once I step across the threshold.

An ethereal glow greets me. Tiny lights dangle from invisible strings across the entire room. There must be hundreds of twinkling strands. The visual display resembles fireflies floating in the air. It takes my breath away. But that's just one portion.

Electric candles litter every available surface, as well as the floor. The fake flames flicker to give an authentic vibe. Yellow flower petals are scattered into the mix too.

In the center of it all is Rhodes down on one knee, with Gage and Payton flanking him. Pressure squeezes my windpipe as I try to remain steady on wobbly knees. My eyes well with emotion, distorting the scene into a bright blur.

I fan the heat stinging my face. "Oh, I wasn't expecting this."

Rhodes smirks, that dimple winking at me. His gaze is solely trained on mine as I stumble forward. "This girl walked into a bar and turned my life right side up."

"Are you talking about me?" I manage to croak.

"As if anyone else would fit. It's been just Payton and me for years. We've decided to expand the clan. Right, Bumblebee?" He slides his focus to her for a brief moment. The love shining from that glance makes the first droplets spill down my cheeks.

She's nodding with extra enthusiasm. "Yep!"

Once I've reached him, he rests one of my palms flat over his thumping heart. "This beats for you and Gage too."

My bottom lip quivers while I look from him to his daughter. "I feel the same way."

Payton and Gage squeak, ready to burst, but Rhodes presses a finger over his mouth. "Just give me one more minute. Then you can steal the spotlight."

They suck in deep breaths to hold. Double thumbs-up are added security.

Rhodes opens the small box resting in his palm. I nearly faint from the sparkle. A massive canary solitaire sits nestled in the blue velvet. He plucks the yellow diamond from its cushion. "For my Firefly. To always chase away the shadows."

The lump in my throat doubles in size. "It's stunning."

"Just like the woman who will wear it." He snags my left hand in his. "Do me the honor of becoming my wife. Agree to make me the happiest man in this life and the next. Spend your days getting me riled so we can keep the heat burning all night. My hand for yours."

"Best trade yet," I murmur.

There's a shimmer in Rhodes' eyes as he gazes up at me. "Will you marry me, Rylee Creed?"

My head is bobbing too fast, sending more tears streaming down. "Yes, of course. Yes, yes!"

He slides the ring on my finger, brushing a soft kiss on my knuckle. "I love you."

With zero grace, my knees meet the floor. I have him snug against me in the next breath. "I love you too. So very much."

A pitchy voice interrupts from right beside me. "Is it our turn?"

Rhodes glances at my son, a watery grin covering his lips. "Yeah, buddy. Go ahead."

"She said yes!" Gage shouts. "Does this mean you're my dad?"

His throat works with a thick swallow. "If you'd like me to be."

Payton leaps toward me, stopping just before a collision can occur. "And you'll be my mom?"

"If you'll have me," I blubber.

She flings her arms around me. "Yay! You're the best, and I love you already. Thanks for making us super-duper happy."

"Love you, sweetie." My eyes slide shut against the fresh wave of heat.

Gage steals her from my embrace. They exchange a high-five with a triple twirl at the end. Payton beams at him. "You're gonna be my brother, like for real."

"And you'll be my sister," he proclaims in victory.

Payton glances at me. "I'm gonna have a mommy."

"Best family ever," Gage whisper-shouts.

"Couldn't agree more, buddy." Rhodes ruffles his hair. Then he climbs to his feet, helping me rise as well.

"Where's the bubbly? We're celebrating!" I thrust my arm straight out, the light catching on the bling.

"I have something better." My fiancé—cue internal squeal— produces a very familiar bottle from what appears to be thin air.

My focus is too concentrated on the label to question his storage efforts. "Is that—?"

Next, Rhodes whips out two glasses and gets to pouring. "Trevor's brew? Yep."

We've shared a bottle once or twice, but it's a precious commodity with very limited stock. The thought is almost sobering. "Our supply is almost gone, huh?"

He pauses in his task to peek over at me. "I was actually going to talk to you about that."

Nerves tickle my stomach. "Oh?"

"What are the chances you want to add a brewery component to the bar? We could build it off the back. I don't think the equipment requires much space."

"A brewery and a bar? We'll be busy." I find myself swaying into him.

"Especially if there's going to be a baby." His breath ghosts across my forehead before he grants me a kiss, sending a flush down my cheek.

"I'm not changing poop diapers," Payton interjects.

My amusement slides her way. "No?"

She plugs her nose. "Nah-huh. Nope. Too stinky."

"Me either," Gage joins in.

Rhodes thrusts a thumb to his chest. "I'll be on poop patrol. Don't worry."

"You're awfully sure I'll agree," I mumble. The smile in my voice betrays any denial I'm trying to enforce.

"The deals have tipped heavily in my favor so far. Might as well go bigger." His palm settles on my stomach.

"Not sure we can get much better."

His lips drift to my temple where I feel his grin. "It's not a competition, Firefly. I just want more of you and me."

Gage giggles. "They're totally gonna spread the love."

Payton nods. "The fire between them is really burning. Like huge flames."

"See? We could have more of this," he whispers in my ear.

I snuggle into his side, my grip extending to Gage and Payton. "Mine and yours."

Rhodes draws the four of us into a tight-knit embrace, like the family we are. "Ours."

epilogue

RHODES

I TIP THE BOTTLE UNTIL A THIN STREAM OF PALE ALE TRICKLES out. Bubbles fizz and froth into the ground, proving that at least our carbonation methods aren't a total bust. "How's that?"

No response, of course. Not that I expected anything different. This isn't my first beer tasting at Trevor's grave. There's not a chance it will be my last, so long as I can control it. The breeze that blows leaves across the cemetery seems to agree.

That gust is a reprieve I tip my face into. Summer has arrived, bringing humidity to clog the air. But the heat is only one aspect of my favorite season. Greenery spreads far and wide. The sight reminds me of growth and fresh starts. Seems only fitting, considering what I'm drinking.

After spinning the bottle in my palm, I treat myself to a sip. A gagged wretch immediately rejects the mouthful. Skunky. Bitter. Charred. The taste combination is horrifically unpleasant. I press a fist to my mouth to trap the liquid. It's a mighty feat to swallow.

Rylee cringes from her spot across the plot. "I burned the other batch of wort. This stuff should've been okay."

I'm still trying to choke the swig down. "It's a very unique blend, Firefly. Quite… invigorating. Beer brewing must run in the family."

"You just don't want to see me cry again." She bites her bottom lip, most likely attempting to stave off an emotional downpour.

"Do I ever? Those tears break me." I clutch a palm to my chest.

"Freaking hormones," she mumbles.

I nod. "You're in a fragile state."

"No thanks to you and your magic sperm."

"What's sperm?" Payton appears next to Rylee, as if she's been there the entire time.

"Sweet salamanders. Where'd you come from?" My wife gasps and widens her eyes at our nosy eavesdropper.

"Uh, over there." She flails an arm in the general backward direction.

Her partner in meddlesome crime is still racing around a tree without a care for our conversation. The pair is more invested in playing interference than ever. But their constant shenanigans don't earn complaints from me.

Things appear nice and rosy from where I sit. The sun is shining and I'm surrounded by those I love. A grin stretches across my lips as I capture the moment.

"Mommy?"

Rylee's breath still hitches whenever Payton refers to her as such. "Yes, sweet angel who just almost made me pee my pants?"

Our daughter squints against the midday rays. "Do you need to go potty again? We already had to stop twice on the way here."

"No, but thanks for asking. You're very considerate of my bladder." Rylee toys with the braid in Payton's hair, which she's responsible for.

In return, the young girl gazes at her in pure adoration. "What's sperm?"

My wife goes still in her absent fidgeting. "Oh, yikes. That's a good question. I don't really know…"

"But you just said something about magic and sperm."
Payton turns her focus to me. "What's sperm, Daddy?"

I'm staring at Rylee. "This is your honor to behold."

She rolls her eyes. "Heaven forbid we stumble into another penis pickle predicament."

Payton giggles, clapping a palm over her mouth. "You said penis. We don't talk about boy parts, remember?"

A blush rises on Rylee's cheeks. "Busted."

"Who's gonna tell me about the sperm?" Payton clasps her palms in a pleading gesture.

"I wanna know too!" Gage races toward us at lightning speed. His new shoes flash with every hurried leap.

The woman who leaked the splooge clue raises her hand. "It's not a huge deal. Sperm is like… a potion to make a baby."

I spew nothing but straight air, making a sputtered racket. "Seriously, Firefly?"

She scratches at the flushed splotches dotting her neck. "What?"

"You could've said anything." I pinch the bridge of my nose.

Meanwhile, the kids have gone quiet. Concerningly so. Their rapt concentration is zeroed in on Rylee's very pregnant tummy. Payton is the first to snap from their shared stupor.

Her eyes are saucer-sized. "Wow, you must've eaten lots of sperm."

Gage appears to connect a few dots if his astonished expression is anything to go from. "Oh, oh! So, sperm helps spread the love between a mommy and daddy when they're ready to share?"

Rylee ducks her chin to hide a growing smile. "Okay, I can see the errors in my explanation."

"We're gonna be in trouble with the square squad," I grumble. There's a particular group of ladies who don't appreciate how open and honest we are with our children.

My wife palms her forehead with a groan. "Oh, crud. They haven't forgiven me for snatching you off the market."

"This is a discussion that stays in the family, okay? Don't repeat anything to your friends." I point from Payton to Gage.

"We won't," they say in unison.

"Talk about a red flag," Rylee murmurs.

"I mean, what's the worst that can happen?"

She holds up a finger. "You should never ask that. That's how I got into this… pickle."

Gage studies his mom circling her baby bump. "Wait. I thought that was from the sperm. Do pickles make babies too?"

Payton freezes. "I'm never eating a pickle again."

"Good call," I praise. "Just stay away from boys until you're thirty."

She glances at her brother. "That's kinda hard when I live with one."

"Gage doesn't count. He's going to protect you from all the others."

Rylee sighs, a wistful smile brightening her features. "Older brothers are good at that."

"No fair. I wanna be older. My birthday is a month after his," Payton complains.

Gage puffs out his chest. "I'll take care of you, Bumblebee. Just like Daddy."

My daughter considers that, ending on a shrug. "Whatever."

"Are we done flapping chaps? I wanna keep running." He bounces on his feet.

"You are adorable," his mother coos. "Go have fun. We'll leave soon."

"M'kay." Gage trots to Trevor's grave and wraps his skinny arms around the stone marker. "Miss you, Uncle. Bye for now."

Payton joins him, dropping a kiss onto the cold slab. "Tootles, Trev."

My heart clenches while the pair dashes off to resume their chase around the tree. "That was special. We have great kids."

"The best." Moisture shines in Rylee's eyes when I glance

over. She swipes at the tears before they can fall. "Now change the subject before I bawl."

That's when I notice the rancid beer flavor is still clinging to my tongue. I pass a glance at the wet spot in the grass. "Apologies for that last drink, man. Let me make it up to you."

"Thought it wasn't bad?" She pins me with a knowing look that demands a confession.

"An acquired taste," I counter.

Rylee crosses her arms, effectively putting her generous cleavage on display. Those supple mounds have grown by the handful since I shoved two buns in her oven. "Wouldn't know since you knocked me up the instant I stopped taking the pill."

A pleased rumble rolls from me. "Yeah, I did."

"With twins."

"Double the fun," I reason.

"On our wedding night."

"Had to ring in the new year with a bang. It's tradition."

She quirks a brow. "Oh, is it now?"

"Yes, it will be from now on."

"Insatiable." Yet her lips flash me a coy grin.

"Have you seen yourself?"

Rylee rubs her swollen belly. "I'm hard to miss."

Arousal spikes in my bloodstream. If it were up to me, she'd be pregnant without pause. I've established somewhat of a breeding kink since this woman sashayed her fine ass into our bar. Then I remember where we are.

"Sorry, brother. Your sister is too damn sexy." I wince and pat the grass. After digging in the cooler by my feet, I whip out a can of reliable Coors Light. "This should even the score."

"I love that you call him that." She melts into her chair with a breathy exhale.

"Cheers to that." I pour a swig into the earth, lift the can to the sky, and take a sip of my own.

Rylee mirrors my motions. "This cream soda is tasty."

"You're welcome." That's far easier to make than beer.

"I didn't force you to drink the swill." She wrinkles her nose at our latest failed attempt.

"One of these days, we'll get it right."

"I dunno, babe." Her gaze moves over our kids to the bump protruding from her abdomen, then lands on me. "We're doing pretty well as it is."

"Couldn't ask for more, Firefly. You've given me the dream."

"It's been almost a year." Her tone carries a somber note, although she's smiling.

"Look how far we've come. Not too bad, huh?"

"I'd say we're expanding accordingly, and not just my waistline."

My throat gets tight as memories surface, especially from when this journey started. "The business is better than ever, man. We're doing right by you and your wishes. I think you'd be proud of us."

"Thanks, brother. For everything." Rylee brings three fingers to her lips, then sends a kiss straight to the heavens. "We wouldn't be together if it weren't for you."

That's the end... sort of. If you'd like to read more of Rhodes and Rylee (along with Payton and Gage), I've whipped up a few bonus scenes that you can read for free. Grab them here!

other books

Want more single parent romances from me?
I have several for you to fall for.
Here's a piece from **Ask Me Why** – a single (extra broody)
dad, enemies-to-lovers romance.

I check the clock again. Thirty minutes until close. I can survive that long. If only a customer or two would come in and take my mind off food.

As if hearing my silent plea, the door swings open. The bell calls out, and a familiar little figure zooms inside. I peer around the display case that's obstructing my view. Ollie sends me a beaming smile and my hunger pains are instantly forgotten.

Oh, this kid is going to break so many hearts when he's older.

"Hi, Miss Braelyn." Ollie strides up to me like we're the best of pals. Maybe we already are.

My depleted energy seems to spring back. I give him a wave. "Hey, Ollie. Glad to see you again."

"Sorry I'm late."

I shake my head. "Nonsense. You're right on time. Is Mary with you?"

His forehead creases. "Uh, no. She went home. We would've been here sooner, but my dad was working." Ollie hitches a small thumb over his shoulder.

That's when the door opens with a bang. A tall man stomps in with the power of a hurricane. Is the ground shaking? If it is, I barely notice.

Holy. Hotness.

Who ordered the sex in a suit?

The guy's laser focus is on the boy beside me so he doesn't notice my slack jaw. He's tall, but not overly bulky. His thick hair is styled in a messy sort of way, and I want to smooth the unruly flyaways. A five-o'clock shadow dusts his jaw, the first signs of stubble barely visible. The contrast between his light eyes and dark features is hypnotic. An impeccable suit covers his broad frame, cut to fit his wide shoulders and trim waist perfectly. He could easily sell this look. Hell, after one glance I'm ready to buy it off him.

He's fucking lickable.

"Ollie, I told you to wait. Selective listening isn't cute anymore. Why do you insist on running ahead of me?" The stranger's boom ricochets around us.

I blink, and the haze evaporates. What the actual eff was that? I look down at the child in question and wait for him to answer. He's squirming all about. Ollie barely gives his father a second glance, too busy studying the assortment of candy on display. But no worries. I'm giving this man more attention than he needs anyway. I can hardly take my peepers off him.

Ollie lingers for another beat, then quickly dashes to the taffy bins. I see him move from one to the next in my peripheral vision.

"Need a camera?"

I startle at the harsh growl. "Huh?"

"Then you can take a picture." His frosty blue eyes narrow on me, and I'm frozen in place.

"Excuse me?" Why is my voice so breathy?

"It'll last longer." He raises a dark brow.

Clarity seeps into my stupor, and the urge to tuck tail streaks through me. But I don't. I raise my chin and openly appraise him. "I like your suit."

"It's custom fit."

"Looks that way."

He crosses his arms and stands straighter. "You're not my type, taffy girl."

I fight the urge to scratch my temple, being stumped again. "Okay?"

"Stare all you want. It'll get you nowhere." He points between us. "Never gonna happen."

For a moment, all I can do is gape at him. I feel my face go up in flames. Is he for freaking real?

"I w-wasn't... no, I didn't mean," I sputter. "I'm not hitting on you."

His smirk is devilish. "Save it for the judge, sugar. I get it."

Before I can defend myself, Ollie zips toward us and smiles at me. "Do you like my dad?"

Everything inside of me skids to a stop. I pop my mouth open, but nothing comes out. My throat is a tight fist, and swallowing is a challenge. How the hell do I respond to that?

I tug at the collar of my shirt. "Uh, well, we haven't really met. I don't even know his name."

Ollie's gaze bounces between us. "He didn't tell you?"

"Nope." There's no hesitation. Throwing this cocky dick under the bus is an easy decision.

The ass glares at me. "We didn't get that far."

Ollie shakes a finger at his dad. "That's not polite. You're supposed to do introductions first. That's what you taught me."

He remains silent, thoroughly scolded by a child. Ollie huffs loudly. I lift a hand to cover my growing smile. Something tells me this imposing man wouldn't appreciate my humor.

"Brance Stone," he finally offers. A weaker woman might wither under that icy stare. Too bad for him, I'm all out of shits to give.

"It's a pleasure to meet you. I'm Braelyn Miller." I plaster on an extra wide grin for good measure.

A muscle jumps in his jaw. "Likewise."

Continue reading *Ask Me Why* on Amazon!

How about a single mama romance? **Loner** is definitely one you should take a peek at. Enjoy this excerpt.

I shuffle forward to meet him between our vehicles. Motor oil, sweat, musk, and gasoline stick to him like a second skin. He smells like a bad boy wrapped in a double dose of trouble and danger. Instinct and attraction have failed me enough that I know to keep my distance.

He gives my car an assessing glance. "Got a flat?"

I sigh at the grizzly grate of his voice. Good grief. "Yeah."

"How about the tools to fix it?"

"That's a negative." I tack on a smile to lighten the static zapping between us. If anything, the electric charge cranks higher. He makes no show of interest one way or another. Am I alone in these feelings?

He crosses his arms, biceps flexing with the shift. Is that for my benefit? "Did you call someone?"

"Not yet." I spy the familiar style of his shirt. "Are you a mechanic?"

"Yeah."

I wait for him to add more. He doesn't. Cool. "At a shop in town?"

"I own it."

"Would I know the place?"

He scoffs. "Doubt it."

"Why's that?"

"I don't do cars."

I blink at him. "Excuse me?"

"Bikes only."

I give him a slow once-over, trying not to judge. There's no harm in having a bit of fun. "As in bicycles?"

His expression turns more frosty. "Motorcycles."

A grin curves my lips. "Ah, gotcha. Do you have a name?"

"Sure do."

What is it with this guy? Calling him resistant is being generous. "Care to share?"

"Not really."

"And why is that? Introductions are polite."

"Never been known for my manners."

"Well, I'm Keegan." I offer him a hand to shake.

He just stares at my open palm, letting another grunt loose.

Stomping my foot feels like an appropriate reaction to his childish behavior. "Oh my Lord. Tell me your name."

"What's it matter?"

"Because."

He rakes through his hair. "Crawford. Most call me Ford."

I roll the word on my tongue. It fits the package, and I appraise him under a new scope. "Like the truck?"

"No, like short for Crawford."

A sting sizzles up my neck. "Sorry I asked."

"Likewise."

I wait a beat, for what I'm not entirely sure. Maybe his friendly alter ego will show up. "Well, thanks for stopping. Can you lend a hand?"

"Maybe."

It's becoming quite clear calling a local garage might be faster. I reach into my pocket, ready to continue where I left off.

A shadow looms over my screen. "In a hurry?"

I peek up at Crawford from under my lashes. "Are you trying to keep me around?"

His laugh is drier than the grasslands in July. "Hardly."

Crawford's special brand of surliness is so heavy that a fog descends around us. I'm well aware he's trying to repel me with his nasty ass attitude. This man is full to the top with piss and vinegar. Lucky for me, I'm fluent in decoding the asshole dialect. Kill 'em with kindness? Been there, definitely done that. I fling some loose hair over my shoulder and offer him a beaming smile. "If I didn't know better, I'd assume you're putting up a front to chase me off. But," I add with a saucy wink, "your type is more common than ketchup on the dinner table. Don't worry about me falling for you, Ford. I've had enough bullshit in my life to open a buffet, but the all-you-can-eat line isn't for me."

His hazel eyes roll to the dusty ground. "You done yapping? I got places to be."

If steam could physically billow out of my ears, I'd resemble a chimney. Instead, I give him the narrowest glare on this side of town. "If my daughter wasn't with me, you'd be on the receiving end of a blue streak so wide we'd never find our way out."

He sobers at that. "You got a kid?"

"Yep."

Crawford scrubs the back of his neck. "Shit, I shouldn't have been so crass."

I slap a palm to my chest. "Because I'm a mother?"

Continue reading *Loner* on Amazon!

One more? Here's a sliver from *There's Always Someday* – a single father, neighbors-to-lovers romance.

A tiny wail cracks into the silence. That's when I remember he's clutching a baby against his chest. I can't imagine having a child at my age, and he can't be much older than me. To further remind us of her existence, a tiny fist thrusts into the air and swats at the air blindly.

I've never felt such a powerful urge to capture the moment behind my lens. My index finger twitches with the desire to click the shot. The picture they create deserves to be displayed.

He begins to shush her while bouncing in place. "Uh, sorry. It's past her bedtime. We've been on the road for hours."

His words finally break me free from my mesmerized bubble. I start talking without conscious thought. "Oh I don't mind. Ha ha. She's adorable, by the way. Long drives can be really hard even for grown-ups." I internally scream at myself to get it together, but my mouth is moving too fast for my brain to catch up. "Hi, um, I'm Clea, we live here—not like 'we' as a couple. That would be super weird since this is my brother. We live right over there. Sorry, I already told you that. Where did you come from?"

Kody gives me an elbow to the ribs to shut me up. "What my nosy sister means to say is that we're glad to have new neighbors. This house stood vacant for too long. I'm Kody."

Fire singes my cheeks. I find myself grateful that it's dark out, or this handsome stranger would see me turning redder than a beet.

"Nolan," he offers. "It's nice to meet you both. Oh, and we're from Madison."

It's safe to assume he's referring to the city in Wisconsin. "What brings you to Minnesota? It's the lakes, right?"

Kody pins me with a glare. I almost wither into the soaking lawn. The last thing I want is to chase him away with an insulting inquisition, but Nolan squashes any concern that I've potentially overstepped. "A fresh start. That's the plan, at least."

I wait for him to say more, biting my tongue to get ahold of myself before I invade his privacy any further. When only the crickets answer, I decide it's safe to proceed. With caution, of course. "Well, you really picked a great place to live. Excellent choice."

Face meet palm. I'm beginning to sound like a welcome wagon on too much sugar and caffeine.

The harsh lines exposing his sorrow lighten just a touch when he glances at me. "I really needed to hear that ringing endorsement. It's a good thing you stopped by."

Whether he's being sarcastic or not isn't important. I'm not ashamed to admit that the hint of a smile on his face sends me reeling all over again.

"Can we help with anything?" I paste on what's meant to be an encouraging smile.

Nolan wears defeat like a familiar cloak. His glassy eyes lift to mine. The man looks close to tears. "Could you hold her for me?"

My tongue sticks to the roof of my mouth. I have zero experience with kids, but that doesn't mean I'm not intrigued by the little pink bundle snuggled against his chest. Denying him, especially in his current state, is impossible. "Umm, sure."

Nolan deposits the squirming bundle into my outstretched arms. My movements feel wooden and odd. The corner of his lips hitch, just the slightest bit, and only briefly. "You'll get the hang of it."

I nod, believing his words deep in my gut. "What's her name?"

"Tallulah." The word is choked from him. "We call her Tally for short."

I stroke a finger down her satin cheek. "She's absolutely beautiful. Aren't you, precious girl?"

"She gets that from her mother." A single tear rolls down his cheek with that broken statement. A tight knot dips in his throat as he swallows. "If only she were here to appreciate the similarities. It's just us now. Tally's mom isn't… in the picture."

Continue reading *There's Always Someday* on Amazon!

acknowledgements

Mine For Yours is my eighteenth published novel. That's crazy to type. I feel extremely fortunate to have the opportunity to continue sharing my stories with you. I'm also very honored that you're choosing to read them. Thank you for that! The fact you picked up my book to read means more than I'll ever be able to describe.

I know I'm not supposed to have favorites. Every book is special and unique, but there are certain stories that just hit a differentnote. Deeper. Make a bigger impact. Unforgettable. Mine For Yours is one of those for me. Fingers crossed your agree.

My son is Gage and Payton combined into one incredible child. He gave me more inspiration than I knew what to do with. Endless hugs and kisses and laughs are shared, just like in this book. Along with my daughter and husband, he lights up my world like a field of fireflies. Along that same line, I need to thank my husband for being patient with me whenever deadline season looms. He picks up the slack and never complains. This crazy amazing author life wouldn't be possible without him. I love you to a galaxy far, far away.

If you don't know Renee, I hope you get a chance to meet her someday. She's the one who makes sure I stay on track and get stuff done. But not only that, she's a wonderful friend. The best, really. I'm extremely lucky that she's mine. Thanks for being the greatest support system and bestest friend.

Heather is the lover of my life – if we didn't have husbands and children, we might run away to the beach together. Day after day, she's there for me. It's difficult to find such a meaningful friendship in an online career, but we've done it. I'd be lost without you, Hover!

K.K. is the extra sister I didn't realize was missing until I found her. Our bond was instant and I'm thankful daily to have her in my corner. We might overinduldge from time to time, but our love can always be a triple shot.

Kate is not only an extremely talented author, but she also created the stunning cover for this book. Mine For Yours has a beautiful design thanks to Y'all That Graphic. But more than that, I'm grateful for our friendship. Thanks for the laughs and love.

Kayla has been my hype squad with Mine For Yours since I first told her I was writing a double single parent romance. Her encouragement and support is irreplaceable. You're fantastic and I'm thankful for you!

Shain is an incredible cheerleader if you're ever stuck in a deadline. We push each other to get it done. Besides, it's more fun to be in the trenches with great friends.

I feel extremely fortunate and blessed to have so many awesome ladies in my corner that I can lean on, and vice versa. I know I can turn to you, no matter what, and that kind of supportive comfort is priceless. Thank you to Tia, Annie, Leigh, Amy, Michelle, TJ, Suzie, Kandi, and many more. Your friendship is irreplaceable. Thank you, thank you.

If you didn't know, I have the greatest group ever. I might be biased, but Harloe's Hotties is the best. My people. I have so much love for our special spot on social media. Thanks for being part of it. You get the inside track for Lover Boy's antics, so hopefully this one hit home for you. And Harloe's Review Crew gets heaps of love too. Your excitement and eager anticipation makes releasing books even more fun. I'm so thankful for you.

Thank you to Candi Kane and her team at Candi Kane PR. My head spins each time she tells me what's on her daily agenda. I have no idea how she does it all, but she pulls it off with ease.

I'm grateful for everything you do. Also, a big thanks to the wonderful ladies at Give Me Books. Once again, your help for this release is invaluable and very much appreciated.

Thanks to Kassey Nixon with Kassey Photophraphy for taking such awesome pictures of Rhylan for the cover. And to Rhylan for posing. This cover just might be my favorite. What do you think?

There are so many vital individuals who assist in the writing and publishing process. Renee reads as I write and keeps me on track. Thanks to Erica, Kayla, Patricia, and Keri for beta reading. Sending a huge thanks to Alex with Infinite Well for editing and polishing Mine For Yours until the story sparkled. To Lacie and BB for proofing. A massive thanks to Stacey from Champagne Book Designs. As always, she once again created the most stunning interior for my book baby. I cannot recommend her formatting services enough!

I need to send out another huge round of thanks to all the readers, reviewers, bloggers, Bookstagrammers, BookTokers, and romance lovers out there. Because of you, authors like me get to continue writing and doing what we love. You're who we strive to reach and aim to be better for. Thank you to infinity for continuing to be there for all of us!

And last but definitely not least, if you enjoyed Mine For Yours and want to do me a huge favor, please consider leaving a review. It really helps others find my books. Thank you for reading!

about the author

Harloe Rae is a *USA Today* & Amazon Top 5 best-selling author. Her passion for writing and reading has taken on a whole new meaning. Each day is an unforgettable adventure.

She's a Minnesota gal with a serious addiction to romance. There's nothing quite like an epic happily ever after. When she's not buried in the writing cave, Harloe can be found hanging with her hubby and kiddos. If the weather permits, she loves being lakeside or out in the country with her horses.

Broody heroes are Harloe's favorite to write. Her romances are swoony and emotional with plenty of heat. All of her books are available on Amazon and Kindle Unlimited.

Stay in the know by subscribing to her newsletter at
bit.ly/HarloesList

Join her reader group, Harloe's Hotties, at
www.facebook.com/groups/harloehotties

Check out her site at www.harloerae.com

Follow her on:
BookBub: http://bit.ly/HarloeBB
Amazon: http://bit.ly/HarloeOnAmazon
Goodreads: http://bit.ly/HarloeOnGR
Facebook Page: /Facebook.com/authorharloerae
Instagram: www.instagram.com/harloerae
TikTok: www.tiktok.com/@harloerae

Made in United States
North Haven, CT
22 October 2023

43057838R00207